Also by DJ Sherratt
#1 in The Morningstar Trilogy
Chasing Charlie

Chasing New York

DJ Sherratt

authorHOUSE®

AuthorHouse™
1663 Liberty Drive
Bloomington, IN 47403
www.authorhouse.com
Phone: 1 (800) 839-8640

Published by AuthorHouse 11/17/2015

ISBN: 978-1-5049-6249-0 (sc)
ISBN: 978-1-5049-6250-6 (e)

Table of Contents

Acknowledgments

I am forever grateful to those who have helped and supported me in my endeavour to write "The Morningstar Trilogy" and specifically, "Chasing New York".

Ann, your willingness to jump to my call is so appreciated. Many thanks to you, your camera and your garden. Your touch brings out the beauty in everything!

James, you are my very dear friend. Thank you for making my baby shine and make sense!

To the Hollomby's, I appreciate you allowing me to use your family's names. I hope I did them justice.

Robin, thank you for all your input and preventing me from creating a new map of Europe! My BBFF!

To my incredible husband, Mark. Your love and unending belief in me is what gets me through. Thank you for that.

I love you.

And lovingly, to Roberta Shepherd, this one's for you!

All my love,
;Dxx

"I think that we are like stars. Something happens to burst us open; but when we burst open and think we are dying; we're actually turning into a supernova. And then when we look at ourselves again, we see that we're suddenly more beautiful than we ever were before!"

— C. JoyBell C.

Prologue

He's sitting on a bed, plucking away at the guitar he holds. The new speakers, purchased for his 18th birthday, sound perfect. He's concentrating on the chords he's playing, repeating them until they are natural to him. As he plays, he can see smoke building around him slowly. He doesn't panic, he doesn't move except his fingers on the neck of the guitar, still repeating the chords.

Out of the smoke he sees a form walking towards him. He continues repeating the chords and the speakers get louder as the form gets nearer. He is now playing frantically, moving his head to the chords, lost in the music. The form becomes clearer and the shape of a woman appears. She is slight of frame, elderly, dressed elegantly and smiling. He looks up from where he sits on the bed and smiles at her, still continuing to play the chords.

Her lips are moving as if in slow motion but no sound comes out. He feels frustration, tenses his body and increases the intensity of his playing as he tries to watch the woman and play the chords at the same time. Her lips continue to move without sound until suddenly she leans forward and her face is all he can see; large, wide-eyed and penetrating. The speakers are now full blast. As the noise builds to a deafening crescendo she takes an obvious deep breath.

"Wake Up!" she shouts above the din, her eyes as large as saucers.

He awoke with a start. He'd been right in the middle of a recurring dream when he jolted awake and heard the sound of crashing glass from somewhere in the apartment. His heart racing and his mind reeling, he pushed himself up off his bed and listened for any other sounds.

Seconds passed in silence. He gently opened the top drawer next to his bedside and, reaching to the very back of the drawer, he grabbed the handle of his gun. With his other hand he snagged his phone from the pocket of his jacket at the end of the bed and tiptoed across the room and into his walk-in closet. The doors were louvered and faced the closed bedroom door. If he crouched low he could pull the laundry basket in front of him and be completely hidden and still see what was going on. Holding the phone in one hand and the gun in the other, he kept his eyes on the door while he managed to call 911 with his thumb.

"911, what is your emergency?" the dispatcher's voice said, rather flatly.

Jesus Christ! he thought, *there's an intruder! You could sound a little more concerned,* but what came out was barely a whisper. "There's an intruder in my apartment," he said quietly, into the phone.

"An intruder?" she asked. "Do you have security, sir? Are you still in the apartment?" she asked.

He could hear her typing quickly. "Yes, we have a security man at the front door," he whispered. "I'm hidden in my closet."

"Can you give me your address?" she asked.

"5575 Riverside Drive. Apartment 1505. Can you please hurry?" he asked, his heart thundering in his chest. "I'm afraid they're trying to kill me," he admitted.

"There's more than one?" the dispatcher asked.

"I… uh…" he hesitated. "I don't know. I ran into the closet as soon as I realized someone had broken in. Are the police on the way?" he asked, his whispers rising in pitch.

"Yes, we have police on the way. Just stay on the line with me, okay? Can you hear anyone? Are they moving around?" the dispatcher asked.

Keeping calm was the name of the game here and this guy was getting too excited.

"I heard glass break. It woke me up." Not true and he knew it, but he wasn't going to go there with the 911 dispatcher!

Just then he heard the faint sound of a hallway closet door closing. His heart was pounding madly in his chest. Someone had definitely broken in!

"Seriously, do you have anyone coming? They're moving around now, I can hear them opening doors." Again his whispered voice rose as he panicked.

Again the dispatcher remained calm and continued asking him questions. "Are you alone, sir?" she asked calmly.

"Yes," his heart now pounding so loud he was barely able to speak.

He still had the gun in his hand and his eye on the closed bedroom door. If he had to he could shoot anyone coming through that door from where he was hidden. He wasn't sure he could kill them but he'd be sure they were stopped before reaching him.

His hand shook as he tried to aim at the door and focus on the doorknob. *How did it come to this?* he wondered. He had never thought this would be the result of telling the world who his father was! Campbell had revealed the details of his past and Kyle had beefed up security, but this was bullshit! If he wasn't so friggin' scared he'd be *really pissed!*

Footsteps! He heard footsteps! *Shit!* They were right outside his bedroom. His mind screamed! *Why were they coming here and why after him?* He needed to get his shit together and try to think straight. He took three deep breaths and tried to remain calm. The shaking didn't help.

"Sir, are you there?" the dispatcher asked. "Police have arrived and are on their way up in the elevator to your floor."

He panicked as he saw the bedroom doorknob jiggle slightly and then turn slowly. His throat constricted as did everything else on him. He could see the door opening just a little… were they making sure they had a bedroom? When the door swung open suddenly, he pointed his gun outward away from his body and emptied it towards the form coming through the door as he screamed into the phone. The body fell to the floor before the hand had left the doorknob.

Shaking all over and feeling tears in his eyes, he dropped the phone and rose from his hiding spot. His heart was racing. He felt like he might be sick.

Four large holes now adorned the louvered panels of his closet doors. He opened what was left of the door on the right side to see the crumpled form of an extremely large man, dressed all in black. He was lying on his stomach, head turned grotesquely to one side. There were three, large, bloodstained marks on his back and the leather jacket had blown open where the bullets left the body. *Holy Shit!* he thought. *What the hell just happened?* His heart was racing even faster and he was frozen where he stood.

Naked, breathing heavy, standing over a dead body, pale as a ghost and holding a gun. That was the description the police officer stated in his report and that was the description that ran in the latest edition of *Star Access!* with a front cover showing his handsome face and a large headline that read: *Chase Morningstar! A Shooting Star?* Oh, he had definitely made his mark! New York was turning out to be a hellish ride!

~

Chapter 1

What's with Campbell?

He was such a funny boy! Always able to make a crowd laugh by either faking an accent, a fall or a faux pas. Even at a young age, he was slapstick before he knew what slapstick was. No matter what, he had the crowd in the palm of his hand and usually they were holding their stomachs.

Before the age of six he was able to play the piano without instruction. That, coupled with his outgoing personality and ability to mimic to perfection, made Mark Hagen a tiny little charmer and a natural entertainer. The large hazel eyes, cherubic face and soft brown hair that curled if left too long didn't hurt either. He took after his father whom he absolutely idolized.

His British-born father was the funniest man Mark knew. He spoke with a funny accent, told silly jokes, played the piano with his feet as good as he did his hands and constantly had a story to tell. He always had an audience wherever he went and Mark paid very close attention.

As a young man of eighteen Mark's father applied for and was granted passage and immigration to the U.S. in January of 1939, just months before Britain declared war on Germany. Liverpool, his hometown, took a heavy beating during the war years and he lost touch with his family when they were dispersed throughout England and North America. He found work off and on in bars around New York but, as the U.S. entered the war in 1941, his dreams of being famous grew dim. To keep himself fed he took employment on the docks helping Uncle Sam move the war machine forward. When he impregnated a young woman whose parents insisted he marry her and provide for her and their unborn child appropriately, it ended his career as an entertainer and any hope he had of being famous.

His main audience nowadays was his youngest son Mark. He'd sing his songs and tell fantastical stories, making Mark laugh so hard he would sometimes pee his pants.

His father taught him how to play the piano from an early age and Mark played whatever his father played. He was a tiny sponge soaking up everything he could, wanting to be like him in every way. Soon Mark was imitating him in front of his friends and teachers at school. He became increasingly entertaining and was encouraged to perform by his parents and older brother, Dex, who was Mark's biggest fan.

As far as Mark was concerned, he was the center of the universe in his small life and all those around him who were physically larger than he, gave in to his every request. He captivated audiences, just like his father. He told stories using multiple accents, just like his father. He always looked for a laugh, just like his father.

The only time his father wasn't very fun was when he'd had too much to drink. Then, he'd become dark, moody and belligerent – a complete contrast to his sober self. Sometimes he'd leave the house in a drunken rage and not return for hours, long after Mark had gone to bed. His dark side was gingerly held in check and caused discord in the house on many occasions. When he was good, he was great, fantastic, there was no one like him; when he was bad, you steered clear of him. He'd become accusatory and violent, throwing things around the room. He even threw hard boiled eggs at Mark's mother once because he was drunk and unhappy with the fact that it was snowing. As time went on Mark's father was drunk more than sober and furious rather than funny.

No matter how dark his father's mood or how violent his actions, Mark still kept his father high upon a pedestal. That is, until he turned eight years old. On Mark's eighth birthday his father left to purchase candles for his birthday cake and didn't bother coming home.

They had waited for hours; he, his mother and brother, Dex, with the cake sitting on the kitchen table, untouched. It was adorned with "Happy 8th Birthday Mark" written in the same color of green as the rest of the icing piping the outside of it. When she finally realized what was going on, his mother simply cut the cake and served it to the boys, without singing "Happy Birthday," without candles to blow out, without any kind of celebration at all. She did, however, have tears streaming down her face.

That night, Dex crept into Mark's bedroom and laid beside him as he too cried. Not understanding the complexities of relationships or of adult minds, Mark could only conclude that his father's disappearance was linked to him and that in some way it was his fault. Dex tried to console him and assured him that it wasn't about him but Mark couldn't be persuaded and turned his tears towards his pillow, crying into the night.

His sorrow lasted for many months, at least as long as it took for his father to contact the household again. When his father called, his mother agreed to make a picnic for the family and visit with him in a nearby park. There, they spent the first 30 minutes as though they didn't know one another. His father made no explanations and gave no excuses for his absence.

Mark's mother was submissive; she'd take him back no matter what the circumstances. Dex was begrudging, not wanting to get hurt again and Mark, who had loved and adored, idolized and emulated his father, wasn't fooled. His dad was an arse and he'd never trust him again. Mark was the smartest of the lot. His father had been his world. All the laughter and attention he craved was from his father. His fall from grace also meant Mark was irreparably hurt, especially for him to have disappeared on his birthday. It was a very deep wound.

As it turned out, Mark's father wasn't interested in coming home on the day of the picnic, he just wanted to touch base. The now family of three walked home with their heads hung low, each having their own struggle with the man who had disappointed them all.

Mark's mother was forced to take on two jobs to make ends meet. She relied on Dex to step in and help out with looking after Mark while she worked at a bakery during the day and cleaned offices at night. Dex did his best to make sure Mark was well taken care of but he himself was just a boy of twelve and could not have foreseen Mark's illness; no one could have.

When Mark was ten years old he got a very bad throat infection. His throat swelled up so severely he was admitted to the children's ward of the local hospital. He was barely able to swallow and lost so much weight he looked like a tiny skeleton. The doctors treated the throat infection immediately with antibiotics, thinking nothing of it, but unbeknownst to the doctors, Mark was allergic and instead of curing him it made him spiral downward, teetering very close to death. His brother went into the small hospital chapel and prayed for hours begging for his brother's life, even offering up his own, at one point. When Dex finally made his way back to Mark's hospital room, he was surprised to find his brother awake and alert requesting Campbell's chicken noodle soup. Soon after, as part of his recovery, Mark began eating Campbell's soup non-stop, garnering him the nickname "Campbell." It never left him.

His father became a non-reliable frustrating pain in the ass as his life progressed. He was unable to move past his own five foot hemisphere and be any kind of decent role model to his sons. His drinking had become an everyday occurrence, which hindered him from working even the simplest of jobs. Now he told jokes and entertained people on the streets who threw him coins, with which he'd buy booze and the odd meal. He had very little to live off and would often call upon Campbell's mother to help him out.

In the meantime, Campbell's mother was so busy working trying to put food on the table and keep her estranged husband from being homeless, that the universe Campbell was once the center of became a black hole of despair that consumed him completely.

The once charming entertainer of the family became a sullen shadow of his former self. The kids at school would ask "What's with Campbell?" but no one knew the real answer. Dex was the only one who still treated him like he was anything special and their relationship grew stronger and closer over time. Dex would make dinner for the two of them, laugh with him as they shared their day, made sure that he and Campbell had their homework done and their ears, hands and faces washed and teeth brushed before bedtime. Dex sacrificed a lot to be there for Campbell and because of it Campbell loved him dearly.

Time didn't improve Campbell's father's conscience, commitment to his family or his antics and before too long another man came calling, wanting his mother's company for dates and dinners.

Mr. Dreyfuss was only two years older than Campbell's mother but seemed years older by comparison. He needed afternoon naps, couldn't stay up past 8:30 at night and complained of his bursitis all the time. Campbell's mother was smitten. Dex and Campbell were not but it didn't matter one bit. Within months, his mother was married to Mr. Dreyfuss and Dex and Campbell found themselves living in a very strict household where there was no piano, no laughter and Campbell was no longer the center of anyone's universe. Both boys felt increasingly unwelcome. Mr. Dreyfuss became a dictator imposing his conservative Christian beliefs on their mother more and more and neither Dex nor

Campbell wanted to follow suit. He offered to pay for Dex's entire college tuition outright as long as he attended school out of state and Dex agreed.

Before he left for college, Dex pulled Campbell aside and spoke to him seriously, worried about leaving him behind.

"You remember what I've told you all along, Campbell. No matter what anyone says to you, you're talented and meant to entertain. Find yourself somewhere to play the piano and practice all you can. And make sure you stay in school! That way you have something else to lean on when times are tough, but entertaining crowds, that's your true calling. Just hang in there for the next couple of years and make your grades and you'll be able to follow me and leave here."

He held onto his arm for a moment staring into those big hazel eyes. He was once so little, so tiny. Dex couldn't help but feel protective. He hated leaving his little brother behind but he had to get away.

Over time the tension in the house became unbearable and the boys were always on edge. Mr. Dreyfuss and the boys were not at all compatible. This was becoming increasingly emotionally difficult for Campbell's mother who, since remarrying, was constantly torn between her boys and her very demanding, very controlling husband. She knew that her husband's generous offer for college was just a ruse. He'd complained about the boys as soon as they had moved into his home. She realized that she had made a terrible mistake by marrying Mr. Dreyfuss but was too embarrassed to divorce him, so she went on every day with her guilt growing deeper and deeper. With Dex gone she knew that Campbell would struggle and he would leave soon too and then she'd be left completely alone with him. She didn't want that. In the end, her mind snapped under the persistent anxiety, pressure and guilt. She committed suicide by leaving her gas stove on while Campbell was at school one November afternoon. Her funeral landed on Campbell's sixteenth birthday, with no cake being served at all.

Dex, who had come home to bury his mother, found Campbell crying behind the church after the service and interment. He sat down next to his inconsolable brother, put his arm around him and pulled him close. Campbell sobbed into his brother's shoulder for over an hour. So, for lack of a better comforter, Dex produced a joint and introduced Campbell to weed, something he had recently found himself. All the writers at school were smoking marijuana and Dex felt it helped him write without inhibition.

From the moment the high hit Campbell, he knew he was saved. The fog lifted and suddenly everything was funny. He had found his smile again! That first time he smoked a joint he laughed until he cried. It was his blessing and his curse especially since it wasn't that plentiful for a boy his age. Dex had a tough time tracking down someone in the area who would be willing to supply Campbell, but he managed to meet up with a guy from his past who was happy to oblige. Before returning to college, Dex left Campbell with a large bag of marijuana hidden secretly inside a canvas duffle bag. There was no other therapy for the boy and he never considered an alternative.

After his mother's death, Campbell was given to his father to raise. He had managed to come off the streets, but that was really just geography. He threw down a mattress on a dirty living room floor and told him *"Oy, you sleep 'ere. And don't be any bloody trouble or I'll boot yer arse."* Gone was the showman, the piano playing, story and joke telling entertainer. The man he once revered he was now repulsed by. His father lived every night in a local club drinking and trying to get on stage, but no one thought a drunk was very humorous. He had no idea what had happened for his father to change so drastically but he would do everything in his power to be rid of him as soon as possible.

Dex went off to college to become a writer. Just like Campbell, he believed he'd found a calling and he immersed himself in his studies and writings. Some helped purge his soul, some helped feed it and although he was glad to be out of his home situation, he worried about

Campbell. He was right to because, without Dex's support, Campbell quickly fell into a lifestyle of requiring weed in order to face the daily existence he'd become begrudgingly accustomed to. After searching the bars, clubs and social places in his neighborhood, he finally found a piano at a nearby pool hall and convinced the owner to let him play for tips. It wasn't exactly Carnegie Hall but it was a start. He'd try out new music, quip with the pool players and even offer background music to a tense shot. It may not have always been appreciated but no one could deny the kid had talent!

The only person who seemed not to notice was his father. This perplexed Campbell and only encouraged his marijuana use. His ability to entertain was his greatest asset; however, in order to perform, he now required getting stoned. For most users, it numbed the brain and caused a sort of dense fog as well as an intense desire to eat. For Campbell it created a funny barrier and an undeniable focus with no cravings other than soup. He was able to forget his shattered heart and crumpled world and devote all of his attention on whatever his mind was centered on at the time. Campbell could give 100% to the task, provided he was higher than a kite when he did it.

***

Still just a teenager, Campbell made great money on tips alone playing piano at the pool hall and was soon trying to get gigs at local night clubs and bars that allowed piano players. Once he got the gig at "Creelman's Corner Club", Campbell soon fell out of school and started working nights full time. Shortly after he was shown the mattress on the floor, he was living in a boarding house and paying his own way entertaining at one of the hottest night clubs in the city; illegally of course, as he was still underage. His popularity grew regardless and he soon made a name for himself with the club circuit. He was asked time and again to sit in with bands playing at other clubs; to entertain for a night somewhere else, but Campbell stayed true to Creelman's. Possibly because Mr. Creelman was such a nice guy, probably because Mr. Creelman fed into

Campbell's desire to smoke weed. Rarely did he stray from his nightly spot at the piano bench at Creelman's. Except that one night.

***

Campbell had moved out from his father's apartment and was living at the boarding house full time when he got a call early one morning from Dex's college school administrator. Campbell and Dex had kept in touch but Dex's school schedule and distance from Campbell made it difficult to even speak to one another let alone get a chance to visit. Some months had passed since the brothers last spoke and now, with Campbell working nights at the club, the boys just couldn't seem to connect. So when Mrs. Sterling, the owner of the boarding house, told Campbell there was a phone call from his brother's college for him, he dashed to the phone and yelled into the receiver thinking it was Dex.

It wasn't. It was someone from the college. A "Mr. Montgomery" regretfully informing him that Dex was found dead in his room that morning. After all the worrying about Campbell and how he was going to survive, it was Dex who, when left alone, couldn't deal with his past or face his demons. At first he found writing therapeutic but after a while it didn't help him. Neither did the drugs and he'd tried just about every one of them.

Where Campbell took after his father, Dex took after his mother; they shared the same mental struggles. As time passed he slowly unraveled. He became isolated, anti-social and tormented. When they found him he had hung himself from his closet rod with his belt. There was no note saying goodbye to Campbell; something Campbell had a hard time understanding. He didn't even know he was having a hard time. Whenever they spoke, he was always cheerful, happy at school. It was the slap to the face after the punch in the guts that Campbell really didn't need. His remedy was to keep himself high for the rest of the day. He locked himself in his room and started smoking.

It was the one and only time that he missed playing at Creelman's. That night Campbell's piano remained dark and covered while he lay in a stoned stupor, drifting in and out of his mind's photo box of stills where Dex and he were the central figures. A day at the beach; Dex was seven, Campbell barely three. Years later on Christmas morning, opening presents; Dex got a toy rifle, Campbell got a sharp three piece suit and top hat for when he "performed." In Campbell's mind he could recall standing in front of the tree, wearing his suit and hat, next to Dex, in his pajamas holding his rifle like the new sheriff in town. Both boys were grinning from ear to ear, reveling in the joy the day always brought as the flash went off.

The day Dex died Campbell remained completely out of it. He stayed in his world of memories with Dex, floating back to a time in his life when he didn't know what it felt like to be abandoned by the man he idolized most, or for his heart to be crushed; a time when he was central to all who loved him. He lay on the bed crying softly, unaware of the time that passed or the tears streaming down the sides of his face and soaking his pillow.

They buried his brother on a rainy Tuesday. Campbell stood next to the coffin at what he presumed was his head and said his goodbyes in his mind. He could envision Dex standing before him and telling him that he was fine and he'd watch over him. Campbell didn't believe him. Another male role model that let him down.

With Dex's death, Campbell plummeted into a fogged up haze of an existence. He stayed happy that way, if only for a while. His performances at Creelman's never faltered but he was always as high as a kite, not caring about the consequences. He gave up on reality and now thought the alternative was a much better choice. He had no intention of climbing his way out of his dazed confusion until, sitting in a shitty diner one cold January, having his third cup of coffee that day, he happened to watch as a young democratic senator by the name of John F. Kennedy was sworn in and gave his inaugural speech as the new President of the United States.

Although Campbell never paid attention to politics and couldn't care less about who ran for what, this Kennedy guy was more like someone he could relate to. He was much younger than previous presidents and had amazing charisma and Campbell respected that. He spoke about things that mattered to everyone and he had great taste in women! Kennedy's "…ask not what your country can do for you; ask what you can do for your country…" practically had Campbell going out to enlist on that cold January morning, but who needed a piano player in the army? Nevertheless, it gave Campbell a new guide and he vowed to improve his lot in life. Campbell let his guard down and made John F. Kennedy his new hero, following his every move for the next few years. He became interested and involved. Kennedy brought Campbell back to life and, for the first time in a long time, Campbell started to think the light at the end of the tunnel was not a train after all.

On November 22, 1963, Campbell was all set to celebrate his twenty-third birthday when the unthinkable occurred. Why did bad things always have to happen on his birthday?

***

Campbell had been on his own for many years. He hadn't seen much of his father although, periodically, he would drop in to Creelman's Corner Club to see Campbell, begging for money or something else he needed. Campbell's father had really let his life fall apart. His example compared to President Kennedy was all Campbell needed to keep him from living his life the way his father had.

Although he now had quite the reputation as a serious entertainer, Campbell still remained very isolated in his personal life. The entertainer lived very much as a loner. So, on his twenty-third birthday, with no one around to celebrate and no presents to open, he opted to spend his special day with the patrons of the diner he often frequented. He spent the morning drinking coffee, gabbing with the waitresses and catching up on some news, watching the small black and white TV that sat on the corner counter. It was expected to be a quiet uneventful day in Campbell's life and instead he once again found himself crying before the day was done. Seemed to Campbell as though his birthday couldn't come without sadness and tears.

Someone had killed the President of the United States, on Campbell's birthday, no less, in Dallas, Texas. Someone shot him while he paraded in an open car. The most charismatic man Campbell had ever seen, who held the highest position in the American Government, had been targeted and shot while riding in an open car in Dallas, Texas. Campbell just shook his head and cried. How was anything ever going to get better when all the good men were gone? Once again he had lost someone who he'd chosen to guide him. With the tragic loss of Kennedy, so too went Campbell's heart.

He watched, mesmerized, as the nation grieved. It seemed the whole world was heartbroken as a young mother mourned the loss of her dynamic and charismatic husband. Her daughter holding her mother's hand showing such grace and poise at such an early age and the youngest child, a son, John-John, spending his third birthday burying his dead father, saluting his daddy in front of the entire planet. Truly gut wrenching.

Campbell made sure he rose every morning during those days and sat in that diner and watched the news footage of Kennedy's assassination, his dead body lying in State in the nation's Capital and his subsequent presidential funeral. Campbell thought it was riveting and, although his heart remained heavy, he found solace in the footage, in the funeral and in the patrons of the diner.

In some strange way by the end of the coverage, all the mutual grieving helped Campbell put things into perspective. Kennedy's passing wasn't what he should focus on but rather the words that had inspired him originally.

"My fellow Americans, ask not what your country can do for you, but what you can do for your country."

Campbell fixated on those rousing words. What could he do for his country? It occurred to him that he definitely had something to offer. He knew how to make people laugh and sing along to his piano playing. He knew how to entertain and right now people wanted to break free from reality and laugh again. Campbell's epiphany occurred right there in the diner. He wanted to help everyone heal from the hurt. He was going to go to Creelman's and play the hell out of that damn piano. He was going to give the audience a chance to escape for a few hours – a chance to laugh and smile.

When the furor had died down, another old man was again in the Presidential Office and making young men go to fight a war in a country that Campbell didn't even know existed. Vietnam caused unbelievable unrest for such a tiny country and he was grateful for his anonymity, never having been conscripted because he never went by his real name, making it difficult for the government to track him down. His paycheck came to him each week as an envelope full of cash. No income statement attached, just a torn piece of paper with his hours multiplied by his rate of pay and how much it totaled. Campbell didn't question their bookkeeping practices and they didn't question his name or his living arrangements. As long as the two understood one another in that regard, all went well.

Campbell became purposeful in his entertaining. He felt in control of his audience night after night and realized that he could manipulate the amount of drinking and partying based on the set of music he played. Some nights he'd have the whole audience of Creelman's jumping and rocking to his piano stylings and other nights they sat in quiet contemplation as he played his heart out on the keys. He understood that he made a crowd of people dependent on him; that *he* became *their* drug.

The problem was, after becoming a staple to the establishment, he soon found himself with a strong case of wanderlust. He realized that by staying in one place he wasn't allowing his own natural evolution as a person or a musician and, after thinking it over, he walked away from Creelman's to head further west and find out what life had in store. Always keeping in mind his priorities; to find a piano and stay high.

Campbell managed to keep his weed supply in abundance in those early days; his ability to make money always at the ready along with his ability to find a dealer close by, tuned in like a divining rod for water. Campbell could spot the one person selling weed in a room full of hundreds of people.

He began to play with other musicians who would jam in the stage areas of local bars. He'd enter a town and stick his head into a bar or club in the late afternoon to see if anyone was jamming. If so, he'd saunter over, smile his great smile and ask if they had a piano man in their group. Often they would have the piano but no player, at which point Campbell would take on the job, usually without being asked. This went off okay most of the time; however, if he sensed there were unhappy feelings, he would request a chance to prove his worth and then, after playing a bit, he'd soon be welcomed into the group. He'd be around long enough for them to get really good and then be gone, sometimes after a few weeks, sometimes after a few months. He never stayed long. This kind of lifestyle went hand in hand with his money troubles. He'd play in and out of people's lives, leaving them with either a good laugh, a good high or broke with Campbell owing them a good deal of money. Staying in town too long meant he would rack up debts. Leaving when no one was looking meant he used fake names with the front desk, but to his audience and as a musician he always went by the name "Campbell."

The truth is, he brought great talent to whomever he played with. He was always well liked, his piano playing only augmenting the rest of the musicians he played alongside and when they'd realize he'd skipped town, most of his former band mates would feel a void. Much like his father, Campbell would gain people's trust and have them adoring him only to disappear when they were least expecting it. Some traits were passed down without even trying.

His life carried on like this for many years. Campbell lived from one motel room to the next finding that life was easier the less shit he carried. He didn't own much, he didn't date much and he didn't make many lasting connections with people.

His dating life was intermittent. A long term relationship to Campbell was maybe three months. They didn't last very long because he didn't stay in one place very long. He had learned to appreciate many aspects of a woman, but still hadn't found one that made him consider settling down. In all the years he'd entertained and moved around, he had never fallen in love.

He was playing with a group of guys called "Cobalt Blue" at a Chicago club when, one evening, they brought in a beautiful female vocalist named Celia Morningstar. It was rare that Campbell bothered with the talent, always finding it to be a hassle when it came time to move on, but something about this woman was different. She had a voice like no other, her look was exotic as hell and lips were magnificent. Right from the start she caught Campbell's attention. She flirted with him and swayed her lovely hips whenever she thought he was looking and he was looking a lot.

He found himself dreaming about her, wondering how she spent her days and with whom she spent her nights. She always arrived with two other men and Campbell wasn't sure who they were or what role they played in her life; he only knew her name and that she seemed to be as interested in him as he was in her. After an evening spent flirting and making suggestive comments back and forth to one another, Campbell ended up in the back seat of his car between Celia's eagerly spread legs. She was exciting and luscious and lovely. She smelled like vanilla and soft musk. It drove him crazy. Her body moved in sync with his beautifully and he was very aroused by her. He enjoyed the hell out of their lovemaking and as his orgasm hit him full on he thought for a split second, *she could be the one!*

~

Chapter 2

Chase Morningstar

Chase Morningstar carried his bag onto the late night flight back to New York and found his seat in first class. Thanks to Lapis Labels, Chase Morningstar would now be flying first class all the time! He'd signed a three million dollar contract to create his first CD with Lapis Labels and was now enjoying what that kind of money would bring him. As he rested his head back he closed his eyes and stretched his legs out in front of him… oh, the benefits of first class!

He let out a heavy sigh and started relaxing, truly relaxing. For the first time in a very long time Chase Morningstar felt at ease and without burden. He reflected back on the happenings of the past few days, months and years. The very large chip he'd been lugging around, comfortably resting on his shoulder was gone. It had built up over time. Over his entire lifetime resentment had grown towards a brother, 15 years his senior who meant the world to him and had left when Chase was a very young boy, for a career playing music in bars across the US. It was only supposed to be for a few short months but it turned into nearly 20 years of rare visits and worst of all, a broken promise. Chase was only a young child but he recalled the conversation he'd had with Charlie the night before he left when Charlie had tucked him into bed.

"Why are you going away, Charlie?" asked the little boy, trying hard to not cry, but his bottom lip wasn't cooperating.

"Mom wants me to play my guitar for more people than just you and her," he said, sounding defeated.

"Why can't I come wiv you?" Chase asked, again his lip quivered.

"Awww... little buddy," Charlie said tenderly, stroking the young boy's head. "You need to stay here and watch out for mom while I'm gone. I want to know she's okay and I know you're the best at keeping her smiling, making her laugh and giving her some good cuddles," he told him affectionately. "Mom is going to need you to do that a lot so I'm putting you in charge of those things, okay?" he said seriously, hoping Chase would understand.

The little boy nodded his head just as a tear dropped down the side of his face. *Poor little guy*, thought Charlie. He scuffed the boy's hair and kissed him on his forehead before standing up to leave Chase's room.

"How long are you going to be gone for? I'm already missing you," Chase said, as he rolled to his side. The question made his older brother stop at the door and look at his baby brother with a smile on his face.

"Oh, it won't be long. Just until the end of the summer. I've promised Mom that I'll try this until summer ends and then come home for school. I'm gonna be a teacher, you know, just like Papa George!" he told the small child and then he smiled wide at him and Chase's whole face lit up as he smiled back. He felt much better about Charlie going away now, assured that Charlie would be home soon.

"Promise?" asked Chase.

"Promise," replied Charlie, as he turned and left the doorway.

It would be the last time Chase believed in a promise.

The captain's voice broke into Chase's reverie and brought him back to the flight to New York.

18

"Good afternoon ladies and gentlemen, this is your captain speaking. I've just been notified that we are going to have to sit on the runway for a bit, delaying our take off approximately a half hour." The passengers let out a unanimous groan. "Yeah, I know. Sorry about this but we're holding for now. I'll let you know when we get cleared for take-off," the captain ended.

Chase sunk lower into his seat and closed his eyes again. He didn't care. He was comfortable and slightly sleepy anyway. Once again his mind drifted back to his childhood. He spent time examining the resentment he held against Charlie for so long and then applied Charlie's reasoning for his long absences and broken promise. To look at it now, Chase realized that he probably wouldn't have been satisfied knowing why Charlie stayed away so much, not as a young boy anyway. As a grown man, Chase understood Charlie's paranoia. It was as if he'd been given clearer vision and with every remembrance, Chase was now able to look upon the account and understand not only his side, but Charlie's as well.

Even recalling his mother's death, Chase could now understand how it had cemented Charlie's fears as well as his own frustration with his brother. Chase believed for years that if Charlie had been home, the two of them could have saved her. That instance alone must have added 100 lbs to the chip on Chase's shoulder. Charlie paid heavily for his mother's death without even realizing it.

Chase sighed and pushed that horrific memory from his mind. He remembered shortly after Charlie took him on the road and together they formed a blues/jazz band called "Chasing Charlie." Chase was up front on stage performing each night with the audience eating out of his hand, but it wasn't enough. He wanted more but Charlie didn't. Charlie made sure Chase understood that if he began this band with his brother it would never be more than a band who toured and played live to an eclectic audience with a discerning blues and jazz taste. Charlie wasn't interested in recording, interviews with music reporters, or becoming famous in any way; he just wanted to play his music live.

Charlie made the deal with Chase hoping he wouldn't change his mind and Chase made the deal with Charlie hoping that he would. After 20 years of touring, Charlie not only stuck to the deal, he became a static house band at a club owned by Georgie and her uncle, Charlie's old touring buddy, Wade McGrath. Once that happened, Chase became a complete asshole. Complete. He treated his band mates and his brother very badly and was a selfish, drunken bastard at the hardest time for Georgie. No wonder she didn't accept his offer of love. In reflection, he had planned today to go so differently.

Georgie. The woman he loved and quite literally just lost. To Charlie. He should feel angry, even jealous but he couldn't. Georgie Pelos had been his secret love for most of his life. She babysat him as a young boy and he always thought he'd grow up to marry her. He even recalled telling his mother nightly that he would. Chase smiled to himself as he remembered Celia's reaction.

One night at suppertime he'd told his mother, "I'm going to marry Georgie when I get big like Charlie!"

"Are you?" she'd say, smiling to herself.

"Oh yes and we're going to live here with you," he stated, matter-of-factly.

"You are?" Celia asked. "Don't you want to live in a house all your own? Perhaps Georgie doesn't want to live with me," she offered, making the small boy think over his plan.

"Nope, I think she'll love it here. I don't want to live away from you, Mommy and besides, Charlie says you have to have me here to keep you smiling," he assured her.

And when he told Georgie of his plans, she had a lot to say about it. Thinking back, Chase knew he had her to thank for his drive to be a superstar. It was Georgie who had put the thought in his head.

Chase surprised her one day when he informed her that he was going to be a star and he would grow up to marry her.

"Oh, well you'd better make a lot of money, Chase, because I plan on wanting the best of everything," she joked with him, laughing.

Chase heard those words and took them verbatim. Thinking on it now, waiting for his flight to take off, Chase resigned himself to the fact that he would be headed back to New York with Georgie as his muse.

In trying to make a grand proclamation of love to her, Chase was made to realize that Georgie's heart belonged to Charlie and always had. They were destined to spend the rest of their lives together. It was a bittersweet result for Chase. He had secretly watched as they professed their life-long love for one another. For them, it was a glorious day but not so much for Chase. Once Chase witnessed their love for one another, he held nothing back – the two brothers addressed all the anger and resentment that Chase had been holding onto, once and for all. Of course, the wedding of former Chasing Charlie band mate, Rosa, was not the best time to lock themselves up in the men's room at the Black and Blue club and clear the air, but when the brothers emerged there was a peace between them that hadn't been there in some time.

Although his day hadn't gone as planned, Chase was leaving with less baggage than when he came, emotionally and mentally anyway. After he said all of his goodbyes to his former band mates and Georgie, he asked Charlie to step outside with him. Before he called a cab he wanted one more conversation with his brother. Charlie came clean to Chase and now it was Chase's turn.

"Charlie, I'm sorry I've been such a prick during all this," he motioned back to the club. "You know when I was a little kid I had no idea why you seemed to want to stay away, you know that, right?" Both men nodded. "I've been resentful of you for so fuckin' long, I can't remember when I didn't feel that way. Everything, from you leaving when I was little, to you barely coming home, to you not wanting to be famous, it all added to the shit I felt. I'm sorry Charlie, really sorry that I acted like I did. I took it all so personally, I guess. You were my idol, you know?" he stopped. He didn't want to say any more without letting Charlie respond.

Charlie shook his head, smiled and reached out and hugged his brother tightly. "If I was your idol, it's no wonder you became such a prick!" He slapped his brother's back, laughing and stepped back smiling.

Charlie continued to smile as he looked toward the ground. "Now it's your turn to leave, Chase." Charlie said, sounding melancholy. "I truly don't want to hold you up any longer but there's something I haven't mentioned. I wanted to wait until things were straightened out between us." Charlie looked at Chase sincerely, as though he wanted to be sure Chase understood the seriousness of what he was about to say.

He tilted his head considering his words carefully. "It's funny this has all happened within the last few months. It's as if life knows when to feed you what you need." He smiled at Chase. Charlie knew Chase had no idea what he was about to tell him. He took a deep breath.

"On the day Wade died, he told me of someone who dated mom and," he hesitated, "he believed he was your father." He waited a moment letting this sink in. At Chase's obvious look of confusion, Charlie continued. "Wade only knew the guy by a nickname he had and it wasn't much help so I asked my father if he could do some digging for me. He's given me the name and number of who his sources believe is your father. The guy lives in New York," Charlie explained to an astonished Chase as he handed him a folded piece of paper.

Chase was floored! He had never known who his father was and Celia never really spoke of it. For the longest time he thought he was the child of someone famous; how else could such charisma be explained? When he offered this suggestion to his mother Celia one day, she just laughed and shook her head and said, "Oh, to be sure, baby!" She never explained it; nor did she deny it.

Wade's death brought out more than its fair share of skeletons. The old family friend and Charlie's touring partner for almost 15 years left more in his will than just unexpected inheritances for Charlie. His machinations would have lasting effects on others long after his death. Chase had been effected by Wade's manipulations in a major way but in the end he was grateful for the excuse to leave Charlie and the band behind and head to New York to make his own mark on the world. He wanted to do it in grand style.

Chase held the folded piece of paper tightly in his hand. He wasn't sure if he wanted to look at it while Charlie stood there, but then it occurred to him that Charlie probably knew what it said.

"Did you look already?" Chase asked.

Charlie smiled a huge smile. "Open it," was all he said, smiling back.

Chase unfolded the paper and read the name, Mark Hagen. He did a double take and reread the name. MARK HAGEN. What the hell was going on? Was this a joke?

"This is the name of the piano player I just met in New York. *His nickname is Campbell*," Chase said, confused. "*I told you* about him. He once sang with mom."

"One and the same, I believe. He apparently did more than sing with her!" Charlie chuckled. Chase was still unsure if Charlie had his information right and Charlie could see he wasn't buying it, so he explained.

"Wade told me your father's nickname was *"Campbell"* and that he was a piano player, but he thought he was dead. Given that, my father contacted a private investigator he knows who had to do some really intense digging but finally found this guy in New York and yes, it sounds like the same guy you just met. How much of a coincidence is that?" asked Charlie, smiling and chuckling while slapping his younger brother on the back. "You should know, Brad says his man had a helluva time finding this guy. He was hidden well and for a reason. Full disclosure little brother."

"I can't believe it," Chase said softly, staring at the name on the paper.

Charlie looked at him intently. "Tell me something," he asked, Chase still grinning from ear to ear, "have you ever seen the elderly black woman that we met in the cemetery that day we left Chicago, after the fire?" He paused for a moment and then leaned in closer and whispered to Chase "Ever see her again? …afterwards? …huh?" He raised his eyebrows at his younger brother, nodding his head.

Chase knew that neither he nor Charlie could explain the elderly black woman who made periodic appearances, almost like a supernatural guide, throughout their lives. But then, Chase had never told Charlie of his recurring dream. Perhaps the Morningstar brothers were protected by many different spiritual guides!

Chase was pulled abruptly from his reverie by another overhead announcement: "Ladies and Gentlemen, once again this is your captain speaking and we have just been cleared for takeoff."

A round of applause rang through the passengers. Chase smiled to himself. With all that emotional upheaval behind him, Chase Morningstar was more than cleared for take-off! He was ready to soar into the stratosphere of the music world. Chase Morningstar was ready to become a Superstar!!

***

Kyle Craven's heart attack was settling down into an easy, slow-moving, pulmonary embolism now that Chase had returned from Chicago. Just days after signing a three million dollar contract, his newest up and coming artist leaves the state to God knows where without so much as an explanation!

Kyle would have to go over the terms of the agreement again with Chase, just so there'd be no more quick getaways without Kyle being informed on all fronts and given 72 hours' notice prior to said getaway occurring. Now that he'd returned, Kyle put eyes on him 24/7. He had a lot riding on this deal and he wasn't going to let this impulsive, brilliant artist blow it.

Chase had talent and charisma oozing from every pore, an incredible musical ability and, in the studio, there was no one like him; he worked like a dog. Chase rocked! There was however, something that ate at him. Kyle was intrigued to find out what made this enigma tick; what or rather, *who* his muse was, so he locked Chase in a hotel room and told him to start writing songs. Once Chase started, it flowed like a torrent.

Chase felt creatively inspired once he left Chicago and allowed his heartache over Georgie to flow through to his writing or his guitar playing or whatever creative outlet he happened to be engaged in. He could write music across a multitude of genres and stretched even as far as soft rock on two of his songs not yet laid down. He always wanted to break into rock, but that was never supported with Chasing Charlie. Kyle accepted anything he wrote and didn't give him parameters, so Chase wrote whatever he felt.

Kyle also made sure Chase and his newly formed backup band consisting of six members, rehearsed with Chase every chance they got. He liked his new band and although they were all brought together in very short order and had yet to be named, Chase was proud of their caliber.

Their ages ranged from a 35 year old bass player to his 74 year old piano player, none other than Campbell, Kyle's first choice because he loved the chemistry between them after they had jammed together a few times. Chase and Campbell had a certain something that Kyle couldn't put his finger on, but he made sure Campbell was Chase's piano player. Kyle and Campbell had a long-standing close relationship, like uncle and nephew and the younger made sure the elder was always working, always safe and always in studio, not playing out in the open in a club or bar.

Chase's band was an eclectic group, diverse not only in their ages, but also in their background and careers. The only novice to the recording studio was Chase and he soaked it all up like a sponge. Kyle got him to work quickly using as much studio time as he could book and whenever Chase was available. Kyle would say his learning curve was 90 degrees!

After only a few weeks, Chase and his band had laid down numerous tracks that Kyle knew would be worthy of shooting to #1 on the rhythm and blues charts, and that was before he'd been formally introduced! It took no time at all before they worked like they had been together for years, with Chase Morningstar finally recording.

Yes, he was known to some as the enigmatic and mesmerizing frontman for the former blues band called Chasing Charlie, but Chase Morningstar had his own galaxy to aspire to. There was no telling how far he could go and Kyle Craven had every intention of being taken along for the ride. He could practically smell the money!

The fact that Kyle had hired Campbell was a small joke to Chase. He didn't go right to the guy announcing, "Hey, you're my Dad!" like in the movies. Instead, he watched Campbell, trying to gauge his reaction, waiting for an opportunity to talk to the guy and see if Charlie and Brad's information was correct.

That opportunity came one evening after a late session in the studio. With Chase on guitar and Campbell on the piano, they finished up some finer details to Chase's latest track and were packing away their gear when Chase asked if Campbell would join him for a drink at the local watering hole. Two hours later they sat at the bar sharing stories of their travels and tours. Apparently they had a lot more in common than they realized. They both secretly loved Elvis Presley, almost to an obsession. Each had seen every movie he ever made; Chase had them all on Blu-ray. They both hated seafood, sauerkraut and steamed rice. They agreed on their preference of brunettes to blondes and were both self-professed boob men over ass and legs. The one thing they didn't share was an addictive nature.

Campbell had smoked weed for years. It was the only drug he used and he used it regularly. That was, until the one and only fateful night when out of desperation for a high and with no weed at hand, Campbell let his guard down and tried cocaine. That night taught him an extremely valuable lesson and Campbell, to that point, had never tried cocaine again.

Chase liked his drink but he didn't lean on it now at all since he'd left Chicago and had started his own recording career. He wrote better when his mind was clear and not fogged up by alcohol and he rarely smoked. Chase was keenly focused and kept his goal in the crosshairs. He was going to work as hard as he could to get his name in every household. *"No press was bad press"* – that was his motto! Little did he know how he would come to regret that saying in a very big way.

As they nursed their drinks Chase took a long look at Campbell as he sat across from him. *For 74 years of age, he's spry, in pretty good shape and has a sharp mind,* Chase thought. *I could have done worse for a father.* He was ready to share this secret with Campbell. Now was the time to let Campbell in on why he'd asked him to go for a drink. Chase sat back and stretched first.

"So, we've got quite a few things in common, huh? Are you surprised or do you think it's a musician thing?" he asked leadingly. If Campbell had suspected anything, Chase was giving him the chance to admit it.

Campbell thought for a moment then let out his breath like a hiss. "No, it's not a musician thing." He paused, shaking his head, looking directly at Chase. He cleared his throat and sat back in his chair, folding his hands and then looking down to his lap. "It's probably more a *Hagen* thing," he admitted, raising his head and looking his son directly in the eye.

Chase waited a moment, considering Campbell's words. He understood what he meant; Campbell already knew they were related. Chase stared at his father, holding his eye then he nodded and poured another shot for each of them.

"Can you believe I sat in on your jam session, out of the blue?" He raised his glass. "To an unbelievable circumstance," toasted Chase.

"To my beautiful Celia," Campbell toasted.

It made Chase hesitate for a moment and then smile once again. "To my beautiful mother, Celia," Chase repeated and clinked his glass with Campbell's and then knocked back his shot.

"I knew as soon as you said your name the first time we met. You don't forget a name like "Morningstar" easily, never mind a woman like your mother. Besides, you look a helluva lot like my older brother, your late Uncle Dex." He laughed. They clinked their glass again and shot another back.

"So… *Dad,*" Chase emphasized the word "…what happened? You spent time with mom and then what?"

"I spent a few weeks courtin' your mom when I was with a group of guys called Cobalt Blue; we played at a local club in Chicago. We moved on and started playing further out of state. I had no idea you were even conceived," Campbell stated as he shrugged his shoulders and lied – at least about how long they dated and the "moving on with the band" part. Chase didn't need to know about Campbell's bad habits and the reason he left Chicago in the first place. *Let him spend ten minutes feeling proud of his paternal heritage* Campbell thought, *even if it would be short lived.*

Campbell proudly told stories of Celia and her performances with Cobalt Blue and Chase listened intently, totally enthralled. He also studied Campbell; the way he spoke, his movements, his mannerisms. Of all the similarities Chase caught, it was the duplication of their head jerk laugh that clinched the deal for him. When something really caught Chase on the funny bone, his laugh was a burst from his chest and his head jerked back, losing himself in the humor of the moment. Campbell reacted the same way, at something Chase had said, no less. Chase couldn't believe he didn't recognize before what, to him, was so obvious now – they were most definitely father and son.

~

Chapter 3

One Thing Leads To Another

The car squealed its tires as it turned around quickly on the quiet residential street. At that hour of night, it would certainly wake up the neighborhood but Campbell didn't care. He was feeling invincible after having had the most amazing time (and sex) he'd ever had with an equally amazing new lady named Celia. She was sexy, sophisticated and smart.

As he drove along the dark streets of Chicago in the early morning hours, he smiled as he thought back to how primal their lovemaking had been. He could barely wait to get at her and she was just as bad; she'd actually torn the buttons right off his shirt! That just meant she had passion and he liked that about her.

He really liked how they worked together both on the piano bench and the back bench seat of his car; she matched him, note for note, stroke for stroke. He could see himself really falling for her.

As Campbell navigated through the quiet sleeping city he allowed himself to imagine a life with Celia. When he drove her home she mentioned a teenage son. Campbell hadn't considered children, either of his own or otherwise, but the thought didn't put him off – in fact it intrigued him. He'd like a son.

Campbell grew lofty in his imaginings and just as he was about to broadside a city taxi he managed to jerk himself out of his reverie and slam on the brakes. He and the cabbie looked at one another, each believing it was their own fault, neither paying attention at this late hour. It was truly a wakeup call and Campbell gave his head a shake, took a deep breath and waited for the cabbie to pull out of his way before continuing forward.

He did have a mission. He needed to score some weed having run out earlier in the evening. The thought made him want to smoke something there and then and he rooted through the ashtray of his car, sure there was a roach leftover worth sparking up. He had run out of options as to who he could go to. Campbell didn't pay his debts. He wasn't great with his money, always finding a "higher" priority, but that meant that he owed everybody for everything; always robbing Peter to pay Paul. When rent was due, he'd given his money to a dealer. When he needed to pay a dealer, he'd paid part of his rent so someone was always owed something. He started out with excellent connections but at this point in time he'd worn out his welcome and then some. This didn't concern him though as long as there was a high nearby. Campbell was in a good mood. Always.

Campbell drove until he came to the small dilapidated block of apartments with the rust brick walls and the rusted iron balconies – the last resort. He wouldn't put a field mouse on any one of those balconies for fear they'd collapse under the weight. He hated the environment his vice took him into but he loved the vice itself; so much so that it was worth all the nasty places he had to visit and the shitty people he had to deal with.

He parked the car on a dark side street at the back of the apartments, entered through a back door and went straight into the building. Any security in place was long since broken and the lock on the door didn't stop anyone from entering. The heady smell of urine and 1,000 dinners hit his nostrils and he took small breaths to help tolerate the odour. Campbell knew it was late but he also knew Hennie, a late 20-something drug dealer would be awake. Hennie had a young wife and two children but that didn't stop him from being one of the most well-known and sometimes ruthless drug dealers in his city. He was tough as nails and Campbell didn't trust him but he knew he'd be up and definitely have some reefer. What else could Campbell do?

The thing is, he already owed him $450.00. He was hoping that Hennie would give him just a little weed until Friday when he got paid. He could pay him some then. As long as there was a piano that could be played, Campbell knew he could earn a wage so money was always coming in, just never enough. His income was from one gig to the next; mainly out of pocket but Campbell never carried his money with him. A lesson he learned after being robbed while carrying all he had on him. The lesson taught him to stash his money in his motel room and carry coins enough for coffee. It never occurred to him to put it in a bank.

He climbed the three flights of stairs to Hennie's apartment and opened the door to his floor. Hennie lived at the far end of the hall and once again Campbell found himself taking in a big breath and holding it while he walked down the passageway. When he arrived at #312 he could see that the door was slightly open with a chain in place across the top. He could hear several male voices talking and laughing inside. He knocked hard four times on the door causing it to open wider only to be caught by the chain. The voices silenced; whispers could be heard and moments later Hennie's bloodshot eye and half of his red chubby nose poked through the slim opening.

"Hey, Campbell!" Hennie exclaimed, rather loudly.

It unnerved Campbell slightly. "Uh… hey… Hennie. How's it going, man?" He kept his voice low, not wanting to wake the building.

"You bring me my money?" Hennie asked, his body still behind the door.

"Well, actually not till Friday, but I was hoping you could front me some until then. Just a little like a dime bag or something, just till I get paid and then I'm coming right back here to pay you off completely, I swear it," Campbell pleaded. Then he flashed him his best smile.

Hennie paused giving him a discerning look while thinking about his request. He wasn't sure if he liked Campbell. He seemed like a nice guy, funny as hell and all, but he couldn't be trusted where money was concerned and Hennie's patience had worn thin. Unlike Campbell, Hennie was excellent with his money and he wanted to teach Campbell a lesson about what happens when you continue to screw around with people and their money. He unchained the door, opened it wide and gestured for Campbell to come inside. Once done, Hennie closed and locked it.

Campbell followed Hennie into his living room where he saw five men sitting at a makeshift card table, playing poker, drinking shots, smoking cigars and passing a joint. They were all rather large, each with a menacing look about him. Regardless of his young family, Hennie ran with a pretty tough group to be sure and Campbell felt immediately on edge. He could see each man had a small mirror next to their drink and white powder covered each one. Cocaine.

He had seen people using it but had never tried it himself. There was a certain tension that filled the room when they saw Campbell. These guys were heavily into their drinks, their drugs and their game. Suddenly Campbell didn't want to be there anymore, weed or not. Hennie introduced him to the men but didn't offer their names in return. No other introductions were forthcoming. They knew who he was, but he didn't know any of them except Hennie.

Hennie took his seat at the game table and spoke rapid fire to the men in a language Campbell didn't know, maybe German or Dutch. When he finished, a large blonde haired man spoke, then the guy wearing the grey sweater, then Hennie again. They stopped talking and all looked at him and then back to Hennie nodding.

"Excuse me, but these men are some of my associates," which got a laugh from most of them. "I have told them what you want me to do and they have offered me a solution. See Campbell, I'm very tired of having my money sitting with you when it should be with me." As he said this he used both hands to gesture to Campbell and then back to himself. "My…" he hesitated, "associates…" he smiled again and then continued, "believe they have a solution to this dilemma by getting you to work for me to pay off your debt," he explained.

Campbell felt incredibly nervous. Now he really wanted out of there! Maybe if he just explained that he only wanted a little and that first thing Friday morning he would be all paid up, Hennie's associates would understand better.

"I already have work, it isn't that. It's just that I get paid Friday and I could pay it all to you then," Campbell explained. He looked anxiously at the men who were sat at the table.

"Ahh… but this work isn't a 9 to 5 job. I just need you to deliver a package for me. If you can do that, then I think I can give you a dime bag to tide you over," Hennie said. He leaned back in his chair, pulled a joint out of his pocket and drew it between his lips, wetting the paper entirely. He then put it to his lips and sparked the end with his lighter. Campbell could tell from the pungent odour that it was of excellent quality. Damn, Hennie always had good shit.

"And will I still owe you $450.00?" asked Campbell.

"Nope, your debt will be wiped clean," Hennie said, assuring him.

Campbell looked over the men sitting around the table. He knew something was going on but wasn't sure what it was. He couldn't tell by their language or gestures what they were up to and hoped it was just a package delivery, nothing more. He could sure use this debt being wiped clean but he worried at what price?

"Okay, so... uh... I guess so. Can I ask what's in the package?" Campbell inquired, hoping he'd at least be told that for a heads up.

"You can ask but I'm not going to tell you," Hennie laughed and slapped the table hard with his hand.

The other men joined in and had a good laugh together. Campbell didn't laugh. He nervously smiled and shifted on his feet. Hennie got up from the table and walked towards a cabinet near the kitchen. He bent down exposing half his ass crack and retrieved a package all taped up in brown paper. He threw the package at Campbell who caught it at his chest. It felt soft and had no scent. Campbell figured it was probably cocaine. Great. Now he was a delivery boy for Hennie and his henchmen. Great.

Campbell was starting to wonder if he could trust Hennie about his debt being paid out. In the pit of his stomach this didn't feel right to him but he wasn't completely sure he could get himself out of it. Shit!

"You'll get your dime bag when you've delivered the package," he said, as he approached Campbell and handed the lit joint to him. Campbell hesitated and then accepted the joint, acknowledging the assignment. He didn't know what else to do and besides, at least he got a joint to smoke while he made the delivery.

"I'm doing the delivery right now, I presume?" he asked, wanting to get his instructions and then get the hell out of there fast.

"Yes. I need you to take that package to this address." He handed Campbell a small piece of paper with "906 Clutterbuck Road" written on it. He knew the area, another equally shitty part of town.

"Okay, well, I'd better get going," he said, turning towards the door.

"See you back here when you're done," Hennie said as he sat back down at the table. He said something to the other men and they all broke out laughing.

Dammit! Campbell thought. *How the hell do I get out of this now?* He gingerly drew on the joint as he found his way back downstairs and outside to where he'd parked the car. The breath holding helped not only for the high but also for the building's pong. He got into his car and tossed the package on the front passenger's seat, staring at it, trying to think.

If he didn't show up, they'd be looking for him. Not a good thing to do if he wanted to live. If he delivered the package and came back here, who's to say they would keep their word? What if none of this was on the up and up and he was being set up? Paranoia was making his mind reel. He decided to drive to the address and see what the place was like and then go from there. Maybe it was no big deal. Maybe the people at this address weren't as intimidating as the men in Hennie's apartment.

It was still the wee hours of the morning and Campbell was feeling very exhausted. He hadn't slept in more than 24 hours and just wanted to find a little weed before going home. *Was it necessary to have to go through all this shit too?*

He drove across town quickly, easily done when there's little to no traffic. He found Clutterbuck Road and turned onto it, turning off his headlights. As he crept silently down the road looking for number 906, he took stock of the houses and neighborhood around him. Many of these homes had seen better days. Some were outright abandoned. Campbell had a nasty feeling that the house he was delivering to wasn't going to be much better and he was right. As he pulled into the driveway of 906 he saw movement from within. There were lights on. There were also threadbare sheets for curtains and it was missing its screen door.

Campbell turned off the car and sat in the driveway for a moment trying to gather his thoughts. If things went south, what would he do? He reached over to the glove compartment and rooted around for anything in there he could use as a weapon should things get messy. The only item of any use was a 9-inch Phillips screwdriver. He grabbed it and dropped it into the inside of his right sock. He also grabbed a pair of brass knuckles he had bought at a pawn shop a few years ago. A deal had turned bad once and he got into a fist fight with the guy which ended up hurting his hands. He couldn't play piano for over a month. After that he bought the knuckles. They'd never been used but they were a great source of comfort when going into circumstances where he wasn't sure what would happen.

He figured he'd be sorry if he found himself in another bad situation and didn't have them with him. He decided to place them in his right pocket, hidden away, unless they were needed. Now, armed as best as he could be, he grabbed the package and got out of the car.

The steps leading up to the front door were in rough shape and he didn't even try using the handrail as it, too, was barely holding on. He knocked on the door and immediately put his hand in his pocket, protectively donning the knuckles.

After a moment the door opened and a tall, skinny woman stood before him. She looked as though she'd been on a binger for years and wasn't even considering a break. Campbell imagined this was a constant for her; she probably didn't even wake up sober. She was wearing bellbottom jeans that hugged her hips and ass very tightly. Her top was a white, sleeveless, ribbed cotton shirt and it clung to her, exposing to all that she wore no bra. Campbell tried not to look directly at her for fear that some wall of a guy would soon come upon them and realize what Campbell could see. Then Campbell would have to pull out the knuckles!

"Uh… I have a package from Hennie," Campbell said, without an introduction. The sooner he could get this done, the sooner he could get back to Hennie's, get his dime bag and get home.

The blonde smiled all glassy eyed, and in a stupor, she held up one finger. "Jus' a minute," she slurred. "WAARRRRENN," she yelled as loud as she could, "Hennie's delivery boy is here!"

Campbell heard footsteps coming towards the door and prayed all went well. Warren came from around the door and nodded to Campbell. He was a big guy with a large upper body and really skinny legs. He was shaped like a cartoon character. His head was square, he had very little eyes and nearly no lips to speak of. He, too, looked rough as hell and when he smiled only four teeth showed.

Must be tough to eat like that, thought Campbell and gripped the hidden knuckles reassuring himself. These two looked oddly paired. They must be addicts. Besides, what kind of people get a delivery of cocaine after 3:00 am if they aren't addicts? Campbell stepped inside the house following after the skinny blonde and the toothless Warren. He handed the package over and stood for a moment waiting to see if there was anything else. His right hand gripped the knuckles firmly.

"Hennie didn't say anything about payment so, I figure you guys are square then?" Campbell asked, trying to get a move on.

"Oh, he didn't talk to me about *my* payment, only yours," Warren said, smiling his toothless grin.

"What?" Campbell asked, confused. "I don't get you, man."

"See, it's like this…" Warren stepped forward and put his hand on Campbell's left shoulder, speaking closely to him while leading him further into the house. His breath hit Campbell hard and it made him move his head quickly to the side, away from the stench, his gag reflex being heavily tested.

"Hennie doesn't like waiting on his money or having to remind someone that he's owed. When he has someone who's dickin' him about for his bread, he sends them to me and I let them know he's pissed off with them and I remind them that they owe him money. In return, I get a big bag of coke. It's the perfect relationship."

As soon as he finished speaking, he grabbed Campbell's arm and twisted it behind his back, causing him to wince in pain. Campbell quickly brought his brass-knuckled fist out and around to connect with Warren squarely in the face. Warren stumbled backwards, letting go of Campbell's arm. Campbell lunged past Warren making a break for the door, but the skinny blonde was quick and tripped Campbell, sprawling him out in front of the doorway. Campbell flipped over and tried to rise but Warren was on him and grabbed him by the throat. He started punching Campbell as he stood over him. Campbell tried punching back, pulling on Warren's hands and blocking his face but Warren's assault kept on coming.

He remembered the screwdriver in his sock and managed to bring his leg up far enough for him to reach and grab it. He swiftly brought it up and plunged it into Warren's abdomen with full force, his adrenaline pumping hard. Having never stabbed anyone before, Campbell was shocked at how hard Warren's abdomen was, but the screwdriver went in to its handle, causing an immediate gush of blood. It shot out with such speed that Campbell's arm and pant leg were soon covered in it. Warren jerked back and quickly clutched his stomach as Campbell drew the screwdriver out. His face twisted in pain and disbelief and his eyes registered his wonderment at what had happened. The skinny blonde screamed and rushed to Warren's aide as he fell to the floor. Campbell wasn't sure if a screwdriver could kill a guy but he sure as hell wasn't going to stick around and find out. Moving quickly, he got himself up off the floor and began to back away, holding the screwdriver like a knife out in front for protection. It was covered in Warren's blood and body matter (of some kind) left behind.

Campbell didn't trust the skinny blonde; she wasn't as out of it as she appeared to be. He noticed the package of cocaine on the ground. Warren and the blonde were too wrapped up in dealing with his wound to see him grab it and Campbell figured they wouldn't notice it was missing for a while, if at all. He was pretty sure Warren would be heading to the hospital – he doubted they'd be calling the police! Campbell clambered out of the door with a large bundle of cocaine that would be just about enough money to help him get as far away as possible.

He made it back to his car, wiping his hand off on a clean dry part of his shirt before reaching for the door handle. Throwing the screwdriver and the package onto the floor in the back, he quickly started the car and gunned the engine, pulling backwards out of Warren's driveway and up the street. It was the second time that night he drove through a neighborhood squealing his tires.

This night did not end up as well as it had started and now he was going to have to race back to his motel room and be gone before Hennie got word that he'd wounded Warren and stolen the cocaine. He couldn't imagine going back to Hennie's now even though Hennie had told him to. What was the point? Did Hennie want to see the result of Warren's beating? Besides, if Warren had been successful, who's to say he could've made the trip? What kind of a fool *would* go back? Campbell realized then that Hennie probably wasn't expecting him. Now he was going to have to make a run for it.

Thinking rapid fire, his heart racing hard and covered in Warren's blood he started to figure out his next steps. He would head out of town, completely away from Chicago and make his way east. His hands had not been hurt and he could easily find a place in which he could play piano and make some quick cash. Meanwhile, there was always someone in a bar looking for cocaine. He wasn't sure what the going rate was but he'd make money from the package he'd taken, for certain.

Feeling as though he had a decent plan, he drove straight to his motel room and rushed inside to change his clothes, wash his hands and face and pack up his things. Campbell didn't have a lot of things. Things got in the way. He made sure to travel light for this very circumstance. He never knew when he might need to leave in a hurry.

He'd be leaving before collecting Friday's pay and running out on quite a few others he owed in the weeks he'd been in town, but at least he'd be alive and still be able to play piano. Nothing else mattered after that.

He doubted they'd follow him out of town and never as far as the east coast (if that's where he ended up) but he knew if he stayed in Chicago he wouldn't be safe. God only knew who else Hennie was associated with. If he sent word around that Campbell had stabbed his enforcer and run off with a package of cocaine, Campbell would be a target for every thug and henchman this side of Lake Michigan. Leaving was his only option, and leaving tonight!

His clothes were wrapped up in a garbage bag and would be thrown out during the drive. He stuffed his things into two small cases, grabbed a box he kept near his bedside and found the last of his stashed money – $51.00. It would fill the tank a few times and then he'd be far enough away for him to safely poke his head out again.

All of his possessions in the world fit into the trunk of his car with plenty of room to spare. As he drove with the city's lights in his rear view mirror, he thought about the events of the evening.

It had all started with a show and then great sex with Celia. Celia, the caramel beauty with the amazing lips and stellar voice. He'd never see her again, probably. At least they had tonight together. He'd promised her he'd see her on Thursday night and was very much looking forward to another back seat romp. Instead, he found himself on a dark road driving away from her and the life he'd imagined with her. Oh how he hated the control his vice had on his life, but oh how he *loved* his vice!

~

Chapter 4

Supernova and the Constellations

For a group of musicians who were so in sync musically they couldn't decide on what the hell they should call themselves other than "Chase's Band." Chase had recorded more than 20 tracks with his new nameless band, enough for his first CD to drop and they needed to agree on a name fast! These were some incredibly creative minds at work but their ability to capture their essence in a name was completely lost on them. Normally, Kyle would have put some whiz-kid with a master's degree in marketing on it, but Chase had insisted that the name come from either he or one of his band members. It must be organic.

In the end, it was Chase who thought of "Supernova." In his effort to find the perfect name, he decided he wanted it to reflect more on him. He'd spent 20 years waiting to break out into the mainstream music industry and he was going to take every morsel offered up on the platter before him. It wasn't so much a selfish flaw as it was a narrow focus – Chase wanted fame.

He learned by definition that a supernova was a star that suddenly increases to incredible luminosity because of a catastrophic explosion and ejects most of its mass. This represented perfectly his break from Chasing Charlie and his desire to rise to fame; a sudden, bright burst of energy as he explodes free from that which held him contained.

Of course, he didn't sell it to Kyle or his band like that. In a studio rehearsal one afternoon, Chase presented his idea to the group, including Kyle, after a fantastic day of work.

"You guys are all so incredibly talented." He gushed, genuinely. "It burns my eyes, you're so bright; you're like a supernova! And I'm like a small meteor, a *'morning star'* shooting off you. You guys should call yourselves 'Supernova!'" Damn he was good!

He flashed his killer smile and the deal was done. They all loved it and agreed it was clever for continuity to maintain an astronomy theme. Chase Morningstar and his band Supernova were born.

Kyle Craven couldn't wait to start feeding it out in press releases and put it on all social media. He got the web designers working on the website and had them upload a few videos of them jamming in the studio. No complete songs, only portions, mostly showcasing Chase's style. They were "liked" on Facebook over 140,000 times before the CD was even named!

Their insignia was a small shooting star racing upwards from a huge bright explosion. The graphics department used reds, oranges and blacks to represent the vast amount of heat and energy the event created, with the universe in the background being a deep lapis lazuli blue, representing Lapis Labels. Perfection.

Tracks were chosen from amongst those recorded and Chase made sure they maintained a certain flow. He wanted everything to be exact. This CD was a representation of his solo career, his first steps forward. If his name was going on it, it had to be of stellar quality. To finish the project, the last thing needed was to name the CD. Once again, Chase was at the controls. When the topic was brought up, Chase immediately had an idea.

"I thought you might!" answered Kyle, laughing. Chase had driven harder and faster than any other artist Kyle had worked with. In seven short months he had done what most artists take sometimes years to accomplish. Once this CD was dropped, Chase had another 15 tracks ready to go on the next one!

"The Constellations," Chase said. With his smile on full display, he continued. "Most of the songs are about surviving heartache and unrequited love. People look for answers in the stars, read their star charts for signs. I want this CD to be the one played when some girl is crying her guts out over a guy who will never love her, or broke her heart into a million pieces… or," he hesitated and shrugged "… vice versa. I want her to look for answers in *The Constellations*," he said, smiling, as he held a mock of the CD cover in one hand and pointed at it with the other. The cover was a series of specific constellations, specific to Chase, that is.

He had researched all the constellations, their positioning and their meaning. When he came upon the constellation "Auriga" and read of it having the brightest star in the sky, Capella within it, he was sold. The easiest way to find Capella was to locate Orion (the Hunter) and Taurus (the Bull). Situated directly above them was Capella. That was all he needed to read. Chase chose Auriga as the main focus of the cover. It meant nothing to the band or Kyle; it meant everything to Chase.

***

Chase had been working non-stop. The pace he kept was grueling and his easy going nature had long fallen victim to arduous nights of recording and days spent working with Kyle and the marketing people, being interviewed, photographed and becoming more his persona and less himself. Chase was now a serious artist who had say in *how* he was marketed and his ideas were excellent, well thought out and sometimes downright brilliant, but all work and no play made Chase a grumpy boy.

After purging his soul in his writings and getting his first CD set to drop, Chase was ready for some fun. The launch party was scheduled and Chase was looking forward to it. It was going to be quite the affair with many big name blues artists, rock artists and entertainers, invited for Chase Morningstar and Supernova's big debut.

~

Chapter 5

Philly First

For the most part, Campbell had it made! He was now only 100 miles from Philly, and more importantly, hundreds of miles from Hennie and his henchmen. He just needed to keep a low profile for the next while until he was well out of Hennie's reach. He also needed to unload the cocaine and find himself some weed.

As he got closer to Philadelphia he decided to stop for the night. He wanted to find a motel on the outskirts of the city and off the highway; it would be the last place Hennie would look. He'd sniff out the clientele to see if there were any potential buyers for the coke. It would be great if he could unload the whole package tonight, find some weed and be underway first thing in the morning, but it didn't go that way. He checked out the action in the main lobby which consisted of a small diner offering a modest menu with their dessert selection circling in a cold carousel near the checkout. Not exactly fine dining, but what did he expect? Those in the diner were not the cocaine snorting type; a couple older than dirt, who seemed as if they were sharing a pair of dentures in order to eat through a steak dinner; a young mother with two children, inquisitive about the diner but wary of their mother's temper, and a truck driver who was constantly smoking and drinking coffee while reading the paper. Not a cocaine user amongst them. Campbell knew this would be a bust. He really needed to find a buyer but opted to get settled before continuing his search. He felt safe here hiding from Hennie and figured he could definitely relax a little. Even if he played a night or two here and there, Hennie would never guess he'd be playing piano out in the open, especially not in Philly.

It had been hours since Campbell had eaten or slept, stopping only at a rest stop once along the way for an hour or two nap, not nearly enough for him to really rejuvenate. He quickly registered at the front desk under a fake name, Mark Harrison; not using his real name of Mark Hagen in case Hennie had exceptional connections. The guy at the reception was a large man and he reminded Campbell of a walrus as he waddled back and forth for the length of the desk. He asked for Campbell's signature, gave him the keys to his room and then Campbell went to drop off his things.

The room was a standard, double double, meaning two double beds and a shower – the bare bones. This one at least had a table and a TV, everything pretty customary but it had all seen better days. The glass on the top of the table was scarred where glasses and ceramic coffee cups had sat and scraped it over the years. Campbell had seen more motel rooms like this than he cared to admit. Some a little shittier; not many much better. He hadn't invested in a home base. He'd lived out of suitcases for so long he could set up house anywhere and that's exactly what he did.

First things first, he put the two cases on the fold out luggage stands available in the closet, never using the drawers in the credenza for his clothes. He did hide the package of cocaine in there however, making sure it was tucked far to the back of the drawer. He also put his shaver and shampoo in the bathroom area, then washed his hands and face, leaving shortly after in search of food.

He ordered himself the roast beef with Swiss on rye sandwich, a beer and a slice of pumpkin pie, all of which he ate down in gulps. The beer helped him burp back up the air he swallowed with eating so quickly. He sat for a moment looking at the other patrons; barely a pulse amongst them. Even the children were quiet, having been given hell by their mother. With no excitement happening in the diner, Campbell went back to his room feeling frustrated. His stash of money was down to $43.00 and he needed to sell some cocaine in order to pay for the motel. Not to mention, he'd still found no prospect for scoring weed and was really starting to feel the usual nagging need to get high. Drinking was an option but he preferred to keep his wits about him and that meant he shouldn't drink.

The TV played a game show while Campbell laid back on one of the two beds trying to figure out how to get high before falling asleep. His eyes kept resting back on the top drawer of the credenza in front of the bed. The TV sat on top so his eyes were drawn to the area, but if he was to be perfectly honest, he wasn't interested in the TV, he was considering trying his first line of coke. What difference could it make? A tiny line of coke out of the entire bundle that he'd pilfered from Warren and the skinny blonde wouldn't make any difference at all.

Figuring he was shit-out-of-luck in finding his drug of choice, it didn't take long before his mind was made up. Lightning fast, he bolted up and had the package out and was back on the bed in a split second. He knew a lot of guys that snorted coke all the time and had told him how intoxicating it could be. The word was that once you tried it, you were hooked; it was *that* good. He almost tore into the package with his bare hands in his haste to try the high it held inside. He'd only ever tried weed knowing full well that cocaine cost a lot more, in more ways than one! However, when you're in a very tight bind, you improvise and he had more than enough to improvise with! Besides, he had survived Hennie and his henchmen; that alone deserved celebrating!

He moved to the end of the bed and dragged the glass top table closer to him, making sure the area nearest to him wasn't scratched or etched. He needed a sharp edge to cut through the tape that bound the package. He went into the bathroom and removed the blade from his razor. It would also serve to straighten the line of coke out as he'd seen many do before. Once he cut through the tape, the package opened at the top. He reached in and pulled out a large clear baggie of cocaine. The snow white powder sparkled slightly and Campbell felt almost giddy. This was a lot of cocaine. It must be expensive to keep an enforcer! He knew full well stealing this much cocaine meant there was no way he could return to Chicago as long as Hennie drew breath, perhaps even while Hennie's kids did as well!

Not having a mirror at his disposal, Campbell used the glass top table to spread out a small amount using the razor's edge. He pulled a dollar bill from his pocket and rolled it into a tube, stuffing it up his nostril and snorting in the thin line he laid out. The powder hit his sinuses immediately and it felt good, not wet like a spray, but dry and good. Really good. Then after a moment, REALLY GOOD! Everything was good. Really, really good. Yup, it was all really good. IT WAS GREAT!

In a very short time, he felt fantastic, as though his worries were non-existent. He could solve any problem. The world was his oyster. This shit was unbelievable and he had a huge bundle of it!

Suddenly he didn't want to sleep or stay inside the room. He wanted to be out and about amongst people. Not sure how long the high would last he snorted one more line up the other nostril. He rooted through his things and found an empty prescription bottle and carefully scooped up a bit more to take with him. He then resealed the baggie, put it back in the package and stowed it away into the back of the top drawer of the credenza. As he tidied the room he sniffed and snorted, constantly wiping at his nose. He put the table back into place, returned the blade to his razor and then left the room, slamming the door behind him. He was now on a mission to find fun! Campbell jumped in his car and drove off down the road. He'd just had a boost of "feel good" after *too many* hours of sobriety coupled with stress and anxiety; now he just wanted everyone to be his friend!

His smile was plastered across his face as he pulled into the parking lot of a local bar called The Rusty Nail. He could hear the crowd from inside before he even reached the doors and just knew that this was a great idea! He pulled the double doors open with great gusto, making quite the entrance for all the patrons to see. Heads turned as he almost fell into the bar. He stumbled only slightly however, catching himself and moving forward so that his step wasn't too altered. He felt so great! He was even able to make moves like Fred Astaire; pretty smooth he figured.

He took a good look around the bar before moving past the entryway. He wasn't interested in sitting at the bar with the three men who all sat separately, choosing instead to head towards the back where the pool tables were and a small stage and dance floor. Campbell spied a piano covered in the corner and walked straight over to it. He could barely hear music piped in over a sound system but was sure his music would soon draw a crowd and raise the energy level. He just felt so damn good, he couldn't help but want to spread the joy. Pulling the cover off the piano he lifted the keyboard cover and tinkled a few keys to test the tune of it. He didn't mind the tone – not that bad for an old piano stuck in the back corner of a bar that probably hadn't been played in ages. He'd make it sing!

With no bench available, he grabbed the nearest stool, pulled it underneath him and began to play. His forte was blues but Campbell was well versed in all sorts of music and cover songs. He knew how to capture a crowd's attention. He started with some Elton John and the room soon began to gravitate towards the piano player in the corner. Before long, Campbell had a line of shots waiting for him along the top of the piano. He played like he never had before; he sang out loud, cracked jokes with the crowd and entertained like only a music man can. The group was absolutely captivated by him and his talent was surpassed only by his humor. He had them eating out of his hand; virtually a one man show and all the while stoned on the highest grade cocaine available.

***

The crowd increased around the ancient piano and its 37 year old player, for this night, named Campbell. The Rusty Nail hadn't seen a night of such entertainment in a long time. Campbell downed every shot of liquor lined up for him and visited the bathroom twice making sure to snort more cocaine both times. When the bartender rang the bell for last call, the crowd collectively groaned and booed aloud. The piano player, feeling incredibly good and wanting to continue that feeling, invited everyone back to his motel room for more fun. The crowd, completely enamored with the charismatic piano player, followed him and when Campbell got back to his motel room he had over 40 followers and nowhere for them to sit. The party went on for five hours with Campbell hosting the entire time. Strangers were in both beds, leaving all sorts of fluids, bodily and otherwise on the sheets. God knows what was in his bathroom. It was overrun with occupants and when they couldn't wait or find a decent alternative they began urinating directly outside his motel room door.

When the sun rose the next morning, Campbell was lying on his bed, his bottom half sitting on the edge of the bed closest to the door, his upper half splayed out; his arms spread out on either side like Jesus on the cross. His jeans were pulled down to just above his knees, his boxers were intact. He couldn't remember how he'd ended up there; his last clear memory was snorting cocaine off of the midsection of a brunette who was lying on his bed with numerous bar flies around him awaiting their turn.

Campbell had very little recollection of his last 12 hours. Cocaine had provided him with the best night of his life and he could barely recall a thing. He did know that he absolutely loved the high that cocaine gave him and that fact alone made him fearful, more than anything. It was an incredibly expensive addiction and he knew from the get go that he couldn't afford to get hooked on cocaine, no matter how much he had.

The remembrance of the stolen cocaine made Campbell sit up straight. He'd slept in his clothes, with his motel room door wide open, on display to whomever walked past. The TV was left on the channel test screen, making a screeching noise and displaying the blue-red-green patterned screen that caused him to look away and blink twice, the colors being so bright. His mouth was incredibly dry and he slowly rose from the edge of the bed, pulled up his jeans and walked into the bathroom. He ran the bathroom tap for a few moments, letting it get cold and then drank down mouthfuls until he felt satisfied. He splashed cold water onto his face and on the back of his neck and let the excess drip from him as he hung his head over the sink.

His bathroom towel had been used numerous times over as evidenced by the dark dirty coloring of its edges and the musty smell of mildew that quickly hit him as soon as he brought it closer. Too many hands had wiped off on that towel for him to want to use it. He quickly swiped his wet hands over his jeans and was satisfied that he'd made the more sterile choice.

When he came back into the room, Campbell took in his surroundings with astonishment. It was stripped, save the TV, credenza and one bed. The TV was bolted to the wall – it wasn't going anywhere. The credenza it sat on was a built-in, so it stayed, but the drawers were all missing including his stash of stolen cocaine. His eyes quickly scanned the rest of the room, taking in the damage.

The bed frame and mattress on the bed he woke up on remained. The other bed, frame, mattress and all was missing completely. The table he snorted the coke from the night previous was gone. His clothes had been ransacked and only the crappiest of his belongings remained including the shoes and jeans he was wearing.

After a panicked search he found his wallet and the last $43.00 to his name. Miraculously, it had fallen out of the back pocket of his jeans and under his bed, all for safe keeping! At least now he could tear out of town. Without it, he'd have really been in a bind! Not giving it a second thought, he quickly gathered together everything that hadn't been stolen, which wasn't much, and got his car on the road without looking back. At least he hadn't given his real name; at least he'd been that smart.

After running out on the motel bill which would've cost probably hundreds of dollars with the amount of damage and missing items, Campbell spent another $20.00 filling the gas tank and driving straight towards New York. He took stock of the greater picture. He was nearly 37 years old and had nothing to show for it. No cocaine, no weed and nowhere to go. All he owned was in his trunk. Perhaps he could find a new life getting lost in a big city. A big city like New York. It could offer Campbell a great place to start a new life. Hennie and his henchmen would have a difficult time finding him there. He could go by his nickname and have no fear of being found.

Satisfied that he was heading in the right direction, Campbell drove on through and arrived at a hamlet of New York in under two hours. He immediately felt better. Something about this city was going to change him. He could feel it. As he drove around, he assessed the energy of the city's streets. No doubt he could find work here. No doubt he could find weed here and no doubt he could stay out of Hennie's reach.

The first cheap opportunity he found, he parked the car. He hoped like hell it wouldn't be stripped clean by the time he got back to it but it was better than a $25.00 parking ticket when he only had $23.00 to his name. If he could find a piano that needed playing he could earn some money. He was doing his best about his weed situation; perhaps a shot or two of whiskey would help, but of course it would cut into his last few dollars.

He had spotted a number of bars and clubs about three blocks from where he'd parked and he decided to walk in that direction and see what he could find. It wasn't quite time for a club to be open for the day but he was hoping there would be someone working in the kitchen who might give him some inside information. The first place was closed up tight, no action at all. Undeterred, Campbell carried on further down the street. There was one spot he was hoping was open, one that had caught his eye as he drove past. It had musical notes and the silhouette of a band playing against the backdrop of the city skyline on its sign and he figured it was his best chance for employment. "Skyline" took up the entire top floor of an old, grey, two-story building. It gave an interesting perspective of the street from its second story and all the windows faced into the heart of the city with its skyline clear for all patrons to see. Campbell pulled on the door leading to the upstairs and it opened easily. Nice!

At the top of the stairs he came upon two sets of doors. One set was glass with gold handles and "Skyline" etched into it with the cityscape under the name. The other door was to the far left and down the end of a hall. He went towards that door. It also opened easily and he popped his head in and called out "Hello?" to anyone who could hear. There was no response so Campbell went through the doors and further into the kitchen area. He couldn't see anyone around. Someone had to be there – they wouldn't leave their kitchen door open. He was wondering where everyone was when a petite blonde woman with high hair, heavy makeup and even heavier perfume, came through a pair of swinging double doors. She stood shocked to see him and as it registered to her that a stranger stood before her, her face went through a range of apparent emotions; surprise, confusion, questioning and then anger.

"Oo the 'ell are you?" she asked.

Campbell realized she was a lot older than he originally thought. Her voice was husky and harsh, like the voice of a 1,000 cigarettes. He detected a British accent but it was more her tone that made Campbell step back. He immediately felt like he'd been caught doing something he shouldn't and he had to regroup his thoughts and remember what he *was* doing there.

"I… uh…" he flashed a wide smile, hesitating. Best to woo her with his charm, not knowing who she was or her importance in the club.

She cocked her head to one side, his smile winning her slightly. She wasn't born yesterday and even though he had a nice smile, she wanted to know what the hell he was doing in the kitchen of her club! Instead of asking the question again, she simply raised her perfectly penciled eyebrow at Campbell and waited for his answer.

"My name's Campbell. I'm a piano player and wondered if I could get a job here. Are you looking for someone to tickle your ivories?" he asked, hoping his suggestive joke would help.

"My name is Pearl. I own this club and I 'aven't been propositioned in a long time. Lucky for you, I'm also not interested. You're young enough to be me son and I don't fancy meself with boys, only men!" she told him straight.

Campbell smiled inwardly. She sounded much like his father. As he wondered about her background his gaze rested on her for a moment. It dawned on him that she was looking at him, rather annoyed. He gathered his wits and tried thinking back through the last few moments and what had occurred. He needed to make amends and quick!

"Er… sorry Pearl. I'm not trying to be disrespectful I just… ah… I could really do with some work and… I play the piano but I'll do anything," he said humbly. He stood with his hands raised before her. He really hoped he hadn't blown it and she'd want to hear him play first before making her decision.

She eyed him up and down. He looked very tired, like he'd been sleeping in his car. His clothes were incredibly rumpled and his hair was in disarray. Pearl felt for him. He reminded her of her younger brother Eric who had moved to America many years before her and was living somewhere in the mid-west. She made a mental note to ask her sister if she had news on him; maybe Alice knew where he was.

Once again Pearl's attention settled on Campbell. She hoped that somewhere along the line someone had helped Eric as she was about to help this poor soul of a man.

"You on rough times then?" she asked him, her one eyebrow raised again.

Campbell tried to look away, embarrassed by the question, but felt as though he couldn't lie his way out of this to her. He ended up looking directly into her eyes and nodded; being truthful with her might help. She came across as a "no bullshit" kind of woman.

"What's your name again, luv?" she asked, as she leaned against the steel racks that lined one side of the broad kitchen area.

"I'm Campbell. Actually..." he explained, "that's a nickname everyone calls me. It's a thing I have with the soup." He shrugged his shoulders and smiled as he blushed and turned his gaze towards the floor.

Humility was also a gift. He didn't know anything about Pearl except that she was the one person he needed on his side right now, so some ass kissing may be in order.

"If you have a piano, I'll play for you and show you that I'm worth the job. I can provide quiet background music or an evening's worth of entertainment, requests, you name it. I can augment your existing band or be a one man show. Just let me give you five minutes of my work and if you don't like it you can tell me to leave," he said pleadingly.

What did he have to lose? Who was going to promote him if he didn't promote himself? As if an epiphany had hit him, he took that moment to look down at his clothes and realize his presentation probably wasn't its best. He ran his hand across three days growth of beard and through his unwashed hair. Good job he wasn't high! She might have picked up on that. Campbell figured not too much got past this lady.

Pearl's heart melted at his plea. How could she turn him away? She couldn't. She wouldn't. Normally, she wouldn't give anyone using this approach a position at Skyline but something inside Pearl told her to help this poor bugger.

"C'mon then, impress me," she said, as she jerked her head towards the set of double doors she had originally come through and turned away, walking briskly.

Campbell wasn't sure of her age, maybe late 60's, maybe older but she was still in fairly decent shape. She wore tight black jeans, rolled up, with strappy black heels and a blue silk shirt with a light black leather jacket. Pearl had it going on! She walked with a mission, flinging her high, blonde, shoulder-length hair as she marched out through the middle of the kitchen and into the main club area. She guided Campbell over to a stage where instruments were set up. Pearl pointed out the piano to Campbell and then gestured for him to take a seat. He did as she instructed and cleared his throat as he played Billy Joel's "Piano Man," first singing it, then improvising with it, quietly, romantically, as if lulling the listener into his every key stroke. Campbell played his heart out to Pearl and it worked!

Pearl was struck by Campbell's ability to go from one genre to the next, making the same song sound different each time. He certainly knew how to play a piano and she already knew he had the charisma to win a crowd; he'd won her over and she'd probably be his toughest critic.

At the end of his performance he dropped his hands into his lap. He grinned at her mischievously as if to say, *"…go ahead, tell me you don't love me."* What was not to love? She couldn't resist him and although the Skyline already had a regular band, she decided Campbell could provide dinner music for the weekend crowd, before the place got rocking. If he managed to work a gig into the whole evening as well, who was she to mind? If he could draw in a crowd and keep them eating and drinking to boot, he was worth taking a chance on.

"You can play during the dinner hour, just piano, no singing. Keep it subtle so that they don't have to shout above it. I hate it when I have to shout above the music durin' me dinner. It totally ruins it for me," she admitted.

Pearl's makeup, hairstyle and energy level made her almost like a cartoon character except for her accent. It gave her a snobby tone, although she was anything but. She'd seen some rough times herself and was empathetic to anyone who needed the opportunity to change their life. She hoped that by helping Campbell out, it would send some good out into the cosmos for her younger brother as well.

"Now, 'ave ya got somewhere to stay?" she asked him, figuring he didn't. From the look of him, he came as is.

"Uh… no… actually, that was going to be my next move. Do you know of a men's mission or YMCA nearby? I'm low on funds and came into town on fumes," he told her, embarrassed at his own predicament. He wasn't even admitting the whole truth to her, keeping his secret of Hennie and the cocaine to himself. No need to give her reason to be suspicious of him, besides, he was an unknown here. So far, he didn't owe anyone anything.

"I do actually know of a place you can stay. A friend of mine takes in boarders and on my say-so, she'd let you board for a week before payday. Mind now, if you piss me off or do me a bad turn, she'll boot yer arse out of there so quick and then have the police after ya, 'til you'd wish you hadn't bothered," she admonished.

Campbell couldn't help but smile at her, she was such a character! "Thanks Pearl. I promise to be a good boy and behave myself. And I will be forever grateful for giving me a job and helping me find a place to stay," he said, grinning at her.

"Just you make sure you do mind yerself, Mr. Clever Clogs. I'll be giving yer arse a boot otherwise," she admonished. She looked sternly at him and then broke out into a smile. She couldn't help it —there was just something about him.

***

Pearl's friend Lucy owned a very large house near where Campbell had parked his car. He would be able to walk to Skyline and save himself money on gas while he stayed. Lucy was equally as English as Pearl and Campbell couldn't help but wonder what their story was. Had they come over together? Were they related? They looked nothing alike but that usually didn't mean anything nowadays. He made a mental note to question Pearl about it once he was alone with her again. He had stowed his things into the last room available, used the bathroom and shower and came downstairs to find the two women talking over a cup of tea – typical English women.

"Where's the rest of your clothes then, luv?" asked Pearl, giving his attire a questioning look.

"They were stolen," Campbell said, trying to straighten out the wrinkles in his shirt. "I was going to try and find a Goodwill or clothing donation store and get some more things."

He'd have to get at least one more pair of jeans and maybe a few shirts. He only had twenty dollars left and until he'd played a few nights at Skyline, it was all he had to his name. Thank God Lucy was willing to let him stay on Pearl's good reference. At least he now had a place to sleep and someone who would feed him. Now, all he had to do was find weed and he'd be back on top!

"I have some clothes upstairs you can go through. Not sure what's there but I'm sure you'll find something that'll suit ya," Lucy said, as she spooned out a thick rich stew and buttered a hunk of bread for Campbell.

She placed it in front of him and before she had pulled her hand away, Campbell had thanked her and was stuffing both bread and stew into his mouth at the same time. He had lived off coffee, a few donuts and adrenaline for the past five days and had now finally found a place where he might be able to settle. He was hundreds of miles from Hennie, had survived his try with cocaine, just barely, and made his way to New York intact. With food in his stomach and a change of clothes, just try stopping Campbell now!

Lucy went upstairs to lay out the clothing she thought might fit Campbell. Pearl sat watching him eat his stew wondering what had happened to this poor lad to find him in this state at this point in his life. She guessed him to be in his mid to late thirties, could tell by the state of him that he didn't have anyone who cared about him and knew from the state of his car that he had nowhere he had to be. *Poor bugger!* Waiting for him to finish his meal before lighting a cigarette, she took a long first drag, letting the smoke trail slowly out of her mouth, circling around her head and up into the air of the boarding house kitchen as she studied him closely.

"So, what's next for you then?" she asked him.

"Well, that depends on you. What time do I show up for work tonight, Boss Lady?" he asked her.

If he was to start at the dinner hour that gave him only a few hours to try and track down some weed. He'd gone too long without getting high, longer than he was use to and even though he could manage in front of Pearl, he was extremely anxious about performing completely sober tonight without so much as a drink in him.

"Once Lucy has found you somethin' to wear, I suggest you ask 'er for a razor and go back in that bathroom and give yerself a good shave. Then be at that piano for six o'clock, fair enough?" she asked him.

He nodded in agreement as he used his last piece of bread to mop up the remaining stew in his bowl and popped it into his mouth. He was about to ask for some insight into Lucy's history with Pearl when the front door burst open and a tall lumbering man in a jean jacket and a dark turtleneck stepped into the kitchen with a big bright smile. His hair was long and straight and pulled back into a pony tail. His features were all dark and intimidating until you saw that grin and then you weren't concerned anymore. He lifted his nose in the air smelling Lucy's stew and made a bee line for the stove.

Drawing in a deep sniff he exhaled with a sigh. "I love Lucy's stews!" he exclaimed, as he grabbed a bowl and started filling it. Campbell didn't know what to make of him except to assume he was also a boarder.

"You're a bloody hollow tube, you are mate," Pearl said, laughing at him. They obviously knew one another and shared an exchange of smiles.

"This is Malcolm," Pearl said, pointing to him as he took a chair opposite Campbell. "Nice bloke but a bit of a wanker!" she chuckled. "This is Campbell, he's also a nice bloke but not near the wanker that you are," she teased Malcolm.

He grinned back at her and stuffed his spoon into his mouth, immediately realizing that it was far too hot to devour just yet. His overreaction to its temperature made them all laugh and for the first time in a long time Campbell felt at ease, almost like a homecoming. He'd find some peace here, he could feel it in his gut.

Pearl stood up and left the room, excusing herself to "use the loo!" Lucy remained upstairs searching out the clothing for Campbell, leaving

Malcolm and Campbell at the kitchen table alone. As Malcolm ate his stew, he kept his eyes down but suddenly spoke directly to Campbell in a quiet voice.

"You need to find something to smoke, man?" he asked quietly, with his head down, eyes on his food.

At first Campbell didn't think he'd heard him correctly, so he just sat there looking at Malcolm quizzically. His hesitation made Malcolm look up and into Campbell's eyes and then Campbell knew right away what Malcolm had asked him. His eyes were bloodshot and his pupils were mere dots in the center. Campbell knew the look well. Malcolm had probably just smoked a joint within the last half hour.

Could this be true? Could he have stumbled upon someone who could get him high right under this very roof?

"Uh… yeah," he laughed. "Is it that obvious?" he asked, wondering what made Malcolm ask in the first place.

"Don't get freaked out now, it's my job to ask, if you get my drift," he said, returning his attention to scraping the bowl with his spoon, getting every last morsel into him. "Damn, but doesn't that little ol' English sweetheart make some fine stew!" he roared when he finished. He banged his hand on the table for effect and wiped his mouth clean with his napkin. Campbell had met a lot of dealers over the years. For a dealer, Malcolm had his finer points.

Later that afternoon, Campbell stood in his new room, which was cozy and warm with a big comfy bed, a duvet for cold winter nights and plush carpeting on the floor to help warm the feet. The bathroom, which was down the hall and very large, had two sinks. He'd share it with the occupant of the only other room on his floor, which was Malcolm.

He stood before a long mirror hanging on the side wall next to a small alcove where a winged-back chair and a stool were placed. He could imagine an elderly gentleman sitting with his feet up, sipping brandy in the alcove setting, reading a book.

He looked in the mirror and took stock of the clothing that Lucy had found. It was quite lucrative with Campbell gaining three pairs of pants, a pair of jeans, four shirts of excellent quality and a jacket that would keep him warm. She had also produced a pack of new underwear containing three pairs and two new pairs of socks. Campbell was shocked as she laid it all out on his bed and left the room for him to try it all on. To his surprise, everything fit! This was more clothing than he had owned in a long time and never had he received it all at once, except maybe at Christmas one year, but that was many years ago now; long since forgotten in Campbell's world.

This was almost as good as Christmas though! He'd found food, shelter, work and weed, obtaining the latter from Malcolm as his long arm extended across the kitchen table to drop two rolled joints into Campbell's grateful hand. He owed Malcolm of course, but already he felt better just knowing that he had a high waiting and an audience to entertain and all of this thanks to meeting up with Pearl. Her name fit her well. To Campbell, she was a treasure indeed!

He'd have to make sure he didn't jack her around like he'd done so many times before to other people who had been friendly to him. It always seemed to end that way with him. He figured his inability to trust anyone played a large role in why he screwed so many good people over, but he wanted to be different with Pearl and Lucy. He caught their humor and Pearl reminded him of a father he had loved many years ago; one who he had long since left behind. Campbell wasn't even sure if his father was still alive or not. They had not been in contact for well over fifteen years.

Now he found himself starting a new life, living in a new city, feeling like he could possibly make something happen. In five short days his life had completely turned around and this time was going to be his time and he was going to take charge of his life. He wondered whether Dex or his mother ever looked down and saw what he was up to. He figured Dex would be fairly impressed with how he'd managed through the last five days, hell the last 20 years, frankly!

Now came his reward. His shave made him look much sleeker; he combed his hair back off his face and brushed his teeth again. He patted his breast shirt pocket where he carefully placed the two joints as he grabbed his new coat and left the room. On his walk to the club, he'd smoke his first joint in more than five days and be ready to perform.

And just like that, Campbell fell right back into his same lifestyle without even missing a beat. The more things change, the more they stay the same.

~

Chapter 6

What A Real Gem Pearl Is!

Campbell had been living at Lucy's boarding house for more than two years. He grew very fond of the two old British ladies who now dominated his world. One ran his life at work, the other at home. Both were funny as hell, kept Campbell in stitches and new material constantly and filled a void that hadn't been filled in years. For the first time in a long time, he felt at home. He was almost 40 years old and only just starting to feel whole again. He found that he was getting stoned less and entertaining more. Campbell had turned his dinner hour into a piano-fest every night where patrons were willing to stand along the back wall holding their own drinks just to be able to enjoy the piano styling's of "Campbell." That's how he was known to the staff and patrons, that's how he was known at the boarding house and that's how he wanted it. He'd decided to not let anyone know his real name thinking one day he might need to have that as insurance should Hennie ever come looking for him. Campbell had not forgotten that night two years back when he stabbed Hennie's bruiser with the screwdriver and ran off with his cocaine. It was always in the back of his mind that he needed to be ever vigilant and not give too much away about himself. He had made a few phone calls to try and find out if "Warren" had died, but with very little to go on other than his address on Clutterbuck Road and his first name, Campbell came up empty handed. At least for now he was hidden away in a small hamlet just outside of New York City happy to be gainfully employed with a funny and welcoming place to go home to. Regardless of his past, Campbell was the happiest he had ever been since his eighth birthday. Unfortunately, his father would make sure it was short lived.

Once again his birthday rolled around and Pearl wanted to throw him a big birthday bash at the club. He let his guard down and agreed, with Pearl taking control of all the organizing. She was in her element! They'd have the patrons all bring him some sort of gift (nothing too expensive) and in his honor Pearl was going to serve all his favorite dishes. Lucy was asked to lend a hand in the kitchen because Campbell loved everything she cooked!

Pearl and Lucy were in the back kitchen of Skyline going over menu ideas when Pearl heard the kitchen door swing open and shut again. A voice called out, "Allo?" Pearl was not expecting anyone at this time of day and was annoyed that, once again, someone had come into her club through a staff entrance when it was clearly marked "staff only" on the door. She had softened when she met Campbell, but he was the exception. This poor bugger was going to get the full belt of her temper.

"Pardon, luv," she said to Lucy as she stormed off around the corner to confront the stranger. She almost walked straight into him she was so mad. They both stumbled and the stranger helped her right herself, making sure to catch her arm before she toppled over. Pearl gathered herself and was about to blast the man when she stopped herself. It took only a moment before she realized who he was and threw her arms around his neck.

"Oh, Eric!" she cried and she hugged him tightly. Her baby brother had finally found her after all these years. She hadn't seen him since he left England but she'd know him anywhere. Pearl held his face in her hands as she gazed at him with her eyes full of tears.

"Bloody 'ell, you're a sight!" she gushed. "God, I've thought about you for so long and wondered how you were. I didn't even know if you knew I'd come 'ere. Wasn't sure what Mum had told ya and whether or not you were still in contact. Last thing she told me was that yer marriage had busted up and that you were back doing your thing." She barely let him get a word in she was so excited. He just kept smiling and laughing and nodding his head to her statements.

"Oh, Lucy luv, come see who just stepped across the doorstep," she called out. She took a moment to dry her eyes before Lucy came from the back area and looked over at Eric. He wasn't a big man, standing at just under six feet. He was lean and a little ragged looking. Lucy took one look at him and knew he'd been a heavy drinker for years. She had worked in the pubs back home and had run boarding homes for decades. She knew the look and Eric had it all over him. Regardless, she put a big smile on her face and went to shake his hand.

"'Ow d'ya'do?" she asked, in typical Lancashire style.

She shook his hand vigorously and when he smiled it caught her breath. *God, he looks familiar!* she thought. She cocked her head to one side as she studied him. Pearl caught Lucy's reaction and wondered what the keen eyed woman had seen. Pearl trusted Lucy implicitly. Lucy had proved her stellar intuition on more than one occasion and with 40-plus years friendship between them, Pearl knew to pay attention to Lucy's reactions, good or bad.

"Eric, I want you to meet my best friend, Lucy. We met on the boat comin' over and 'ave been by each other's side ever since. Seen each other through several 'ard times, 'aven't we luv?" she said as she hugged Lucy's shoulders.

"Lucy, this my baby brother, Eric! 'E's been missing in America for the past… what's it been? Decades?" she asked Eric, squeezing his hand.

"I've spent years trying to track you down," he explained quickly. "You changed your name when you married and I didn't 'ave yer married name. I knew you'd be ownin' a club or sumthin' so when I found out yer married name I started asking for a club owner named Pearl Duncan and lo and behold here you are! Doesn't surprise me that you've done this well for yerself, you were always so clever with yer maths and you were a bloody little drill sergeant from what I remember," he laughed and once again Lucy was taken aback.

She couldn't shake this feeling that she had met Eric somewhere before and she rattled her brain to try and think back. All this time she had known Pearl she had never met the family but knew there were plenty of siblings. Still, she had difficulty getting past the fact that Eric and she had met before. Not giving anything away to Pearl just yet, she told them to carry on with their reunion at a table in the main room and she'd go and make them a cup of tea and something to eat.

"Have you a place to stay?" Pearl asked Eric as she took him into the dining lounge.

He shook his head and looked down. "No... I... uh... I've just come into town. I was 'oping to find a place to kip and then 'ead into New York shortly after. I want to see if there are some comedy places about that might have an open mike night or somethin'," he lied.

He hadn't been in front of an audience in years. Eric lost all his motivation to be funny shortly after his marriage broke down. So many things had transpired since then that he'd begun drinking to try and cope and that was the end of that.

As Eric finished his explanation Lucy came backside first into the room carrying a large tray with a teapot and three cups, a cheese plate with grapes and olives and another with crackers. She'd also sliced some roast beef and buttered some bread for a sandwich.

As she put the tray on the table to unload it, Pearl stated, "I'm sure Lucy wouldn't mind puttin' you up, would ya luv? You've got the spare room right now and I'll cover whatever costs Eric racks up until he can get himself back on his feet. Right?" she directed the question at Eric.

She then looked at Lucy for support. It was obvious to both women that Eric needed some help and his big sister was in a position to do so; what could Lucy say but "yes, of course." 40 years of friendship or not though, Lucy was going to be asking Pearl all sorts of questions about him once she could get Pearl alone.

"I dare say I can put 'im up, I suppose," she offered. "Long as you get on with the others stayin' there and don't cause trouble. I'm the same whether or not yer family; if you're a trouble maker, yer out on yer arse," she stated, making sure it was clear to both Pearl and Eric that there would be no exceptions. For some reason she felt like she had to make sure that was said.

Pearl and Eric sat for another hour catching up and reminiscing about their childhood in England. She informed him of several family deaths including his favorite uncle and he informed her that he had lost his eldest son and ex-wife within a few years of one another. He didn't go into details and Pearl didn't push him, but she assumed that that was all it took to make him lose himself. He told her that his younger son went his own way and he hadn't spoken to him in many years. Eric had lost touch with him too and spent the last few decades alone and drunk. It was just a few short months ago that he started trying to sober up and walk a straighter line. It had been difficult and he stumbled a few times but every day he woke up believing in his goal; he'd get through the day without a drink and if he made it to bed that night with his goal accomplished then he had the strength to wake up and do it all over again. That was how he got through each day. At least, that was what he was wanting Pearl to believe.

Pearl fought back tears as she listened to his plight. He had lost so much and the fact that he had been able to start turning things around for himself was heartwarming. It may be difficult for a little while but Pearl planned on helping him in any way she could. First things first, she wanted to get him settled at Lucy's.

When Lucy came out to take away their dishes, Pearl asked, "Will ya be a luv and take Eric 'ome with ya so he can get settled?" Lucy nodded her agreement and Pearl looked to Eric. "I'll not be too much longer after ya. I'll get this place locked up and be there in a flash. You go and get ya things tucked away and we can have a nice big dinner back at the 'ouse."

Eric nodded, finished his last sip of tea and bent to kiss his sister on the cheek. "Thanks Pearl, ever so much. Right nice of you both to 'elp me out. Promise not to be any trouble," Eric said. He seemed grateful for the room and board.

"C'mon then, sausage," Lucy said to Eric. "It's a short walk from 'ere and we can 'ave a chance to go over the 'ouse rules."

"Aye, she runs a tight ship does our Lucy, so you'd best mind what she says," Pearl warned.

Eric gathered his bag up and followed Lucy out of the dining room as she began listing the do's and don'ts of living at her boarding home. Pearl let them get out of earshot and then went to the phone and placed a call overseas. It would be nearly bedtime but she had to make sure that she spoke to her sister before she went back to Lucy's. It took a moment for the call to go through and when it did, it rang nearly five times before it was answered.

"Allo?"

"Alice?" Pearl asked. "Can you 'ear me?"

"Yes, luvie, I can hear you just fine. Are you alright?" Alice asked her. Pearl usually rang her on Sundays near suppertime, not every week, but at least once a month.

"Yes. Alice, you'll never guess who walked into my club earlier today. You'll never guess," she said excitedly.

"So tell me then if I'll never guess, ya daft bugger," Alice laughed at her older sister.

"Our Eric. It's 'im, I'm not kiddin'. 'E looks a bloody mess and says 'e's only just found out my last name so 'e's been able to find me," Pearl said all at once. The news went unanswered and once again Pearl wondered if Alice was having trouble hearing her.

"Did'ja 'ear me then? I've just told ya that our Eric has finally found me in America," she repeated.

"I know, I did 'ear you but… er… well I don't understand it Pearl. You said 'e'd finally found you and that 'e didn't know your last name but I gave him that information years back. 'E rang me and asked for it. 'E told me that 'e was going to surprise you with a visit one day so I didn't say anything hoping 'e would. In all this time you've never mentioned it and then I didn't bother saying anything to you because I didn't want to upset you. E's known for a lot longer than just a few days, luv. Sorry t' tell ya this, but 'e's 'ad this information for quite some time. 'E was even told about your club there. 'E's either really down and out or 'e's up to sumthin'."

This floored Pearl. Why had he not called on her? If he'd known all these years, why had he not come to see her? Alice's words were dead on, maybe the bigger question here was, *why* had he come to see her and *why now?* She said a quick goodbye to Alice and told her she'd call her on Sunday when rates were cheaper.

She ran into the kitchen, checking to see if any main kitchen staff had arrived to prepare for the night. Ralphie was just coming out of the freezer when Pearl came through the doors. She explained that she was leaving for a bit and that he was to manage things until she came back for the night's entertainment. She gave him her spare set of keys, just in case he needed anything and grabbed her handbag and left Skyline for Lucy's. There was a reason Eric was lying to her and she wasn't sure why. Whatever it was, she wondered if Lucy had sensed it too. Pearl had caught her reaction to him and was now very interested in what she had to say. Something here wasn't right and Pearl worried she had now brought it into Lucy's home.

***

Lucy and Eric had made it to the house just as she'd finished going through all the rules. He followed her like an abandoned puppy and didn't move until she gave him the go ahead. He actually waited at the door until she invited him in.

"What are ya, a bloody vampire then? Waiting for an invite? Get yer arse in 'ere and close the door. It's bloody freezin' in November and yer lettin' me 'eat escape the 'ouse!" she admonished. She didn't care whose brother he was, he'd better not be costly; she wouldn't tolerate that at all!

Eric followed her into the kitchen and stood by the table. She was still struggling with the sense that she knew this man, but how could that be? She had never once met Pearl's younger brother – both she and Pearl would have remembered when and yet it was eating at her that there was something about him that was so familiar, but there was also something about him she wasn't so sure of. He seemed a bit fidgety, perhaps he hadn't had a drink today. He was looking around as if to try and figure out the layout of the house.

"All the bedrooms are on the second and third floors. I'll put you on the second floor. The bathroom is at the end of the hall, towels are in your room in the bottom drawer of your clothes chest," she explained.

"Thanks," he said, as he dropped his head.

He seemed slightly ashamed and for a moment Lucy felt a pang of sorrow for him. "Go on then, get yerself upstairs and sorted out. Yours is the first room on the right," she directed him in a slightly stern voice.

He didn't need to hear anymore and off he went to the room on the second floor, first on the right. Lucy busied herself in her kitchen, going through her ritual of mindlessly putting the kettle on and preparing the teapot to make tea; her thoughts elsewhere. She could hear Eric's footsteps briefly moving around up in the room upstairs and then heard his bedroom door close as he started descending the stairs to return to the kitchen. At that moment, the front door opened and in came Campbell, walking straight into the kitchen. When he saw Eric on the stairs he stopped cold.

"What the fuck are you doing here?" Campbell said angrily.

At the sound of Campbell's voice, Lucy had the epiphany. It was Campbell! The reason she felt as though she had met Eric before was because he was so like Campbell! Lucy then put the whole train of thought together. The connection was Campbell; Eric had the exact mannerisms of Campbell, he even looked like him too. She looked back and forth from one to the other trying to determine how that was possible.

"Allo, Mark," Eric said quietly.

"What? Who the 'ell is Mark?" Lucy asked. She was bloody confused, she knew that. How did these two know one another and why was Pearl's brother calling Campbell "Mark"?

Just as Lucy was about to start getting answers, Pearl burst through the door. She also froze right where she stood. Standing beside one another, Pearl and Campbell looked at one another and then looked back at Eric who was still in the process of coming down the stairs.

"I can't believe you came 'ere. I never even told you about yer auntie Pearl. How'd ya find 'er then?" Eric asked Campbell. He then turned to Pearl and said to her, "What do you think of our Mark then, Pearlie?" using a pet name she hadn't heard since she left England.

"*Our Mark?*" Pearl and Lucy said in unison.

By this time Campbell was in shock. He was trying hard to figure out how his father had found him here and what was he talking about. *Auntie Pearl?* He had been careful not to leave behind any loose threads yet somehow he had managed, after all these years, to track him down.

Eric straightened out all the questions everyone had in a few simple sentences. "Pearl, this is my youngest and only surviving son, Mark. Mark, this fine lady is my eldest sister, Pearl."

Lucy's hair stood straight up on the back of her neck. Campbell looked quizzically at Pearl. She also did the same.

"How can that be? I came here not even knowing you existed," he said, not understanding how certain things in life were completely out of our control.

Pearl looked at him equally shocked. In the two years since Campbell had shown up she'd grown extremely fond of him and found herself making sure that Campbell had full time hours at the club, a roof over his head at Lucy's and that he kept out of trouble. It didn't bother her that he was a grown man of almost 40 years, she felt like he needed family and she was more than willing to provide that.

Perhaps it had been instinctual. Perhaps Pearl's innate sense of being a blood relative was what made her soften to Campbell that day he wandered into her kitchen. A deep down recognition of a familial trait. Now, seeing her youngest brother and nephew in the same room together, she wondered how it hadn't come to her before. Campbell was just like Eric. It was really uncanny that he'd had no idea of who she was and yet had still managed to find family within all the hundreds of thousands of people, places and miles across the U.S. Blood really was thicker than water.

***

Although all the dots had been connected, Lucy was still unimpressed. Pearl may have been slightly enamored with Eric, but she wasn't so easily fooled. She really needed to talk alone with Pearl and find out what the hell was going on. If it was all just a fluke that Eric had shown up, why had he not been more surprised when his only son, who he hadn't seen in umpteen years, walked into his long-lost sister's best friend's boarding house out of coincidence? Why had there not been tears of joy – a reunion? Instead, both men just stood staring at one another across the room creating tension that could've been cut with a knife. These two men may be father and son but there wasn't a lot of love or respect between them. Lucy didn't need a psychology degree to figure that out. Nor did she need anything else to tell her that Eric's return wasn't as coincidental as Pearl might think. She trusted Campbell a lot more than she did Eric, *even if* Campbell wasn't his real name.

"Pearl, do you mind if we have a word alone for a minute, in the other room?" Lucy asked, motioning her head towards the door of the "other room." She then walked out of the room with Pearl following closely behind her.

When they got on the other side of the door, Lucy turned quickly and said rather dramatically to her friend, "Listen, luv, I'm not so sure about your Eric. I think 'e's 'ere under false pretenses. I can't tell you why bu' I don' trust 'im as far as I could pick 'im up and throw 'im!" she warned in a fierce whisper.

"I know sumthin's up," said Pearl, "I'm just not sure what. I rang Alice up after you left the club and she told me that Eric's 'ad me address and number for many years, and 'e's known about the club. So, the first thing 'e does when 'e sees me is lie to me? The little bastard! That means 'e's up to no good. And how did 'e know about Campbell?" she asked, feeling like, between them, they should be able to figure out what the hell was going on.

"I think we need to watch out for Campbell," Lucy said quietly.

"What do you mean? I don't think 'e's a bad sort, do you?" Pearl asked worried.

"No… no… don't worry. I think 'e's fine. But what I do think is that Eric isn't and 'e's shown up because of our Campbell. I think we need to watch out for 'im just in case Eric wants to do 'im 'arm. I really don't trust 'im at all," she told Pearl. The women both agreed, of the two of them Campbell was the one they could trust.

As Pearl and Lucy were in the other room, Campbell took the whistling kettle that Lucy had put on the stove and made a fresh pot of tea, putting the cozy over the teapot just as Lucy would have done.

"What are you doing here?" Campbell asked angrily. He suddenly felt on edge like he needed to be watching over his shoulder.

"I came lookin' for me sister, Pearl," Eric said, with his hands held out innocently. "'Ad no idea you were 'ere. Surprised the shit outta me, I'll tell ya," he said almost hesitantly, with a weak smile.

"Bullshit," was the only reply Campbell gave him.

"Now is that any way to speak to yer Dad? I 'aven't seen ya in 'ow many years and that's the first thing you can say to me? Where's your bloody manners?" he said almost angrily, but he knew better. His son could beat the shit out of him if he'd wanted, so keeping his temper in check was necessary.

"*My* manners? What about *your* manners? Leaving to get birthday candles for your son's birthday cake and NOT returning doesn't sound like good manners to me," Campbell threw back at him. "As if you have any right to expect respect out of me. You ruined my life at the age of eight years old and all you've done since is bring me sorrow. Now, years later, you think you're going to walk back into my life and fuck it up all over again? Do you need money? What do you want?" He paused, catching his breath, his temper full on. "Tell me right now what you're doing here. How the fuck did you find me and what is it you want?" Campbell insisted.

Eric came towards Campbell with his arms outstretched but Campbell backed off. "'Onestly Mark, I'm an old man who's seen some really crappy times. I've sobered up and come to find my sister. I didn't know you were 'ere; I really had no idea. It was pure shock to see you as I'm sure it was for you to see me here. How did you find Pearl?" he asked his son, with real interest.

Eric couldn't remember ever telling either Dex or Mark much about his eldest sister, Pearl. She was many years older than he was and had moved out of the house when Eric was just a lad. They didn't have much time together, only ever seeing one another at family functions until Eric went off to America. Pearl heard about his life via their mother and sister but not for many years now. So, how was it that his son managed to find her? Eric wanted to know.

Campbell shrugged his shoulders. "I came into the city and stumbled into the Skyline purely because the other club's door was locked. I had no idea Pearl was related to me in any way until you told me so today," Campbell explained, truthfully.

It didn't seem to satisfy Eric. The fact that he had found her particular club in and amongst the hundreds there must be within the city limits was astonishing. He found the only club with an open door and a family member.

Eric looked at his son. *I don't even know him enough to know if he's lying or telling me the truth,* he thought. His only living child was standing before him as a full grown man and the father didn't know the son at all.

Eric decided he would continue on with his plan. To hell with it – it wasn't like Mark ever tried to make his life any easier, always acting like he was weary of his presence whenever Eric showed up. He didn't need that, not at his advancing age. He had come this far and would reap a great reward if he was able to see it through. He just had to play it all cool. Eric could do that; he could play into Pearl's kindness and live off the generosity of Lucy until he touched base with who had financed his little trip. Once he let them know of his location, they'd pay him his reward and he could be on his way, probably not stay long enough to mess up the room. Pearl was never a consideration, she was only collateral damage. That was just the cold hard fact of it and Eric was a cold hard man now. Not even his gem of a sister was going to change things now.

***

Campbell didn't feel any better after his spirited conversation with Eric. He didn't believe him at all and needed to talk with Pearl and Lucy to gauge their feelings about Eric's sudden appearance and what they thought was behind it. It was just a few days before his birthday – did that have anything to do with it? Was it some sort of trigger, or due date or something that Campbell wasn't aware of? The first thing he would do is pull the ladies aside and have a talk with them. If Pearl knew anything he was sure that she'd tell him. The thing is, they hadn't had one moment alone since Campbell walked through the door. He was still standing in the kitchen wearing his overcoat, his scarf and his all-weather boots.

When Lucy and Pearl came back into the kitchen, Campbell tried hard to get Pearl's attention and when their eyes met she knew right away what she needed to do.

"Why don't you 'ead upstairs and have a kip before dinner, Eric? Campb... er... Mark 'ere works as the entertainment at Skyline and both of us will be leavin' shortly after we've 'ad dinner. We'll make sure that you're up before then and we've 'ad a chat." Pearl's voice wasn't so much a question as it was a command.

Eric looked from Pearl to Campbell and then Lucy, who had a look of pure rage on her face. He probably needed to listen to his sister and head upstairs. He needed to take care of a phone call anyway and could do with the time alone to weasel out a phone where he might have some privacy. He turned on his heels and went straight back up the stairs without another word. Better to think he was playing by the rules, that way he could get his pay and be on his way. As Eric went back upstairs both ladies looked at Campbell for an explanation.

"What the 'ell is goin' on? What the 'ell are you up to? Who the 'ell is 'Mark'?" Pearl asked directly, confusion and anger stinging the tone of her voice. Campbell had never seen her this annoyed. He knew he needed to play damage control.

"Campbell's a nickname, remember, I told you that the first day we met. I have a thing for the soup, okay? I never give my real name in case I need it one day to go into hiding. You never asked me for it and it never came up in conversation, so I didn't really feel like giving it up," he explained, all in one breathe.

Both women stood staring at him, not knowing what to say. Part of each of them wanted to box his ears and another part wanted to make sure he was protected and safe from harm.

"So, why don't you tell us what you think 'as brought 'im to town and why you think you'd have to go into hiding?" Pearl stated, as she pointed her thumb towards the stairs Eric went up.

She pulled a chair out from the kitchen table and sat down. Lucy did the same and soon Campbell had no choice but to pull up a chair and make himself comfortable. Lucy poured each of them a cup of tea and made sure the milk and sugar was placed in the middle of the table. As Campbell started talking he began undoing his boots, not making eye contact with them.

"Eric, my father…" he paused, "…left our family during my eighth birthday party." He paused and shook his head, still feeling the resentment. "Anyway, he then contacted my mum after more than a year and acted as though he hadn't done anything wrong. I washed my hands of him and barely saw him until my mum died and I was sent to live with him. I didn't stay long and he certainly didn't care about me. He's a heavy drinker and he went through a lot of years where he wasn't sober at all. I've moved around a lot without leaving any forwarding addresses, you know? I'm a starving musician. For a while, he'd always seem to find me and drop in just when I least expected it," he explained. "I thought we'd lost track of one another some time ago. I haven't seen him for years." At this point he stopped, hoping they wouldn't need to know much more.

"But… don't ya think it's funny that 'e's shown up just now to see *me*?" asked Pearl. "After all these years? Personally, luv, me and Lucy think 'e's up to no good on you," she said outright. "And why would that be? What's 'e got on you?" she asked Campbell directly, cocking her eybrow.

Once again, Campbell felt the familial bond with these women. No wonder he had been so at home here. Pearl was true blood family to him and now it all made sense. Lucy, who was always there to greet Campbell when he came home, whether it was late at night or sometimes into the wee hours of the morning, was also family where he was concerned. She was another mother figure to Campbell just as Pearl was and these women deserved that level of respect. They deserved the truth, the *real* truth!

Campbell heaved a heavy sigh as he finished untying his boots, removed them and placed them beside his chair as he sat back. He was resigned to spill his heart and soul to them both – to confess all sins.

"I think I might have killed a man in complete self-defense," he said, head hung down, ashamed to admit it but unsure of its truth. "And I think Eric has been coerced into finding me for some kind of payment," he explained, as he raised his head and watched the two women change their looks of total acceptance to one of worried astonishment.

"Okay, well... I... uh..." he stammered, stopped, caught his breath and then started again. "A couple of years ago, I got caught up in a real load of shit that I wasn't expecting. After a show one night I went looking for some marijuana. I went to the place of a guy I knew and he said if I delivered something for him, he'd give me some weed." Campbell hung his head and took a breath.

"When I got to the address I felt uneasy. I armed myself with a screwdriver." He paused again noticing both women were hanging on his every word. "The guy inside was a bad dude and when he thought I wasn't looking he tried to attack me. We struggled and he got me down and was choking me so I grabbed the screwdriver and stabbed him with it. I didn't know what else to do so I grabbed the package and took off from there. I mean literally, I left the town, the state... I friggin' left." He emphasized the last sentence by gesturing with a hand slice through the air. "I don't know what happened to the guy I stabbed. I figured if he died, Hennie would be after me. If he didn't, well... then Hennie would still be after me 'cause I got away with a large package of cocaine and a debt. Either way, I needed to lay low for a bit."

"But you aren't sure the fella died then?" Pearl asked, scared to know the answer.

Campbell shrugged his shoulders almost in defeat. "I tried contacting some of the city hospitals but I didn't have enough information to be of any help. I figured after being here a while I was pretty safe. That is, until I walked in to find my father on your stairs," he said directly to Lucy with a nod. "I have a gut feeling Eric is here to rat me out. Not too sure how he found out I was here, but I can guess there aren't too many guys who play the piano named Campbell."

"So, this fella that might be comin' after you, 'e's a really bad sort then, is 'e?" Pearl asked. If Eric was intending to bring this man into her club, or worse, Lucy's home, Pearl was determined she would make it so that neither happened.

"Yes, he's all sorts of bad," Campbell explained. "And like I said, it's not just his "enforcer" I stabbed and possibly killed, I left with a large quantity of his cocaine and a few hundred dollars in his debt. I'd say I'm in some pretty deep shit if I'm right about why my father has shown up here."

"Bloody 'ell," both ladies said in unison. How could they protect themselves against this? In all their years together, they had never had anything like this upon the doorstep.

"I'm sorry, ladies" Campbell said softly. He felt awful that they were now in direct line of danger and he was responsible for bringing it to them.

Pearl's mind was reeling as she sipped her tea, racking her brain for a way out of this mess and with the best possible outcome. She did have an idea, but it was going to take a few other good friends to pull it off.

"I 'ave to make a few phone calls. You two keep trying to think of a way to stall Eric if 'e goes to leave. We must keep 'im with us until we leave for the club, right?" she told them.

"Right," they answered together.

"What are you up to Pearl?" Campbell asked her. "I can just leave here and make sure he follows. That'll get him out of your hair and away from causing you trouble or harm."

"Yes, luv, I realize that, but the best scenario would be that 'e's gone for good and the fella you owe is gone too. That way you can live your life freely without constantly looking over your shoulder," she said. Pearl knew people who could help her immensely and they were loyal to her for a good turn she had done for them once.

"What do you mean by 'gone'?" Campbell asked, getting worried. "Nothing illegal, right Pearl? I'm already running from something like that" he said, with a slight nervous smile.

"No, you daft bugger! Who do you think I am?" Pearl smacked her new found nephew's arm. "But, I'm going to have it so that they'll be too bloody busy dealin' with their own problems to care very much about you." With that she got up and left the room, leaving Lucy and Campbell perplexed at what she had in mind.

***

Eric made his way back upstairs and tried listening through the air vent in his room to the conversation going on in the kitchen. It was an old trick he'd learned living amongst those he didn't trust. Sometimes air vents would carry your voice to another room connected through the venting system and sometimes it allowed for eavesdropping. Unfortunately, the three down below were talking too quietly for him to make out much at all. He could tell the difference between the speaker but not what they were saying. He decided to take the opportunity to find a phone and make his call. He gently turned his doorknob and quietly opened his door. Their voices weren't much louder even with the door open but he could still hear them talking which meant his coast was clear.

He made his way quietly down the hallway ready to step into the next room when he spotted a black rotary phone on a table in the corner of the hallway. Perfect! When he got in front of the phone he pulled out his grubby wallet and found the scrap piece of paper with a phone number written on it. He lifted the receiver and heard the hum of the connected line. He smiled wide. Placing his body in front of the phone so as to somewhat deaden the noise of the rotary dial, he dialed the number and waited. It rang three times and then was answered.

"Yes?" the man said.

"It's me... Eric. I found him!" he said, in an excited whisper.

"You did, huh? Well done!" the man said, pleased with his minion. "Tell me where you are and I'll come to you immediately!" he told Eric.

Once all the information was given, Eric filled him in on what was going to take place that night. "We are going to go to the club after dinner where he'll be performing. You come in and sit nearby until I give you the okay. I'm not sure what time he works until but once he's done you can grab him and go."

"I see you've thought it all through. Not a lot of love between you and him, then? I don't know of any man who would sell out his own son. If I cared, I might want to know what has transpired between you to do this, but... I don't!" he laughed, amusing only himself.

"When do I get my money?" Eric asked. As soon as he was paid, he'd be out of there, back on the road. He wouldn't say goodbye to Pearl; it would be better that way, just bugger off and be gone.

"You'll get paid when I see you tonight. I've waited long enough for do this. It happens tonight. If I'm to get there in time, I must leave now! I'll be flying into LaGuardia," he said, as he looked at his watch. "Good work. I'll see you tonight," and he hung up the phone.

Eric hung up his end and thought about how pleased he felt for successfully finding Campbell. When Eric had first arrived in Chicago, he began hearing through the seedy underworld grapevine that Hennie, a drug king-pin, was willing to pay a huge price for Campbell's whereabouts. What else was he to do, a down-and-out man but, find his son? He knew of only one entertainer named "Campbell" who might have a connection with a drug dealer. It had taken more than a year of inquiries but he finally spoke to some tourists from outside New York who were impressed with a guy named Campbell playing piano for patrons at the Skyline club, which he knew to be his sister's club. That was all Eric needed to hear. The next move he made was to buy a bus ticket to Westchester, New York. Eric spent his travelling time thinking of the coincidence that his son would find his sister out-of-the-blue. What were the odds?

No matter how hard he tried to fake it, his stage skills failed him when push came to shove. He fooled no one when he and his son, Mark, first saw one another after so many years. His son's reaction triggered anger in him that after all this time the kid still held so much bitterness and resentment towards him. Eric thought that he might feel a pang of guilt for tracking him down at Hennie's request, but when Mark still showed him such a lack of respect and caring, Eric quickly rid himself of his guilt and went back into plan mode.

***

Pearl's blood ran cold as she stood in Lucy's bedroom holding her hand over the mouth end of the phone, listening in on Eric's conversation with God only knows who! The mean bastard was truly willing to sell out his only remaining child! For what? Money? His child's life for probably no more than what Eric could piss away in a fortnight. Her heart was thumping as she held her finger on the disconnect button before quietly replacing the receiver and then picked it up again listening for the hum. Making sure no one was eavesdropping on her call, she began calling in some favors.

Her first call was to Paul Craven, a rookie producer in the music industry and onetime lover who stole her heart and kept a piece of it. Paul had taken an older woman who was perhaps insecure after two failed marriages and years without a decent man and made her feel fantastic! Their sexcapades were unbelievable! Neither of her husbands had ever made Pearl feel like the sexy, wanted woman that Paul did. They had met at her club 10 years earlier and it was lust at first sight. They had great sex in almost every part of the club and when that grew old they still remained close friends, each appreciating the others friendship and company and sometimes body, when there was no one else.

After their lovemaking, Paul would hold her and tell her about his dream of opening his own recording studio. He wanted musicians to be able to come through his doors and have the freedom that wasn't offered to them from other big name studios. Paul Craven was out to help the underdog and Pearl loved that about him; however, it was clear to both from the very get go that there was no commitment expected. Perhaps because of that, they were able to be themselves and it created a very open and honest bond that grew between them.

As a surprise one day, Pearl had given him $5,000.00, practically a lottery win to Paul, so he could build his own recording studio and begin making and marketing music. She told him that it wasn't a loan, it was a gift because she believed in him. She asked only that if he should come across someone that needed his help he should give it freely, remembering that he was once given that kind of a gift.

He took Pearl's money and turned it into a very profitable recording studio. Paul had helped many a struggling but talented musician because of Pearl and when his son, Kyle, had been born just a few short months ago, he made sure Pearl was sent a birth announcement and new family picture. That alone was payment enough for Pearl. Paul deserved every ounce of happiness.

When Paul answered the phone Pearl hesitated a moment, remembering all she knew about him, intimately; his smell, his demanding sex drive, his amazing passion! She briefly explained to him what she was hoping he could help with and Paul very quickly agreed to do all he could. From his positive response she was thrilled to hear how quickly he could swing things together. She thanked him profusely and his "… anything for you, my darlin'," made her eyes mist for a moment. Pearl took a deep breath. He really was a terrifically passionate man!

With that call done, the next was placed to a friend who had some real pull. He'd boarded at Lucy's for more than three years and Pearl had got him a job at the club, but his real desire was to enter the police force. She saw a decent young man in Christopher Hollomby and wanted to help him out. She had talked with her ex-brother-in-law, a cop himself, to see if he had any pull. He met with Christopher and found that he was a very good candidate for their training program and pulled the necessary strings to get him enrolled. Christopher had excelled and was now a lieutenant on the Westchester Police Force. Although she and the brother-in-law rarely spoke since then, she and Christopher were in regular contact.

Pearl always liked having a good friend who was a cop, especially as a club owner. It had been a benefit once or twice in the past when she had some dodgy sorts come around her club causing trouble. She only needed to call Christopher and he'd either send around a squad car or drop by himself, letting all patrons know that he had Pearl's back and not to mess with her or her club.

This time, she needed him to help out with whoever it was that would be coming for Campbell. Christopher was more than willing to do her bidding, taking down all the information she had and then easing her concerns by letting her know he'd take care of everything. All she had to do was go about her night as if nothing were any different. She assured him she could do that and, satisfied with their plan, they ended the call. Pearl made her way back into the kitchen smiling at Lucy and Campbell who still sat at the table looking concerned.

"'Ave you ever seen the 'Sound of Music,' luv?" she asked Campbell directly.

"Yes… why?" he asked her back, wondering what that had to do with anything.

"Because tonight we're going to re-enact their escape from the Nazi's, only you won't be climbin' bloody mountains!" she laughed. Lucy and Campbell tilted their heads at her to question what the hell she meant. Pearl just smiled and whistled, "So long, farewell, auf wiedersehen, goodbye…" as she put the kettle on for dinner.

She quickly captured Lucy and Campbell's attention as she quietly laid out her plan to them. Campbell and Pearl would go over to the club taking Eric along with them. Once they were gone, Lucy was to have a look around Eric's room to see if she could find any information. If she found anything, she was to call Christopher Hollomby right away.

Pearl and Campbell would go about as if it were a normal night. Pearl would sit Eric on the right side of the room near to the kitchens where she could keep an eye on him without him knowing. Christopher was to show up during Campbell's last set and sit close to Eric, watching to see if he could spot who he was to meet up with. Campbell was to take his final bow and go into the crowd like he usually does, wait for a few minutes, then excuse himself for just a moment and then make his escape. Christopher would quietly leave, following him and keeping him safe until Campbell got into his car. Unbeknownst to Eric, Lucy will have also gathered up all of Campbell's things and loaded them into his car, so he could just jump in and go.

Pearl gave Campbell Paul Craven's address and phone number. Paul had promised to take Campbell into his studio, using his creative talents behind some of the names his studio was recording with now. Paul would keep him working and help him get a place to stay and teach him how to have the best of both worlds; creating and playing music while keeping an extremely low profile.

Once Campbell had safely left the city, Christopher would make his way back up to the club and watch Eric for signs of whomever it was that was out for Campbell. If the guy was in trouble with the law, Christopher would find that out and nab him before he even left the club.

The plan was all set. The only thing missing was the identity of the man that had hired Eric.

***

In Lucy's house, dinner was served promptly at 5:00 pm so Pearl and Campbell had a chance to get to the club and prepare for the show. Lucy made steak and kidney pie with mashed potatoes and steamed vegetables – a welcome home-cooked meal for a cold November night. Campbell's favorite meal, actually. Lucy planned it that way knowing it would be his last night in her home and so close to his birthday. Now, this was to be his big birthday bash, without all the fanfare, celebration and happiness.

When Eric finished his dinner and left the room to get his things together to go, Pearl quickly grabbed Campbell's hand and said with a bit of a catch in her throat, "I'll miss you, luv! I understand now why you tugged at me 'eart like you did. You keep out of sight until all this blows over, you 'ear? And when you do finally get the chance, give us a ring and let us know you're doing okay. I'm sorry about yer birthday party. It'll be all bolloxed up now that yer leavin', but better you live to celebrate another, eh?" she said good naturedly, while wiping a tear away. She thrust a large wad of cash into Campbell's hand and he was astonished at the size of it.

"I... I can't accept th..." he tried to say, but she wouldn't have it.

She shushed him and closed his hand over the money pushing it back towards him. "Call it a family inheritance," she said. She turned around and left the kitchen, stopping the conversation there.

Campbell dropped his head feeling so grateful for his Auntie Pearl. She really was a true gem!

***

As the night played out, all went well. Campbell's ability to entertain his audience was on full display, being sure they were getting their money's worth. He certainly drew in a crowd! Pearl wondered how he'd do in the studios not playing for an audience, but knew it was for the best, at least for the foreseeable future. She gazed around the room, slowly letting her eyes rest on Eric. She watched Eric watch Campbell and what she saw shocked her. He seemed enthralled with Campbell's antics and his face was lit up, practically beaming at him. She wished for more insight into what had happened to him that would turn him into the kind of man who would sell out his own son...

Lost in her thoughts, she almost missed the casual head nod that Eric gave to a bald headed, short and stocky man who had just walked past him as he entered the club and sat at the table next to Eric's. The man said something to Eric without looking at him and Eric shook his head slowly in response.

This must be his connection! Pearl thought. She kept her eye on both men throughout the evening, making sure they had a drink in their hand. She closely observed the man sitting near to Eric. He kept his hand inside his coat pocket, not removing the coat, even while in the club. *That's odd*, thought Pearl. She'd be sure to point him out to Campbell during his next break.

But Campbell chose not to take a break. He had taken notice of the man sitting near to his father's table as well; he'd seen him right away! It was Hennie himself! He wasn't fooling around this time and wanted to be sure Campbell paid his debts in full – *all* debts owing. Campbell's mind reeled while he played for the crowd. He went over and over the night that started him on this journey. Stabbing Warren was what turned everything around and put him in a race for his life. Now, he could be facing death if Pearl's careful planning and loyal friends fell through and Campbell was scared that he'd made a mistake in thinking he could easily ditch Hennie and get away. What if Hennie's henchmen followed his car? What if there was a miscommunication and Christopher Hollomby didn't get here in time?

Suddenly, Campbell felt very anxious and started looking for Pearl to help calm his nerves. As he continued with his music, he managed to catch Pearl's attention and she nodded towards the bar. When he looked over he saw a lone, very tall, very large man standing against the bar with his foot resting on the foot rail below. He looked like he was about 30 years old but was built like a castle wall. Campbell hoped to get his attention and get him to notice Hennie, to point him out in some way.

But Christopher didn't need Hennie pointed out to him. When Lucy searched Eric's room she found the crumpled piece of paper with Hennie's phone number on it and called Christopher immediately. He traced the phone number to a known drug king in the Chicago area called Hennie Vander, aka Hennie Walder, aka Heinrich VanderWaulde. He was of Dutch descent, got his product in mailed shipments from Amsterdam and was watched by law enforcement, although they had yet to nail him. Along with the rap sheet, the Chicago PD gave a clear description of Hennie. Armed with this and a handgun, Christopher and several undercover officers drove to the Skyline club.

***

Hennie flew into LaGuardia and was on his way to the Skyline Club in plenty of time. He couldn't conceal a gun so he had to stop along the way and buy one. He wasn't going to make it a long drawn out affair; no torture or having Campbell beg for his life, which he was fond of having his victims do. Something about someone begging you for their life was invigorating to Hennie. Often, he'd make them beg; usually it came naturally. He'd even had Warren beg him, but it was a foregone conclusion that Warren must die.

When his skinny blonde girlfriend called Hennie screaming into the phone that Warren had been stabbed by Campbell that night, Hennie knew right away that Warren would have to die. He told the girlfriend that he would call for an ambulance and just to stay put near Warren making sure he was kept comfortable. He hung up the phone and continued on with his card game without calling for any help. When the game was over and his henchmen left, he drove over to Clutterbuck Road and entered the house. He found Warren lying, extremely weak, in a large pool of his own blood. Beside him was his skinny blonde girlfriend, completely wasted in a drug induced daze. She had snorted a large amount of cocaine in order to deal with the situation. *Great coping skills*, thought Hennie.

When Warren realized Hennie had come into the house, he started begging him for help but Hennie shushed his cries and quietly and calmly took a gun out of his jacket and screwed on the silencer. Warren understood what Hennie was going to do and his cries became louder, but still too weak to attract anyone's attention.

"Why?" he cried to Hennie. "Ain't I done what you always wanted me to do? Please, Hennie, please man, I beg of you. Don't do it," he pleaded desperately.

"If you hadn't been so careless as to let yourself get stabbed, I wouldn't have to do this. But you must understand, I can't have you seen by a doctor or risk them coming to the house. If they were ever able to link you to me I would be arrested right away. I can't have that happen. So you see? It must end this way for you and your girlfriend. But, be happy. You will die together," he smiled at Warren and with that, Hennie pointed the gun at Warren's head, took aim and shot him through the right eye, killing him. He then turned and shot the skinny blonde girlfriend dead too. Collateral damage. He would get his henchmen over to clean up the mess and have the house ready for its new tenant as soon as possible. His enforcers always lived at this address; the address never changed, only the enforcer.

Now, two years later, he was going to make sure that Campbell paid the ultimate price for his actions. Nobody screws over Hennie and survives! He watched as Campbell sang and danced his way across the piano keys, becoming increasingly uncomfortable by the amount of people in the room. The crowd had piled in and now the room was full to overflowing with people wanting Campbell to continue all night with his incredible piano playing and fun-loving energy.

Hennie didn't like witnesses and right now he wanted nothing more than to get Campbell out of there, into his car and drive him somewhere to kill him. Once done, he'd throw the gun into the Hudson River before flying home. It shouldn't take very long. He just had to wait until Campbell was ready to leave.

Eric had done a good job tracking down his son. Hennie slowly reached into his inside coat pocket and took out a thick white envelope. Eric was absolutely transfixed on his son and didn't notice Hennie's envelope at first. When Hennie tapped his arm with the packet, he turned, shocked and looked at Hennie wide-eyed, then down to the white envelope that contained his payment for services rendered. He stared for a while at the envelope and then back up at his son; his only surviving son who was right now entertaining a room full of people, just like he had once done. He hesitantly took the payment, looking at Campbell with regret on his face.

Once again, without looking at him, Hennie spoke to him. "Do not lose your interest now. That money will buy you a new life. Your son chose his fate, make sure you choose better."

Eric stuffed the envelope into his jacket pocket and sat with his head down for the remainder of the show. The lump in his throat matched the ache in his gut and he wondered if there was any way he could stop what had been set in motion. He looked around to find his sister and saw that she was across the room, sitting at a table near the bar. When he caught her eye they both smiled weakly at one another and Pearl wondered if her youngest brother felt any remorse for what he had done. This would be the last time she would see him as she would never allow him back into her life after tonight.

As the night came to an end and Campbell finished his last song, the audience erupted with applause. Pearl watched him as he took his last bow. She was going to miss him. Maybe one day, when all these bad characters were no longer around, she and Campbell could reunite. Almost on cue, Campbell walked straight over to Pearl and hugged her hard, whispering his thanks for all she had done. He then kissed her on her cheek, squeezed her arm twice and went over to a few other audience members who were wishing to tell him how marvelous he was. Pearl felt saddened by his goodbye and hoped he'd be in touch once things settled down.

Eric made his way over towards the piano, spotting Campbell's jacket hanging on a hook on the wall. He touched it gently, thinking back to when his son was just a young lad and would entertain the whole family for hours. His breath caught as he held onto the jacket's sleeve. In a burst of inspiration, he secretly slipped the white envelope into Campbell's inside jacket pocket and left the room, making his way to the bathroom. After splashing cold water on his face he decided his best chance was to distract Hennie long enough, forewarn his son and then get him the hell out of harm's way. He hadn't thought it out much past that; he wasn't very good at planning or being very strategic but he had brought this all upon them and he needed to try and make it right somehow.

When he made his way back to his table, Hennie was gone. Shit! Eric's first thought was, *where was Mark?!* He found him across the room still chatting with audience members and joking with the crowd. Still the entertainer long past his show. Good. That meant Hennie wasn't watching, he was trusting that Eric would do his part and bring his son out to him, as he'd been paid to do.

Hennie would be waiting in the dark to jump as he and Mark made their way back to the boarding house. That was the plan, but now things had changed and he wanted nothing more to do with the plan. Now that Hennie was gone, Eric grabbed his coat from the back of his chair and made his way over to Pearl. He sat down at her table with a nervous look around the room.

"Listen here, Pearlie. There's sumthin' I 'ave to tell ya, see? I've done sumthin' really rotten and I'm not sure how to make it better," he explained nervously, his hands shaking as he spoke.

Pearl could tell he'd had a change of heart and desperately wanted to blast him for it, but she knew doing that now was useless, especially if he could shed some light on what Hennie had planned.

"Does it 'ave anything to do with your son and 'is wellbeing?" she asked. He hung his head at her question and she knew right away he was caught.

"I'm sorry, Pearlie. I'm a useless selfish bastard, I know," he said pitifully, almost in tears, nervously looking around the room.

"Do you realize that that arsehole who 'ired you is going to try and *kill* your son? You do know that, don't you? And you've brought this onto my doorstep and Lucy's doorstep? You're a bloody train wreck, you are!" she spat at him.

She motioned to Christopher at the bar and Campbell from across the room and had them come over to join them. When Eric saw the large man walking towards them he panicked believing he was there to hurt him. He stood to leave but Christopher was suddenly blocking his way. Pearl caught his hand and pulled him back into the chair.

"This is my friend, Christopher. Christopher, this is my pathetic little brother, Eric. Now tell Christopher everything you know and you'd better make it bloody quick," she said angrily.

He looked at Christopher with relief on his face. This may work out after all! He told the large cop of Hennie's intention and that he was carrying a gun. Christopher nodded in understanding. He asked Eric if Hennie had anyone with him and although he doubted it knowing he had just flown in, Eric couldn't be sure. Christopher had been watching when Hennie left the club; he made no visible signal to anyone and Christopher didn't notice any other men leave within a 10 minute period. Unless he had men waiting outside, Christopher suspected Hennie was working alone. On that basis, Christopher came up with a new strategy.

"I say we go through with Hennie's plan. I think we still have you and Campbell leave as if to go back to Lucy's. I brought backup with me and we'll be close behind. Hennie will want to get you in the car so you need to act as if you're going along with him but don't worry, it won't go down that way. Are you sure you're willing to do this?" Christopher asked, as Campbell nodded his head. "Once he pulls the gun on you I can arrest him, but I'm not too sure how long I can hold him for or even if I can get him put away," he told them outright.

"Which is why you should bugger off, Campbell," Pearl said. "Not that I don't love 'avin' ya 'round 'ere but I want to know that you're safe and you won't be safe until that bastard is gone, and by gone I mean dead!"

"I have to agree with Pearl. Depending on what he does, a decent lawyer could make it so that he hardly sees jail time. I've seen it happen too many times. If he's gone to the trouble to hire your father to find you, all in an effort to bring harm to you, for whatever reason…" he held out his hands, palms facing the three of them, "…and I don't want to know why this thug is after you, I really don't. Any family of Pearl's is family to me but I'm thinking it would be good to go away, hide away until you know for sure that he's not a threat to you anymore, just like your Aunt says," Christopher explained.

Both Eric and Campbell nodded in agreement and they stared at one another from across the table. Campbell now had to trust his father and he hadn't trusted him in over 30 years. Something seemed to have changed in the old man, something Campbell couldn't put his finger on. Over the course of his show, Campbell watched Eric's reaction. He beamed and smiled wide throughout the entire time and clapped the hardest when the audience gave him applause. Could it be that his father actually felt proud of him; that he had discovered worth in his only living child? It certainly seemed as though he felt regret for being a part of Hennie's plan, but was it truly sincere? If Hennie's plan was to ambush them all with his henchmen and Eric was setting them all up even deeper, Campbell would be caught in an all-out gun fight without a weapon and would probably not live through it. This played heavily on Campbell's mind. Now, trusting his father could cost him his life.

Realizing that Hennie was possibly getting skittish waiting for Campbell and Eric to leave the building and with their plan in place, they stood and prepared themselves. Pearl hugged her nephew, then her brother. She turned and placed herself at the window where she could spot Campbell's car two blocks over parked at the side of Lucy's house. Although she couldn't see Hennie anywhere, she knew he was lurking, somewhere, waiting like a predator, ready to strike.

Christopher gave Campbell some last minute advice and they shook hands. Campbell thanked the cop for all his help and for being so good to Pearl.

"Pearl's been very good to me. She calls and I come running. I'd do anything for her," Christopher admitted.

This made Campbell feel happy knowing that she'd be well looked after. Christopher was a good man.

Campbell patted his father on his back. "Well, dad, what do you say we get this show on the road?" he punned.

His light hearted attempt was appreciated by his father and he tried relaxing his shoulders and jaw. Eric was so tense he could barely breathe. He took one last look around the room and followed Campbell out the door of the club and down the stairs. His heart was thumping in his chest so loudly he was afraid Hennie would hear it once they stepped outside. Before Campbell's hand reached the door to push it open, Eric stopped him.

"I'm sorry, son," he said quietly.

Campbell looked at his father, a sadness creeping into both their hearts for the years lost. Campbell smiled briefly at his dad as his hand pushed the door open and let the cold night air into the stairwell. As both men pulled their jackets closer, Campbell suddenly noticed a bulge inside the pocket of his coat. He couldn't look now but when he had the chance he would investigate what the hell it was.

Christopher and his backup moved with stealth down the stairs and waited until the father and son had crossed the street. Suddenly, Hennie popped out from behind a garden fence and followed them. Christopher had his men spread out to surround Hennie, Campbell and Eric. He kept his men in sight as he ducked behind a wall, still watching Hennie follow the father and son. They were feet from Lucy's house when Hennie stopped them.

"That's far enough, Eric. I'll take him now. Turn around and come with me, Campbell. I believe you and I have some unfinished business to attend to," Hennie said, making both men turn to see him with his hand jutting in his pocket. Campbell couldn't be sure but he figured Hennie had them at gunpoint.

"Walk slowly to the car, Campbell. No sudden moves or I'll kill you right here in front of your loving father," he threatened sarcastically.

Campbell's heart was pounding in his chest and he hoped like hell that Christopher and his men were witness to what was going on. Campbell turned to look at Hennie. He thought it might help Christopher if Hennie kept his back turned and facing Campbell, so he started talking to him as a distraction.

"Shit, Hennie, what did you expect? I was gonna let Warren beat the shit out of me? I had to fight back somehow," he said, in his own defense. He knew it was a long shot but maybe Hennie would understand about a will to live and not wanting to be beaten up.

"No, Campbell, I expect you to take whatever I throw at you when you're in my debt. Warren and his girlfriend's death are on you. Had you taken what you deserved, things would have stayed the same; but, you forced me to take things into my own hands."

This information shocked Campbell. So, both of them died and he wasn't to blame.

"You and I are going to go for a drive and have a talk. When we're done, sadly only one of us will return," Hennie explained.

Eric stood stock still. If Hennie thought he was still following along with the plan then he was safe and could possibly be of some help.

Christopher continued moving with stealth and gaining ground behind Hennie's turned back.

"So, you killed them both?" Campbell asked.

"Yes, it's really a shame. You only managed to weaken Warren, but I couldn't let them live. She was also killed. Collateral damage, of course. You understand," he said, smiling.

You bastard! thought Campbell! That poor girl didn't deserve to die and Campbell was pretty sure that if Warren had been taken to a hospital, he'd have lived. Hennie had made sure that neither lived past that night and then placed the blame and the memory on Campbell. He really was an evil son-of-a-bitch.

"Now follow me and get in the car," he said, with a face as stone-cold as gray granite. He motioned toward a silver car parked a few feet away. Campbell knew he couldn't stall him any longer. He stepped backwards towards the car and started to reach for the door handle when Christopher called out.

"Drop the weapon and raise your hands!" Christopher commanded, his voice deep and resonating in the quiet black of the cold night.

Hennie tilted his head as he stared at Campbell. He hadn't expected this. He froze for a split second – long enough for Christopher to take action. He lunged forward out of the shadows, surprising both Eric and Campbell at how such a very large man had managed to creep so close without detection. At that point, two other men stepped out from hiding with their guns drawn on Hennie.

"I said, drop the weapon," commanded Christopher, once again.

Hennie slowly raised his hands but kept the gun in his hand. When one of the cops stepped forward placing the muzzle of his gun against Hennie's head, Hennie finally relented and dropped the gun.

"Don't think that this is finished. Not at all, Campbell. I will find you and I will fuck you over. I will ruin you. Just when you least expect it, just when you have forgotten I exist, I will fuck you over. I WILL GET MY REVENGE!!!!" he screamed, before he was handcuffed and marched off.

"Hey, what the fuck was that?" Campbell shouted at Christopher. His heart was racing. "He had that gun pointed at me for the past 10 minutes. You couldn't have stepped out any sooner?"

"He was talkin'. You got him to admit to two murders. Hopefully, we can make those charges stick. Now go on, get outta here, Campbell," Christopher told him. "My guys are good and won't mention your involvement but get your ass going now!"

Campbell needed no more convincing. He got to his car in seconds, unlocking the door and starting the engine as quick as can be. Campbell was ready to pull away but Eric stopped him.

"You amazed me tonight, son. You have talent, real talent. I'm sorry I put you in this situation. I'm sorry I haven't been there for you." He hung his head. He then said softly, "I'm sorry I left you. It was just too hard to look you in the eye anymore." He tried to say more but his voice caught in his throat and he was unable to continue. His eyes welled up.

Campbell stared at his father for a moment processing what he'd just said. *He couldn't look him in the eye.* Could that be it? After all these years, Campbell finally had the answer! His father had felt that he couldn't live up to his son's adoration. The more his son loved him, the more Eric hated himself. Anger replaced every emotion he felt and he carried it for many years.

Now with finding his sister and his son showing such incredible, obviously inherited talent, Eric felt like he was once again amongst family, after all these years. But it might be short lived. He stared hard at Campbell not knowing what to say, hoping his son understood. He tapped the car and Campbell nodded and pulled away.

Eric stood alone in the night watching Campbell's car drive off as Hennie was being pushed head first into a squad car up ahead. Before Eric could make his own escape, Christopher called him over.

"Don't try to run off on me. You and I have to have words and I'd ask that you take a ride with my partner down to headquarters. We have some questions for you," he said, more as a statement than a question.

Eric thought of running for a split second, a knee jerk reaction for him, but something inside told him not to. Something told him to stop and try to do the right thing. His hesitation was noted by Christopher but when he turned towards the squad car and began walking with his head hung, both knew he had good intentions. Seeing Campbell perform was overwhelming for Eric. He wanted to be a better man so that his son, the entertainer, would want to have a relationship with him. It was possible but it had to happen one step at a time and that first step had to be towards the cop car.

***

Campbell drove away from Westchester and towards Paul Craven's New York City address. Another city, another address. After spending many months being static, he was once again on the move. His mind was reeling with everything that just happened. Hennie held a gun on him for a good 10 minutes and he'd managed not to soil his drawers or cry like a little girl. He'd never been so scared in his whole life and he thanked his lucky stars that it all worked out like it did. Campbell put his hand to his heart to feel his heartbeat, hoping to settle it down with every mile he put between him and Westchester. He quickly felt the thick package that had been placed there by Eric. He reached in and pulled out the white envelope. Unsure of its contents, he steered the car with his knees as he used both hands to open the envelope. Inside he found a thick stack of 100 dollar bills. Probably 30 or 40 of them, totalling three to four thousand dollars. Once again, Campbell's heart started to race. Add that to the money that Pearl had given him and he was driving away from Westchester with almost ten thousand dollars. Plenty to start a new, underground life in the heart of New York City.

Finally, Campbell felt himself start to relax. When he thought to look at the back seat he noticed that Lucy had not only packed his things but also food including sandwiches and three different pies. This meant he could drive to Paul Craven's and arrive with offerings. Lucy thought of everything!

As he drove towards a new life, his mind went back over all that had happened. Although things had gone according to plan, Campbell was sorry to say goodbye. He had finally found family again; at the last moment, his father seemed to come around, something he thought would never happen and now he was driving away from him and his little boarding house family. Compared to what the outcome could have been, he was just grateful to be alive.

Campbell patted his pockets until he found his stash. He pulled out a joint and lit it as he drove down the highway towards New York City. He had somehow landed back on his feet with money in his pocket and a joint filling his lungs. It was sweet how things worked out!

***

Paul Craven took Campbell into his studio, "The Blues Station," and found him steady work as the go-to piano player for whoever needed one on a recording. Campbell stayed with Paul and his small family for just a few weeks and then found an apartment close to the studio and was able to set himself up, not only with steady work, but also with a steady flow of weed. Without missing a beat Campbell was once again living his easy going life, getting high at every opportunity and playing music.

It had been almost two years since the whole nightmare began and he'd gone on the run from Hennie. He was satisfied with how things had resolved themselves, but only to a certain degree. At times he wondered about his father and how he was doing. He wished that he and Eric could try to have a relationship but time was ticking away and Campbell was still very much underground. He'd have to leave Eric in Pearl's good care. If anyone could straighten him out it would be his Aunt Pearl!

Campbell became an ardent tea drinker and with every cup he drank, he was transported back to Lucy's kitchen, her cooking and the camaraderie. Damn, he missed them all! Campbell had spent many years without a family to call his own and they were as much family as he could imagine.

Only once had he daydreamed about a wife and family. Sometimes, when he really treated himself, he'd reminisce back to one glorious moment and imagine how differently his life could have been with the wildly exotic and amazingly gifted, green eyed Celia Morningstar!

~

Chapter 7

The Launch Party

By this time Campbell was barely maintaining. He had spent many years in the recording studio, out of the public eye, playing piano on some of the best musical recordings out there with only his initials *"MCH"* listed as the "Man on Keys." After his aunt Pearl and Paul Craven helped him lay low for a while, he'd landed a gig for a group that just so happened to have lost their piano player to a burst appendix. Literally, the guy died.

Paul Craven set Campbell up with an audition for the band and they hired him right away. One gig led to another which led to another and before he knew it, he'd spent thirty years in the studios near the heart of New York City, recording with some of the industries finest, with no one any the wiser as to who Mark Hagen really was.

Now, thanks to a son he didn't even know existed eight months ago, he was playing in a band full-time, a *friggin' incredible* band! He'd finally made it at 74 years old! His lifestyle had improved a fair bit and money was better, although *he* wasn't any better with it and his weed use was ramping up with the same trajectory as his employment with Chase and Supernova.

With the launch party only hours away and Campbell running low, he placed a call to a girl he sometimes bought from. Her name was Sonya; a very attractive thirty-something, hazel-eyed blonde with a decent rack and an even better set of connections! She agreed to meet up with him at a nearby coffee shop. When she showed up, she handed him a grocery bag with a few things in it.

Campbell had been through this with her before. The weed was wrapped up in butcher paper within the grocery bag; Sonya was very careful. She was also drug free, never having tried anything she sold. She didn't like selling drugs, but she had few alternatives. She had tried a regular 9 to 5 job and hated it. She liked her freedom, she liked her money and she liked to have the freedom to do what she wanted with her money. With no one in her life who was willing to support her, Sonya had been introduced to selling drugs thanks to her brother, Johann, a sleazy, greasy-haired, hard-assed, evil son-of-a-bitch who was very well known within the drug underworld as "Clippity-Clop Man"(the clippity-clop came from the noise his multi-ringed hand created when tapping rhythmically against his cane as he held it in front of him; a favorite posture of his). Sonya made decent money, lived a decent life but couldn't find a decent man.

"So, buddy, what've you been up to?" Sonya asked inquisitively. She wasn't sure of Campbell's age, probably in his late sixties, she figured.

"I've been recording with my son," he said proudly.

Sonya was so impressed, she almost spit out her mouth full of cappuccino. "Really! I didn't even know you had a son!" she said incredulously.

"Neither did I," Campbell admitted. "I've only known him for eight months but you listen to me, he's going to be a huge name. We're about to skyrocket overnight with the drop of our CD," he gushed, but didn't give anything else away. He smiled wide at her and nodded his head for effect.

Sonya had her doubts. A lot of her buyers told tall tales and she'd learned not to believe everything she heard. She did know that Campbell was a great piano player who mostly played on tracks for other recording artists. She knew he'd met some fairly high profile blues recording artists, but his own son, suddenly out of nowhere, a major recording artist? Please.

"Well, sounds like you've got yourself one hell of a great son! Good luck to him," she said.

Campbell could tell by the tone of her voice that she didn't believe him. "I know you think I'm full of shit, but it's the truth. We're launching our CD tonight at a party with Lapis Labels footing the bill and a lot of big names are gonna to be there." He waited, hoping that might convince her. When she didn't budge on that he blurted out, "Hey, don't believe me? Come for yourself. Everyone who's anyone is gonna be there," he suggested. He hoped she'd say yes, only so he could impress this young, attractive woman who sold him his weed.

Sonya studied Campbell for a moment. How can an old guy like this suddenly be in a newly formed band that was going to play for the next huge recording artist?

"Which label are you with?" she asked, testing him.

"Lapis," he told her matter-of-factly.

She knew Lapis Labels well, even sold some of her product to a few of the IT guys working there. They had mentioned something about ramping up for their next biggest star. If he was telling the truth then a launch party at their expense would be a huge deal and get loads of big names out to celebrate. Not that she didn't know her fair share of celebrities, but it would be nice to be out amongst them without her drug persona. It was breaking Johann's rule for certain and she knew that, but she'd be careful and stay close to the elderly Campbell.

"Are you serious? You want me to come out to your launch party?" she asked, wanting him to confirm it. If he really meant it, he'd have to give her name to security or the person organizing the event, at least.

"Seriously," he stated. "You can be my personal guest. I'll make sure they have your name so you can come right in."

Campbell wrote down the address of the venue and took Sonya's last name to ensure her access. They spent five minutes more chatting about the evening ahead and then went their separate ways, both agreeing to meet up for 7:30 pm, neither aware of what lay in store for them that evening.

***

Chase Morningstar checked his look in the mirror one more time. He felt nervous as hell and hoped that he could get it under control before arriving at the party. He wasn't worried about the party itself; Kyle had people to take care of that. He was more worried about who would show up to celebrate his new solo career. How would he be received now that he had dropped his first CD in under a year's time and the first two releases, which began saturating the radio stations nationwide in the last few weeks, had gone straight to the top of the R&B charts?

If there was one thing Chase could write a song about, it was his broken heart. Not to mention that he had received word that Charlie and Georgie eloped a few weeks back not wanting a big fuss, just simple vows spoken between them with the minister and his wife present as witnesses. Charlie hoped Chase would understand their decision; after all, would he really want to be best man at his brother's wedding and watch him marry the object of his heart's desire? Better to write a number one hit about how it feels to have heartache, unrequited love and loneliness. Chase understood their decision and appreciated it.

Tonight was his chance to celebrate all his hard work for the last several months. Kyle had let him call all the shots when it mattered most and it showed in the compilation of songs on "The Constellations." He was also showing the music videos for his first two releases tonight so it was all on the line. He felt like an over protective parent sending their child out into the world on their own, vulnerable to the criticisms and judgments that would be cast upon them when the parent thinks they're perfect just as they are.

The room buzzer broke into his thoughts indicating the driver was waiting for him downstairs to take him to the party. He glanced at the mirror, the black Armani suit making him look sharp, sleek and in control. The crisp white shirt unbuttoned to mid-chest made it sexy and Chase's million watt smile culminated into one of the most eligible bachelors about to soar into the R&B celebrity stratosphere. Chase was ready for his atmospheric ascent but his heart still sat in his shoes.

***

Sonya showered and put her lovely blonde hair up in a nice chignon, leaving curly tendrils falling to one side of her face. She took her time, carefully applying her makeup. She wanted to make sure she looked absolutely perfect tonight. There were going to be a lot of people there, beautiful influential people and Sonya secretly hoped to find the man of her dreams.

After all, she was a good looking woman and she took excellent care of herself. She barely drank, except for the odd glass of wine when she was out socially. She walked vigorously every day and ate properly. Neither her schooling, nor her resume were stellar, but she was making the most of selling drugs. She didn't need a real job as long as she sold to the right clientele. What she did do was use both her abundance of time and cash to her advantage. She had ideas on how to improve her education and possibly expand her marital prospects. She took courses on money management and learned how to follow the stock market so she had a much better understanding of how to handle her money. She also spent many hours studying art, classic literature and fine wines all in an effort to seem refined to the right kind of man. After almost 10 years of selling, she was hitting 35 years of age, had no serious commitments, and was fearful of her life passing her by with no husband or child to share it with.

Everything she did was for the purpose of trying to attract the right guy; "Mr. Right," not "Mr. Right-For-Right-Now," or "Mr. He'll-Do-In-A-Pinch." She wanted *the* guy, the one that would make her world complete. She'd been alone for too long. Her brother, Johann, was the only male role model she'd known as a young impressionable girl and, although she knew what a sleazy piece of shit he was, in his own way he wanted the best for her and she deserved to have a husband who wanted that too.

Johann was paranoid about publicity. When Sonya started dealing drugs to daytime actors, he was not pleased and let her know it. Brother or not, he could be very intimidating when he wasn't pleased.

"If they expose you, you're dead to me, you understand?" he would tell her. She understood well.

With this in mind, Sonya treated her clientele with kid gloves, maintaining the utmost level of discretion between them, and they, in turn, treated her like gold. They wouldn't dream of ratting her out or referring her to someone who couldn't be trusted. She provided them with a reliable and discreet way to forget their troubles, worries and sometimes responsibilities. They remembered her birthday, sent her flowers and gave her expensive Christmas presents. It was a symbiotic relationship.

She didn't look like the average dealer, not like Johann did. Sonya was a well-dressed woman who could look as though she was just about to broker a large business deal with some of New York's Wall Street sharks and in the next minute dress for a casual stroll through Central Park, sleek and well put together. She always knew exactly what to wear and how to wear it.

On this night, she wore a simple black dress that graced her shoulders exposing her collarbone and small frame. It clung to her shapely body and stopped above the knee. The neckline fell in folds above her breasts, exposing enough cleavage to draw the interest of any red-blooded male who was close enough to see. She wore only gold accessories. The Michael Kors watch, her newest gift from a grateful client, made her wrist seem teeny-tiny. It was the latest trend.

Her customers included a fair share of celebrities. The females, if they smoked pot, were usually lovely; some of the nicest women in entertainment smoked weed. On the other hand, if the female celebrity was a hard core drug user, Sonya had no time for them. They were the worst – insecure cats always at the ready to throw themselves on you and scratch your eyes out. She never trusted them.

The male celebrities were all the same no matter what their drug of choice. They all thought they were God's gift to women, but if they required her services as a dealer then Sonya wasn't interested in dating them. It was difficult to meet a guy who didn't have something to do with the drug industry, so she rarely dated anyone in her crowd.

Tonight was a gift; a great surprise she didn't expect. She'd learned to take advantage of situations when they were thrust upon her and she was going to make the very most of tonight. It wasn't like she was invited to launch parties for some new up and coming music star all the time – far from it. Her social status was only as high as her celebrities wanted to be and that generally meant they didn't want to be out in public, especially not at a party with paparazzi and publicity when they bought their drugs.

When Sonya did get together with friends outside of the drug trade, she found she couldn't be herself completely. When asked what she did for a living, she'd tell them she helped run a family business. When asked why she was taking a course, she'd always have to lie about her goals and aspirations. Who wants to hear that you make a ton of money selling drugs but you'd like to find someone to take you away from all of that? No one, that's who.

So she lied and her friends never gave it another thought. Just once she'd love to have someone who knew her truly for who she was, drug trade and all. But that was probably asking too much. For tonight, she'd settle for giving her number to some really great guy. *If only the stars would align*, she thought to herself.

***

Campbell had dressed in his finest suit and new silk shirt. He was very excited about the launch of Chase's CD with Supernova backing him. He couldn't be prouder. He lit a joint as he carefully greased his hair back making sure not to get anything on his suit. He looked at his reflection in the mirror and was shocked to see the old face staring back at him. Still feeling like a man in his 20's, Campbell marveled at the time that had flown by. Enough for a son of his to be the same age he was when he first met Celia and they created their son. Tonight would complete the circle for Campbell. He'd celebrate his son's great talent, the drop of "The Constellations" CD and hopefully be able to show up with a very beautiful blonde on his arm! Such a stellar event.

Once satisfied with his look, Campbell left the bathroom still smoking the joint as he finished gathering his things. Lapis and Craven's people were sending a limo separately for the band. Chase would arrive alone. Just fine by Campbell. He preferred to be in the background. Campbell liked to keep the spotlight on the artist. He'd performed like that for many years. Only a very close inner circle of perhaps 10 people knew his real name.

He gave himself a sign-of-the-cross pat down to check for all the essentials; testicles, spectacles, watch and wallet. Confirming all were there, he left his apartment. He'd wait for the limo outside of his building. There were no buzzers where he lived. In fact, there was no security at all.

***

The launch party for "The Constellations" CD was gearing up to be quite an event. Kyle Craven and his team had really outdone themselves. Every A-list celebrity, music mogul and R&B artist had confirmed and paparazzi were lined up along the building entrance to the Lapis Labels offices. As each limo pulled up, camera flashes were so blinding it made a strobe light seem tame. Each celebrity's name was called from every direction so that the perfect shot was captured. Just one decent shot could payout $15,000.00 to the right magazine, newspaper or entertainment cable network.

As the limo carrying the band members stopped in front of the entrance, the overhead announcement of Supernova's arrival was blasting through the fan base, paparazzi and beyond. Loud whistles and calls were heard as the crowd showed their appreciation of the fine group of musicians emerging from the vehicle.

Campbell was out second to last and caught the eye of the beautiful blonde Sonya standing off to one side with a very large man standing next to her, practically dwarfing her. He went straight to her and gave the large man the "OK" that she was with him. When she was allowed past him and over to where he stood, the smile she gave Campbell could have melted glass.

"Oh thank God you spotted me," she said gratefully. "I wasn't sure if you and the band would come through the main entrance or not," she admitted.

Campbell didn't like that. Was she saying he wasn't worth all the fuss and bother of coming in with all the paparazzi there? As though the elderly piano player wasn't important? Little did she know he was the father of the newest rising star on the R&B Billboard Music charts. Although the world would never know who he was, he wasn't worried to admit to Sonya that Chase was his son. She only sold weed after all. These days, weed was hardly part of the hardcore drug ring. Resigned, he let the slight from her pass.

"Looking good there, young lady," he said, taking in her appearance from head to foot.

Even though he was double her age, his look made her blush. She looped her hand through his arm and entered the building as flash cameras erupted behind them, missing their entrance completely, much to the relief of both Campbell and Sonya.

Seconds behind them came Chase's limo. Before the announcer could declare that Chase Morningstar had now arrived, the screams from the gathered crowd deafened everyone within a half mile radius. There was no disputing the fact that Chase Morningstar had made a definite impact on mainstream R&B music, on women ranging in age from 25 to 50, and every kind of social media. Although only two singles had been released through the internet, there was a huge amount of interest circling Chase. After all, he had the looks, the voice, the presence and the broken heart enough to be a serious R&B artist. Chase and Kyle had made sure the video for each single was ready to go on screens placed throughout the Lapis offices during the launch. There were photos of Chase and Supernova on nearly every wall and the large conference room had been turned into a reception hall with dining tables and a dance floor. Kyle had taken care of every detail. All 300 guests would be wined, dined and entertained, all to the music of Chase Morningstar's first CD. The interview requests were lined up. Chase would have to sit with every major news entertainment agency and most of the morning shows from all the big networks. It was going to be a very busy evening and Kyle checked his watch for the millionth time as he watched Campbell and a pretty blonde walk off the elevators and into the office area, temporarily changed into the entrance of a club. Chase's voice filled the entrance from the reception hall and Campbell's face broke into a huge smile as he approached Kyle with his hand extended.

"Kyle, this is outstanding," gushed Campbell, as he shook Kyle's hand enthusiastically. Kyle, too, smiled and not only grasped Campbell's hand hard but also put his arm around his shoulders and pulled him into a hug, slapping him on the back with his other hand.

"You old dog, can you believe it? And who knew that day when I walked him into the studio? What kind of coincidence was that? Who knew?" Kyle said loudly, as he kept his arm around Campbell's shoulder and squeezed him to his side. "I bet you never thought this would happen to you at 74, huh? Bet my dad's just beaming at home!"

"I'd never have guessed it at all," Campbell admitted, laughing, especially with an attractive blonde standing next to him.

"Sonya, this is Kyle Craven, our Lapis Rep. Kyle, this is Sonya… eh… Kel… uh…" Campbell stuttered, trying to recall her last name.

"Sonya Kellerman," Sonya said, as she extended her hand to Kyle and smiled.

Kyle shook her hand and nodded his head at her with an inquisitive look. "Nice to meet you, Sonya," Kyle said. He gave her an appreciative look and turned his attention back to Campbell who wasn't forthcoming with any answers. Campbell winked at Kyle as he placed his hand on the small of Sonya's back and led her into the reception hall.

Kyle was still busy trying to sort out how and why Campbell knew a woman like Sonya when Chase stepped off the elevator and the flash bulbs and music increased tenfold, right on cue. Kyle loved it when his instructions were followed perfectly.

115

As Chase was being bombarded with photo ops from Lapis executives and a few celebrities that were fortunate enough to be on the previous elevator, Kyle made his way over to his new rising superstar and, after a few photos taken with them shaking hands in front of the cover of the CD, Kyle took the opportunity to pull Chase aside.

"You doing okay there, Buddy?" he asked, squeezing Chase's shoulder hard. Both men were smiling wide as if they had a great secret between them.

"I'm doing just fine, Mr. Craven. Just fine!" Chase answered, almost having to yell over the pumping sounds of Supernova's acoustics, the extended version of one of the released singles. Kyle brought Chase's ear closer to his mouth so he didn't have to yell.

"I'll be introducing you in about 20 minutes. You good with that?" he asked him.

Chase nodded his head in answer. Kyle had warned him that he'd be expected to say a few words so Chase had taken the time to write down a few things. He patted his breast pocket and winked at Kyle. As Kyle ushered him into the reception hall, Chase was blown away by the décor. It was as if he had stepped off a ledge and was falling through space. The usually bland conference hall was completely encased in black velvet draping that covered the four walls and joined all together at the center of the ceiling, almost like a circus tent. Hung from that center point was a ball that spread stars throughout the blackness. On the furthest wall was the CD cover; Auriga, the constellation standing out against all the other brilliant dots, with the brightest star "Capella" beaming for all to see. Chase stood for a moment and took it all in. His vision was before him, his rising star moving at the speed of light. The room had numerous tables, all dressed in dark linens in keeping with the space theme. The floor was even darkened by filtered lighting. You truly felt as if you were floating in space. The dance floor was lit with the Milky Way galaxy and as dancers took to it, they became washed with its stars and planets. Chase's music played from the strategically placed speakers and the room became still with his voice accompanying his entrance.

The opposite side of the room displayed the new release video "Capella," a bluesy song about a bright spot in a person's life that defines them and makes them stand out. When he wrote it Chase was referring to his break away from Chasing Charlie and the strength it gave him to make his own career decisions. It was a very defining moment for Chase and the video reflected that with each frame; Chase encased in a wall, unable to climb over, push through or go around until he uses his mind to make the wall explode before him.

When the VJ was informed that Chase had arrived, he and Kyle were suddenly blinded by bright white light as the entire room's attention turned to them and then erupted in applause. Kyle took just a moment and then stepped away from Chase allowing him the applause and recognition he deserved. After all, every song on the CD, every creative step along the way, everything about his music was Chase's creation and under his control.

He took his bows graciously and waited for Kyle's introduction before uttering a word. For a brief moment, he was happy to take the praise before walking over to where most of the band members of Supernova were seated, thereby including them in the applause and appreciation. All the band members took their bows and then the lights took to the podium at the front of the hall. Kyle stepped into the spotlight clapping his hands enthusiastically as he leaned into the microphone.

"Ladies and Gentlemen…" he started, trying to silence the crowd. It took a few moments and then they quickly settled. "Ladies and Gentlemen, I'd like to take a moment to introduce you to the worst kept secret of my entire career," he joked. The crowd laughed along with him and he let it take a moment before he continued.

"I've worked with plenty of artists over the last 15 years and many of you here tonight have experienced your first CD launch so you know the excitement Mr. Morningstar and his band Supernova are also experiencing. All of you listening to the music and watching the charismatic Chase Morningstar in the two music videos that are playing on the plasma screens around the universe..." he twirled his finger around his head pointing out the room, "are the first to see these videos. Not only is this launch party being viewed by millions through a webcast but at midnight tonight those videos will be played for the first time on MTV and then released on the internet probably going viral by the time we are all having our morning coffee." The crowd erupted in applause and whistles and Kyle paused. *This crowd is on fire,* he thought. Better to not keep them waiting any longer.

"The talent of this man pales only in comparison to his work ethic, his energy level and his enthusiasm. Remember his name, remember his music and you'll never forget his face!" Kyle called out over top of the already fevered audience. "Ladies and Gentlemen, I have the honor of presenting to you, Mr. Chase Morningstar!"

Actual screaming was heard. Chase lit his million watt smile as he bounded toward the podium, with Kyle whistling sharply and clapping his hands hard for his new rising star. They embraced as Chase reached the microphone and the entire audience heard their exchange.

"You're a fuckin' shooting star, man," gushed Kyle, as he hugged him.

"Well hang on tight, buddy. I'm only getting started!" Chase said, laughing over the roar of the crowd.

***

Campbell stood to the side of the room, where the rest of Supernova were seated. He and Sonya were caught up in the moment and laughing and clapping, enjoying the crowd's energy. Before Kyle took the podium, Sonya was lost in the video playing on the screen closest to her table. Her eyes didn't leave the video's main character and the song was intoxicating. The words made her believe the artist singing was finally finding the path they were meant to travel and being open to the sensation of creative freedom for the first time. She was completely overtaken by the sights and sounds around her and the face of that man whose music made you feel as if you had intruded but he let you continue on in anyway.

As Chase came to the podium, Sonya's heart fluttered as she realized that her video Adonis was here and about to speak! She felt like a fifteen year old girl again with a schoolgirl crush on the stereotypical bad boy. Lost in her thoughts, Sonya nearly jumped when Campbell leaned over and said in a low voice near her ear, "I told you, my son is going to be a super star!" he bragged.

Sonya's head practically snapped as she looked at him astonished. She knew he'd never hear her over the crowd's energy so she gestured with her thumb towards Chase at the podium and mouthed *That's your son?*

Campbell nodded and smiled a huge smile. A proud papa indeed!

Sonya took a moment to study Campbell and then thought about the man she'd been watching in the video and at the podium. Yes, she had to admit it, she saw the connection. The two men were alike, very much in fact. Campbell was definitely Chase's father, but Chase also had a certain quality that didn't come from Campbell's genes. Sonya would have liked to have seen the other part of this equation but didn't know enough about Campbell's story to know if he'd been married to Chase's mother or not. Regardless, they made one fine looking human being that was for sure! When the chance came, she was going to ask Campbell a lot of questions.

***

"Good evening," Chase began, as the audience hushed and shushed itself to a low murmur. "Thank you all for coming tonight and celebrating the launch of my CD, "The Constellations!" Again, the audience applauded. He let them settle before continuing. "You know, I say *my* CD when really there are a number of people who have supported me through this project, namely my band Supernova and Kyle Craven, of course, from my favorite label Lapis Labels." Another round of applause and whistles with Chase steering the audience as always. They hushed once again when they saw him lean into the microphone.

"This journey for me has been about finding out who I really am as an artist, as a performer and as a man. I think the one thing that can help guide you through life is to know who you are and from where you came. It took me 37 years to find that and I'm not too sure how many are aware but I am thrilled to introduce you to our oldest member of Supernova and..." he paused a moment "...my father, the fantastic piano man, Mr. Mark Hagen," Chase called out with pride.

Camera flashes were going off in rapid fire as the spotlight highlighted Campbell. Sonya was also drenched in white light and felt blinded, suddenly not able to see three feet in front of her. After getting her bearings, she slowly stepped backwards out of the light allowing Campbell to have his moment.

"C'mon up here... Dad," Chase encouraged Campbell, waving him up towards the podium.

Campbell froze for a moment not sure what to do. He heard Chase use his real name, Mark Hagen. It never occurred to him to tell Chase that he shouldn't be announcing his name to the whole world like that, considering his past and all, but then, he hadn't really told Chase about his past. He didn't really want to admit to him all the mistakes he'd made and was still somewhat hiding from.

Campbell shook off the feeling of dread and made his way up to where Chase was. As he approached, Campbell held his arms out and Chase instinctively hugged the man, his father, essentially for the first time. They had only ever spoken the one time about being father and son and since then had never really broached the subject again. For Chase, this was another defining moment. He had let the world know who his father was, and that he was a very talented musician. Mark Hagen had been in the shadows long enough and without realizing that was how "Campbell" wanted it, Chase was all about bringing his father along for the ride as much and as far as he could.

The room was momentarily stunned by the news, some present having used Campbell's talents on their own recordings and having known the man for many years didn't know of a son who was so gifted, such a creative musical genius that his first CD was ready for launch in just seven short months. Others were not aware of what they had witnessed and applauded only because Chase commanded the room and at his every whim the audience responded positively. And then there were those who caught every single moment, most notably, the name "Mark Hagen."

After Chase and Campbell shared a brief moment, Chase said into the microphone, "Okay everyone, tonight is about celebration, it's about exploration and it's about the first step out into a whole new universe for me and the band. Thank you for sharing this night with us. Eat, drink and make very merry on the dance floor!"

He grinned as he stepped away, hooting and clapping with the audience following right along. He hadn't been on stage once during his entire time in New York and yet, with only a microphone before him, he was able to raise the energy level in the room tenfold. Chase was on a 90 degree trajectory and everyone in the room knew it.

***

Sonya remained at the table she had been standing at with Campbell when the spotlight hit them. She felt as though she had been caught in the middle of a bomb blast. Her heart was racing and her mind was reeling. She made a mental note that she'd better not touch a single drink of alcohol because she was already out of control. She could see Campbell leading Chase over to the table as the music started blaring, the bass pumping so hard her chest hurt. She knew he wanted to introduce her to his son and she was barely able to swallow and collect herself before Chase Morningstar was standing before her, smiling his brilliant smile as Campbell leaned into Chase's ear to introduce Sonya to him. She just smiled back at Chase, grateful that the music prevented a lot of conversation. He took her hand to shake it but instead held it in his hand a moment and then flipped it over and raised it to his lips. He said nothing to her, just looked her directly in the eye and kissed the back of her hand slowly and seductively. She couldn't tell what he was thinking, whether or not he meant to be so incredibly sexy, she just knew that when his lips touched her hand it sent jolts of electricity through her hand and straight to her groin. She held her breath as his eyes held hers, not wanting the moment to end. He slowly lowered her hand but still held it in his and gently smiled at her. *Did he just feel that as well?* she wondered.

***

Chase was intrigued by the gorgeous blonde his father had brought to the launch party. Without knowing too much about the woman, not to mention the inability to really be heard with the party just starting to get going around them, Chase could only use gestures to show how he felt. He was compelled to kiss her hand although it wasn't something he normally did.

What the hell is my 74 year old father doing with this stunning woman? he wondered. She didn't look like a gold-digger to Chase; she looked like an elegant respectable woman who had been invited to his party and was as new to this setting as he was.

He broke his gaze on her for just a moment and realized that there were many people vying for his attention. He drew her close so he didn't have to shout and said into her ear, "I'm gonna be very busy for the next couple of hours, but if you can stick around for a while, I'd love to spend some time with you," he said against her head.

He squeezed her hand and kissed it one more time before letting it go. He was hoping it convinced her to not go anywhere for the foreseeable future. It had been a very long time since he had been intrigued by a woman other than Georgie and now that he had purged his heart ache over her into his music, he felt like his heart was free to care again, to even love again. Perhaps his father had introduced him to someone who would be monumental in his life. Wouldn't that be something, he mused as he reluctantly stepped away from Sonya to greet other well-wishers.

***

Campbell's smile was glued to his face but inside he was an absolute mess. He kept trying to shake it off but the more the cameras flashed and the more he stood watching the interaction between Chase and Sonya all he could think about was his own destiny.

Chase had used his name, his *real* name. He had managed to be "Campbell" for thirty years, skirting so many thugs, gangsters and all sorts of city scum. He let only a select few know his real name, having learned that lesson while staying at Lucy's. He learned back then that he had burned too many bridges to ever be who he really was and instead was forced to remain Campbell in his musical career in order to live as the anonymous Mark Hagen in his everyday life. It meant that anyone recognizing him from decades ago could never track him down. His apartment didn't list a "Campbell" as a first name or a last so even if followed they would come up empty handed as soon as they got to the apartment listings. Now, at the biggest launch party of the year, with every entertainment news network present and all in the room hanging on Chase's every word, he had uttered the one thing that had Campbell now feeling anxious as hell and nervous about whose attention it might grab.

He really needed to get high. Immediately! That would help calm him down. Campbell didn't like to drink in this kind of a situation, it made him sloppy. He needed focus and to think clearly and he needed to calm the hell down. It probably wasn't great for a man of his age to have heart palpitations like he was experiencing and he knew if he could get a joint into him, he'd settle down for certain. Not thinking he'd need more than the few that he'd smoked before arriving, Campbell had no more joints on him. Now, when he needed it the most. *SHIT!*

Chase had been enveloped by the party and Sonya was still in a daze over her introduction to Chase. For a brief moment, Campbell felt a pang of jealousy but then realized it was foolish of him to think that a stunning girl like Sonya would be remotely interested in him at all. He was more than double her age. He needed to remember that. He needed to keep things in perspective. What he really needed was to get high. Campbell managed to catch Sonya's eye and motioned as if smoking a joint, then pointed to her. She shook her head in the negative and held out her hands, empty; she hadn't brought any drugs with her, never having been to something like this before she wasn't sure if she would be searched before being allowed to enter. She had decided that she would leave all product at home and if an opportunity to market herself arose, then she'd jump at the chance. After having met Chase, she didn't know his take on the whole drug scene and didn't want to ruin anything just yet. She'd be happy with him not finding out that she dealt drugs for a living at all, if possible. So Campbell's request went unfulfilled.

When he realized that she came empty handed, Campbell started to panic. Someone, somewhere, here tonight, had to have something that would help ease his nerves and settle him down. He decided he needed to go to the bathroom and splash some water on his face. He excused himself, leaving Sonya watching the dance floor fill up and pushing a few appetizers around on her plate as she sat, star struck. Campbell had never seen her outside of her usual drug selling persona so he wasn't sure if this was normal for her or not and right now he didn't care; he just needed to stop feeling so damned anxious.

He made his way over to the bathrooms inside the reception hall, grabbing the door handle and hoping there wouldn't be too many others in there. Another stroke of bad luck. Three men stood near the bathroom sinks, blocking his way. As he came through the door they moved suspiciously with their backs towards him so he couldn't see what they were doing.

He stepped to one side and cleared his throat. "Uh… excuse me there guys, but I was hoping to use the sink," he said, trying hard not to disrupt them too much but eager to get some cold water on his face.

One man stepped aside exposing their activity to Campbell; they were snorting cocaine off a small mirror. Campbell eyed the situation and then eyed the men. He was sure they were Lapis executives by the way they were dressed and he wondered if that was the only shit they had brought.

"Any of you have anything a little more suitable for an old fart like me?" he asked, as he ran the cold water over his wrists first and then brought his hands full of the cold water up into his face. He repeated this twice more and then grabbed five or six paper towels to dry his face and hands off. When he finished, he smiled broadly at the perplexed men. Did they think he was joking?

"Seriously, anyone carrying a joint?" he asked.

The men looked between one another and then one reached into his inside breast pocket and produced the highly sought after marijuana cigarette.

Campbell nearly cried out he was so happy to see it. "So spark it up, what are you waiting for?" he asked, anxious to get his happy on and put his worries aside.

The executive smiled and wagged his finger at Campbell. "Now, now. We can't smoke in here. You'll have to take it to the stairwell or an empty office space without a smoke detector," he said, obviously having given it a lot of thought. "Be careful, ol' man, this stuff has one hell of a kick," he laughed, as he handed Campbell the joint.

Campbell took it from the exec's hand and smiled and winked in appreciation. He could deal with anything as soon as he found a place to smoke it. He thanked the group of men again and left the bathroom quickly to the sound of them laughing as the door closed behind him. He rushed off to the entrance of the reception hall and out to where the elevators first opened into the Lapis Labels offices. He headed for the stairwell door and pushed through it, stepping onto a landing in front of flights of grey painted stairwells going up and down as far as the eye could see. Campbell walked down three or four flights before sitting on one of the stairs, producing the joint from his jacket pocket and lighting it with great enthusiasm. Had he known that this night would cause him so much worry, he'd have better prepared for it, but he couldn't possibly have imagined that Chase would use his real name and in front of all the news people and with all the video cameras rolling. Campbell just didn't know what to expect from that sort of exposure. Chase's lack of discretion could cost Campbell a lot and, as he sat in the stairwell smoking the joint, he contemplated revealing to Chase his deviant past, including who might come looking for him and what it might bring to their doorstep.

The marijuana smelled sweeter than most and Campbell sat back leaning against the stair as he relaxed, allowing the weed to do its thing. He could tell its potency when it hit the back of his eyelids, straining the tiny muscles there and letting Campbell know that the weed was of excellent quality. He could feel the stone overtake him and he rested his head back against the stairs and thought about his circumstances. He let his mind work with the idea for a moment, enjoying the remaining smell in the air and the solitude of the stairwell.

Suddenly, everything cleared. Everything started feeling great, really great and he was instantly convinced that he was in no peril whatsoever. The weed was working, making him feel better and better as each minute passed. *This is some excellent shit,* he thought to himself. By now Campbell was positively sure that Chase's slip of the tongue would go unnoticed with no one being aware of his outing; meanwhile, he was feeling incredible and wanted to go back out to the party and knock the whole damn place over with his great talent. It also didn't hurt that he was Chase's father!

He took one more toke before putting out the joint and saving the other half for later. This shit was far too good to use up all at once. After carefully putting it out, he wrapped the unused half into a napkin and stowed it in his jacket pocket. He practically bounded up the few flights of stairs back onto the Lapis Labels floor and into the pumping launch party. His heart was racing, almost matching the beat of the song the VJ was tantalizing the dance crowd with. He may have been 74 but Campbell felt like he was 21. When a few girls encircled him as he tried to make his way through the dance floor and onto the other side of the hall, he was caught up in the music, the movement and the moment and couldn't help himself. His dance moves were strenuous and a little exaggerated but he kept up with all the girls for the full five minutes of music and, as the strobe light went off, his face pulled tight, he clenched his chest and quickly dropped to the floor, hitting his head and knocking himself out cold.

***

Chase was caught in the middle of a drunken conversation between two musicians who wanted him to record with them on their next album. They began by trying to outdo the other's promise for what they would offer to Chase for his sound and name on at least one track. After only a few minutes, and probably many more alcoholic beverages, the two musicians were locked in a heated competition and started firing insults back and forth at one another. Chase stood between thinking what a waste of time these two were. They may be big on the Billboard Music Charts but they were losers and duds in Chase's eyes. He, too, almost lost himself in alcohol once. Getting himself out of Chicago and centered in New York gave him back his perspective and he no longer cared to lose control like that. Besides, look at the sloppy mess people see you as. He wanted to be taken seriously and, if you're a drunk, that doesn't happen. Chase decided he was going to zone out of their conversation and see if he could find Sonya in the crowd and zone in on her for a while. He scanned the room thinking it should be easy to spot her very beautiful blonde hair, especially in a room made to look like space. He didn't see her immediately and had to go back and look more closely but he did finally spot her on the other side of the dance floor. She was bent over with a concerned look on her face. Chase had to stand up to see what she was looking at and as he did he realized that someone had gone down on the dance floor. Probably someone knocked someone over and she happened to be near and was offering some assistance. He watched her for a moment as the crowd grew bigger around the fallen dancer. As though on cue, the idea hit Chase as Sonya's eyes lifted in search of someone and they both locked eyes. He only had to see the look on Sonya's face and instantly Chase knew it wasn't just any dancer that had gone down, it was his father.

~

Chapter 8

Love Is the Drug

Campbell awoke feeling groggy and sore. His head hurt like it never had before, as though his brain had smacked against his skull. He tried to focus on the room around him; brown drapes hung to either side of his bed, a rectangular window exposed the very early morning and he could make out an empty chair across the room. He had a thousand questions but couldn't manage to utter a word. His head was pounding, his heart raced in his chest. What the hell was going on?

***

Sonya and Chase left the launch party together and followed the ambulance to the hospital. They were ushered in through the Emergency Department and put into a quiet room awaiting a doctor to see Campbell and then let them know what had happened. No three hour wait in the waiting room. Thank God for Kyle and his magic phone – the man had connections!

Left alone, Chase had a moment to appreciate Sonya's company. She was a welcome sight for his very tired eyes, still dressed in her black dress from the party and even after all the distress she still looked as though the night had just begun. He gave her a big million watt smile.

"You're very sweet for staying. He probably fainted when it hit him that he escorted *you* into the party," Chase said, easing her tension and giving her a reason to smile. She was grateful to him for it.

"Well, Campbell's a charmer," she said shyly. "I wouldn't dream of attending the party at his request and not staying with him, regardless of the circumstances. He's my date," she stated, matter-of-factly. She meant it too and Chase could tell. She continued describing the events as if remembering in her mind's eye.

"I don't know what happened. One minute he was dancing with us, the next his eyes had rolled back and he fell like a stone," she explained, her large brown eyes filling with tears at the thought of Campbell's face as he fell.

Chase's heart melted. His arm instinctively went around her and he pulled her to him as they sat side by side.

"Hey… hey… it's okay. He's gonna be alright. I'm sure the doctors would be in here by now if it was anything too bad," he said, trying to reassure her.

Sonya replayed the evening to Chase numerous times, insisting he was fine the last time they spoke which was just after Chase had introduced him. Sonya told Chase everything she could, stopping short at admitting that Campbell had asked her for weed at the party. She didn't need him knowing that and she was sure Campbell would agree.

"I wonder if it's his heart?" asked Chase out loud.

I wonder if he found something to smoke thought Sonya.

Regardless of what the other was thinking both agreed it had to be his heart. They exchanged a few "Campbell" stories and then conversation led back to each other. When it came to Sonya's story, she chose to edit it somewhat.

"I was raised by my brother, basically. My father was never around and my mother died when I was young. Johann was always there for me, but its tough 'cause he's… difficult to like," she admitted openly.

Chase didn't know to what degree she had confessed, but he knew it was a lot for her. She looked down as if ashamed. He thought of her story and came to a realization.

"It's a carbon copy of my life," Chase told her, smiling wide, arms held open. "I didn't have a father and after my mother died I went on the road with Charlie, my older brother." He wanted her to feel as though whatever fucked up rationale was the cornerstone of her childhood, he could accept it because he'd lived it too. He'd also had an abnormal childhood and was open to anything, especially if it was opposite of the all American upbringing with the nuclear family and church on Sundays. It just wasn't how Celia Morningstar had raised her boys. Instead, they were surrounded by blues and jazz music and their church was the fellowship of musicians and clubs within the city of Chicago.

They waited while tests were being run on Campbell. Eventually, the doctors determined that he had suffered a very serious concussion after having a bad reaction to an illicit drug; probably cocaine. They told Chase that they would be moving Campbell to a private room and keeping him in for observation due to the concussion.

"You're welcome to sit with him if you wish," said the short female doctor. Chase could only make out her first name, Corinne. "I'll get a Porter to bring in another chair," she said, smiling at Chase.

Corinne may have been doing her residency and working 36 hour shifts but she knew Chase Morningstar when she saw him. He'd been all over the radio, web, blogosphere and twitter accounts all week.

Chase had cleared things with Kyle, done a few phone interviews in the hallway outside the Emergency Department and promised himself to several other network entertainment shows after the crisis with Campbell stabilized, all while Kyle frantically managed the vertical ascent of Chase Morningstar.

By the time Campbell was moved and settled into a private room and Kyle had managed the publicity side of things, both Sonya and Chase were exhausted. As Campbell began to regain consciousness, Sonya and Chase were sitting in the corner of the room, both with their heads drooped and asleep in their chairs.

***

He's sitting on a bed, plucking away at the guitar he holds. The new speakers, purchased for his birthday, sound perfect. He's concentrating on the chords he's playing, repeating them until they are natural to him. As he plays he can see smoke building around him slowly. He doesn't panic – he doesn't move except his fingers on the neck of the guitar, still repeating the chords.

Out of the smoke he sees a form walking towards him. He continues repeating the chords and the speaker gets louder as the form gets nearer. He is now playing frantically, moving his head to the chords, lost in the music. The form becomes clearer… the shape of a woman clearly appears. She is slight of frame, elderly, dressed elegantly and smiling. He looks up from where he sits on the bed and smiles at her, still continuing to play the chords. Her lips are moving rather slowly but no sound comes out. He feels frustration, tenses his body and continues with his guitar playing trying to watch the woman and play the chords at the same time. Her lips continue to move without sound until suddenly she leans forward and her face is all he can see – large, wide-eyed and penetrating. The speakers are now full blast as the noise builds to a deafening crescendo…

He awoke with a start, his heart racing. Even when he napped, it plagued him.

***

Campbell's mouth was extremely dry and he felt like a truck had hit him. His head hurt like hell, as if a vice were holding it in place. There were two needles secured into his arms and taped in place and both were connected to machines monitoring some sort of bodily function that would be pertinent to a doctor or medical staff, but nothing he could understand.

He remembered the launch party and Sonya meeting him at the entrance. He remembered Chase's entrance, the cameras flashing and then everything went rather blurry. He lay listening to the whirring of the machines and the beeping of his heartbeat on the monitor. As the mechanical sounds filled the room, Campbell tried hard to fill in the gaps of his memory from the previous night.

Giving it sound reflection, Campbell realized that Chase's entrance seemed to be the catalyst. Something happened at that point. Campbell tried relaxing and going over what he knew was accurate. Meeting Sonya first, then meeting Chase. The cameras flashing, lots of people smiling, Chase's speech and then Chase telling everyone that Campbell was his dad. Campbell felt proud that his son was so successful and willing to acknowledge him worldwide.

As he lay in the hospital bed, his mind kept flipping from the past to the present, going far back into his memory and then back to the circumstances surrounding last night's launch party that ended with him being rushed to the Emergency Department.

Just then, from across the room, Chase's head snapped up as he awoke with a start. It took him a moment to orient himself and he immediately looked over towards Campbell who weakly waved "Hi." Chase jumped from his seat, waking Sonya from her slumber and rushed to stand to the side of Campbell's bed.

"Hey buddy. How're ya feelin'?" he asked gently, taking his hand and holding it.

"Rough… dizzy… uh, my head is throbbing… foggy… confused," were the words he used to describe his present state.

Sonya, now fully awake, came to stand at the other side of the bed. "Geez, you had us worried!" she said, concerned for the old man.

Campbell looked into her pretty face and recalled that very sight as he looked up at her from the ground, but it all seemed very hazy, like a dream, as though his memory was struggling to remember all of the events that ended up landing him in the hospital.

"You gave yourself quite the knock to yer noggin' when you fell," Chase said.

"I fell?" Campbell asked, rubbing his head and then feeling a large swollen sore spot on the back of his head. He groaned as his fingers ran across it.

"Yes, you fell and hit your head on the dance floor," Sonya explained. "I thought I saw you clench your chest like you were having a heart attack but the doctors assure us it wasn't that. You were a dancing machine with all of us; it wouldn't have surprised me if you did have a heart attack! I should call you the "Dancing Machine!" she laughed and both Chase and Campbell smiled at her.

Prettiest drug dealer I've ever seen, that's for sure, Campbell thought and that's when it hit him. He'd smoked a joint in the stairwell. He'd been given a joint from the three guys in the bathroom and taken it to the stairwell to smoke. He remembered feeling really great, really acutely aware of his surroundings and wanting to go back into the launch party and get the party started. But what the hell was he thinking? He didn't know those guys in the bathroom. What the hell did they give him? It was unlike any weed he'd ever had!

Sonya's voice cut into his foggy ponderings when she said, "You probably got yourself all worked up from the dancing and your blood pressure rose and you blacked out and hit your head giving you a nice concussion and a good sized goose egg on the back of your head. Don't worry, I still think you're a Dancing Machine," she smiled. "You suit that more than you do 'Mark'," she laughingly teased.

Campbell's face fell at hearing her use his real name as the final puzzle piece fell into place. The evening began with meeting Sonya outside in front of the building then seeing Chase arrive, the flashing cameras, the large crowd there just for him. Chase then admitted to the crowd that Campbell was his father before bringing him up to the podium, and then he said it – Campbell's real name. Only a select group of people knew his real name. Very select. Campbell even questioned why he'd told Chase his real name when they were first introduced over a year ago in the studio. It was a careless move he hadn't made in thirty years.

Yes! Campbell realized, resting his aching head back on the pillow and looking up at the ceiling as he envisioned how the events unfolded. It was Chase's announcement that sent Campbell running into the bathroom and straight into smoking a joint in a panicked effort to try and cope with the fact that Chase's announcement was to a worldwide audience. In 30-odd years he had never worried about it being revealed; his circle of "people" never extended past those he knew were trustworthy.

To have had it broadcast on such a scale meant many people will be able to find him; through Lapis Labels, through Mark Hagen and worst of all, through Chase Morningstar. Kyle had said that the launch would be the beginning of a meteoric rise for Chase and Supernova's career. Now, everyone knew that Mark Hagen was not only a member of the band but father of the superstar himself. This could potentially bring trouble to Chase. Even though more than 30 years had passed since Hennie had come to kill him, Campbell didn't believe for a second that he was stopped that night by Christopher Hollomby. He figured that, if anything, Hennie got some jail time for the two murders if they managed to make the charges stick and was probably living somewhere with a large, healthy grudge growing like a cancer for Campbell. After all, not only had he stolen a large package of cocaine but he ran out on a debt he owed and then (possibly) had him thrown in jail.

Campbell knew Hennie would be in his 60's at this point. The thought of watching two elderly men fight it out made Campbell smile as he pictured himself trying to punch Hennie and him trying to hit him with his walker; if only! Instead, he came back to reality knowing that a gun stops anyone in a second and can be used by young and old alike. Besides, what if Hennie had passed his grudge on down through his henchmen. At that thought, Campbell went noticeably pale.

"Hey, are you okay, Campbell?" Sonya asked, as she noticed the color drain from his face.

"Yes, dear. You're such a lovely girl," he said, patting her hand. "I'm so thankful it was your beautiful face that I saw when I came to!" he said, smiling at her.

She blushed at the elderly man's flattering words and Chase noticed. He noticed a lot about this girl, actually. When a more appropriate time presented itself, he and Sonya were going to have a proper date. He was going to make sure of that.

"I wonder if you would mind giving my son and me a moment alone, Sonya. Can you please find me some water?" he asked her.

"Of course! Chase, can I get you something? A coffee?" she asked, as she turned for the door.

"Sure, thanks. Just black, thanks," he said to her, as he smiled his million watt smile.

Sonya was an extremely strong woman, but even she couldn't resist that smile: she melted into her shoes!

When she was gone, Campbell turned his head toward Chase and said to him ominously, "I have to tell you something. Something you need to be aware of…" he stopped, making sure Chase understood the importance of the moment.

Not knowing what to expect and seeing the look on Campbell's face, Chase replied, "You have my attention," and leaned into the bedside.

For the next 30 minutes Campbell told Chase everything that happened on the night he was conceived. Campbell told him everything from the moment he dropped his mother off to the moment he dropped to the floor last night, including admitting that he had smoked a joint in the stairwell. He also told him why.

When he believed that Chase had listened and heard his story, he then said, "Which leads me to worry for both of us and the label now. I have no idea where Hennie ended up and whether or not he has a lifelong vendetta against me. Assholes like him will stop at nothing. I bet he's kept this grudge for some 30 years. We haven't got a clue who means us harm, now that they've seen my face and know my real name," he ended with, hoping that Chase would focus on the concern about the future, rather than his indiscretions from his past, even if some of them were only hours old.

Chase allowed a silence to take over the room while he contemplated all that he had been told. There were layers of problems, the complexity of three decades overlaying all of the troubles that were now before them. Chase was obviously not aware that Campbell's real name would cause such difficulty. Chase wasn't telling Campbell that cocaine *as well as* marijuana were found in his system. *Note to self,* he thought, *find out where he got the joint from.* Chase sighed as he envisioned the negative headlines this could create.

"I don't suppose you know much else about this Hennie guy? Do you still know the cop Hollomby? Maybe he knows something. Do you think we could contact Hollomby to see if he'd have anything on him?" Chase asked, thinking Kyle could get an investigator on it and maybe help with damage control.

Campbell shook his head solemnly. "Christopher died more than 20 years ago. Some guy went nuts, blasted him with a shot gun." Campbell shrugged his shoulders with no further answers. "The only other person, or people who might have kept track were my father, my aunt Pearl or her friend Lucy. Of course, they're all dead too. Face it, Chase, we're up a creek without a paddle," Campbell said sadly.

"I know you're concerned, Campbell, but I think you're safe in here and I know my apartment building is safe, so I'm going to assume that we're good to go for tonight. I'll talk to Kyle and see about getting some security in place."

He wanted Campbell to know that he took the threat seriously but that he felt confident that he and Kyle could handle it. He wanted Campbell to be able to rest and hoped he'd be discharged the next morning. What he didn't want was for Campbell to know how royally pissed off he was that Campbell had not divulged the importance of keeping his real name secret, after months of knowing him. Then, to have chosen to get high at the launch, at an elderly age; what was he thinking?!

Campbell was definitely a loose cannon that Chase just couldn't afford right now. He needed to keep him on a short leash and monitor his actions. If media, social, news or otherwise got hold of this, it could destroy Chase's image, his creative process or ultimately his dreams. Chase wasn't about to let that happen.

He studied Campbell as he fell back to sleep and began snoring. Chase was thinking he should leave the room when Sonya came through the door carrying a large Starbucks cup. She held it out to him smiling and looked at him sadly.

"You guys okay?" she asked instinctively, sensing something in Campbell's request for her to leave.

Chase nodded his head and smiled back at her then let his gaze fall back on his father. "He revealed his secrets to me, although I don't know if I'm happy about knowing them." He paused, his smile faded. The seriousness of the moment took over and after allowing his thoughts to drift he was brought back to the moment. He wanted to make sure Sonya got home safely.

"I'd like you to be taken home with my people, actually, in my personal limo. No funny business, I promise," he said, smiling his smile with his hands up in surrender.

"Oh, you have no idea, do you?" she said, with a strange smile on her face. "Seems that your launch's live webcast was huge and so many people logged on that it crashed the site for a bit. They've also crashed the website for the CD. That means that beyond the main doors out there are about 400 paparazzi and news media, not to mention fans who not only saw your launch, but reported on your father's fall and want to speak to the superstar himself!" she said, matter-of-factly. "You may have come through those doors as a rising star, but since the webcast and all the social media buzz, you're a friggin' universal name, Mr. Morningstar!" she told him, not knowing how he would take the news.

"What...? You mean there are photographers outside?" he asked, amused by her perception of "a universal name."

She could tell that he wasn't grasping the enormity of the situation beyond the hospital doors so, with Campbell sleeping in the bed, she grabbed Chase's arm and dragged him outside of the room and towards the main Emergency Department doors. He got within 30 feet of them and could hear a very large and raucous group gathered outside, causing havoc for anyone entering for real emergencies. Upon realizing what he and Sonya would hit ahead of them, Chase grabbed her hand and veered left down a hallway that was more geared to the administration of the hospital. He checked the time – it was 8:00 am. Chase hoped that someone would be at a desk at this time. He led Sonya into an office and was grateful to see a receptionist on duty.

He asked the girl if she could call Kyle and provided his number. At first, she seemed stunned by his request, trying to accept that Chase Morningstar just walked through her office door! She had just spent last night watching his CD launch online and now he stood before her! When he explained that he needed to leave the hospital under the highest security and secrecy possible, the receptionist swung into action. She immediately called security, explained the situation and then requested a different entrance be secured for them. She also arranged for security to escort them through the underground tunnels to the secured entrance where they would be able to leave with no one knowing.

When she explained this to the couple, Chase hesitated a moment and then said, "I won't be leaving from that entrance, only you will, Sonya."

He looked at Sonya hoping she understood the publicity opportunity he faced. If it weren't for Campbell's fall, Chase would be making news for his launch alone, focusing on his talents. Instead, now the focus would be on how his father was doing. If Sonya was beside him as he tried to navigate through the throng of photographers and news reporters that would also be something he'd have to explain.

"Listen, Sonya," he said, turning her towards him, "I know I have to face them, but you don't. I asked for this but you didn't and an invitation to a launch party shouldn't end up with having your face plastered all over the morning papers." He smiled his gorgeous smile and Sonya's heart raced.

"I think my life is about to become rather crazy and exposed. It's going to be hard for someone to date me; my schedule is nuts." He laughed, dropped his head and ran his hand through his hair, messing it up, as though it were representing his current life. Sonya wondered where this was leading. She was about to stop him but he brought his head up, smiled at her again and took her hands in his.

"What I'm trying to say is… if you're willing to take me on, I'd like to see you. Like… a date. Dating, I mean." He laughed again and this time shook his head. "Damn, I haven't been tongue-tied by a beautiful woman before, but you mess me up somethin' fierce," he admitted shyly.

Sonya just smiled wide. What could she say? "I'd like that too, Chase. But…" she started to say something and he interrupted her.

"But? Shit, please tell me you aren't already in a relationship; there's no ring on your finger, I checked!" he said, letting her know that he'd done some homework.

The "but" was instead, "But, you're about to become a major superstar. You sure you want to be stuck through a whole dinner with me?" She was teasing him, but there was some trepidation in her statement too. She knew she couldn't be completely honest with Chase. That was going to make things very difficult.

"I can't think of anyone better," he smiled, and asked the efficient receptionist while motioning towards a few chairs around a small coffee table, "Can we have a seat over here?"

The receptionist nodded approval and Chase led Sonya over to the chairs, had her take a seat and he sat beside her turning his chair towards her.

"Look, I've heard about your dysfunctional childhood and have been able to compare it to mine. You obviously like my music, I saw you dancing to it and having a great time until Campbell's fall and you

141

take my breath away with those eyes. You sound like the perfect dinner date!" he said proudly.

She laughed. *If only it were that easy!*

He noticed her hesitation and wondered what was stopping her. Was it her work? Out of the blue he asked, "What do you do for a living?"

She hesitated to answer him, wishing she could be completely honest with him, but she couldn't, not yet anyway. "I… uh… help run the family business. Pharmaceutical sales," she told him.

"Oh! Does it take up a lot of your time?" he asked her, really interested. He wouldn't have thought she was lying; she was far too sophisticated for bullshit.

"Well, it's just my brother and I now sort of running it," she said, thinking about what Chase would think of her brother.

"What's his name?" Chase asked.

"Johann," she answered. *Mr. Clippity-Clop Man to anyone in the drug underground.* Boy, she couldn't be telling Chase that. She couldn't even imagine a time when they could or would meet. Chase would see straight through his sliminess and know right away that he was an evil prick. Johann didn't disguise it well.

"You close to him?" Chase asked tenderly.

Sonya nodded and then shook her head but said nothing else and Chase took it as a sign to not ask any further.

"Okay, so anything you want to know about me, just ask. Or go home and read all about me on whatever computer site you want. I'm an open book at this point," he offered her. She looked at him, grateful for his intuitive understanding and with that look he blurted out, "You have the most incredibly beautiful blue eyes I have ever seen." He smiled wide, sitting back in his chair with his hands held out. "What more do I need to know than that?" he offered her.

In her head, she told herself that this shouldn't happen, but her heart screamed for her to go for it. This was exactly what she had hoped for! Meeting someone like Chase was why she had educated herself, polished herself and brought herself up to a level that would be worthy of a man like him, but in her gut something was nagging and she knew it.

"So, are we on? You'll give me a chance and a date? Say dinner... tomorrow night, you pick the most expensive or most sought after reservation in the city and I'll have all the arrangements made. What do you say?" he asked.

What could she say? "Yes," she answered, smiling back at him. That was where their conversation ended as Kyle came through the office door in full command.

"Holy shit, what a night! I can't believe the number of paparazzi out there and even news reporters! You can't buy this kind of publicity," he said excitedly. He looked at Chase, smiling, and then turned to Sonya and said, "Oh hey! You're a friend of... Campbell's, right?" he asked her. Before she could answer, Chase jumped in with, "and now mine. We were just making dinner arrangements for tomorrow night. Can we exchange numbers so we can finish this up?" he asked her, smiling.

She agreed and they spent a few moments loading each other's information into their respective phones. Once done, Chase led Sonya out to the hall where a security officer was waiting to take her to the secluded private exit. Before he let her go, he pulled her to him and kissed her. He pulled away for a moment and then pulled her back to him giving her a long, languishing kiss.

"Sorry, I couldn't let you go without doing that or I would have regretted it and I'm trying to live without regrets now," he said cryptically. "Thanks for taking care of Campbell the way you did and coming here and staying until we knew he'd be okay. You're a real sweetheart for doing that," he said softly. "And lastly, please don't forget about our date. I'm really looking forward to it."

He kissed her again, tenderly holding her to him for a moment as their lips lay against each other's then he stood back. She didn't take her eyes from his for a moment, even when she turned her body towards the exit, following the officer. When she did look forward she had a funny feeling that she and Mr. Chase Morningstar were about to start an exciting journey together and it gave her butterflies.

Sonya was led to a running black limo with darkened windows. As she stepped out into the morning light she took in a deep breath of the cold, crisp air and paused. The driver opened the door for her and she climbed inside and got comfortable on its large back seat. The sole occupant, she stretched out thinking of how things could change for her if Chase and she were to become an item. He had taken such good care, even ensuring that she stay away from the milieu he would be heading into right after she left. It had kept her face out of the limelight which was a good thing. Johann wouldn't be happy to see her face all over the news. Johann wouldn't be happy at all. He liked keeping publicity to a minimum, but he LOVED selling drugs. Perhaps there were those at the party that she could make a drug connection with, making it beneficial for her to be there. Either way, she knew Johann would have an opinion and she anticipated hearing from him soon.

She tried not to think about her brother, wanting to remain positive and in the moment. The limo was large and she imagined herself being in the back of many limos if her future was with Chase. He could change everything for her. She could quit selling drugs and be his wife or even find something within his world that she could do. Her mind wandered through all kinds of scenarios until the car came to a stop.

She looked through the darkened window and could only see a quiet city street, not nearly awake enough for all the traffic it was already seeing. She was only blocks away from her apartment, but had given the driver this address, not wanting him to take her to her real home and neighborhood. Always trying to keep her secret life secret.

As the driver opened her door, she thanked him for the ride, exited the car and started walking towards a brownstone as if she were to enter it. The limo driver, satisfied that she was home, pulled away from the road and drove off. She waited a moment, just in case he was looking in the rear view, pretending to hunt her keys from her handbag. When he turned a corner and drove out of sight, she descended the brownstone's steps and started walking towards her own apartment. If she hadn't spent the night at the launch party only to end up sleeping in the chair in an emergency room, to anyone watching, this could look like a walk of shame, but Sonya knew all too well the reality of what had happened and hoped that the contrast of the night to the stark, cold morning she faced was not a precursor to the adventure she was about to embark on!

***

Kyle and Chase stood in the hallway planning their strategy for maneuvering through the reporters. "I want you to tell them that Campbell had a bad fall and that the doctors are keeping him in for observation. Tell them he should be released by tomorrow and that he'll be just fine. Don't say anything more and don't answer any questions," he told him quickly.

Chase nodded and Kyle urged him towards the Emergency Room doors where the eager faces of the reporters were anxiously dodging and rising to try and see. Chase briefly wondered how long these guys had waited.

Just before they got to the doors, Kyle told him, "Just stop out front for a moment, say your piece and head straight for the open door limo pulled up right beyond them." He patted Chase on the shoulder and smiled wide and he pushed his weight against the doors and opened them up. "Hang on Buddy," was all Chase heard him say as he left the Emergency area and entered the crowd.

Immediately he was mobbed by hundreds of reporters and fans. Microphones were thrust in front of his mouth and so many people were throwing rapid fire questions at him that Chase was dumbstruck for a moment. Kyle was standing off to his right watching him carefully, ready to jump in if Chase fell to trouble. His fans wanted to know what they witnessed on last night's live web cast. Just as Kyle was about to step forward to make a statement, Chase cleared his throat and tilted his head as he let out a heavy sigh.

"Thank you to all of you for being here. We had a little scare last night when my... er..." he hesitated, "...piano player, Campbell, fell on the dance floor at the launch of our new CD. He banged his head pretty good, has a nice goose egg at the back and a hell of a headache but the ol' guy is just being kept in for observation one more night and then they'll send him home with a clean bill of health. Now, if you'll excuse me, I've had a hell'uva night and I need my bed."

With that, he did just as Kyle had told him and started pushing his way through the mob surrounding him and towards the open door of the limo, disregarding the avalanche of questions and call outs and people screaming his name. Kyle also started moving in that direction and, as a large crowd, they moved with them.

Chase stayed quiet, until someone yelled out, "Does Mark Hagen have anything to say?"

Chase knew it was a fair question but in light of Campbell's confessions, Chase didn't want to hear people use his name. "Yeah... about that..." he paused. The crowd within closest proximity went quiet. Chase simply shrugged his shoulders, "He actually goes by Campbell, that's how we all know and love him, as Campbell," he said loudly, hoping all could hear him while keeping his temper in check.

When he finally reached the limo he turned to see where Kyle was, saw and grabbed him by his collar and dragged him into the limo with him. The door was quickly shut as hands started tapping and slapping against the darkened shut windows. Chase and Kyle both took a moment to straighten their clothing up and take a deep breath.

"Holy crap that was a lot of people!" Chase said. He had seen his share of large audiences but had never had to wade through them and they weren't all out for answers from him. This was going to take some getting used to, for certain. However, inside, in his stomach, it gave him butterflies!

***

Kyle's phone started buzzing and as he answered it the caller yelled out, "What the hell are you doing?!" Kyle sighed and put his ear to the phone and spoke to the caller. "Dad, what's the matter?" he asked reluctantly. Chase couldn't make out his words but he could definitely hear Kyle's father's anger and not just because Kyle kept taking the phone away from his ear to avoid the ear blasting his father was giving him.

"I know… Yes, I didn't tell… uh-huh, I know… I will. Yes dad, I know. Okay, okay… yup, you too. Bye now." He sighed again and turned his phone off and put it back in his pocket before leaning back on the seat.

"He's freaking out because you said Campbell's real name on the World Wide Web. He's flipped his lid! I swear," he said, trying to explain away the awkwardness of his father's actions.

"Well, I think he may have a valid reason," Chase said. He then explained to Kyle exactly what Campbell had confessed to him.

After he had finished, Kyle nodded his head. "Yeah, I knew a lot of that had happened. See, when Campbell left Pearl and Lucy he came to live with us for a while. I was just a baby at the time. I don't remember him living in our home but he's always been a part of my life and a family friend, almost like an uncle. He and my dad are very close friends and he's kept him working and slightly hidden for all these years. That first time he met you that day in the studio I was surprised that he told you his real name. He never does that," Kyle admitted to Chase. Campbell had said the same thing. It gave Chase pause.

"I had no idea of all of this, you gotta know it, man," Chase said, almost apologetically. "I would never had said *anything* had I known. I did it 'cause I thought he'd like to be known after all these years. I guess in some way I thought he felt trapped like I did with Chasing Charlie and I wanted to give him the spotlight. Anyway, it was a terrible failure and I can't take it back. So, how are we going to handle it?" he asked his Lapis representative. Kyle had all the answers. He'd been groomed for exactly this by first his father, then his schooling.

"I'll get security all over you and Campbell. Next, I'll get someone to do some digging into Hennie. Maybe we have nothing to worry about; maybe he's long since dead and his vengeance along with him," Kyle offered positively.

"From your mouth to God's ear," Chase said, as he sank back in the seat and closed his eyes.

***

In a penthouse apartment overlooking the city, a greasy haired man sat in a chair in front of his extremely large computer screen, brooding and unhappy. Even at the early morning hour, he nursed a drink. The picture was paused, holding in frame a beautiful blonde as she was just coming up from being bent over a body lying on a dance floor of a party. The blonde's mouth was open as if she was shocked.

The greasy haired man clicked on a screen button and the picture changed to a still of Chase and Campbell standing side by side, Chase's arm around Campbell, both smiling wide. Anyone with eyes could see that they were related, easily father and son. He leaned forward in his chair, staring intensely at the picture. The faces before him caused a physical reaction in his gut. He flipped the picture back to the beautiful blonde. His gut reacted even more. He sat back in his chair and let out a heavy sigh as he tapped his many rings across the brass handle of the cane he held. *Clippity-clop, clippity-clop.* He kept making the noise as he studied the picture and zoomed in on the blonde's face. He finished his drink, slamming the glass down on a nearby side table as the rage grew inside him.

***

Sonya showered and had some breakfast before checking her phone. She had four messages. She sipped a coffee as she listened to the first two, writing down a few notes as she listened. She deleted those and carried on listening to the third message. As soon as she heard his voice, her blood went cold. He was such an evil prick that his voice could give you shivers. She could tell he wasn't happy so she was going to have to lie to him. She decided it was better not to mention Chase or that he was someone she was interested in. Not yet anyway. His message was just a few words: "Call me when you get this." Enough for her to be cautious. She took a deep breath and dialed his number. She knew he'd been drinking and that was confirmed the minute he answered the phone.

"Your face is all over this fuckin' launch party for the "star" guy last night. What, you turned into a fuckin' nurse? What were you going to do, give the guy CP-fuckin'-R? Doesn't look like you're in the shadows too much. What if someone had recognized you and called you out?" He roared at her without any kind of inquiry as to how she was or how the night ended up.

"A person dropped to the floor right in front of me; what did you want me to do, leave the poor guy lying there?" she asked, in her defense. The less he knew, the better.

"You weren't stupid enough to sell the guy coke on the dance floor, right? Hopefully, the guy died and he can't identify you," he said. God, he was an asshole!

"It wasn't drugs that took him down, Johann!" she shouted into the phone. Insensitive bastard! "He had a heart arrhythmia or something and went light headed but he fell and hit his head hard. It knocked him out with a bad concussion. He's an elderly man for Christ's sake! Besides, the place was crawling with celebrities; no one wants to admit they know a drug dealer," she ended with. Already she was fed up with the conversation but she had to be careful, Johann had no patience for disrespect, sister or not.

"Listen to me you stupid little bitch! You step into the spotlight *and* try to stay in hiding, IT AIN'T GONNA WORK! They stay in their world and we stay in ours, you get it? You become one of them, you expose yourself and all of us along with you. You understand? Be careful what you're doing, Sonya. Don't end up regretting your decision," he warned her and hung up the phone.

She tossed her phone away from her onto the couch in anger. What a prick! God, she regretted ever getting involved with drugs. Now that she was so close to getting what it was she really wanted, it became such a hindrance. Now, she could really do with leaving it behind her but Johann was making it seem like it was impossible. Shit! Why did it all have to be so complicated? She laid herself down on her couch grabbing the tossed away phone to move it out of her way when she realized she hadn't listened to the fourth call. She played the voicemail and instantly smiled. It was Chase. He sounded tired, dreamy and very sexy. *"Hey beautiful lady, just wanted to make sure you got home okay. Much as I have to do today, all I keep thinking about is our dinner date tomorrow. Don't forget to let me know where you want to eat. I'll make sure we have some privacy. Hope you're resting after the night we had. See you soon, bye!"*

Sonya could hear the soft sexy smile in his voice and she groaned as stretched herself out on the couch. Chase was like the forbidden fruit and all Sonya wanted to do was take a nice juicy bite. All the while she could hear Johann's warning, *Don't end up regretting your decision!*

***

After a power nap, a quick shower and a high protein breakfast, Chase spent the day in a series of interviews, one right after the other, all to promote the CD. Regardless of how masterful a creation the CD was, almost every interviewer asked the same question, "How's your father, Mark Hagen?"

Chase cringed at each mention of his name. If it hadn't been heard last night, it was most certainly getting heard all over the morning news shows. ABC, CNN, NBC, FOX, CBS and E! were putting the main emphasis of their reporting on Campbell's fall. Chase dodged them brilliantly and when the last interview ended at 5:00 pm, he sat back, feeling tired of talking.

Throughout the hectic day, Kyle kept in touch with the hospital and was told that although Campbell's concussion was concerning, they would be releasing him into respite care early the next morning. Kyle arranged for him to be picked up by limo and taken to a respite house where he'd be watched carefully, not only by medical staff, but also by security.

Kyle made sure his hospital door was also guarded while he was an inpatient. Apparently, a flower shop of arrangements had been sent to wish him "Get Well Soon" by anyone and everyone so, for such a private guy, he was feeling quite overwhelmed.

Chase was kept up-to-date on Campbell's condition as well as the status of the investigation into his past. There were very few leads but maybe someone knew something. It was the not knowing that was eating at Chase.

He left the studio at last and asked the driver to take him back to his apartment. He had just a few short hours before he needed to get ready for an exclusive dinner party with some of the Lapis Executives. It was their night to celebrate Chase's CD launch in a much more sedate style than the launch party. These men and women were the stakeholders and they celebrated in fine elegance. Chase wasn't used to such fare but he understood that he needed to be open to new ideas and possibilities and was willing to learn from any situation.

Kyle would walk him through it and instruct him. They came from completely different worlds but they had developed a loyalty and friendship that transcended their differences. Kyle respected his mega multi-talented superstar and Chase respected his extremely keen business sense. He knew enough to know when to let Chase have full control of the creative process. That was a smart businessman.

Before leaving for the dinner party, Chase checked his phone. There was a text from Sonya from earlier in the day:

~3:23 pm~

I've always wanted to try Hotel Chandler. Are you up for it?

SKx

He smiled when he read it. He didn't care if they were to dine in a Subway. He just wanted to look across the table and see her beautiful face looking back throughout the dinner.

4:10 pm

Sure! I'll make all the arrangements. I'll have a car pick you up at 7:30 pm. Reservations for 8:00 pm – time for a drink at the bar?

CMx

He copied her signature hoping she'd think it was sweet. She replied promptly.

~4:12 pm~

No car is necessary, I can meet you there. But a drink at the bar would be nice. I'll be there for 7:45 pm. Looking forward to it!

SKx

He quickly called and made the reservations requesting the most private table and promising a $100.00 tip if the request was granted. He also requested a fresh bouquet of wild flowers be nearby their table with a card that read, "Your beautiful smile makes these flowers pale in comparison – Chase." He asked that some quiet John Legend be playing in the background. He wanted everything perfect.

Chase had never really wooed a woman before, always having it handed to him during his many years on the road. The one and only time he had put his heart out there was his attempt to tell Georgie Pelos his true feelings and have her come back to New York with him. It fell completely flat. He had learned his lesson; first make sure the lady is interested in you then make every effort to make her yours. The planning and detail that he was undergoing in making sure his date with Sonya was perfect, made his anticipation of the evening more enticing.

Once all the arrangements were put in place, he concentrated on dinner with the Lapis Labels stakeholders. These weren't people to be uncomfortable around and Chase needed to be in top form tonight. Another black Armani suit but this time with all black accessories. Black on black. A nice sleek look. Since his departure from playing with Chasing Charlie, his look had become far more polished. New York crowds expected that. You could look casual during the day, but

153

at night you needed to dress your best. That was all there was to it. He had adjusted quite nicely to being a millionaire, finding an excellent money manager through the Label's connections and following a lot of Kyle's advice where major purchases were concerned. As for his sense of style, Chase had invested in some high end suits, shoes, shirts and ties. He'd pierced his earlobe and found a half carat diamond that he kept in permanently. He bought a Rolex watch and a gold identification bracelet to complete his jewelry accessories. It was more than his older brother Charlie would wear but then, the whole point of doing this was to move beyond Charlie and out into his own world. It may not have been his upbringing but it felt right. Chase Morningstar was about to soar beyond this realm and into another and he was dressed for success!

***

Chicago was only one hour behind. At the same time that Chase was preparing for dinner with Kyle and the stakeholders, an investigator walked into City Hall showing his identification and asking for housing records going back to 1977. The clerk made a face at him not sure if they kept records going back that far. She punched a few things into the keyboard, stared at the computer screen in front of her, wrote something down on a post-it note and handed it to the man.

"Those records are now public so they're held in a storage warehouse about six blocks from here. They have the files you're looking for. Here's the address." She thrust the post-it note towards him and basically dismissed him as the next person stepped forward to ask for directions.

The man read the paper: "1757 E26[th] Street, 15th floor, room 1533." He was hoping that he could get there before it closed. He grabbed a taxi and paid the driver an extra $10.00 to get him there within a few minutes.

When he entered the building, signs directed him to the elevators. He took one up to the 15th floor and walked off the elevator checking each door until he reached 1533, City Housing, Office of Public Records.

He entered the office, showed his credentials and asked the lone clerk behind the screen about accessing files from 1977.

"You'll have to be a little more specific, sir. There's a lot of files back there and if you don't narrow down your search you'll be here for hours," she explained, rather irked that he had shown up at this hour. She closed in 30 minutes.

"Okay, how about this address." He handed her a piece of paper. It had the last address Campbell could remember that Hennie lived at. He didn't even know if Hennie was his real name. If it wasn't he might never be able to locate him. But the address and the year was a start. Campbell was only in town a few weeks before he left in a hurry so he hoped that Hennie had lived there longer than one year.

The clerk looked at it, typed it into her keyboard and waited for her computer screen to tell her what she wanted to know. After a few moments she hit a button under her desk which activated a buzzer and opened the gated area for the man to enter.

"Aisle 22, Row 5, right in the middle. The box should be labelled with the year and street name."

He cocked his head at her. "No chance they're on a database, or even microfiche?" he asked.

She laughed and nodded, "You got that right." She laughed again. "No chance!"

She nodded at him and he nodded back, smiling to himself. He'd asked for that. Anything older than 1995 was usually still held in hard copy. He turned down the corridor as row upon row of large shelving units came into view, filled with bankers boxes each neatly labelled. The shelves were at least 30 deep and 10 high. *Good job they had a clerk at the front desk*, he thought!

He followed her instructions and soon found the aisle and then the shelf. The boxes were piled three high per shelf and with one heavy sigh, he pulled the wheeled staircase over to the area he wanted and climbed up it to pull out the bankers box. He brought it down to the second tier of the staircase, where he placed it on the landing and he sat down on the three stairs below. He removed the lid and started going through it paper by paper looking for a name. He wasn't really sure what the name would turn out to be but he knew Hennie was a start. Each paper contained 30 or 40 names that he had to read through and then the street address. He had gone through maybe seven pages when he came across the name, "Hennie K. VanderWaulde," and then another with, "Heinrich Vander," and, "Heinrich Walde." There were more pages with a few more possible aliases for Hennie, each of them giving a different address, all of them he'd have to investigate. But he knew he was onto something. The man lifted his large frame up off the stairs, put the lid on the box for a moment and walked the papers he was holding over to a nearby photocopier. He took copies and then took the papers back to the box. He quickly rifled through the remaining papers but found nothing more. With this he could pull police records and see what they told of Hennie or "Heinrich's" story. He loved to dig into people's backgrounds. He loved to find out about those who would remain mysterious to the rest of us. He was driven to expose those who didn't want others to know about their incredibly secret lives. Hennie was of particular interest to him. Numerous aliases usually meant a very prolific illegal life. Lots of secrets there!

He left the office one minute before closing, making the clerk very happy. He didn't like imposing on other's time. As he walked from the building he was already texting Kyle, letting him know that he'd picked up a lead. He was excellent at what he did. For this case, he had personal reasons.

***

Kyle received the following text:

~4:59 pm~

Heinrich... several last names used. Digging deeper.

He knew it meant a lead from his investigator and he felt confident that this man would be able to track down Campbell's past. It was all he needed to know. Tonight was equally as important as the launch party the night before. Even though it attracted a ton of publicity, Kyle would have preferred it without the drama of Campbell's name revealed and then having him drop to the floor.

Tonight was about showing the people who gave Chase his $3 million to create and make music, how much he appreciated it and how hard Chase was going to work to make them even more money. The sooner Kyle could get this resolved for Chase, the better. Chase needed to keep his focus on his career and not worry about distractions that came along. That's why he was here, to deflect those distractions as quickly as possible and keep Chase on course. In return, he would earn a king's ransom for all of them and that was Kyle's goal. He would be able to live the high life, with New York City splayed out before him.

Nothing gave him a better thrill than standing on the rooftop of his apartment building, drinking wine and taking in his city. As far as he was concerned, he owned it. His father never reached these heights, figuratively or literally. Kyle would excel even further than that. His business card would read: Kyle Craven, Label Rep to the Superstars.

***

Campbell awoke in his hospital room. His head still ached and his stomach felt off. He was disappointed to find he was still in hospital, thinking that he could have easily been discharged that morning. He would have got a much better night's sleep without all the whirring and buzzing of machines. He only had a few monitors around him but they made enough noise that Campbell couldn't rest easily. He looked around the room and saw all the floral arrangements that had been delivered. *Dear God* he thought, *is this how it'll be when I die?* So many flowers! He had been in hiding for so long he wasn't really known but to a handful of people and now he had dozens of well-wishers.

He really had his Aunt Pearl and Paul Craven to thank for getting him out of Hennie's crosshairs and keeping him hidden. After a few years and once everyone felt the coast was clear, Paul called Pearl and made arrangements with her to bring herself, Lucy and Eric out to visit with Campbell at his home. It was great to see them all again. The biggest surprise was his father, who had completely sobered up since that night at the Skyline and was now living at Lucy's full-time and helping Pearl out in the kitchens at the club. Gone were his entertaining days. He was just happy to be working and surrounded by family again.

When they visited at Paul's, Eric let Campbell know he was sorry for all the problems he had caused. Life with Pearl was great for Eric and Campbell felt happy that his father had finally found happiness. They visited twice more after that and then within two short years they were all gone. All three died, due to old age and natural causes. Lucy was found dead in her bed at her boarding house one Wednesday morning. It broke Pearl's heart. She and Eric tried to continue running the boarding house, but Pearl really had her hands full at the club and Eric couldn't manage it alone. They were about to sell it when Eric took ill, went into hospital and never came out. His funeral was sad, only his sister Pearl and a few workers from the club attended. Campbell wanted to attend but Paul and Pearl both thought it was a dangerous risk. Not four months later, Pearl had a heart attack at the club one afternoon, dying right where she sat and loved to be the most; the table at the furthest point from the stage nearest the bar, so she could see everything. She died working on some accounting. No one realized for a bit – she just looked as though she was concentrating on her books, busy working away, so the staff let her be until someone thought to ask if she wanted anything. When the staff member went to check on her, she'd been dead for over an hour. There was nothing anyone could do.

Paul thought it was a bad idea if Campbell attended her service so he spent the day of her funeral in a small chapel saying prayers for her, Lucy and Eric. The Elderly British Contingent. He still missed them now after so many years and now an elderly man himself.

His thoughts came back to his hospital room and all the flowers and cards he'd been sent. Not having had much of a chance to read them he gathered them all up, even the small cards that adorned the many floral arrangements, climbed back into his bed and began to read them all. He struggled with it as the letters jumped all over the page. His head throbbed and he had to take his time with each one in order to read what it said.

Many were from Lapis Labels co-workers, office staff and fellow studio musicians. A few were from some very famous musicians that he had played with incognito on some very successful CD's. Sonya's card was lovely, sentimental and caring. She wrote simply, *"You owe me a dance! Please take good care and get well soon so you can pay up!"*

He remembered smoking the joint in the stairwell and then feeling incredibly good and returning to the party and dancing with the girls, like he was a maniac or something. Funny thing was, he only remembered smoking half of the joint given to him by one of the guys he'd met in the bathroom. Never did he ever get that wrecked from half a joint. What kind of shit were they growing now? He pushed aside the cards and went over to the closet in his room. Inside was the suit he was wearing on the night of the party. He reached into the inside jacket pocket and felt the half joint safely tucked away. He pulled it out and brought it over to the bed to study it. Grabbing a tissue from his bedside table, he tore apart the remaining joint and studied its contents. It looked normal, nothing different. He smelled the weed. It didn't smell much different, maybe a little sweeter. He shook his head, confused by the experience he'd had. He scrunched up the contents of the joint into the tissue and put it inside his bedside table. He'd have to ask Sonya about it when they had a private moment.

He continued to read more of the greeting cards piled on his bed. He felt overwhelmed by the amount of caring some had shown and then he came to one that made his blood run cold. It read simply: *"Mark, did you think you could hide forever?"* It was signed "H." Hennie. Hennie! After all these years, Hennie. Nothing else was on the card. Not even the floral shop where the arrangement came from. Campbell looked over at all the flowers lined up along his shelf not knowing which one belonged to this card. None of the arrangements stood out to Campbell, besides what was he looking for? The card said it all; Hennie, or one of his henchmen had been notified that he had been found and now he wasn't safe. No one was.

He laid his head back on his pillow and let out a heavy sigh. This had dogged him for so many years now. He was tired of living in hiding. Maybe Chase and Kyle could help him find a way out of this once and for all. If it was Hennie who had personally delivered it, he now knew there was more to Campbell's life that could be affected, and others besides Campbell could be a target. He now had a son. Rising superstar Chase Morningstar.

***

As Chase entered the dining hall he was greeted by Kyle. They shook hands warmly, smiled and Kyle tried to calm Chase down, recognizing that he was nowhere near his comfort zone.

"Just imagine everyone in their underwear. It helps to put you at ease," he said, to Chase's nervous look around the room.

"Are you kidding me? There isn't anyone in here I want to see in their underwear! Never mind putting me at ease, it'd put me off, possibly forever!" Chase laughed as he looked from one high-nose stuffy bugger and his ancient wife to another.

"Yes, well these are the people that "put" $3 million in your pocket so make nice with them. Remember your manners, your charm and your million watt smile, at least three times!" Kyle joked with him.

He took Chase by the arm and started introducing him around the room. Chase met university professors, a judge, many lawyers, an over-obvious socialite and a few elderly business men who he guessed had never worked a hard day in their life and probably ate from gold plates. They reeked of old money. Chase bet that not one of them had heard his music or seen his videos. All they did was sit in their fat cat offices deciding whose dreams they will and won't make come true, like a puppeteer with many marionettes. Chase hoped they didn't cut the strings just yet; he was only just getting started.

Not all of the stakeholders were old. Chase was surprised to see three men, probably in their mid to late twenties, huddled together on one side of the dining hall. Being a few minutes before dinner would be served, Chase was interested in meeting everyone he could. God only knows what the dinner conversation would be like. He doubted they would show him any interest at all. He'd be better off trying to impress upon them his gratitude and ideas for the future in smaller groups rather than en masse. Kyle was deep in conversation with an old man and his wife, who looked like George and Martha Washington. Chase chuckled to himself as he stepped away and moved towards the younger stakeholders. They were having a good laugh amongst themselves when he approached.

"Hi there, Chase Morningstar. How ya doin'?" he asked as he shot his hand out to the first man. His hand was accepted, shaken and then offered in turn to the two other men.

"I'm Ron," the first man said, then pointed to his friend to his right and said, "This is Greyson and this is Andy," finishing with the last guy on the end.

Chase shook all their hands, spread smiles all around and then stood awkward for a moment. "Greyson, huh? Is there a story to it? I mean, I got called "Chase" because I loved chasing my older brother around constantly," Chase told them, trying to break the ice before diving into what he really wanted to know.

"It's a family name," Greyson told him. "My grandmother's maiden name. My grandfather insisted and I guess back then he had a lot of influence!" he said, with a good sense of humor.

Chase felt comfortable enough now to try and get the answers he wanted. "So… uh… I hope I'm not being indelicate here but how do you three end up being at this dinner? Aren't you about 100 years too young?" Chase asked, smiling. They all had a good laugh at Chase's slight towards the average age of the room.

Ron then turned to Chase and confided, "We're computer geeks," he explained. "We came up with an idea for a program that works with sound boards and mixers to create a new level of recording with unbelievable sound. The clarity is unreal. It makes Lapis envied throughout the industry," he said confidently and shrugged his shoulders. "When we showed them what it could do they jumped all over it. They knew what potential it had to make them a leading recording label. But…" he smiled really wide, "instead of being paid in dollars, we only accepted shares in the company. We knew who they represented and we also knew that once those artists had a chance to work with the program we designed and the interface was so sweet," he gushed, "well…" he scoffed and looked at his friends nodding, "the label's earning potential would go through the roof. Like taking candy from a baby really. Now, every few weeks or so we get invited to these boring dinner parties and watch them fake interest towards the newest money maker," Ron said, as he downed his drink and motioned for the waiter to bring him another.

Chase stood watching Ron thinking he was rather cocky and full of himself. It gave him some insight into how he must have looked to his band and especially to his older brother Charlie during their last few months together. When his focus came back to Ron, he felt ashamed. This guy was a dick! Charlie and the band had probably thought that numerous times about me. *Note to self: Call Charlie sometime soon and get caught up with him, the band and the club,* Chase thought.

The three men received fresh drinks and had them half gone before the waitress had time to turn around. They looked as if they were just itching to be at a frat house and bust a huge bash out rather than a sedate elegant dinner party.

"Yeah… we like parties, man. Like… your launch party is more our style. That was fierce! We did some blow in the bathroom and just got ripped!" Greyson said.

Chase kept the smile on his face but inside his respect level for these men plummeted. "Yeah?" Chase said, "Good job you didn't get caught, there were police crawling all over the place.

"Oh, we aren't stupid. We may be younger than the dinosaurs here but we know better than to pull out a joint and start chugging it in people's faces. Not like that old guy, huh? And man, when he went down, *he went down!*" Andy laughed, emphasizing the point by smacking his palms together to represent Campbell's fall.

Chase kept his anger in check. If he was to find anything out he couldn't give away too much. Maybe these guys didn't pick up on the connection between Chase and Campbell.

"Oh, I saw that. What the hell happened to him?" Chase asked, leading Andy on.

"He came running in as we were doin' some blow in the bathroom. He asked me for a joint. The joints I had on me were laced with coke. I warned him that it had a hell of a kick but he grabbed it and took off," Greyson said laughing.

So, that's what happened! Chase had been very disappointed to find out from Campbell's doctors that they found traces of cocaine in his system. He now knew that it wasn't there by Campbell's own volition. He made another mental note to stop by the hospital on his way home to see Campbell.

Although these three men had smarts, they had no conscience or kindness. To have allowed an elderly man to take off and not make a point of stopping him before any harm had been done was unforgiveable. Chase made another mental note about these three assholes.

The dinner bell rang and Chase excused himself from the three men and found Kyle. He would spend the next hour and a half trying to explain his music and his future ideas to elderly people who had no idea what he was talking about. The one thing they all agreed upon was that Chase was going to make them a lot of money; to this they toasted.

All the while the three young men giggled and whispered at the end of the table, as if they were having their own separate party. At a table full of old money and elegance, their odd behaviour and ignorance was on full display. They really put the "ass" in class.

Chase took note of it all, remembering to keep it in check because one day, the knowledge he gained tonight would be used to not only better himself, Campbell and his band Supernova, but he suspected it would be at a heavy cost to those who were underestimating his own smarts and abilities.

***

When he entered the hospital room it was after 11:00 pm. He'd promised the nurse he just wanted to check in to see if Campbell needed anything, quickly say "hi" and then he'd leave, but when he poked his head in,

Campbell was asleep sitting up, his mouth open and dragging air into and out of his mouth with a high wheezing sound. He was surrounded by cards and Chase took a moment to gather them up and put them beside him on the table. He reached for the small card Campbell still held clutched in his sleep and had a hard time not waking Campbell in doing so. He looked at the one line sentence, froze and read it again. *Jesus*, he thought, *he was right!*

He studied his sleeping father and wondered how it must have been for him to live in hiding all these years. Trapped by your own name. Chase knew how it felt to be trapped, but to have to live in hiding, now that would be a bitch! Chase felt responsible for bringing this on Campbell, even though Campbell should either never have told him or told him the truth and let him know that it would be dangerous to share his real name with others.

Chase picked up the other cards and notes and quickly went through them, making sure there were no others from whoever this was. The card Campbell held was the only one of its kind. The fact that he held it told Chase he'd seen it and knew he wasn't safe. Chase let out a heavy sigh. All these years he'd gone without a father and now that he'd found him it was far more complicated and complex than he could have ever imagined.

He placed the cards and notes into the bedside table and found the crushed tissue. He was about to throw it out when the pungent smell hit him. It was a joint, or what was left of a joint. The one Campbell had smoked in the stairwell perhaps? He would keep this and see if the doctors could determine if cocaine was in it. He looked back at Campbell, squeezed his father's arm and gave him one last look before he left the room. Let Campbell have what little rest he could find now. Until they found this guy, Campbell wasn't safe.

***

~2:52 pm~

How was your night? Another dinner with big-wigs?

SKx

Chased smiled to himself. If only she knew how badly he wanted to have seen her instead of being around all the stuffed suits that financed his creativity.

~3:01 pm~

I spent it with too many old people. You were on my mind. I'm looking forward to dining with you tonight. How was your night?

CMx

~3:06 pm~

Spent dealing with some serious idiots! I hope my next meeting goes better. I thought about you too! I could get to the Hotel Chandler earlier if you want. 7:00 pm??

SKx

~3:07 pm

YES!

CMxx

Sonya couldn't help but smile. Mr. Chase Morningstar seemed very interested! She'd have to be careful about how much she shared with him. Telling him she was "dealing" with idiots was her way of being truthful without actually telling the truth. She had spent her previous night delivering to her many customers.

At that very moment she was sitting in the living room of a famous soap actress named Darla Dawson. She and Sonya had been introduced by another soap actor. It was a great industry for referrals. Darla had been buying from Sonya since she started on "Closed Curtains," a soap about three sisters who run a fashion magazine. Darla's character was the youngest sister who had one major crisis after another. Unlike her character, Darla's major crisis right now was debating over whether to buy the small bag of cocaine Sonya had brought or just stick with the regular weed she'd been buying for a while.

Sonya liked Darla, she had a good head on her shoulders and wasn't swayed by her peers who were all into using cocaine, especially in the daytime drama industry. Sonya sold to a lot of soap drama queens.

Darla held both bags in her hands and thought it over, stroking the small bag of white powder as if it were some exotic pet. Sonya could almost see her weighing the pros and cons. Suddenly, Darla quickly stood up and handed the small packet back to Sonya.

"I think I'll just stick to my regular shit, girlfriend," stated the actress. It was rare that this happened and Sonya's respect for the woman climbed with her decision.

"Okay, so just the quarter pound of grass then?" Sonya asked her, as she took the packet from Darla and put away the cocaine.

"Yeah... what's that, $650.00?" the actress asked.

"Uh-huh. My special price for bulk buying," Sonya said, smiling.

"Man, you're like a friggin' Costco or Sam's Club," Darla laughed, and soon she and Sonya were in fits of laughter as they compared fictional bulk drug buying at the popular stores.

"What do you usually use?" the actress asked Sonya, as she sat back on the couch. "Do you have a preference?"

"I don't use the stuff personally," she explained to Darla, shaking her head. "I... uh... guess I'm just high on life!" she lied. There were times when Sonya tossed around the thought of smoking weed or blowing coke, especially when she battled bouts of depression but she had always managed to get through her tough times without it. So far, she had never met anyone who did themselves a favor by getting caught up in using drugs.

"Huh! So tell me your secret, 'cause even though I've done well with my life and make a great paycheck, I still like to get into an altered state of being," she said, as she tossed the large baggie of weed next to Sonya on the couch.

Sonya smiled at the petite actress. This might be someone she could finally be a friend with. *Wouldn't that be nice?* she thought.

"Well, it's rare that I see someone hold their own against temptation, especially cocaine, Darla. You should be proud!" Sonya said with her fist raised for a fist bump. Darla fist bumped back and the girls laughed together. They each felt the connection of female friendship, something foreign to both, something wanted by both. A nod was exchanged and they understood; their secrets were safe.

***

Later that night, as Sonya took a seat at the bar, she felt several eyes upon her. She wasn't imagining it. Sonya was a gorgeous woman. It was both a blessing and a curse, especially in her line of work. She had been harassed by more sleaze balls than she cared to remember. She tried to ignore the gawkers around her and ordered herself a rum and sprite. She had positioned herself so that her back was towards the main entry but she could see the comings and goings of the patrons in the mirrored wall behind the bar.

She saw Chase walk in and her breath caught. He was such a handsome man and so very talented. She wondered if she'd ever be able to open up to him about her life, her brother and her occupation.

When he spotted her he stopped dead in his tracks and just took her in. The chocolate-eyed beauty was wearing a deep blue dress that clung to her body. She sat with her legs crossed so that her lovely shaped legs were on full display. Chase had it bad and he knew it. There was only one other woman who had held his interest this much and he had purged her from his heart with his CD. He truly felt like he could have an honest relationship with Sonya and not worry that he wouldn't be able to give her his heart.

She showed her appreciation of what she saw as her face broke into an enormous smile. He came over to her chair and instinctively leaned in for a kiss. It surprised both of them but didn't stop either. When they broke apart, he rubbed his nose to hers and smiled.

"Hello, beautiful lady," he said softly, and then took the seat next to her and motioned to the bartender for two more drinks.

"Hello, handsome man," Sonya replied back. It was all she could manage; her heart was racing.

"You must have been here for a few minutes. You've got the entire bar area of men straining to have a look at you," he said, smiling. Chase had given the bar the once over and counted eight or nine men that were very interested in the beautiful blonde.

"I didn't notice any of them; besides, with your smile I was too busy swooning at you. They all know they don't stand a chance," she answered back, as she took a sip of her drink.

They chatted about Campbell, the CD, her apartment and Chase's life in Chicago. She listened intently to him as he explained Celia's and Campbell's relationship and how it brought about his conception.

He told her of Celia's death and how he and Charlie formed the band Chasing Charlie and spent 20 years touring. She asked questions about the success of the band and when Chase told her about Charlie's paranoia and explained his family's lineage she nodded her head in understanding.

"So now you've been here almost what… a year? And you've already got your own CD out and it's fantastic! Is Charlie kicking himself?" she asked, laughing.

"I highly doubt it!" he laughed back. In his mind he pictured Charlie and Georgie enjoying a night of great music at their club Black and Blue and then going home together. He let his imagination stop there.

"Charlie is truly living his dream. I'm really happy for him. But I always wanted more, you know? Always wanted to break free. I guess I'm not very good at a simpler life."

"Oh, I see stars in your future, Mr. Morningstar," she purred at him before sipping her drink.

"Awwww," he groaned at the pun. "There's nothing but stars in my future, Sonya." He suddenly got very serious. "I plan on breaking through the stratosphere and going beyond. There's so much I want to do and Kyle is going to help make that happen."

Sonya wasn't sure about Kyle, although she'd seen Chase with him. He seemed to be a force to be reckoned with and a keen businessman, at least where Chase was concerned.

"Are you guys close… like, best friends?" she asked Chase directly. If so, she'd need to be on alert. Kyle could possibly expose her. For some reason, she wasn't worried about Campbell. He wasn't going to tell Chase who she *really* was, she knew that for sure.

"Uh… I wouldn't say *best friends* but he's been a great person to lean on since I got here. I never forget that I'm making him a shit load of money and that's a great incentive for him," Chase said frankly, and then broke into a wide smile.

Oh that smile! He leaned in closer to Sonya and she followed suit thinking he was going to tell her something very secretive, but his lips landed full onto her and he started kissing her. His hand reached up to cup her face and the other gently held her arm above the elbow. Everywhere he touched was soft and smooth. Her kisses back were warm and when he pushed his tongue gently against her lips she opened her mouth up to allow his tongue in to dance with hers. Chase knew it was probably driving the male patrons nuts to see him kiss her and when the thought hit him, he smiled breaking the moment between them. Sonya broke into a smile the minute she focused on his face and asked, "What?" laughingly.

"Nothing… I'm just thinking about the amount of men in here that are wishing they were sitting where I am," he admitted.

He quickly took a glance around the room and counted three or four who quickly turned away from staring. The bartender came over and told Chase that their table was ready.

"Good" he said. "I'm tired of sharing you with everyone in here."

He took her by the hand and they followed a small waitress who led them to their table. The level of conversation quieted and then grew as they walked through the room. They were definitely noticed. The reserved table was located in the back left corner of the restaurant, closeted, cozy and lit with candles and John Legend music playing softly, enveloping the room with his beautiful voice.

Sonya was completely enthralled. So far, all her expectations were either met or surpassed! She felt as though she was being swept away by him when in fact, both were experiencing the rip tide.

The table was a small semi-circle so that Chase could seat himself closer to Sonya. What an added bonus he didn't expect! She didn't seem to mind and scooted right up against him as well, a definite in! They ordered two more drinks and perused the menu for a moment. Having made up his mind, Chase sat against the plush back of the curved booth and gazed at Sonya as she made her dinner choices. She was nothing like Georgie, not in looks or in style. Sonya had a different approach that was compatible with Chase's mindset. She seemed a go-getter, someone who could make something happen for herself, someone who was not afraid to try to evolve. Chase realized that he very much liked that. It fit in well with his new life style and his wanting to leave a very big mark on the world in every way.

When the waitress came to take their order they both wanted the steak. Sharing a smile between them, they clinked their glasses and toasted their similar tastes. With their proximity being what it was, it wasn't long before hands were being held and placed possessively. This was driving Chase crazy and he soon found himself feeling aroused for Sonya. Maybe more than he should have been out in public at a very swanky New York restaurant. Chase Morningstar's erection splashed across the New York Post would not be considered great advertising.

He had to settle himself down and was grateful when their meal arrived and he could place a napkin over his lap. Even the weight of the linen didn't help matters and while Sonya started making light work of her dinner, Chase drank sips of water and thought about the elderly stakeholders of Lapis Labels in their underwear.

***

Kyle had arranged for Campbell to be moved into his respite facility that night. Better under the cover of darkness and at off hours when no one was expecting it. If Hennie was watching or had someone else watching, chances are they would be on alert during discharge hours. Regardless, Kyle wasn't taking any chances. Everything was secretive and hush-hush and the ailing Campbell made it safely into his guarded and temporary new home.

Once Kyle had spoken to security at the front entrance and introduced *his* security to them, all was well. Campbell's personal room would be watched and monitored via hidden cameras and Kyle's man would be allowed access to those monitors at all hours. They also gave him liberal entrance to the grounds and facility. Campbell would be safe.

The last thing Kyle did was speak to the medical staff and get an idea of how long Campbell's concussion would take to heal. Supernova was going to be doing a lot of publicity in the coming weeks with Chase's CD launch and the group really needed a piano player.

The medical team all agreed that the brain mends on its own schedule. One doctor went as far as to say that given Campbell's age, it could take quite a few weeks before he could live on his own without some sort of help again. Kyle listened to all their professional input and came to the decision that Campbell would need replacing, at least for the foreseeable future. He couldn't be expected to keep up with the rigorous schedule that Chase Morningstar and Supernova were going to be keeping; it wouldn't help his condition or recovery at all. Kyle also decided not to tell Campbell any of this just yet. It might cause a setback and all Kyle wanted was for Campbell to recover, or he'd never hear the end of it from his father.

On his way home for the evening Kyle placed a call from the bluetooth in his car to a piano player he knew.

"Talk to me..." Cooper Jack answered the phone.

"Coop-*Dawwwg*," Kyle said, drawing out the name, making not only himself but Cooper smile. Cooper was a super cool, very nice guy and Kyle was hoping he'd be able to take on the gig.

"It's Kyle Craven, buddy. I wanna know what your schedule's like for the next few weeks, possibly longer," he said, almost crossing his fingers on the steering wheel.

"Uh… I got some projects coming up but nothing I can't put aside. What's up, Kyle?" asked Cooper.

Kyle smiled again and punched the air with his fist. Score! Cooper would make a great addition to the band. Chase Morningstar and Supernova were about to experience a solar flare!

***

The waitress cleared away the plates from the table and Chase sat back in the booth and stretched his arm out across the top, almost cuddling next to Sonya. She turned her body towards him and pulled her glass of wine off the table and nestled it as she smiled at him. The wine was making her feel relaxed; the wine and Chase. They had spent the evening talking, each flirting with the other and enjoying every moment of the time they shared. Neither wanted to end the dinner or the evening.

Trying to gauge her reaction, he studied her face a moment and then tilted his head and hesitated before asking his question. Sonya knew what was coming.

"Would you like to continue this conversation somewhere more private?" he asked, stroking her leg with his thumb and trying to control the electricity surging through his body.

Her inner self screamed, "NO!" She didn't want him to take her for granted, she didn't want him to think she was easy. She wanted this relationship to be right and start out properly. Under no circumstances was she going to allow him to talk her into going back to his place. Under no circumstances.

As he stroked her thigh, he flashed her his best smile.

"Sure, I'd really like that," she answered softly. In complete frustration, her inner self threw her hands up in the air. So much for willpower!

***

It took only three minutes of being in the back of the limo before Chase and Sonya were locked in a desperate embrace. They were clawing at each other's hair, clothing and limbs trying to get at one another. Neither could explain their chemistry, but both felt it and both were helpless to stop it.

By the time they pulled up to Chase's building, they were practically naked. Chase gave instructions to the driver before they gathered themselves together and left the limo heading for the elevators. They could barely make the fifteen floors to Chase's floor, with Chase crushing Sonya's body against the wall of the elevator and thrusting his tongue and groin into her as his hands thoroughly explored her ass and breasts. He ravaged her and she loved it! Many months had passed since she'd even had a decent kiss. Chase's attention and obvious desire was exactly what she'd hoped for, and then some!

The doors opened on his floor three times before he realized and pulled himself from her, grabbed her hand and got off making their way to Chase's apartment. It all played out on the monitor in the security office and the guy on the night shift laughed out loud at their antics.

Chase unlocked the door swiftly and brought Sonya through with his hand around her waist, pulling her into his home and closing the door behind her with a kick of his foot. They were still grabbing at each other and kissing passionately as Chase led her further into the living room. She took a moment to open her eyes and orient herself to the space. When she was able to focus it made her gasp.

Chase's home was gorgeous and not in a, "I found the best interior designer," kind of way. His apartment had large open ceilings and he had a very large mounted photo of an exotic looking woman with a wild mane of hair, smiling, during a performance of some kind. She looked like she was in her late 20's or early 30's and she was dressed in a black sequined dress. She was beautiful, exquisite. Sonya wondered who she was for Chase to have her grace the wall in such a large manner. The picture took up the entire wall on one side of the room.

Dozens of framed pictures placed symmetrically graced the opposite wall, like a rogue's gallery. Sonya broke free of Chase's kisses and looked over the pictures as his mouth explored her neck and his hands explored her breasts. His desire was making her head spin and she continued falling under his spell and then pulling herself out to focus in on the picture of the woman.

Sonya suddenly stopped Chase by pulling from him gently. He looked at her worried, a bit out of breath, his eyes heavy with lust and passion.

"Shit! Am I going too fast?" he asked, almost apologetically. Damn! He didn't want to fuck this up! She was such a different woman than what he was used to. He hadn't even felt this way about Georgie who he had claimed to love, had flown back to Chicago for and written a full CD's worth of songs about. Georgie didn't electrocute him whenever they touched. Sonya did.

"I'm sorry Sonya... I really don't want to rush through this. I don't want you to think all I want is your body. Although..." he hesitated and broke out into his full million watt smile as his eyes took in her full image, "...I'm also not dead from the waist down." Sonya smiled too. He was quite the wordsmith! She was still processing his words, when he said, "It's been a while since I cared so much about a woman..." he admitted, looking directly into her eyes, "and I care about you."

Sonya was shocked by his words. *He cared about her!* The fact that he admitted it so easily made her practically melt in her socks. God! She felt like she was 15 again and Greg Watson was trying to get a kiss from her in smoker's corner at high school.

As she went to speak her eyes moved up to the large photo of the exotic woman and she held her words. Chase followed her gaze. Without letting her go, he turned them both to face the large photo.

"That's my mother," he explained. "Celia Morningstar. She was about 34 years old when this was taken. She had extraordinary talent. My brother's wife sent me the picture and I had it enlarged and properly mounted. She always told me I was larger than life and I wanted her to be like that in my home. I know it may seem strange but it's also what she represents to me. She overcame a lot and gave everything she could to my brother and me. She died when I was 18 and..." his voice trailed off as his shrugged his shoulders. They stood in silence for a moment, Chase cradling her as he stood behind her, both studying the photo.

"She's stunning," Sonya said honestly.

"I know," Chase replied, looking up at his mother's face. "I never appreciated how beautiful she was until I put that picture on my wall. Such an exotic beauty," he said studying her. "Her voice was fantastic, like liquid gold."

"No wonder Campbell fell for her, huh?" she said smiling. No wonder indeed!

Chase turned Sonya to face him as he looked down on the petite blonde and studied her face, her eyes, and her lips. She was lovely and Chase was completely smitten. The night they'd spent together in the hospital after Campbell's fall was a gift. They had learned so much about one another and although this was supposed to be their first proper date, Chase felt as though he had known her for much longer. Sonya made him feel like he could be completely comfortable with her. He knew that as he started this rise in his career he'd need someone to keep him grounded and Sonya could easily be that someone.

With that in mind he said to her quite seriously, "I don't want to do anything tonight that will ruin anything we have a chance of making happen tomorrow, know what I mean?" he asked her, his face showing concern.

She looked at him, remembering her own thoughts earlier in the evening when she demanded that she not allow herself to be taken for granted. He had told her he cared for her and was displaying unbelievable restraint in order to prove it. She looked down for a moment debating her next move. He was thinking he'd really blown it when she suddenly broke into a quick smile and threw herself into his arms kissing him with every ounce of sex appeal and wanton intent that she had in her. It took him by surprise, but only for a second. He felt her soft luscious lips pressed against his and then the tip of her tongue sliding across his lips and he hungrily opened his mouth and began to kiss her back. He hiked her into his arms, lifting her to straddle his waist and turned to carry her into the bedroom, grabbing her ass lustfully as he did. She giggled as they went through the door with her last sight of the living room being Celia Morningstar smiling high up above on the wall. It was inappropriate as hell, but she winked at the exotic woman and she could swear that she saw Celia wink right back. It was a very good sign!

***

The investigator was up late, staring at his computer. He'd been granted access to archived files on Hennie's cases from Westchester, New York. The City of Westchester had charged Hennie with two counts of attempted murder. They also sent their information on to the Chicago Police Department to see if they had any cold case files that fit with

Warren and his girlfriend's descriptions. From just the Westchester files, the investigator learned that Hennie, or "Heinrich K. VanderWaulde" was born August 8th, 1950 in Rotterdam, Netherlands. He immigrated to the U.S. in June of 1969. From the moment he arrived the police had their questions about him. He owned a shipping company that transported Dutch goods to the east coast and from there all over the U.S. Heinrich had tapped into a need and built a decent business out of it. But there was also the business that went on behind closed doors and within the lower cargo holds of the ships he owned. Amsterdam was ripe with marijuana and poppy growers experimenting with all sorts of different growing methods. Not only did Hennie provide Dutch crockery, linens, dry goods and specialty items to the Dutch community where he lived and across the U.S., but he also provided the best Dutch weed and cocaine straight from Amsterdam, within just a few weeks of being harvested, and because he hid it in his own ships already making the voyage, transportation charges were nil. His henchmen also worked aboard his ships and provided Hennie with the perfect circle of secrecy.

Much like his business, his private life had dual purposes as well. His wife and three children provided the perfect cover. He also had two other children with another woman that no one had any idea about. No one that mattered anyway. His second family rarely saw him, lived in a crappy apartment in an even crappier neighbourhood and it was this family that he used for his secret dealings.

The investigator rubbed his eyes, yawned and stretched away from the monitor. He crossed his arms across his chest and leaned back in his computer chair staring at the screen. The files ended with Hennie dying in jail in 2009. He wasn't likely to leave jail alive anyway, sentenced to life in prison without parole.

That meant he had someone carry on his vendetta, someone very close. Like a family member, a child. The investigator had five of Hennie's children to choose from. It should be fairly easy to track down the VanderWaulde children. They probably had no new information. He knew where Hennie did his illegal dealings and that brought the number of children down to two, but nothing more to go on. No names, first or last and no addresses. He'd have to travel to Chicago to find out any more. Resigning himself to the task before him, he opened a new tab on his internet browser and typed in, "American Airlines." He'd rather fly in and out than drive. He didn't like to drive in Chicago.

***

Chase was spread out across Sonya's naked body, trying to catch his breath. He could hear her heartbeat thumping up against her chest, almost matching the rapid beat of his own. He was also still inside her.

Chase had just experienced the most amazing orgasm he'd ever had and next to breathing, stopping himself from having aftershocks was his greatest priority. His mind was blown, his breath was taken and he was sexually spent.

"Honey, you're crushing me," she whispered beneath him.

"Oh God!" he jerked upward immediately. "I'm sorry!" He looked down upon her as she stretched out underneath him and smiled dreamily.

"Awwwww… that's better," she said, enjoying the stretch. "That was amazing!" she gushed.

"I know! I mean… really… mind blowing!" he laughed, as he gently lowered himself and kissed her head and neck and shoulder. "Hmmmm… you're yummy! You're… like candy… like… a drug," he murmured into her neck, as he snuggled closer into her. *If you only knew,* she thought, the irony not being lost on her.

They enjoyed their completely intimate embrace and neither wanted to break free from the moment. It was Chase who finally moved, lifting himself off of Sonya but staying close to her side afterwards. They drifted in and out of sleep for more than half an hour before Sonya arose fully and realized where she was. She looked down at Chase, sleeping beside her. He could be her future, if only she didn't have a connection to a major drug kingpin. Maybe it wouldn't matter; maybe Chase would be okay with that. She had ten seconds of listening to her inner self and then her deep desire broke through. *Do what you can to make him yours!* she screamed and Sonya was all ears!

***

He stood outside the window watching closely. It was his third night in a row and so far he hadn't found anything worthwhile. His client had asked for a clean job and given the parameters, this couldn't happen at this location. He'd have to check out the next address and see if that had any more promise. If so, then they'd move the assignment to the new address. It didn't matter to him, a job was a job and as long as he got paid, he was easy going. After all, he had mouths to feed!

~

Chapter 9

And Baby Makes Three

In its first week of release, "Constellations" sold more than a million copies sending it into the #1 spot on every music chart from Billboard and R&B to pop-rock. Chase Morningstar was an overnight success and had only just started! Millions of females from the age of 15 to woman of 45 thought Chase Morningstar was the sexiest man alive – even if People Magazine didn't!

After his first date with Sonya, Chase was in demand! Their time together was spent either very late at night or on a weekend when Chase wasn't busy performing, interviewing or recording for the new CD. But, no matter how busy he was, he always made time for Sonya. She was very understanding. She had been there to witness his emergence into the mainstream music world and now he was wanted by some of media's biggest names, playing with the best of the best with Supernova and making a name for himself. Sonya was trying hard to avoid her clientele through the day and seeing Chase at night. This was wreaking havoc on not only her professional connections but her bank account. In the first three weeks of dating Chase her income dropped by 65%. Not that she couldn't afford it, she'd made incredible money for years, but still, she couldn't continue doing this. After a while, her brother would be calling.

On the opposite end of the spectrum, Chase was never better. His creative juices were continually flowing and he had written more songs than the band was ready to record. Kyle smiled all through meetings, recordings and interviews. It was the success his father had always dreamed of.

***

He'd been on the job for a few weeks now. Nothing new. Shift change at 11:00 pm, same guy took over until 7:00 am. Always has a nap between 3:30 am and 4:15 am. Relieved by 7:10 am. If he was going to strike, he'd pick 3:50 am. Everyone would be in a deep sleep by then.

***

Campbell had been in rehabilitation care for almost a month. He still suffered headaches, dizziness and sensitivity to light. He still felt like shit by 3:00 pm and he still didn't feel competent to be living on his own. Given that, and his sense of guilt over knowing he'd brought danger to Chase, Campbell was destined to stay in the rehab centre for a while which meant he wasn't playing piano for Chase. It broke his heart.

In the meantime, Cooper Jack had immersed himself into all things "Constellations." When he and Chase met for the first time, Cooper asked him why he had chosen the star "Capella" as his centrepiece for the CD cover and it stopped Chase.

"I'm impressed. Regardless if you already knew or if you studied up, I'm impressed," he admitted. "It's the brightest star in the sky and that's exactly what I want to be!" Chase said, as he broke into his million watt smile. Cooper smiled a huge grin back.

"You're my new piano man?" Chase asked Cooper. He nodded back to Chase and stuck out his hand.

"Cooper Jack... nice to meet you," he said, shaking Chase's hand in a firm grip. "Your CD is incredible. I've had it on my iPod ever since it dropped. I'm the one who's impressed," he gushed.

"Thanks man, I appreciate it. Let's get in there and see what you got. Grab a drink later, huh?" Chase asked. He wanted to get to know Cooper Jack, his new piano man. After all, if he was going to replace his dad, Chase felt as though he should find out a bit about the dark-eyed, curly haired piano man with the easy grin.

They played for more than three hours, part jam session and part recording session, before Chase stopped the session and applauded Cooper.

"You've got one hell of an ear, Coop," he said, clapping his hands, amazed at his talent. "You've either listened to it non-stop or picked it up by ear and judging by your improvisational work, I'd say it's by ear."

All of Supernova agreed and continued the applause. They decided to break for a meal and a drink and Chase made sure he and Cooper sat alone together in the restaurant to continue getting to know each other. They talked about their life choices, their music likes and dislikes and well after they should have returned to the studio, Chase and Cooper remained sitting, just like Chase and Campbell had that first time. Family and friendships were the topic of their conversation when Chase asked Cooper a question. As he finished his beer and ordered two more he sat back in his chair thinking he couldn't remember the last time he had enjoyed having a drink with a friend like this.

"Tell me the funniest thing you did as a kid," Chase asked Cooper.

With large dark eyes looking wide at Chase, Cooper said with a straight face, "Well, I don't know if it's the funniest but... I peed on my best friend," he said, swigging the last of his beer and placing the bottle on the table and then breaking into a huge grin.

Chase broke out laughing. "Why'dja do that? Did he get stung by a jellyfish or something?" he asked Cooper.

"Oh, hell no. Nothing that heroic. No… I uh… wanted to get his attention and I had climbed up in a tree and saw him down below. And I uh… couldn't get him to look up and see me so I… peed on him," he said. "I drove my mother crazy. She took about two more years of my bullshit and then signed me up for piano lessons. I hated it at first, the practicing and all the rules but when I realized that I could make my own music up and could play things easier by just listening to them rather than reading it on paper, well… then everything changed."

He smiled and pointed upwards as "Mess Around" by Ray Charles began playing over the restaurant's sound system. Immediately, Cooper began moving his fingers across the edge of the table, the worn Formica becoming the keys of his imaginary piano.

Chase enjoyed watching Cooper and his antics. It reminded him of himself. Cooper was a few years younger than Chase and had the confidence of a man who'd been playing in studio for years but still had the wide eyed wonderment of a little boy. His piano playing was on the same calibre as the rest of Supernova and Chase knew he would seamlessly slip into place. Chase was thrilled with his talent but even more by his exuberance, zest for life and the fact that he had once peed on his best friend to get his attention. Now THAT was the kind of guy Chase wanted as a friend!

The restaurant closed around them while the two men remained at their table, still talking well into the night. It was the first of many late night conversations they would share over their fifty-five year friendship.

***

Sonya had been expecting his phone call for a few days. She had geared herself up for it and was almost anticipating a proposal she could make to him, something that might appease him and would allow her to still be with Chase. Sonya had it all planned. But then, so did he and, as always, his timing sucked.

She'd just awoken and entered the bathroom feeling rather sickly. Her stomach had been queasy for a few days and at first she figured she'd probably got the flu or a stomach bug. She'd been spending her days on campus taking another course in business management. This put her in very close proximity with mere children, germ carrying eighteen year olds who were all sneezing and coughing and looking rather sickly.

The idea that it was anything other than a stomach bug never ran through her mind as she stood at the pharmacy counter at her local Walmart. She stood in line ready to pay for her Gravol when her eyes drifted over the pregnancy tests. Suddenly, it was as if she had an epiphany, doing her reckoning of dates, times spent with Chase and her mental calendar of her monthly cycle. When things didn't add up she stared at the boxes in front of her. Pregnancy. *GEEZUS!* her mind screamed. *Could that be what was wrong?* In a panic she grabbed a box from the shelf and threw both the Gravol and test kit on the counter.

"I'm not sure if you can take these if you're pregnant," the young clerk said. "If you want, I can check with the pharmacist?" she asked Sonya.

Sonya was sure she was just trying to be helpful but she didn't care for her helpfulness at this point. She just wanted to buy the medication and other item and get the hell out of there.

"No, there's no need... thanks," she said meekly, trying to raise a smile. She paid for her items and left before the clerk had a chance to reply.

Now she was sitting in her bathroom peeing onto a stick hoping like hell she hadn't put the cart before the horse. She finished up placing the stick on the counter's edge awaiting its results as she heard "Candy Man" playing on her phone. *And there it is,* she thought. The call she had been anticipating; practically dreading.

She answered the phone and awaited the onslaught.

"Hello," she said.

"So, you wanna tell me what the fuck is going on?" he said, rather sweetly, but she wasn't fooled. She could tell he was pissed.

"I've been taking some time off. Taking some business classes again but these are during the day," she stated matter-of-factly.

"And what the hell are the clients supposed to do?" he asked her, his rage kept in check only slightly.

"Oh, for Christ's sake Johann, get someone else to take them on," she answered angrily. Her courage came from the fact that she was angry at how he thought he controlled her and how she almost let him. "Listen to me. These classes can help me take over as like… a silent partner. I can do all the different accounting and transactions for the company keeping everything above board. I can keep it all legit for you and still be able to have a life." She went quiet for a moment and awaited his response.

He took a deep breath. "Does this 'star' guy mean that much to you?" he asked her, his voice almost a whisper.

She hated it when he did this. She could almost believe he cared about her but then he'd turn nasty and abusive and she would realize that all he really cared about was the money.

"Yes, Johann, he means that much to me," she admitted. "I can't keep doing what I'm doing and be with him and I want to be with him. But if I run the other business I can make it work," she said confidently. Her heart was racing. She had never stood up to Johann like this. She knew he was a very dangerous man but he was also a very smart man and she knew she was appealing to his business sense. This would appease him, surely.

"I think you're wasting you're fuckin time with him. He ain't goin' anywhere," Johann said viciously into the phone.

"He's already on his way, Johann, and he wants me to go with him and I want to. He's my one last shot at happiness and a decent future and you have to let me try. Don't I deserve that much?" she asked him.

"Now, c'mon. You can have someone else look after my client list, except Darla, I'll keep her, she's a good shit." She hesitated, wondering if he would agree. "Give me the shipping yard and the few ships you run the Atlantic with. I swear to you I'll make you a huge profit in the first year I have them," she told him, keeping her fingers crossed as she walked back into the bathroom. As she moved about her apartment the reception on the other end of the phone cut in and out.

"What the fuck are you doing? Your reception isn't worth a crap," he muttered angrily.

"Oh… just preparing for a test," she said, tongue in cheek. "Do we have a deal?" she asked him, standing just outside the bathroom so the phone wouldn't cut out, straining to see the stick.

"No, we don't have a fuckin' deal! Are you stupid? I won't allow it," he shouted. "You can't leave a family business like this. You don't leave it, right? You get that?"

"Listen to me, Johann. I'm not your business partner here, I'm your sister, your only flesh and blood. Doesn't that mean anything? Don't you want me to be happy?" she asked him calmly, hoping the tone of her voice would settle him down.

"You're gonna regret it, you know. Don't come fuckin' cryin' to me when it all goes to shit. I told you once before, we aren't part of their social public circle. We're supposed to be in the shadows. It don't mix, you hear me? We don't mix! You expose me or any of my associates and you'll pay for it dearly. You know that, right?" he yelled one more time and the phone went dead.

She put her phone down and ran into the bathroom. She reached the toilet just in time and vomited. She hung over the bowl for a moment waiting to see if she was finished. Once her stomach settled, she turned to the sink to rinse out her mouth. As she ran the water she saw the test stick and grabbed it. She focused in on the digital reading. Plus sign for a positive result, minus sign for a negative. She dropped her hand holding the test stick and let out a heavy sigh as her brother's words rang in her head. *Please God, don't let him be right!*, she prayed.

***

The man's phone buzzed earlier than usual. It must be important because no one dared to call him this early, not if they knew what he did for a living!

"What?" he answered gruffly, still half asleep.

"You'd better get this fuckin' job done and over with quick, or else!" came the threat. The man hated being threatened.

"Don't threaten me!" the man shouted. "I ain't gonna take a risk and be stupid just 'cause you want a hurried job. I know exactly what time he's gonna die and it'll be within the next 24 hours. But I ain't gonna do it 'cause you told me to, get it?" he told him and hung up the phone.

Johann tapped his rings across the head of his cane. He didn't like being spoken to like that and he'd have to make sure this guy knew that one day. But for right now, he'd allow it. If he was successful in hitting his target then Johann's obligations and worries would be gone. If he wasn't, then perhaps Johann would take his business elsewhere and have him taken out by the new guy. Made no difference to him; one hired thug is as good as another, as long as they get the job done and keep his name and identity out of it. If Sonya insisted on this stupid plan of hers, he had no choice but to take out the source of her defection and distraction. If she wasn't going to be loyal then she deserved no loyalty in return. He'd take out anything and everything she loved until she came back crying for her former clients and forgetting she ever wanted to get out of the family business. He'd make her stay. It really was that important to him.

***

"God, I missed you," Chase said into Sonya's neck, as he kissed her and took in her scent. She always smelled so wonderful and fresh as if she'd just stepped out of a shower. He wasn't sure if it was her soap, her perfume or just her own personal scent but he loved it. He loved her. He loved her and felt compelled to tell her.

They were lying on his bed, having ordered dinner in and now had a chance to finally be together. Chase's schedule had been hectic for weeks. He was always flying in to or out of somewhere, sometimes with the band, sometimes without, being interviewed and recorded by God knows who, all in an effort to keep the almost vertical trajectory of his CD going. Copies of "Constellations" were selling out of stores as soon as they were getting stock in. Downloads of his CD off iTunes were in excess of 370,000. He had started to see his long-time dream finally coming to fruition and now he lay with the one woman he wanted by his side. It was just over a year since he left Chicago and what a year he'd had! After pondering for a moment, Chase sat up resting on his elbow and looked down onto Sonya's beautiful face. Her eyes were so dark chocolate brown, it was hard to tell where her pupil actually was. Chase couldn't help but lean over and kiss her.

"I love you, Sonya," he admitted to her, softly, taking her hand and raising it to his lips. He paused for a moment and let her catch her breath. He could tell she was thrilled to hear him say it, but he knew she'd be really thrown by what was coming next.

"I want you to stay with me… forever. I want to have our home together, our lives together. I want to make you happy and make every day exciting and fun for both of us. And there is only one way I can see that happening," he explained.

He sat up further, raised himself up off the bed and held out his hand to her. She took his hand and stood up. Chase dropped to one knee and produced a ring box from out of nowhere. Sonya was stunned and stared, wide eyed.

Chase had shown great affection, attention and admiration to Sonya over the course of their dating. Although it had been a very short time, she knew she loved him and was hoping that at some point this would all naturally progress. She never expected it so soon but she was thrilled!

"Will you marry me, Sonya?" Chase asked her, grinning large and feeling slightly nervous.

She yelped and threw her hands to her mouth, then reached down to pull him up and threw her arms around his neck.

"Yes, yes… oh my God, yes, Chase. Oh my God, oh my God," she kept repeating, as they kissed and laughed and hugged.

Chase was never happier! He once again nuzzled into her neck and thought that he would smell her lovely fresh smell for the rest of his life. God he felt amazing!

Their kissing was going from excitement to lustful and wanting. Before they got too far, Chase stopped, took the ring from the box and placed it on Sonya's finger. She looked down upon a stunning two carat diamond in a beautiful setting with baguette diamonds flanking the large rectangular stone.

"Chase, it's so beautiful. I can't believe this!" She gushed as she tried to focus on the ring through her tears. He took her by the waist and gently guided her back down onto the bed as his hands began undressing her. He made fast work of her blouse and skirt and within moments she was lying naked beside him in all her beauty. He remained lying beside her as he traced his finger over her shoulder bone and down between her breasts, circling each lovely rose colored nipple as he went. His finger traveled further down until it reached into the soft curly hair and found her little sexual bud. He dipped his finger inside her and gathered her juices using it to help lubricate the little bud, worrying it softly, over and over again. She reached up and pulled his head down to hers and kissed him deeply as his fingers began to play with all of her. At first, he touched her gently but as they continued, his erection and desire grew and before long he was kneading her breasts, using his finger to stimulate her and feeling more and more aroused. She struggled with his shirt and jeans until he quickly rolled off the bed, removed all his clothing in record time and joined Sonya back on the bed. As he started kissing he positioned himself over her and entered her with as much restraint as he could manage. He was so aroused he was afraid he'd hurt her with force so he held back a bit allowing her to enjoy the full erection as it slid inside her. Her body curved up towards him as he leaned over her and they began the rhythmic dance of lovemaking, matching the other thrust for thrust in perfect time.

The sensations were almost too much for them both. Neither had experienced such delicious sexual responsiveness and knew that this only happened when it was true love. Their eyes met as they continued, Chase over her with heavy lustful eyes looking down into Sonya's deep, brown, passionate gaze. He increased his thrusting slightly and watched Sonya as her eyes closed and she began to quiver from within. Her mouth opened into an "O" but no sound came out of her. He could feel her interior muscles convulsing and a gush of warm liquid surrounding his erection as he again increased his thrust a little more. As Sonya continued to orgasm, Chase's was building. He grabbed her hands above her head and allowed the orgasm to wash over him as he exploded into her, taking his breath, his mind and his senses with it.

He fell on top of her but held his weight so that she wouldn't be crushed. She brought her hands down around his neck and held him close to her. As he tried to regain focus and relax his body, she whispered into his ear.

"I love you, Chase Morningstar. I can't wait to be your wife," she told him, kissing him along his ear and side of his face.

He smiled as he rose up above her, again looking down on her. He looked completely satiated and at peace.

"I love you too, Sonya, and I can't wait to be your husband," he smiled at her. She was so beautiful he couldn't help but say, "I can't wait to see what our children are going to look like; with your eyes and smile. God, if we have girls, they'll turn me to mush!" he joked, but part of him was serious.

"Well, I don't think it's going to take us too long to find that out... Daddy," she said. She kept her eyes on his, waiting for what she'd just said to register.

When the train finally pulled into the station, Chase's eyes went wide as can be. He broke into a huge smile and said in disbelief, "What's this? Are you sure? You know for certain?" She nodded to all of his questions as he stared at her incredulously.

"Oh my God," he exclaimed, throwing his hand over his mouth.

"Now you're starting to sound like me," she giggled, and pulled the sheets up over her for warmth.

He quickly tucked the sheets closer around her and made sure she was comfortable. "Are you okay? I didn't know... I hope I didn't hurt you or the... uh... the uh..." he hesitated.

"The baby?" she asked him, ending his sentence.

"Yes, the baby. Can we hurt it?" he asked, as his hand instinctively ran over her stomach. She didn't feel pregnant but he was certain things were working and growing away in there.

"No, I don't believe we can. You know people have been having babies for thousands of years," she teased him. "I'm fairly certain that a few of those women have had sex during pregnancy and all their babies have been born just fine," she smiled at him. It was lovely to see how he was taking this. This morning she was nervous as hell to tell him she was pregnant but after having been proposed to, with a ring as well, it could only mean good things, and good things were certainly coming their way!

Chase let out a very long and satisfied sigh. "It's all come together, you know? My CD, you marrying me and now a baby on the way. It's all coming together," he sighed. "It must be true what they say, good things come in three's."

***

He watched from his car in the darkened lot near the corner. He could see the night watchman sitting at his post. He was waiting for the girl to leave. He hadn't been instructed to kill her and he didn't want to fuck up. He'd wait until tomorrow night, providing the guy came home in time and without the girl.

He'd wait just a few more minutes to ensure he had everything down, watching as the night watchman fell asleep at 3:35 am – right on cue. *This should be fairly easy, like taking candy from a baby*, he thought pulling away for home.

~

Chapter 10

Now That You're Here

With the news of the impending marriage and baby on the way, Chase felt compelled to finally call his brother Charlie and fill him in on some things Entertainment Tonight wasn't telling him.

Charlie answered after the first ring. "Damn, Charlie, you always grab it on the first ring! How'd ya do that?" Chase asked him, not bothering with a "hello" or a "hey, how ya doing?"

"It's 'cause I've got this world famous brother who's CD is friggin fantastic but he NEVER calls me anymore!" Charlie said, smiling into the phone and giving Chase the full guilt trip, tickets and all!

"Ya, shit, I'm sorry Charlie, don't take it personally. I'm just so busy now and haven't had a chance to fill you in on everything. But... I've got some really exciting news so I wanted to make sure you heard it from me first before TMZ or some paparazzi finds out and tells you," Chase explained, and then held his breath, taking a moment for Charlie to be ready to hear him.

"Okay, so... what's the news?" Charlie asked him, playing along.

"I'm getting married and I'm going to be a dad," he blurted out all at once.

Charlie could hear the joy in his voice and could practically see Chase's million watt smile over the phone. Charlie was thrilled for his little brother.

"Holy shit! When did all this happen? What's her name? When's the wedding?" Charlie asked him, rapid fire.

"Uh... actually, we'll probably get married as soon as possible. Sonya wants to be able to wear a designer gown and she's already six weeks along so, we'll probably just have a quiet celebration. I was thinking of taking her to Cancun for a weekend and arranging it there. Think you can make it?" he asked Charlie. He figured he already knew the answer, but wanted to be sure that Charlie was invited and that there were no hard feelings left anymore. Charlie had Georgie and Chase had Sonya; everything had worked out as it should.

"Well, we'll have to see how it goes, Chase. I promise we'll do everything we can, but Rosa and Marlon are going away for three weeks to celebrate their one year anniversary so if it's within that time frame we might be screwed," Charlie admitted. "Let me know when it is and Georgie and I will work out the logistics. It would be great to see you, get to know Sonya and watch you get married. God, I'm so happy for you little brother. And look at you now, carrying on the Morningstar name! I love it," Charlie gushed into the phone.

He missed Chase terribly and had kept watch on all the entertainment networks and shows for how his little brother was doing. He made great news and his music was everywhere. Chase had certainly done what he had set out to do and Charlie was immensely proud of him.

"I'll keep you posted, Charlie. The minute I know, you'll know, okay? And how are things with you, man? You and Georgie doing okay?" he asked sincerely.

"Absolutely, little bro. Never better. Can't say as I miss anything about touring with the band. Chilling Charlie is killing it here in the club and I've started going back on stage once in a while. The bar's doing great, making us money and keeping us entertained. Can't ask for more than that," he said contentedly.

"You deserve it, Charlie. You really do. Listen, I gotta run but please kiss Georgie for me and tell her I love her and I love you too, Charlie. Take good care and I'll call when we know a wedding date, for sure, okay?" he told his brother.

"Okay then. Tell Sonya how happy we are for all three of you! You keep aiming for the stars, Chase," Charlie said.

"That's the plan, Charlie, that's the plan!" Chase said, laughing, as he ended the call.

They had spent 20 years touring together and only one year apart and Chase was missing him as though the reverse was true. His older brother had been such a mentor to him after his mother died and Chase learned a lot from Charlie. He had put it all to good use when he was on the road but once in the studio, Chase had to learn from scratch and he was proud to show Charlie how far he'd come in such a short time. Not to rub his nose in it but more for proving to Charlie that he had always known he would be famous one day. Now his hard work and determination were coming to fruition.

∗∗∗

Chase entered his apartment just before 10:00 pm. It would be nice to have an early night for a change. He and Sonya had agreed not to move in together right away as Chase was on the move a lot for the next couple of weeks and Sonya was suffering morning sickness and spent a good portion of every morning in the bathroom. Chase felt badly that she was going through it alone and spent as much face time with her as he could. She was easy going about it all and understood the logistics but they both promised that by two weekends, they would be under the same roof and shortly thereafter, married.

Their news of marriage and a baby on the way would not be shared widely. Chase was nervous about the safety situation as it was, to go putting his newly pregnant fiancé out there before she'd even had a chance to get through her first trimester was not recommended, so only a select few people knew. The couple had visited Campbell to inform him and he was completely shocked by it all.

During a quiet moment between him and Sonya, he agreed it was for the better that they never tell Chase how Campbell came to know her. Sonya assured him that those days were behind her now and she was back at school and was about to become the business manager of a shipping company that had a few boats in its inventory. Campbell nodded as if he understood, but he didn't. Campbell felt exhausted from the visit and trying to settle his mind down on what had been told to him. It took him much longer to process things these days and he wished he could go back to when his mind was sharp and he felt in his twenties, not like now, not like he was seventy plus years. He felt every inch of it now and Chase could tell.

That very thought was crossing Chase's mind as he showered before getting into bed. He could really do with a good night's sleep before the start of another rigorous schedule for the next 14 days and to be sure that happened, he went into the kitchen, got himself a glass of water and took a half sleeping pill. He drank half the glass and absentmindedly deposited it on the living room side table along the way to his bedroom. He climbed into bed and settled, letting the pill do its thing. As he drifted off to sleep he thought about the changes that were going to take place in the next little while. He knew they were all life changing and he was smiling to himself with the excitement of it all.

***

He entered the building through the front door, bold as you please, not concerned about cameras or being seen. He could see the night watchman fast asleep in his chair just off the main entrance, the door to his office area ajar. It was a joke to call this a "secured" building with this going on, but who bothers checking what goes on at 3:50 am? He does, that's who and once he had picked the front door lock he was into the building and inside the security office quickly. He knocked out the night watchman with one left hook to the chin, the guy didn't even wake up, just went from asleep to unconscious in a matter of moments. Once the watchman was taken care of, he disabled all cameras and reversed the tapes and restarted them, taping over them with a fuzzy screen.

He then took the elevator up to Chase's floor, confidently, not concerned about anyone seeing him. He found Chase's door and pulled out his toolkit; a small leather pouch that rolled out to expose a criminal's stash of objects and tools to pick the lock of any door. He had even manufactured a tool that could take the chain off the door without as much as a jingle from the chain. He was that good!

He got the door unlocked without too much bother, a simple pin needle dropping into two chambers – piece of cake. Chase had locked the door using the chain and once again the man's nifty tool came in handy. *I should sell this thing*, he thought to himself, chuckling. *Thieves would pay a fortune for shit like that!* he mused.

The apartment was almost pitch black. This was unusual for most apartment dwellers living high up in the air. Most liked the windows uncovered or with the slightest of draperies, allowing the sky to be their fourth wall, but this guy obviously liked it dark. It made his job more difficult but not impossible. He had fairly decent night vision and it took him a moment for his eyes to adjust. He could barely make out shapes of furniture, but enough to not trip over them at least as he made his way to doorways and tried each handle. He wasn't expecting the half glass of water that sat precariously close to the edge of the living room table and as he passed it he caught it with his hand. The glass crashed to the floor and the man's heart lurched as he stood silent holding his breath.

SHIT! He couldn't believe it! That had never happened before! He was always so stealthy; the best at what he did and he prided himself on it. Trying to calm himself down, he waited to hear if it had awoken the occupant but his heart was beating so hard, it was difficult to hear anything else. It took a moment for him to get back on track and focus on what he was there to do. The glass had not managed to bring anyone out so he continued to quietly try each doorknob. He had been down the hallway and tried the two doors producing a small bedroom and a linen closet. His hand touched the knob on the last door nearest the end of the hallway. He wasn't sure if it was the bathroom or the last bedroom. He figured he should get himself ready to shoot if he came upon his target still sleeping. That'd be two guys in one night that would be caught sleeping with neither knowing what had hit them, one knocked out, one dead, hopefully. That amused him too. As he turned the knob on the door and pushed it open he heard gunshots but they weren't from his gun. He fell to the floor so quickly his hand hadn't left the doorknob. The man didn't have the chance for a last thought.

***

He'd been home for only an hour and his phone hadn't stopped. He spent most of the day answering questions and making statements and swearing on this form and that form that the unidentified man broke into his apartment and came through his bedroom door with the intent to kill him. The fact that they found the night watchmen still unconscious and all cameras destroyed and tapes recorded over, added greatly to Chase's recount of the events. He came back to the apartment to find there were still plenty of investigators and forensics people all about taking pictures; the doorway where the guy broke in, the glass that was knocked over, doorknobs he'd tried and then the 6 foot 5 inch behemoth of a dead guy still lying on Chase's bedroom floor. *Christ! How long does it take until you get rid of the body?* he wondered.

The amount of activity inside his apartment paled in comparison to the amount of activity going on outside his building. Once again, the paparazzi caught wind of the story when police showed up and found Chase still on the phone with the 911 dispatcher 15 floors up. A crowd had gathered by 5:00 am and grew steadily to include onlookers, fans and news stations alike. The morning newspaper read: "Chase Morningstar, A Shooting Star?" and all the morning shows focused heavily on the shooting from every angle. They even managed to find the one and only person Chase had ever met in his building and interviewed her. She told the morning viewers that she knew who he was and that he had a lovely blonde girlfriend who he was very smitten with.

This was a game changer for Chase. Fuck the pomp and circumstance, he and Sonya were getting married as soon as possible, damn the schedule. He also wanted them to move into a house within a highly secure gated area and he was going to put Kyle on it immediately. If he couldn't own his own house right away, he'd rent for now but he had to get him and Sonya and their baby safe and secure.

Chase answered what seemed like his hundredth call when he heard Charlie's voice.

"Christ, Chase, what the hell happened?" asked Charlie, his voice full of concern.

Chase told him what he could, explaining that he had sworn under an affidavit to not say anything while the police were still investigating, but that they could see it was in self defense; he was okay because he did have a licence and permit for the gun. Past that, he wasn't saying anything more.

"Are you okay?" Charlie asked him, worried for his mental state. "I mean, you just had to kill a guy; you might want to take some time to absorb it all," he suggested wisely.

"Yeah, well, I'll have time to reflect on it later. Right now, I'm pushing the wedding up to basically tonight if I can. I want to jump on a flight to Vegas and get this done. Sorry man, but this makes me want to get Sonya and the baby safe under my roof and married to me," he explained to Charlie.

But there was no need to explain it to him, Charlie understood completely. "Do what you gotta do to protect your family, Chase. We're just happy to know you're safe. But, are they letting you leave the state just yet?" Charlie asked him.

Chase smiled. "No, probably not, but the minute I get the go ahead, I'm on a flight. I probably won't be able to give you much of a heads up. I'll try and keep you posted." He sighed for a moment and the brothers shared a pause. "This sure isn't the kind of publicity I was hoping for, you know? And now, the media is horny to figure out who the "mystery blonde" is in my life because some old biddy in the building met us once in the elevator."

"Not our elderly woman, the one we've seen, you know?" Charlie asked him, surprised he would mention her.

"No… but… uh… you know, Charlie, I think I dream about her." Silence greeted him, so he continued. "I keep having this recurring dream and it's either that same woman or," he hesitated, worried to say the words, "…or, it's Mom. It woke me up last night just before the glass broke. That's how I knew there was someone in the apartment," he told his brother, again not divulging everything to him.

"Well, thank God it did, Chase, or there would be completely different news hitting all of us this morning. You get Kyle working on a secure place for all of you and don't worry about the wedding. If making her your bride tonight is what makes you happy, then do it. Georgie and I are just grateful everyone's okay, except the dead guy," Charlie said, laughing a little. "Sorry... too soon?" He chuckled again and got another smile out of Chase.

"No, buddy, not too soon. The fucker tried to kill me. One of us was going to die; better him than me," Chase said, ending the conversation.

***

As Kyle began making Chase's requests happen and doing damage control where he could, he also managed to make a call to a lawyer who would represent Chase in case he should have to answer to any charges, although that wasn't the feeling he was getting from the police. They were going to grant him the time to go to Vegas and get married as long as he did it quietly and he returned within 24 hours. Considering his face was being splashed everywhere, he couldn't go on the run if he tried. Besides, to the police investigating, it seemed pretty cut and dry but they were still digging into the large man's involvement. He was a hired assassin, but hired by who? Kyle gave them information regarding Hennie as well as the investigator he had hired to try and find something on him. Maybe their combined efforts would be able to find out who hired this guy to kill Chase Morningstar.

The questions had been asked. Was it a crazed fan? A woman with a warped sense of reality? A jealous peer? Right now it could be any one of these scenarios but Kyle knew deep down that none of them were the case. His gut told him that it had everything to do with Campbell's past and it wasn't necessarily over yet.

***

"We're marrying tonight?" Sonya asked, shocked. She wasn't even close to picking out a dress yet. She hadn't even told her brother yet. She needed time to get everything set up so that she could remove herself seamlessly from selling drugs and disassociate with her clientele. She needed more time.

"Listen, this whole thing has made me want to circle the wagons, you know. I want to marry you, have you and our baby safe where I can protect you. Please say yes, honey. Please," he pleaded with her. "I want to make you both safe and I can't do that if we're apart living in separate homes. The police are granting us 24 hours to get ourselves to Vegas and married and then get the hell back here. They want us to do it quickly and quietly with as little fanfare as possible."

"And how will that be possible? You're known to everyone, especially after the shooting. Are you kidding?" She felt anxious and rushed.

"Kyle's got this lawyer and a publicist on it. They're going to arrange everything. No one is going to know. And it's the last thing they're expecting so they won't be looking for it. C'mon, baby, please?" he asked her.

"But Chase, we don't have to marry to live together," she told him, not understanding the rush to marry.

"Look," he said, taking her hands in his and looking directly into her deep dark eyes. "You and that baby you're carrying are the most important people in the world to me. I just spent a night scared out of my mind not knowing if I would live or die. Thank God I did live and it's made me appreciate this situation with us. I'm going to be a dad. I want you to be mine. I want you to have my name and I want us to be married immediately. I'll promise you the biggest, fattest wedding you ever saw whenever you want if we legally marry tonight. Deal?"

This was stressing her out. How the hell was she going to get everything arranged now? She'd have to work hard and fast after the fact and maybe even go underground for a while. Lay low. The one unknown to her was Campbell. Would he tell Chase who she really was? So far, he'd said nothing. Should she trust in him? Could she pull this off so quickly? Once again, her inner voices screamed *NO! You need more time!*

She looked into the beautiful hazel eyes of Chase, pleading to whisk her away and get married. She hesitated and then she smiled at him. She nodded her head, throwing her arms around his neck. "You give in too easy, I'd have been happy with a simple wedding. You've agreed to a big fat one. S'gonna cost ya," she teased him, bringing her body into a warm hug from him.

"Oh no, not me. I would've gone as far as a Clooney wedding. YOU gave in too soon! SUCKER!" he said, smiling and squeezing her gently but tightly, taking in her smell once again. He just couldn't get enough of it. Of her.

Seven hours later they stood before a justice of the peace in Las Vegas and were speaking their vows with reverence and honor as if they were before the Archbishop of Canterbury in front of 1,600 people. Sonya found a dress extremely quickly thanks to a phone call to Darla who then called her show's costume department. Sonya had three dresses to choose from with a seamstress standing by willing to alter as much as she could, given the time constraints. She chose a close-fitting designer dress which folded in soft layers downward across the body in white satin. Swarovski crystals adorned the bust line and brought some beautiful bling to the altar! Sonya would never have picked so glamorous a dress to wear, but it was at her disposal, only for the Vegas wedding and she looked extraordinarily fabulous in it. A bit over the top, but hey! it was Vegas after all. She asked Darla to stand in as her maid of honor and Cooper Jack was Chase's best man. Both were sworn to secrecy. Kyle needed to stay in New York and continue to mop up after the shooting mess. Even though it was determined that Chase had been targeted, the news and social media outlets were wreaking havoc on Chase's image.

The publicist brought in to handle the deluge of requests for interviews and comments and sources for comments was top notch at what she did and she soon settled everyone down with three phone calls. With that, the focus was taken off of Chase and onto her statement. She now became the focus of the cameras, speaking on Chase's behalf. If they wanted Chase, the needed to go through her. This gave Chase time to whip away to Vegas, get married to Sonya and get back. Of course, the publicist maneuvered the wedding party onto Lapis Labels' company jet and into a wedding chapel at a very elite hotel along the strip. Even the chapel minister and his wife weren't sure if they were truly witnessing Chase Morningstar marrying a blonde woman; it seemed so surreal. It was only yesterday they were watching him being questioned by police after the shooting in his apartment. Now, he was before them, dressed in a fine dark suit, white shirt and dark tie with an equally well dressed party in tow marrying a beautiful blonde named Sonya. It was all under the highest secrecy with both the minister and his wife signing confidentiality forms.

When they were married, the four witnesses clapped their hands and wished the couple well. Chase got a handshake from Cooper Jack and a kiss on the cheek from Darla. Both kissed and hugged the bride. No pictures were taken to mark the occasion, no shot of the bride and groom, lest it end up in the hands of the media.

Sonya ignored the nagging worry that stuck in her stomach all day. She wasn't going to let it ruin her day, even if she was going to have two weddings. She pushed it down deeper and deeper until she almost didn't know it was there at all.

Regardless of the circumstances behind the rushed wedding, Chase felt at peace. Sonya was now his wife and their baby was going to be born a Morningstar. It was really that important to him.

***

Their first visit, once they got home, was to see Campbell. When they told him the news he held his smile and looked directly at Sonya but said nothing. She feared that Campbell's concussion would cause him to forget their understanding; not to mention how Campbell came to know her. She prayed in her head that he wouldn't blurt out that she had been his drug dealer for a number of years. She prayed that he was as happy to keep that news to himself as she was, but his look didn't look happy. Not at all. When Chase told him about the baby, Campbell seemed confused as if he didn't understand or wasn't sure what to think about the news. Either way, both Chase and Sonya left the rehabilitation centre believing he hadn't taken the news very well and both were quietly thinking, "What's with Campbell?"

***

Within a few weeks, the excitement of the shooting was surpassed by some other celebrity news story. Chase did a series of interviews about the incident and satisfied the curiosity of the media and his fans. His version: Someone broke in with the intent to kill him and he shot in self defense; end of story. He had no information on the assassin nor could he think of any reason why someone might want him dead. The police corroborated his statement and with that, he hoped he'd put everyone's questions to rest. Besides, there were plenty of other celebrities, sports figures and politicians who were willing to become the next big story, so Chase's shooting quieted with each day that passed. Per his request, Lapis Labels didn't mention anything about the wedding of their hottest superstar. It made no headlines, it made no breaking news reels and no cover shots were taken for People, HELLO! or US Weekly. It was as if it never happened, which was exactly what the groom had hoped for. Behind the scenes, the investigation was on-going with the police playing their cards very close to their chest. They visited Campbell in the rehabilitation home, but he wasn't much help. Still suffering from the effects of his concussion, he couldn't remember much about Hennie other than what he'd already told Chase and Kyle.

Even Kyle's father, Paul Craven, was interviewed. The police were hoping he would have some long time insight into Hennie, but Paul was no help either. Hennie was sent to jail and never came out, that was the story Paul knew. If he had anyone working for him on the outside who's to say they could ever be traced back to Hennie? As it was, the trail ran completely cold to the police, which pissed off Chase to no end. He had high hopes for the investigator Kyle hired who was still working the case. He'd done a better job than the police and at least he was doing something by trying to track down Hennie's children.

Chase moved Sonya and himself into a very tight and secure community. The house had an abundance of computerized security cameras and Chase would be notified immediately to his phone if a leaf moved outside on the driveway. Chase figured Sonya wanted to be in hiding because of the unknown figure who might still want Chase dead. Sonya wasn't worried about him as much as she was of anyone who might let Chase know of her former occupation and her drug king brother, especially since she had yet to talk to Johann and explain everything to him.

Regardless of the reason, publicity right now was only for his CD promotion and then Chase always went alone or with Supernova. For protection of their newest rising star, Lapis Labels paid to have a recording studio built into Chase's basement, all to his and Kyle's personal specifications. Supernova would come over, either all at once or at times separately to lay down tracks, work on individual parts of a song or just to jam. Music was always either playing or being created in the house, although the soundproofing was so good, you could barely hear it!

The only problem was, they no longer lived in the city which meant a long commute and Sonya felt isolated inside all the tight security. She tried to work from home as much as she could with her schooling and business management. Her brother completely exploded on her when she finally told him they had married and where she was living. When she mentioned she was pregnant he became really enraged.

"So, you did this purposely?" he spit at her. "You bitches are all the same. You'd trap a guy into marrying you because he knocks you up," he sneered, bitterly. "I told you before but you're too stupid. You don't get it, do you? I won't allow you to stop selling, do you hear me?" He paused and then said, "What do you think he's gonna do when he's finds out what you do for a living? Huh? What your family is involved with? You think he's gonna like that, for his career? I told you that you couldn't do this. Now you've sealed your own fate. You're not my worry now, only a problem that has to be resolved. This'll piss off a lot more people than me. Hope yer happy, bitch." He then cut off the call.

God, she hated him! She knew he'd be awful about it. She told herself that she shouldn't worry about Johann and that she should just look forward to all the good that was in store for her. Johann couldn't hurt her; hell, he couldn't get to her at all. Not with them living within the *bunker* as she referred to it.

She tried very hard not to let Johann's words bother her but they became the nasty voice she kept hearing in her head and it started to weigh on her. What would Chase do if he found out about her other life? Her brother? He would probably leave her because he wouldn't want anything to fuck with his rising star, and who could blame him? The more she worried about it the more she became fearful of exposure, fearful of Chase's reaction and scared to death of losing all she had. The worry and fear slowly consumed her.

She grew quiet, sullen and spent many days lying around the house in a dark mood with her baby growing within her. Chase did all that he could to talk to her and figure out what was bothering her, but she never came clean with him about Johann. How could she? Explaining him and his nasty remarks would only open up a huge can of worms she didn't want to get into. So, she went deeper and deeper into depression, and eventually into despair. She lost her desire to travel into the city, she lost her desire to dress up or go to school, and she lost her desire for everything. Sonya should have been trying to get online for her courses, checking in on the shipping company's accounts and shipments or, at the very least, preparing for the birth of her first child, but she wasn't.

Her pregnancy became more and more daunting and doing anything became difficult. Her morning sickness continued past the first trimester, longer than most, and her stomach never felt quite right. Everything plagued her, plunging her even deeper into her depression. Chase was worried sick and tried to talk to her, cuddle with her, help her in any way he could but she wasn't coming out of it. He even spoke to the doctors about her downward spiral, thinking they would certainly do something but she couldn't be honest with them either, not about her brother, not about her guarded secret life so she lied to the doctors telling them that she was just uncomfortable, worried about her safety and just anxious about the baby coming. Being used to lying about her life and her level of happiness, she won them over. They told Chase to take her home and await the birth of the baby, she should be fine after that. On the drive home, in the back of the limo, Chase pulled Sonya closer to him and snuggled with her as the car moved down the highway.

"Remember, just a few short months ago when we practically tore each other's clothes off in the back of a limo?" he said, squeezing her and nuzzling his nose into her hair. He missed her so much.

She stiffened slightly and kept her head turned away from him, letting the tears slip down her face. He continued the snuggling but let out a heavy sigh as he held onto her and stared off into the distance.

"I wish I could help you, sweetheart. I wish I could understand what it is that's got you so sad. This is supposed to be the happiest time of our lives and it breaks my heart that you've spent more days sad and in tears than you have smiling and happy." As he spoke to her he held onto her wrist, never noticing how very tiny it was until now. He stroked the small wrist with his thumb. "God Sonya, if you shared your worries with me, maybe I have an answer that you aren't aware of. Maybe I could resolve them for you. Please, honey, trust in me. Tell me your worries. Share them with me, please."

He really wished she'd offer up something. He had talked to a few of the doctors about mental illness, but he didn't think that was what was going on with her. At first, she seemed very happy to be pregnant and to get married. Now, it seemed such an insurmountable task and Chase had no idea what the hell had changed, but something had!

He felt badly for the baby whose mommy wasn't acting as if she was happy about its impending arrival. She didn't wish to have the ultrasound to determine the sex, she wasn't interested in a baby shower, baby shopping or any of the traditional events that would make the time waiting for the baby to come so much fun. She wasn't interested because, who would she call? Who could come out to celebrate? Her former drug clients? The only one who could be considered a friend was Darla, who she still saw periodically.

She had seen Darla only a few times before being holed up inside the bunker. After that, she spoke to her just a couple of times and Darla came out to see her just once.

"Shit, girl," Darla said, as she hugged Sonya and smiled at the size of her tummy. "You're practically ready to pop, aren't you?" Darla only had to look at Sonya to know something was up. She wanted answers right away.

"What the f...?" she stopped herself short. "You look so sad. What's going on?" For a split second Sonya thought about telling the same old lie to Darla but then realized that Darla knew the real score. Darla was the one person she could trust with her secrets and worries and so she started talking.

"Chase doesn't know about my former occupation or my family connections. He has no idea," she explained tearfully.

"None?" Darla asked incredulous. "How do you manage to date and marry the most famous musician there is and he doesn't know about your background?" She was shaking her head.

"I never told him. Campbell never told him and my brother has basically told me I'm dead to him because of me not wanting to sell the shit anymore. He thinks I'm going to expose him either intentionally or unintentionally. He thinks I got pregnant on purpose and he didn't even let me tell him how it all went down. I phoned him only to tell him that Chase and I had secretly married but I got defensive when he got so nasty and it just came out. So, now he thinks I've trapped Chase into this marriage, that it isn't based on anything real. He's not going to let me leave the business, Darla. He's not going to believe this is real for me and let me be happy, I know it."

Sonya had been crying quietly but by the end of her explanation, her sobbing was uncontrollable. Darla did her best to try and console her, but Sonya had kept it choked in for so long, it wasn't going to stop anytime soon. Darla didn't have any answers. This shit was above her calling or ability so she just rocked Sonya back and forth for a while and let her cry it out. She didn't stop by again after that, although they spoke once more on the phone. When she heard that Sonya was doing no better she decided to give her some advice.

"Listen, Sonya, you gotta get your shit together 'cause unless you tell Chase exactly what's been going on he's just gonna think you're losing it. If you can't be honest and you gotta live a lie, then do what the rest of us do," she told Sonya.

"Which is?" Sonya asked.

"Try some of the shit you once sold. Improves my mood 100%. Don't do it while you're pregnant, but once you've had the baby, try smoking a joint. You'd be surprised how it can help!"

Darla wasn't kidding but Sonya wasn't convinced. She wondered what the hell she ever saw in Darla if that was the best advice she had. Now she felt completely lost.

Chase's schedule kept him busier than ever. He did his best to be home as much as possible but sometimes he wasn't even in the same state. He'd FaceTime Sonya to make sure she was okay but really nothing had pulled her out of her depression since she started sinking into it. After trying with doctors and Sonya herself, Chase took his frustration to his music. He wrote about the changes in their relationship in a haunting ballad called, "I Thought I Knew You." Kyle didn't catch on and wanted it to be a new release; thought it could reach into the heart of everyone either single or a couple, but all Chase hoped for was that it reached through Sonya's despair and into *her* heart.

I can't recall the last time we were okay.
The future is fast approaching but we're miles away.
Our thoughts and emotions are at different ends,
And I want you and need you,
to come back to where it all began.

I thought I knew you, I thought we were there.
But now it's messed up and going nowhere.
The life I imagined seemed there in my hand,
So easy to touch and hold onto,
now I'm not sure of anything.

I know that our love was meant to be,
I can't deny what's true,
There are so many wonderful things,
That I love about you,
And I thought I knew you, I thought I knew...

Kyle released it just after Labor Day. It hit the airwaves and went straight to number one on all the top 40 charts. It was such a lovely ballad. It represented everyone who had ever felt lost inside a broken relationship. It taught Chase a valuable lesson about fame; it didn't accommodate privacy.

October came and went with young trick-or-treater's practically needing winter coats over top of their costumes, the weather had turned so cold. Sonya sat on the couch feeling fat and miserable and keeping the lights dark so that no children came by. She couldn't bear to see them. One day, she'd be expected to be a creative mom and make her child a Halloween costume. At this point she couldn't take the pressure.

Her due date came and went with no baby in sight. No cramps, no water breaking, nothing. She went four days past her due date and was ready to bust. Her worry and depression had kept her from enjoying the pregnancy and now, with the baby being late, she was at a very low point. Her doctor was going to start inducing her when she finally started labor pains on the evening of November 9th but the baby wouldn't come and she labored for 36 hours before they decided to give her a C-section, something Sonya had secretly feared all along. She cried all during her pregnancy, all during her labor and as they wheeled her into the operating room, she said to her very famous, music star husband, "I don't know if I want to live through this." The hospital staff all heard it and made note of it. Mrs. Chase Morningstar wasn't coping very well at all.

The C-section didn't go as smoothly as hoped but the exhausted baby was born screaming her lungs out and angry as can be at 11:15 am on November 11th. Quite fittingly, her little legs and arms were drawn up close to her tiny body and her face was as red as a poppy. Chase took one look at her with tears streaming down his face and decided *that* was to be her name – Poppy Celia Morningstar. Of course, he'd have to make sure Sonya agreed, but for him, whether her mother agreed or not, she introduced herself to her daddy as "Poppy" and she would always be so. As it was, her mother didn't care what she was named and said Chase could name her whatever he wanted.

Sonya's depression had not lessened since the baby's birth and, after the C-section, Sonya could not find anything to be happy about. Her incision was sore and became infected, making her incredibly sick.

While Poppy was discharged and sent home with her daddy in days, Sonya stayed in hospital longer than expected and Chase had to hire a live-in nanny for Poppy while Sonya healed physically and hopefully mentally, in the hospital.

The nanny was a girl named Luisa who was born in Switzerland and came to the US to stay with family, work as their nanny and eventually attend school. It surprised Chase that she had none of the stereotypical attributes you'd expect of a girl from Switzerland named Luisa. No blonde hair in braids. Her legs weren't long and she wasn't model material at all. She was a very plain looking girl, who didn't accentuate her features or show off any of her assets. That wasn't important to Chase, but her background was. Her schooling was in early childhood education and, although she came very highly recommended, Chase was sure managing a four-day-old baby was not what she expected.

When he handed his new born daughter over to Luisa, she didn't hesitate for a moment and dove right in. She had a good sense of how to take care of Poppy, better than he, and so he paid close attention to everything Luisa did. Chase was torn between visits to Sonya, being in the studio and being at home with Poppy. Thankfully, Luisa was very dedicated to her job as nanny and soon had the infant on a strict feeding and sleeping schedule. Chase took part in her parenting as often as he could. He fed her most of her bottles and would stare into her eyes, wondering what color they would become, what and who she would become and how much he wished her mother was there to enjoy it all.

He tried sneaking her into the hospital for a visit with Sonya but the news media caught on. It didn't take long before they were reporting that Chase Morningstar was not only married, but his wife had delivered a baby girl in a New York hospital and the mother remained there with an undisclosed illness. It was out now; he couldn't get away from it.

At the suggestion of Kyle and his publicist, and in an effort to quell speculation and take the focus from Sonya and her ill health, Chase proudly tweeted a picture of him and Poppy out through social media. His twitter account went ballistic! Poppy Celia Morningstar had made her debut in a bright red onesie with a red knitted cap on her beautiful little head, yawning a big yawn in her father's arms. Her rosebud lips were on perfect display with daddy's million watt smile gleaming as he looked upon her. The picture made every major news headline that day: "The Newest Morningstar!" New York's Daily News read. "Poppy Morningstar makes her debut!" Entertainment Tonight began with.

Gifts started arriving from everywhere. Her Uncle Charlie and Aunt Georgie sent a very large pink teddy bear and a tricycle with a huge bow. Chase broke out laughing at their gifts. He knew the tricycle had to be from Charlie. Everyone wanted to see and to celebrate the beautiful little baby girl. Everyone, that is, but her mother.

His visit to Sonya's hospital bedside with Poppy hidden under his coat did not go well at all. Her incision wound had started healing but her mind was still very unwell. Sonya became tearful and began shaking when Chase walked in with Poppy in his arms. Instead of making her feel better it made her anxious. Chase couldn't understand what had happened to his once vivacious, beautiful and loving wife. He stared at the frail, broken, frazzled woman before him and felt sick. Something had crawled inside this girl and eaten her away from the inside out. Something had made her afraid of living and he wasn't sure what it was, but it made his heart physically ache to see his beautiful wife in such a sad state. He listened and agreed with the doctors when they told him she was suffering from severe post-partum depression and needed medication and monitoring for the time being. He listened when they told him she had been speaking with suicidal ideation and talking about ridding the world of herself and the baby too. Her doctors were very disturbed by her level of depression and worried about allowing her back home with the baby until she completed weeks of intensive therapy and was put on appropriate medications.

Chase visited Sonya as often as possible, at least once a day, and even stayed overnight in her room when he was in the city. He also spoke to her over the phone periodically. She didn't seem to be improving. Although the medications seemed to stop her from being psychotic, they also put her into a very dopey state. Their conversations were generally very one sided.

Poppy was already a month old and Sonya had only seen her twice. She had never held her, fed her or had any bonding with her whatsoever. With all her worry about being exposed and Johann's threats, she came to believe that the baby was better off without her. Johann would make it impossible for her to have this life and enjoy it. She had no choice but to give it all up or Johann would force her to and she had no idea what that would mean. In the process, she gave up her sanity too.

Chase went back to writing. He wrote a song for Poppy called, "Now That You're Here." It was meant to tell her how she had opened his eyes to being responsible, being a parent.

He recorded both the video and the song in his basement with only Cooper Jack, now his closest and best friend, on the piano, all the while cradling Poppy, singing to her the soft, sweet lullaby he had written. It wasn't corny or campy; it was beautiful and touching. If the real story of his wife's mental state were known by the millions that would eventually hear the song or see the video, they'd be heart broken by the scene; Chase shirtless, in a pair of jeans, looking tired, sitting on a piano bench in front of a mike, holding baby Poppy in his arms, a clock nearby focusing for a moment on the time, 2:45 am. Poppy, dressed in red, fast asleep, happy and content. Cooper sharing the piano bench, providing the musical accompaniment.

Now that you're here,
I understand why wars have been fought,
I'd do the same for you to live the life you dream of,
the life you were meant to have.

It isn't enough to tell you,
I have to show you that I care.

And now that you're here,
I have to be the dad you deserve.
To let you know how a man should treat you,
and that I'll be always be there.

Now that you're here,
I have something to say, The love that I feel,
will grow deeper by day, it won't ever go away.
I'll always be Daddy and have no fear,
You can count on me to wipe away tears,
or brush through tangled hair.

Now that you're here,
I want you to know, daughter of mine
You're so precious to me,
Your life is what I hold dear through time,
I promise to keep you safe from all harm.

Go to sleep sweet baby girl, you're safe in my arms.
Go to sleep sweet baby girl, you're safe in my arms.

It took only once to record it and just as the final note ended, Poppy awoke from her sleep, stretched and made the sweetest little cooing noise. Chase raised his head and smiled wide into the camera. Perfect. They kept it on the recording. Both Kyle and Chase insisted that it be released as a single, no CD compilation attached. The Label agreed wholeheartedly and "Now That You're Here" was made available on iTunes, YouTube, and every other music media outlet within days of being recorded. Kyle made the incredible deal of selling 750,000 copies of the song to one of the android phone companies that had a music library. They offered it for free to their subscribers and the response was phenomenal. It became an instant hit. Chase was so incredibly sweet with his new born daughter and the release timed perfectly with the upcoming holiday season. "Now That You're Here," became the new favorite for anything to do with Christmas and, though he didn't even try, he'd brought a whole new fan base to his audience. Chase and Poppy Morningstar were the newest sensation, going viral within hours!

~

Chapter 11

Sonya, Luisa and Poppy: New Beginnings

Chase had seen to everything. Sonya was coming home! He was so excited he cleared his entire schedule because his wife was coming home! She spent nearly two months in the hospital, but her incision had healed and the doctors finally found her the correct medication. Her mind was on the mend. The fact that Luisa was so good with Poppy would be a relief for Sonya. She could relax and take her time getting used to the routine. Chase was sure that once Sonya felt competent, they'd let Luisa go and carry on as their own little family; but for now, Luisa stayed.

This was perfect for Luisa. She had grown to love the little baby girl and, with no mother figure around, the situation suited the nanny just fine. Luisa couldn't breast feed her, but longed to. Unbeknownst to Chase, she sometimes slept in the child's bedroom. She feared for the tiny little girl with no mother and she kept a close eye on her, especially in the early days. As the weeks passed, Luisa didn't worry so much about that but just loved sleeping near the baby and whenever she could, she did.

In many ways, Sonya's homecoming was bittersweet. Luisa was happy that the baby finally had her mommy, but she wanted it to be her. Chase was thrilled that Sonya was finally coming home, but was concerned about making sure Sonya's mental state could be maintained, and then there was Sonya. The medication they gave her helped her to feel less anxious, but there was a price to pay for that. She lived life in a fog. Of course, there was still the problem with Johann that hadn't gone away, but the medication helped with that too. She didn't care about much of anything when she took those pills.

While in the hospital, she hadn't spent time with Poppy, even when her mental state cleared up. She was still resistant to having Chase bring her to the hospital. She felt like all eyes were on her and she didn't trust herself to do the right thing. She wanted to get home and become Poppy's mommy in the privacy of her own home. She didn't know she had competition.

***

Johann saw the front page as he ate his morning breakfast. Her face was splashed all over it. "Mrs. Morningstar Heads Home!" with a photo of Sonya and Chase taken from a distance at some restaurant. He was furious. They even wrote her full name underneath the picture. Damn it! Now she was completely identified. He stared at the photo and knew it wasn't recent. *They mustn't have any recent shots*, he thought wisely, as he sipped his coffee, cigarette smoke circling his head. He cut into his sausage, dipped it into his egg, hungrily stuffed it into his mouth and continued reading.

She was going home after two months in hospital. Johann had let the fervor die down after the first attempt had failed. He needed to regroup and figure out another plan. It had taken him some time to find another assassin willing to do the job. It's not like he could find one in the Yellow Pages or advertise online. He didn't want to use any of his associates because it could be traced back to him; frankly he didn't want any of them to even know. Someone completely out of his circle, out of his realm, who wouldn't draw attention to him. Then, of course, he had to consider the kind of security they had around them.

As he continued to read he got angrier and angrier. She was such a stupid bitch!

***

It had taken him almost a full year to trace all of Hennie's children. A task that he figured would be easy instead grew more and more difficult as time went on. Finding the first three children was fairly easy but getting them to talk wasn't. It seemed Hennie's "public" wife knew nothing of his mistress or her two children so there was no information there.

The other woman never used Hennie's last name and neither did her children. All he knew was that there was a boy and a girl born to Hennie when he was in his late 20's. He didn't have names, dates or photos. He exhausted all resources, called in every favor given or that he could offer up and in all these months, he'd come up empty handed. All he had was Hennie's name, date of birth and some of the aliases he'd used. The file he kept everything in sat before him with a picture of Hennie in the top left hand corner of the inside cover. The man had haunted him for so many years. His name and face were so burned into his mind that he lived his life driven to uncover the truth, where Hennie was concerned.

As he sat having his morning breakfast, his eyes were attracted to the morning newspaper, something he didn't normally bother with. The headline was big news. He'd been working on the Chase Morningstar assassin case for all these months and had never met the man. He was looking at the picture of the famous music superstar, had even watched the video with him and his baby, but had never seen his wife, until now. It figured. She was gorgeous. He continued reading the article and as he began to crack the shell on the top of his second soft boiled egg, he stopped. He leaned in closer to the picture and read the print directly underneath the photo. It read, "Sonya Kellerman and Chase Morningstar having dinner earlier this year."

He cocked his head in interest, lifted his glasses and leaned in as close as he could to get a better look at the beautiful blonde sitting with the music star. He sat back staring at the picture. *Are you serious?* he thought. *It can't be possible, can it?* He grabbed his phone and called the newspaper immediately. This was ridiculous! If his instinct was right this could turn everything around.

***

When the limo pulled into the driveway, Luisa put Poppy into her bassinette in the living room, and straightened her little outfit. Luisa hoped Poppy's mother would be pleased with how Poppy looked; well fed and cared for. Luisa really was very proud of her beautiful baby charge. The child had such a sweet disposition, a very calm nature and the most interesting eyes Luisa had ever seen. Most people would call them hazel but, if you looked closely, they had grass green specks through them; and, if the child wore green, her eyes would somehow appear green as well. She was bright and alert and soaked up everything like a sponge and Luisa was completely in love with the baby girl. She was also in love with the infant's father. This she kept to herself but she loved Chase Morningstar with all of her heart and wanted nothing more than to be his wife. Except now, his wife had arrived home. Luisa straightened her buttoned up white blouse, tightened her ponytail and stood up straight. She wanted to make the best first impression she could. She drew in a deep breath and held it as the door swung open.

***

Sonya was appreciative of Chase's supportive attention to detail. Although the story leaked that she was ready to go home, no one was able to snap a photo of her. She was even taken down to the pass-through for ambulances where no paparazzi or fans could possibly go and put into the darkened limo with Chase waiting inside, surprising her, and ready to bring her home. He presented her with flowers and a beautiful gold chain with a bright red ruby hanging from it. It was

223

meant to represent Poppy but it was too deep and dark and it made Sonya think of blood. Strike #1.

Chase cuddled Sonya the whole way and couldn't stop talking about how much he was looking forward to her being home and them being a complete family, how surprised she was going to be at how smart Poppy was, and how the color of her eyes was just like his mother's and his brother's. Even though Chase had done everything to make her arrival home as comfortable as possible, his enthusiasm scared the hell out of her. Strike #2.

And then she met Luisa. Strike #3.

Right away she sensed Luisa's territorial nature. Chase might have been oblivious to the plain looking young woman, but Sonya could tell right from the start that Luisa had her claws plunged deeply into her daughter and her heart saved only for her husband. Immediately, she felt on edge. Luisa hovered nearby the entire time Sonya looked into the bassinette. As Poppy was asleep, Sonya opted not to pick her up for fear of waking her. Chase was disappointed; Luisa was disgusted. Sonya excused herself and made her way upstairs and put away some of her things. She took a look around the bedroom. *Had Luisa been in here too?* she wondered. She tried to quell her nerves. Chase had been extremely considerate and attentive coming home. *Out of guilt?* her inner self questioned. She shook off the negativity and took a deep breath. The smile she wore was completely false but she would continue to wear it as long as she could stay at home; being in the hospital was killing her.

Downstairs, Chase had brought Poppy out of her bassinette so that when Sonya came back into the room, he handed her over immediately. Sonya hesitated and made some awkward arm movements until Chase showed her how to hold Poppy properly; then he placed the baby in her arms.

Sonya's emotions were all over the place. She held her so gingerly that she stood rigid until Chase took her elbow and led them both over to the couch. Sonya gently sat down and carefully leaned back into the soft cushioning, holding the sleeping child. It was incredibly overwhelming not only for the mother but the father as well. Her senses were on overload. Sonya brought the child's head closer to her nose and took in the scent of her, as if she were making sure she was hers. Poppy smelled intoxicating. Sonya took in quite a few deep breaths of her. She had never smelled anything so incredible. She studied Poppy's little hands clutched together; her fingers were unbelievably long. A piano player! Sonya smiled to herself. Her daughter cooed and groaned slightly, pulling her face into several contortions until her perfect little lips formed a beautiful smile as she stretched and became more comfortable in her mother's arms. Sonya's eyes welled up. She looked up at Chase who was also tearing up. She smiled at him and for a moment he saw his beautiful vivacious wife again for the first time in a very long time. Poppy took that moment to awaken and cry out with another stretch. Suddenly, the smile dropped from Sonya's face and it was replaced by fear. Chase sensed it right away and stepped in, comforting Sonya.

"It's okay... it's okay. She's alright, just waking up hungry as usual. Here, Luisa will you please give Poppy her bottle? Mrs. Morningstar has had enough for now. She still needs to watch herself and take care," Chase said, as he gently took Poppy from Sonya and handed her over to Luisa.

Luisa's smile grew extra-large as she took the baby. It may have seemed normal to Chase but Sonya read more into it than that; however, she didn't want Chase thinking she was making waves already. She would bite her tongue for now but, regardless of her pills and their deadening effect on her, she still trusted her gut when it came to judging someone's character and her inner voice was screaming at her, *Get rid of her!!*

***

He had done his homework. He knew that the only way to be sure his instincts were correct was to do something very dangerous and daring. He made one more phone call before starting the ball rolling. Better he keep someone informed of his findings and intentions.

***

Sonya began adjusting to her new routine. Chase didn't allow her to overdo anything and Luisa was always annoyingly there to step right in when needed. Some days, Sonya was grateful for Luisa's help and some days not so much. Luisa watched everything Sonya did and internally scrutinized her every move. Poppy didn't feed properly when Sonya held her and Sonya couldn't burp the baby sufficiently after a feeding. Chase was always so understanding of Sonya and, when Luisa and he were alone, he assured Luisa that Sonya was getting better.

Although Luisa nodded her head slightly she wasn't thinking the same thing at all. Sonya seemed stiff with the child and Poppy didn't rest very well with her. Luisa could get that baby to sleep in a heartbeat but when her mother tried, she fussed and fretted and after much complaining, would finally fall asleep. It was as plain as day to Luisa; she was a far better mother to Poppy than Sonya was.

On an afternoon out to gather groceries for the family, Luisa was approached by a man who introduced himself as Donny Doan, a specialty photographer. When she inquired about his specialty he played it cool, stating that he did photography of any kind on commission. Luisa guessed him to be a paparazzi. He must have done extra surveillance to know who Luisa was and although security was in place, it wasn't surprising that someone had managed to follow them.

Donny Doan did not present himself as an upfront photographer and Luisa made note of the chiseled, muscular, tattooed arms, secretly recognizing that some of them had come from being in jail; Donny Doan was a convicted ex-con with a thing for Luisa and a hatred for the man she loved, Chase Morningstar.

***

Sonya had good days and bad, but as time progressed, the good days started to outweigh the bad and no one was happier than Chase. He spent his time at home for the first few weeks, writing, playing guitar, composing music for the lyrics that were flowing out of him. Apparently, having his family complete was a creative goldmine. He wrote six songs that ranged from a bluesy love note to Sonya, to a fun-filled, rip-roaring number about enjoying your friends and family and everything else but the kitchen sink. He even wrote a song about Charlie called, "Black and Blue," referencing not only his blues club but his emotions as well.

I'm right where I'm supposed to be,
Chasing and catching my dreams.
You're the reason I wanted more,
but I never understood the need to thank you, it seems.

It beats me black and blue that I don't see you every day,
And now we're worlds apart.
It beats me black and blue to know how much you cared,
Now that I know what was in your heart.

If time passes and we don't connect,
I'll raise my glass in your name.
Whether or not we are side by side,
Our blood remains the same.

You've tried to teach me less was more,
And so it was for you.
But dreams can push through anything,
And make us black and blue.
And make us black and blue...

He'd spent the entire first CD mending his heart of Georgie. He realized it was saving him loads in therapy – actually making him money! Sometimes he would think of a phrase, just one phrase, and write it down, later building an entire song around it. Just something that moved him at the time. He even came up with a silly little ditty he'd sing to Poppy when she didn't want to sleep.

All small things must go to sleep,
So that they grow strong.
If you don't, you'll flip your lid,
Kookie-nuts ding-dong!

It was really more describing him than anything, but he was usually smiling when he sang it.

Little did he know that sometimes Sonya would be watching from a dark shadow, not knowing how long her utopia would last. It had been ages since the attack with no other concerns in over a year. She started to wonder if Johann would allow her this life. Assuming he'd seen some of the pictures of Poppy, that Chase had sent out into the social media world, she wondered what he thought of his beautiful little niece. Did she soften his hard, nasty heart? Sonya prayed for that because she had fallen in love with her family all over again and just wanted things to stay the same; but that wasn't to be.

***

His phone rang early. Interesting. He looked at the number and took a very deep breath. Unknown.

One more deep breath and then, "Hello?" he asked quietly and quickly.

"I'm looking for Luke," said the voice.

"That's me, who's this?" he asked abruptly.

"I'm a businessman who would like to do business with you but not over the phone. Will you meet with me and hear my proposal?" asked the voice.

"I don't meet with people who know my name when I don't know theirs. Nuthin' personal, just a policy." He baited his hook and hoped the big fish took it.

There was a pause at first and Lucas wondered if he would hang up, but the voice quickly said, "I'm Johann."

Johann could respect a businessman who worked with names. Even in the most discreet circumstances it was important to know who you were working with. Luke had come highly recommended by an associate who Johann trusted.

The bait was working beautifully. Lucas wiggled the bloodied severed leg in front of the shark's nose hoping it would bite. His heart raced to the point where he was afraid Johann would somehow hear it. He cleared his throat.

"Okay, Yo-hannnnn," he said, stretching out the name. "Suppose you find us a nice place to meet and we'll talk," he said with confidence. Johann would sense bullshit if he wasn't careful.

Lucas knew Johann was a very smart and intuitive man. He'd been running two businesses for some time from what Lucas had found out and, from his perspective, Johann Kellerman had managed to keep very much under the radar. Perhaps because his money was laundered through a shipping business and out through the large ethnic community he was surrounded by; but more than likely because he had killed off anyone that crossed him and had never been caught. Johann knew all the tricks of the trade, all the ways to hide whatever needed to be hidden within the paperwork, money and large steel containers that were gingerly placed onto Johann's ships, never mind its hull below. His father had taught him well. All those long talks inside the prison had paid off. Hennie taught Johann all he knew about how to run the dual businesses and expected Johann to run it just as he had.

Lucas had followed all the loose threads and they all led back to Johann. Lucas knew this for sure. He also knew of a cop long ago that died at Johann's request and this could be the moment he'd been waiting for. If he could just get Johann to take a big juicy bite.

"I don't do public. I prefer we meet somewhere private but if you wish, we can meet at a restaurant I frequent. They keep a room for me," Johann said, his bravado on full display.

"That works," Lucas answered and quickly wrote down the name and address.

"7:00 pm tonight. Tell them you're there to see me." Then he hung up the phone.

Lucas tossed his phone on the bed and sat down putting his head in his hands. He thought his heart was going to go into arrest, it was beating so fast. After all these years. After all this time. He leaned over and grabbed his coat and found his other phone. Quickly he dialed the number. It was answered right away.

"Hi Mom," he said.

"Lucas!" his mother, Jenna, cried into the phone. "I wondered what you've been up to!" she said teasingly. Oh, just wait till he told her!

***

Chase's ability to create music was working on such a high speed that he had enough songs written and composed for the release of his next CD, which he called "New Beginnings." The entire CD was recorded in his basement studio with Poppy and Sonya looking on.

Little by little, Luisa wasn't required anymore. She was expecting Chase to tell her any day now that she was no longer needed but that day hadn't come yet. It confused her and irritated her because it was obvious the mother was doing better. It was obvious that it was just a matter of time before they'd want to be a family all their own, without Luisa there at all. She still slept in the child's room every now and then. Just in the very early hours of the morning and just for a bit. If she got caught there, they wouldn't like that. They'd let her go for that, she was sure, but occasionally she took the chance. Poppy was her baby, no matter what they said.

This started the creation of a plan for Luisa. A master plan. One that would require several phone calls to those in her past whom she could manipulate and one in particular who would do anything she asked. She started with a phone call to an old employer; one who had the pull to get the ball rolling. She had waited a long time for this and finally her long held silence would pay off.

For now, she would concentrate more on the housework and cooking, leaving the family of three to themselves, and being useful for the baby only when necessary. It could be great insurance, making her more of a housekeeper than a full-on nanny. All the while, in secret, she would begin to call in the rest of her favors and manipulate those she knew she could.

Just a few days later Sonya gave her an envelope from the Bureau of Consular Affairs. Her work Visa was up in five weeks and if she didn't have viable work, Luisa couldn't legally stay in the US. There was a part of her that longed for Switzerland. It was a much simpler life than what she had seen here. She'd relish showing Poppy the land she'd grown up in and loved, especially if Chase would join them.

***

"Jasmine's" was a small, unknown, East Indian restaurant, complete with an East Indian sitar player and a woman's vocal accompaniment playing in the background. All colors were cinnamon and spice, turmeric, cumin and curry. Yum. Lucas' mouth watered as he entered and the smell of curry hit his olfactory senses. He hoped for a chance to try the fare but doubted that his meeting with Johann would also include dinner. He figured when someone was hiring an assassin, he wouldn't make the meeting long enough to break bread. He figured wrong.

The room that they kept for Johann was small and intimate with a table and four chairs. Dark drapes could be drawn to envelop the room and make it even more intimate, if the mood or company called for it. Tonight, the company called for it. As Lucas sat at the table, the drapes were drawn and he realized that Johann, who sat with a freshly lit cigarette burning away, had ordered several Indian dishes and a large steaming plate of basmati rice with cloves. The smell, curry mixed with cigarette, was terribly powerful and before he knew it, Lucas was wishing the drapes were kept open.

"Please," offered Johann, "help yourself to some buttered chicken or beef vindaloo. My favorite is the prawn bhuna, but be my guest and try all three. Or, order for yourself. This is the best Indian food in the city."

Johann's demeanor shocked Lucas. It took a moment for him to regroup. He wanted to appear as legit as possible. He had never been this close or this deep into an investigation before and he really needed to keep his cool.

"I prefer to do business if you don't mind, Johann," Lucas said sternly.

"Ah, a serious businessman, I see. Very wise. Business first, then we eat."

Johann smiled, tore himself a large piece of naan bread and swept up the last of the rice and sauce on his plate with it, popping it into his mouth. It made Lucas' stomach turn. He couldn't break bread with this man.

Johann wasn't near the man Lucas expected. He had pictured him in his mind for a while and the reality was a disappointment. A drug king with ties to the Netherlands, Johann was neither blonde nor large looking at all. Sonya had Hennie's face but she and her brother must have taken after their mother in the physique. Both were small boned and thin. It looked nice on Sonya but Johann reminded Lucas of a weasel. A small, pointed-face man with greasy thin hair barely covering his scalp. The lenses of his glasses were fairly thick, circular and tinted. His shirt was colored and his pants were flared at the bottom. It was too funny. Johann was certainly stuck in the 70's except it was 2015 and he looked ridiculously out of place. Especially his heavily ring-adorned right hand that tapped, annoyingly, against the chromed handle of his cane. Lucas couldn't tell if the cane was to assist in helping or hurting. All he knew was the tapping was driving him crazy; and who ate while smoking a cigarette? In this day and age? And, what kind of a restaurant allowed it?

Regardless of his look Johann was a very powerful, very influential, weasel of a man. He'd best show him the respect he expected, despite his churning stomach. Baiting the big fish was great but catching him and reeling him in was essential.

"I'll probably take a doggy bag, thanks. Ate before I came. I don't do business *and* dinner. No disrespect," Lucas said to him, as his eyes returned to Johann's ringed hand and the cane he held.

"I'm not offended, Luke. But you'll allow me to enjoy?" Johann asked, as he spread his hand across the table full of food and then, not waiting for the answer, he carried on, trying to find a common ground between them. "I have done my fair share of dirty work. I respect your methods so far," as if to make Luke feel flattered by his approval. "I carry the cane as a reminder of a vendetta I paid off for my father many years ago.

233

The bastard got a shot into my leg but I got him right through the eye, just as my father had requested. This cane reminds me how very delicate our business is and that we must never get sloppy, wouldn't you agree?" Johann asked, as he shoved more naan and curry into his mouth.

Lucas nodded, keeping his eyes on Johann but saying nothing. Partly because he couldn't believe what Johann just confessed to him and partly because the sight of him eating was making Lucas feel ill.

"You should know that someone has already failed at this task. I find myself in the unfortunate position of needing to find someone else to do the job," he smiled, showing teeth filled with curry and rice. Lucas held onto the contents of his stomach, but barely.

"I suppose you want to know who the target is, am I correct?" Lucas nodded his head, keeping his eyes on Johann. Johann nodded back. *This Luke is a man of few words,* Johann thought. He hoped it meant Luke was competent and not stupid.

"The target is Chase Morningstar. I want him dead. And in honor of my father, I want him shot through the eye. Do you think you can reach him? Do you think you can do this?"

Lucas nodded, showing no emotion, but inside his head he was thinking *Holy shit! The shark just took a big ol' bite!*

***

Chase was just finishing up with a recording, when Sonya walked through the door holding their daughter. Poppy was an incredible mixture of Chase, Sonya and Celia. Her hands were expressive and she used them to grasp at, point at, or pull at whatever was before her. She had been chatting for a while and even though she was not yet fluent in her language, she spoke certain sentences. Sonya would laugh and swear she was speaking in another tongue and sometimes Poppy was.

One afternoon while recording, Chase motioned for his wife and daughter to come through into the studio. She grabbed the stool and rolled it over beside Chase's chair. They shared a kiss and then Chase kissed Poppy's head as she reached up and grabbed his cheek in her chubby little hand. He grabbed her arm and kissed into her hand, making gobbling sounds as she giggled and laughed with glee. The scene was perfect. Exactly where they should have been months ago.

Chase's CD, "New Beginnings," was breaking all records and "Constellations" was nominated for six Grammys. He was in high demand, but stayed away no more than a day at a time, working mostly from home with Kyle, the publicist and Lapis Labels all behind him. Life was good.

"There's something I've been meaning to talk to you about," Sonya said, as Chase and Poppy played peek-a-boo and both were in fits of laughter.

Chase looked up at his wife and held his smile. His eyebrows raised wondering what was on her mind. "I'd like to give Luisa her two weeks' notice," Sonya said, watching Chase closely for his reaction.

He held her gaze for a moment and then looked down at the baby. "I don't have a problem with that except I think we'd starve and become sloths," he joked. "We have the time on our hands because of Luisa. You've had the chance to get better *because* of Luisa. She does the mundane shit that neither of us want to do, y'know? The cooking and cleaning," he stated. "And when I can't be here, she helps out with Poppy. She's good with her."

"I know. She's good to have around. She's a huge help but maybe we can find someone else," Sonya suggested openly.

She didn't drop her gaze and Chase caught on to her meaning. He wanted to compromise with Sonya. If she was feeling threatened or anxious then he needed to accept that. He could find them another housekeeper especially if it meant that Sonya would be doing the majority of the parenting. He was waiting for her to make the suggestion, for her to be certain before he made that call, but here she was suggesting it. It may as well be done.

"Alright then. I'll talk to her tomorrow," he said, putting his arm around Sonya and drawing her close. Her smell surrounded him and once again he was taken back to the beginning, to when they first met. Only now, they had new beginnings.

***

The house had been dark for some time. He was two blocks over with a great view including the yard and the neighborhood. Although well lit, the sub division was built in a semi-circle with the back yards connecting, and none of them were well lit. Access through the security gates wasn't possible but he knew exactly how to get into the back yard and moved up through the side yards to the side of the house. If everything was in place, he should be able to get into the house fairly easily. Pulling on a pair of latex gloves he tried the garage side door and it opened easily. He silently slipped inside. He shut the door waiting to make sure no one had been alerted. No one had. He moved past the cars and tried the door leading in to the laundry room of the house. It too opened easily. He made sure that there was no sound as he closed the door and moved further into the house. It was dark but he could easily find his way through. He would silently check through the main floor before going upstairs. As he passed through the kitchen he quickly had to dodge behind a corner wall as a man came down the stairs carrying a young female child. He was saying something to her and singing something about sleeping and ding-dong.

The man carried the child to the fridge and opened it, chatting and cooing to her all the while. The light illuminated the two and the intruder could see the face of both quite clearly. He held his breath as he studied them, both very striking, both half asleep. The man retrieved a bottle and placed it in the microwave, all the while kissing and cooing the young child. She put her head on his shoulder and yawned and then reached out towards the microwave and opened and closed her hands repeatedly. The man chuckled, called her a "piggly-wiggly" and proceeded to take the bottle from the microwave, test it's temperature and offer it to the hungry child. She grabbed it from the man and started tugging at it greedily. The man laughed, nuzzled into her and carried her off up the stairs. The intruder watched as the man and child walked down to the end of the hall. He could hear the father's quiet chatter to the baby and, after a few minutes, he came out of the room and back up the hallway, stopped for a moment holding his stance in front of the middle doorway, then proceeded to the first doorway, entered the room and closed the door behind him. The intruder let his breath out slowly and relaxed his tense position. He'd need to wait until the house went quiet again before he could make his move. He returned to the living room area and had a more thorough search through the items in there. He found a small pure silver sculpture that would bring a few hundred, a gold Rolex watch on an end table and eighty-five dollars in a lady's jacket hung on a chair. Satisfied with his take, he went back towards the kitchen and stopped, surveying the staircase. He heard and saw no activity.

He hurried up the stairs and slipped into the hallway. While no one was the wiser he secretly opened the door into the first bedroom on the left. It was extremely dark. It took him a moment to adjust his eyes to the lack of light. Even so, he could see clearly that only a sole figure occupied the bed. He was expecting this to be the master bedroom but it looked like a guest room, probably smaller than the others in the house. He had watched the man enter this room and could only make out the lone body in the bed. He was told to be sure that the baby was nowhere near and to hit only the target, no one else. He could verify both things easily. He pulled out the gun with the silencer already affixed and taking quick aim, shot the figure twice in the head through another pillow. Once done, he quickly left the way he came. No alarms sounded, no one was alerted. As a matter of fact, it took another hour before the body was found and by then the intruder was long gone.

***

He's sitting on a bed, plucking away at the guitar he holds. The new speakers, purchased for his 18th birthday, sound perfect. He's concentrating on the chords he's playing, repeating them until they are natural to him. As he plays he can see smoke building around him slowly. He doesn't panic – he doesn't move except his fingers on the neck of the guitar, still repeating the chords.

Out of the smoke he sees a form walking towards him. He continues repeating the chords and the speakers get louder as the form gets nearer. He is now playing frantically, moving his head to the chords, lost in the music. The form becomes clearer... the shape of a woman appears. She is slight of frame, elderly, dressed elegantly and smiling. He looks up from where he sits on the bed and smiles at her, still continuing to play the chords.

Her lips are moving as if in slow motion but no sound comes out. He feels frustration, tenses his body and increases the intensity of his playing as he tries to watch the woman and play the chords at the same time. Her lips continue to move without sound until suddenly she leans forward and her face is all he can see – large, wide-eyed and penetrating. The speakers are now full blast.

He woke up with a start. The baby was crying. He wasn't sure if Sonya had heard Poppy's cries – she wasn't in bed. Chase could hear the baby continue to cry as though she had no one comforting her, so he got up and went to see to Poppy.

The baby met him with a wet face, a wet bum and a cheeky smile. Chase couldn't help but melt at the sleepy sight of her. He reached into the crib and grabbed his little girl up into his arms.

"What's the matter, Poppy-poo," he said, using his nickname for her. "You need a dry bum, don'tcha?" he asked her, as he moved her over to the changing table and began removing the child's wet diaper. Her chubby little legs began kicking around as the diaper came off and she felt the freedom of being naked. Chase giggled at his daughter and made quick work of disposing of the old diaper and putting a fresh one on. Once done, he put her pajamas back in order and picked her up. The baby radiated a smile to her daddy and hugged his neck, nuzzling into it.

"Bubba?" she asked her daddy.

"Are you hungry, sweetie? Do you want a bottle?" he confirmed with her. When she nodded her head, he headed out of the room. Alright then, we'll go get you a bubba," he said. He began singing his silly sleepy song for her.

All small things must go to sleep,
So that they grow strong.
If you don't, you'll flip your lid,
Kookie-nuts ding-dong!

She giggled and said "Gen!"

"Again?" asked Chase. "Okay, again."

He sang the song again as he made his way down the stairs and into the kitchen. The fridge light blinded them both and they blinked and squinted at its brightness. Chase reached for a ready-made bottle and put it into the microwave to warm. His hungry anxious baby snuggled into him again and yawned, reaching for the bottle. Chase rubbed her back, smiling to himself, wondering how on earth he ever made it through a day without all the extra love she showed to him. Poppy was extremely loving and her daddy was her number one man.

When the microwave finished, he removed the bottle, made sure it wouldn't burn her and gave it to her and took her back to her bed. He placed her back in her crib and helped her lay down with her blanket and bottle. He rubbed her back and stayed a little longer with her watching as her eyes grew heavy even while sucking hungrily on the bottle. He gave her little arm a loving rub and quietly left the room. Heading down the hallway he stopped to enter the bedroom and remembered that Sonya was not in bed beside him. He wondered where she was and, before getting back into bed, he went to the guest room to check and see if she'd crept in there. He walked into the room and could see her in the bed. He sat on the edge and she awoke slowly and rolled over to turn on the night stand light.

"Hey," Chase said, to his beautiful wife, rubbing her leg.

"Hey, sorry hon. I couldn't sleep," she said, while stretching.

"Was I snoring?" he asked. It was a problem. "Sorry."

"Yeah, 'fraid so. Poppy woke up?" she asked him.

"Yeah. She was wet and hungry. We should have named her that," he joked. They shared the laugh. "Are you coming back to bed?" he asked her.

"No, you go ahead. I'll be up in a bit anyway and you're a buzz saw tonight. I think I need ear plugs," she said seriously.

"Okay, we'll get you some. I'm sure there are some here around the house somewhere but if not, I'll get Luisa to pick some up the next time she grocery shops. Get back to sleep. I love you," he said, as he got up, kissed her head, turned the light out and left the room.

As he entered the master bedroom he had a strange sensation and stood stock still to listen to the sounds in the house. Was he hearing things? He waited again and listened for every hum and creak he could make out. Nothing but the normal house sounds. He had an uneasy feeling and poked his head down the hallway and looked down the stairs but the house was quiet and empty. He turned and closed his bedroom door, climbed back into bed and hoped he could get back to sleep. He could. Again the dream started.

He's sitting on a bed, plucking away at the guitar he holds. The new speakers, purchased for his 18ᵗʰ birthday, sound perfect. He's concentrating on the chords he's playing, repeating them until they are natural to him. As he plays he can see smoke building around him slowly. He doesn't panic – he doesn't move except his fingers on the neck of the guitar, still repeating the chords.

Out of the smoke he sees a form walking towards him. He continues repeating the chords and the speakers get louder as the form gets nearer. He is now playing frantically, moving his head to the chords, lost in the music. The form becomes clearer... the shape of a woman appears. She is slight of frame, elderly, dressed elegantly and smiling. He looks up from where he sits on the bed and smiles at her, still continuing to play the chords.

Her lips are moving as if in slow motion but no sound comes out. He feels frustration, tenses his body and increases the intensity of his playing as he tries to watch the woman and play the chords at the same time. Her lips continue to move without sound until suddenly she leans forward and her face is all he can see – large, wide-eyed and penetrating. The speakers are now full blast. As the noise builds to a deafening crescendo she takes an obvious deep breath.

"Wake Up!" she shouts above the din, her eyes as large as saucers.

He jolted up again in bed. His heart was pounding in his chest and he waited a moment, allowing himself to calm. He looked at the clock; it read 7:23 am. Luisa, Poppy and Sonya should be up already and in the kitchen having breakfast. He could smell the brewed coffee and got himself dressed in track pants and a t-shirt before heading down to have breakfast with his family. He found only Luisa and Poppy in the kitchen.

"Good morning ladies," he greeted them, as he kissed the soft, blonde, curly head of his baby girl and smiled at Luisa. He then grabbed a coffee cup and began to pour himself a full hot cup.

"Sonya not up yet?" he asked Luisa. She shook her head in the negative and continued working away on her laptop while eating some toast.

"Huh… maybe I should try sleeping in the guest room. She seems to get a better sleep in there than in the bed in our room," Chase said to Poppy and Luisa. Poppy just smiled at her funny daddy.

Luisa raised her head for a moment and smiled at him. "I thought it was because of your snoring that she can't sleep beside you. It's nothing to do with the room, it's YOU," she said, laughing.

He smiled at her and nodded his head. "You got a point there, Luisa. She could probably sleep anywhere as long as I wasn't beside her," he laughed again.

He grabbed another coffee cup, poured it full and carried it upstairs into the guest room, feeling slightly guilty. The minute he opened the door he knew something wasn't right. The door was closed and there was a heady smell in the room. He came around to the side of the bed and put the coffee cup on the bedside table and turned on the light. At first, it didn't register fully with him. He couldn't tell what he was looking at.

"Sonya?" he asked her, touching her shoulder. She was cold. He looked more closely at the scene before him and could see a dark red mass behind her head and continuing down the pillow, bed sheets and the rest of the bed. He flew backwards with his mouth wide open, unable to speak. How could this be? He saw her just an hour ago – even spoke to her. He flew to the door of the room and ran down the stairs. Luisa looked up as he came running through the kitchen looking frantically around the room. He was breathing heavily and was white as a ghost.

"Where's my phone? WHERE'S MY PHONE?!" He screamed. "I put it with my watch. Where the fuck…" he stopped as he spotted his phone on the end table and grabbed it dialing 911.

Within minutes the house was full of cops and the street full of cop cars. Chase sat in the living room with Luisa and Poppy sitting next to him. The young housekeeper was quietly crying as she tried desperately to keep the child happy and unaware of the fact that her mother had been murdered upstairs in the guest room. Chase seemed as if he were in shock, his eyes red, wet and swollen. He couldn't get the sight of Sonya out of his mind. He now realized that he had seen her head blown through, with blood soaking the entire pillow and area. It was the kind of thing that you never forgot, like seeing his mother fall through the burning floor of his childhood home; it never left him.

His phone, now cradled in his left limp hand, rang. It was Kyle. Chase hadn't thought of calling Kyle as yet, he was too busy trying to figure out what the hell had happened. Kyle was not aware of the situation within the household. Kyle was only aware of the broken records in sales numbers that "New Beginnings" had achieved. He called with the great news.

"Mr. Superstar!" he called into the phone. "How does it feel to have the fastest selling CD in history? Eh, buddy? It's surpassed a million; probably well into three million sales by the end of today," he gushed.

It seemed that the more the arc of Chase's professional life went up, the more his personal life went in the polar opposite direction.

***

Once again the police were asking questions about the dead body in Chase's home. Once again Chase went over and over the details to the detectives working on the case as the forensic photographer snapped hundreds of pictures of the crime scene upstairs. Only this time, the dead body was his beautiful wife and there was no claim of self defense. It was murder. The police listened intently as Chase described the events of the night and very early morning, recounting going to see Sonya in the guest bedroom before heading back to bed. He realized that his last words to her were, "I love you." He was glad he'd said it. It was true. He loved her with all his heart and soul and now she was gone.

After months of Sonya's post-partum depression turning their joy into some really hard times, they were just starting to get back into some sense of normalcy. He was just about to let Luisa go. He would have given her two weeks' pay plus vacation and sent her on her way. Now he couldn't imagine her leaving as he stared absentmindedly at his young baby daughter sitting in Luisa's lap. She'd become a godsend at this time. He wouldn't know what he'd do without her.

After many hours of interviews and statements, the police removed Sonya's body from the house. Luisa and Chase stood in the living room as they carried the gurney down the stairs and out the door; the body wrapped in a white body bag. Luisa broke down crying and had to hand Poppy over to Chase as she ran from the room. He looked at Poppy in his arms and tried to raise a smile, then looked back to where Luisa ran off to. *Poor kid, she sure didn't sign up for this! I'll have to make sure she's not traumatized by this. I'll have to make it up to her,* Chase thought.

***

"You stupid FUCK!" Johann screamed into the phone. It was another early morning call from him and Lucas was barely awake. This guy had a lot of nerve.

"Good morning to you too, Johann," Lucas said nonchalantly. Johann nearly broke his eardrum.

"Do you know what you've done!? You fuckin' fool, you've killed the wrong person!" he yelled so hard into the phone it made Lucas' phone vibrate.

Lucas was confused with what he was saying. "Wait… what? What do you mean I killed the wrong person? I haven't…" but Lucas was cut off by Johann.

"I told you it was *him* I wanted out of the picture you idiot. What the hell happened?" he demanded, but Lucas had no idea what he was talking about. He hadn't listened to the news yet.

"Who are you talking about Johann? Who's dead?" Lucas asked, fearful of the answer.

"Sonya, my fuckin' sister," he barked. "You killed my fuckin' sister and when I track you down, I'm gonna kill you, do you hear me?!"

"I haven't done anything, Johann. I wasn't going to do it until tomorrow night," he admitted.

There was a long pause on the other end of the phone. Lucas could hear Johann's anguished breathing as he took in what he had said. He jumped up and grabbed the remote and turned on the TV to CNN. Anderson Cooper was delivering Breaking News: Chase Morningstar's wife had been murdered in their home very early this morning. *SHIT!* She'd been shot in the head as she lay sleeping in her bed. Lucas froze when he read the CNN banner. His hand pulled on his mouth as he stared at the TV and waited for Johann to speak.

"What are you sayin' to me?" Johann finally asked.

"I'm saying it wasn't me," Lucas said calmly. "Whoever killed your sister, it wasn't me. I had it planned for Friday. I'm outta state right now – been here for two days. I wasn't anywhere near their house." It was true. He'd flown home for a few days before coming back to finish the job.

"You need to watch your back, my friend. I'm not sure I believe your story," Johann said threateningly.

"Johann, listen to me. This is someone else's fuck up, not mine. Obviously, someone else has it out for him too," he said, hoping it would turn Johann's attention away from blaming him.

Again, his statement was met with silence. Then suddenly, "Find out who and do it quick!" he demanded harshly and hung up the phone.

***

Even bad publicity is good publicity. Exactly. This fact was indeed true with Chase Morningstar. The headlines, be they good or bad, sent his record sales through the roof every time! This time however, the whole world mourned with him. He received sympathies and condolences from people clear across the entertainment and celebrity spectrum. Even those in politics that enjoyed his music sent flowers and cards. His twitter account erupted and there were more #sympathies used than ever before.

Sonya's funeral was attended by many who knew Chase, including Georgie and Charlie who flew in as soon as they heard the news. The brothers hadn't seen one another in more than two years and so much had changed since then.

At the airport they embraced for a long while; Charlie hoping to heal his brother's broken heart. *It didn't seem fair. Chase had seen too much tragedy in his life. More than the average person deserves,* Charlie thought, as he held onto him. It brought Chase to tears and just about everyone around them. Georgie, standing in the background holding onto Poppy and watching the brothers she'd known for most of her life face tragedy yet again, was having a hard time holding onto her own emotions. It was too much seeing Charlie cry for Chase, who sobbed. The paparazzi snapped a few pictures and it made news for three nights. All the while, Chase's records were selling through the roof.

Chase, Charlie, Georgie, Poppy, Kyle, Cooper Jack and Campbell all sat in the front row for the United Church service. The rest of the Supernova members sat in the row behind. With no family coming forward, Chase didn't know what Sonya would have believed in but wanted some sort of God to wish her home. He did try contacting Sonya's family and had no luck. The name and address she had given for her brother was outdated and Chase had nothing else in the house that identified him. He couldn't even find anything on the business she ran. Nothing. It confused him.

Lost in the sea of attendees at the service was Luisa. Teary and sad, she was comforted by those close who knew she was the nanny/housekeeper. There weren't many. After running from the room crying that day, she did her best to be there for Chase and Poppy. Right now, he was surrounded by his family and they could take care of him but after they left it would fall to her, she hoped.

Charlie and Georgie stayed for a few weeks and helped Chase deal with some of the shock and recovery. They insisted he have extra security installed in the house and once the police were finished with the room, Georgie called in a cleanup company who did just that. The room was stripped down of everything including the carpet and replaced with all new carpet, mattress, linens and pillows. Chase never entered the room again; no matter how the room changed, he couldn't face going in.

He enjoyed having Charlie and Georgie around and loved showing them how magnificent his beautiful daughter was. Poppy was a very bright light at a very sad time and she was extremely entertaining to the three adults and nanny who were now safe and secure inside the house.

The police determined, after several interviews of both he and Luisa, that there was an intruder who had been in the house for some time on the night of the murder; that he/she had entered through an unlocked garage door. Chase wasn't sure if he had locked it or not. He admitted that he'd become complacent recently. No security cameras were on that night which Chase found strange and couldn't explain. All security ran through a main computer application which he believed was up and running. They took his laptop but found nothing out of the ordinary. The neighborhood was so secure; how could anyone get past the gated security whose security cameras showed no one passing through?

A search of the house found no match to the weapon used. Forensics reported that the bullet was probably shot through a Berretta 92FS and the fact that neither Chase, Luisa nor Poppy heard the gun shot, meant it was more than likely outfitted with a silencer.

They tested Chase, Luisa and Poppy's clothing from that night and found nothing. No traces of blood or gunpowder residue. They did find Sonya's hair on Chase's pajama bottoms but it, too, was without any residue or blood.

The information provided led the police to believe it was another foiled attempt by Hennie's people. Chase was definitely targeted, they figured, which put his daughter at risk now, too. They were on it, they assured him!

As Georgie and Charlie were leaving to return to Chicago, Chase embraced Georgie and thanked her.

"You've been awesome, Georgie. My daughter loves you and I love you. You're good for Charlie; he's become more relaxed with you in his life. I'm grateful for that," he admitted.

"You don't have to thank me, Chase. We're family. I love you too. I always have. I promised your mother many years ago when I babysat you to take very good care of you regardless of your size or age. I'll always keep that promise," she said with assurance. She smiled at him.

She was still such an attractive woman with her dark chocolate eyes and her dark hair, but his feelings had changed now and Georgie truly felt like family to him, like a sister. Nice to have another family member that knew the early years, that shared the same memories of his incredibly talented family.

Charlie hugged him and told him to stay strong. "We are just a call away and Marlon and Rosa will take care of anything if you need us back here. Don't be afraid to ask, okay? You've got your hands pretty full," he said, pointing over to Poppy who was in Luisa's arms, smiling and sucking on three chubby long fingers.

"Her eyes are mom's, you know that right?" Charlie said, studying her little face. Chase nodded in agreement. They embraced once more.

Charlie kissed Poppy's head and said, "Be good for daddy and Luisa." Poppy reached out to her uncle and put a sticky wet hand on his shoulder. "Take care and thanks for your help," he said to Luisa directly. She nodded back in reply and rocked Poppy on one hip.

Georgie and Charlie walked away to board their flight, both taking a moment to look back, not realizing that the next time they would see one another again would be a completely different setting all together.

***

It had been a few months since Sonya's murder. The police were still no closer to finding her killer and for a while their focus was on someone from within who would have unlocked all the doors and stopped the alarm. They questioned Chase thoroughly and Kyle got him the same lawyer that represented him when he killed the first intruder. Her name was Dana Rose. She was an incredible lawyer; went straight for the jugular and had the police at bay in no time but, she didn't like Chase and he knew it. That didn't bother him. She didn't have to like him, she only had to represent him and, for what she got paid, she did her job very well.

The investigation into Chase came up empty handed and he was crossed off the list. They then focused their investigation on Luisa. They were really interested in her and even checked into her family in Switzerland. She'd started in the U.S. as a nanny for four years to a family member on her mother's side. They had two children. She attended school here and looked after the children for four years. When they no longer needed her services, she was recommended to another family and then another after that before landing the job as Poppy's nanny. Luisa was also questioned at great length but she wasn't a wealth of information; her story was she was asleep and heard nothing.

The police soon turned their attention back to a connection to Hennie and the possibility that someone under his hire was out there gunning for Campbell or his family. Chase had security tightened and double checked the doors every night. *A little late,* he would think as he made sure each bolt was turned, each chain in place. *A little too late, indeed.* Each time he checked them, it made his heart ache for his wife who paid the ultimate price for his complacency. How would he ever forgive himself?

It was the sound of Luisa softly crying that alerted him at first. He had been wrapped up in all the details of Sonya's death and had put other things on the backburner. When he had a moment alone in the house, he heard her crying. He remembered thinking he would need to make sure she was doing okay and feeling badly for the circumstances she was unlucky enough to find herself in so, with that in mind, Chase knocked on Luisa's bedroom door one night.

"Luisa, can I talk to you for a minute?" he asked, knocking again gently. "I'm just wondering if you're okay. I can hear..." the door opened abruptly. Luisa's sad face was looking at him, tears staining her cheeks.

"What's going on, honey?" Chase asked, suddenly very concerned for her. She looked awful and he felt extremely guilty for what she'd experienced because of him.

She turned and walked back in her room and Chase reluctantly followed. She slumped down on the bed, cast her head downwards and reached to her left on the bed, to a white piece of paper with an envelope underneath. She said nothing, just held them both out to Chase who questioned what she was holding out to him. He finally took the paper and turned it so that he could see what was written on it. It was from the Department of Immigration, Work Visas and Travel Visas.

This is to inform you that you are asked to report to the Offices of Deportation to determine your request for an extension of your work visa. Please be prepared to prove viable employment for the requested visa extension period.

If it is determined that your work visa cannot be extended you will be deported to your home country with 48 hours.

If you have any questions or concerns, please contact the administrator with your file number.

Shit! He looked at Luisa whose sad, weepy eyes told him that she had been carrying this around for some time. Really? He couldn't believe this! How could he lose her now? Poppy had lost enough – had been through enough. Chase couldn't have this happen now.

"What can we do, do you know?" he asked her, in disbelief.

She shook her head; she didn't know. His mind reeled. He was shocked and felt overwhelmed at it all. Without thinking, he sat down on the bed next to Luisa as they both stared down at the floor.

"If you can prove viable employment for the next while, you can stay, as I read it. I'll have Kyle look this over and make sure we know the ins and outs first, but if it's just a matter of employment, hell, I can guarantee you that!" Chase said, thinking this might be an easy fix.

He put his arm around the sullen young woman and comforted her. She was ecstatic at his touch.

***

The court date for the extension to Luisa's work visa came. She attended with all the legal papers she needed signed by Chase, Kyle, Lapis Labels and several others who had written on the young woman's behalf. Regardless, the judge deported her and told her she needed to be on a plane in 48 hours.

When she returned to tell Chase, he was in disbelief. His call to Kyle who informed him that the recent security measures through Homeland Security and the fact that she had changed employers numerous times, more than was allowed, meant that they threw the book at her. Although Luisa didn't fit any racial profile, she had, for some reason, raised a flag to the judge who sat on the bench that day.

"She'd have to be married or have a child by an American. That's the only way they'd allow her to stay," Kyle told Chase, after the hearing. "Beyond that, she's going home," he said nonchalantly.

This wasn't so nonchalant to Chase. It essentially meant losing the next best thing to her mother that Poppy had and Chase knew it. The loss of both women within such a short period of time would be unbearable. He thought of his own mother and how she did all she could for him while she was alive. She encouraged him, she inspired him and she supported him. She died too young but gave him so much in such a short time. He wanted Poppy to feel that way. As though she had a mother and father who loved and cherished her. He wanted her to know that he would do whatever was in her best interest. Chase believed that keeping Luisa around was in Poppy's best interest and so, within 48 hours of her deportation hearing, four months after his wife's murder and for the second time in his life, Chase flew in secret to Las Vegas to marry again, this time to Luisa. It was simply a formality; the only chance Chase had of keeping her in the U.S. Once again, no pictures were taken, confidentiality forms were signed by all in attendance and no one was the wiser. When they kissed to seal the deal, it was on the cheek. Chase wouldn't kiss her on the lips. This hurt her but she didn't let it show. She needed to be patient. Chase had been through such a terrible ordeal. She knew that, given time, he'd come around. She made her phone call just as she had planned and after the conversation ended she felt confident that things would go her way. They always did.

When her court date arrived and she stood before the judge with her marriage documentation and Chase's representative from Lapis Labels, the judge not only approved the work visa but pushed forward her application to become an American citizen. She thanked the judge respectfully and left the court room smiling. She may be Mrs. Chase Morningstar in name only but now she really carried weight! Her investments had certainly paid off!

When she arrived home she collected the mail. Usually it contained household utilities or junk mail. Today, however, there was a hand written envelope with an obvious card inside. This intrigued Luisa. It had been many weeks since Chase had received condolences or cards of sympathy. Normally, fan mail was filtered through the administration of Lapis Labels so Luisa was very interested in what the hand written envelope contained.

She strategically placed the envelope on top of the mail pile so that Chase would see it first and went on busying herself with dinner preparations. Since Sonya's death, Luisa had inserted herself quite nicely as the woman of the household. She took care of Chase's and Poppy's needs quietly and efficiently, and gave Chase the time he needed to regroup.

Chase usually spent his time in his studio, writing, jamming or sometimes just holding Poppy and listening to his music. His writing increased with Sonya's death but he didn't believe any of the songs would make it onto a CD. He just felt that he needed to write his emotions out and he did.

When he came upstairs from the studio carrying Poppy, it made Luisa stop and take a breath. The two people she secretly loved most and now she was legally a part of their world, even if it was a secret. Even if he didn't really love her, she still had him all to herself and that was exactly what she had hoped for.

Chase briefly smiled at her and placed Poppy in her high chair. He strapped her in and then went to the fridge to get both of them something to eat.

"Everything work out at the court house?" he asked, without even looking at her.

"Yes. My work visa was extended and the judge even pushed through my citizenship request," she answered, pleased with the outcome.

Chase's head snapped around quickly. "What? How'd that happen? What have you got, pictures to blackmail with or something? I've never heard of anyone going from nearly deported to having their application for citizenship pushed through that quickly before," he said.

"Yes, well, I suppose when you marry a famous music star, you get all sorts of perks," she smiled at him sweetly.

Chase smiled back briefly. His heart wasn't in the marriage, it was simply for practicality. At this point, Chase doubted he'd ever feel like marrying anyone again, especially out of love. His heart was shattered by Sonya's murder and he was quite willing to lose himself in his next musical project and keep Poppy safe. Those were his priorities.

Noticing his lack of enthusiasm, Luisa drew his attention to the mail sitting on the counter. He walked over and leafed through it quickly before coming back to the hand written envelope on top.

"Hmmm…" he said to no one. He grabbed a butter knife from the drawer and used it to open the envelope. He pulled out a card with a large floral bouquet on the front. No words at all, just the bouquet, filled with Poppies. Chase opened it up and his heart froze for a moment.

"The baby is next," was all that was written.

Luisa watched him closely. She heard him gasp when he opened the card. She knew it couldn't be good. Chase had become pale.

"I think I need to give this to the police," he said, as he reached for his phone.

"Why?" Luisa asked. "What does it say?"

"That Poppy is next," he told her, his anger starting to boil. "Like *hell* she is!"

He turned his attention to whoever it was that he called and walked away explaining what he had received. Luisa stood for a moment watching him, calculating his moves. What could this mean? Would they have to get further security? Luisa made Poppy something to eat and then proceeded to make lunch for her and Chase. As he returned to the kitchen area, he was just getting off the phone.

"That was the detective working on the case," he said to her. "He's gonna drop by and pick this up for forensics to go over it. Don't touch this anymore in case your DNA gets on it, okay? They're hoping to be able to pull something from it," he explained. Luisa nodded and said nothing.

He called Kyle next and asked him to come over as soon as possible. Within 15 minutes, Kyle was standing in the kitchen.

"I don't think Poppy is safe here, man," said Chase. "I need to get her somewhere safe. I want you to find me a place where she can be safe and they can't touch her, can't get to her," he told Kyle, showing him the card but not allowing him to touch it. He was terrified that whoever it was had the means to kill again and it was only a matter of time.

"Do you have a plan?" Kyle asked. He already knew the answer. Chase always had a plan.

"You're fuckin' right I do, but I'm gonna need Lapis Labels to back me on this and I'm gonna need to make sure everything is completely underground. No one can know, right?" Chase stated. He needed his music life to be fully public but his private life to be on lockdown.

"What are you thinkin', my friend?" Kyle asked.

He had no idea what Chase was about to say, nor could he. It had been brewing in Chase's mind for a couple of days now. The "Plan B" he never wanted to set in motion, but would if things got dire enough. The card arriving at his home address threatening the life of his child after his wife's murder raised the "dire" to new levels.

"I want to move to Switzerland with Luisa and Poppy," he said firmly.

Luisa's head snapped up as she was quietly feeding Poppy in the background while eating her own sandwich. Sometimes, she just blended into the scenery.

"You want to live in Switzerland?" Kyle said incredulously. "How's that gonna work? You expect Supernova to all uproot and join you?" He was not good at hiding his dislike of the idea.

"No, it isn't a permanent thing for me. I'll go with Poppy and Luisa to get a place and get them settled and then I'll return and work on my music for a bit and fly back when I can," he explained to Kyle.

Luisa dropped her head and continued eating her sandwich.

"Look, Kyle, I've just been through a shitload of hurt and tragedy here. Now this asshole is threatening my kid! I can't have that. Before I can get back to work and be my creative self I have to know she's safe and she isn't safe here," he emphasized the point. "Now, I've already lost the one person I thought I'd spend the rest of my life with. Are you gonna stand in my way while I try to make sure that the other person who means the world to me is secure?"

When put into a question like that, Kyle knew he had to support Chase's idea. He'd have one hell of a time making the executives and stakeholders understand, but then they were all lining their pockets on the blood and sweat of this guy; surely they'd allow him some grace from his recent tragedy, which continued to bring in boatloads of money to those fat cats.

"I can see your point and believe me, I'm with you on this. But, why Switzerland? Why not somewhere closer?" Kyle asked him.

Luisa knew the answer. Luisa knew what Chase was thinking and she cleverly kept her head down. Ever quiet, ever listening.

"Because it's where Luisa is from, but no one knows her or that we've married. Regardless of the reason, I can leave Poppy with her, feeling good knowing Luisa isn't at a disadvantage there like she is here. She knows the place and can fit in with the culture. She can give Poppy the life I can't, now that I'm famous. I've been thinking about this a lot, Kyle, and I don't want my daughter around anymore harsh negativity. I think she deserves a good simple life until she's old enough to make sense of what I do. And frankly, her life is in danger here." Kyle nodded his understanding.

"Whaddaya say, Luisa? I know we've just gone through all this maneuvering to get you to stay here but, what say you take me and Poppy home with you, show us your world for a while? I'll make sure you have all of your needs met. A great house, money for anything you want." He waited a moment, trying to gauge her answer. "Are you willing to move back to Switzerland and raise Poppy there? I'll come back for extended visits – I mean, it's gonna kill me not having her around here every day but the worry of her safety is so distracting. At least I know she'll be safe there."

Chase worried that Luisa's last want in the world was to return to Switzerland, especially if she was enjoying the American way of living.

He also hoped that by setting her up financially, her new lifestyle in Switzerland would appeal to her more. It would certainly be an easy ride for her.

Luisa played her emotions very close. She didn't want to come across too eager or indifferent. She waited for a moment making them think she was weighing the pros and cons. She then broke into a weak smile and nodded her head in the affirmative.

Chase slapped his hands together and let out an enthusiastic "Yes!" He quickly side-hugged Luisa, very non-affectionately, but it made her smile from ear to ear. Something Kyle noticed.

"God, I feel so relieved. I promise you, Luisa, you won't regret this," he said to her. Her smile grew wider with Chase's promise and his attention.

But you may! Kyle thought wisely to himself.

~

Chapter 12

Campbell This and Campbell That

Since entering into the rehabilitation home for recovery of his concussion, Campbell's progression back to normal cognitive health had been slow. The long weeks of ringing in his ears drove him mad. His memory was all jumbled up and he now suffered migraine headaches. Add to that the constant dizziness and his inability to find the right word sometimes, and it made him feel very vulnerable. Campbell wasn't able to be left alone for more than short periods of time.

It took him a while to settle in, not being your average 70-odd year old man. He was antsy. There were many in the home who were never going to leave and Campbell could see that. He didn't want to be one of them but, apart from doing his best at memory games, Campbell couldn't exercise his brain like a knee or a hip.

Inside the gymnasium was an old piano. It intrigued Campbell and he often hovered near it and would run his fingers lightly across the keys, in fact so lightly that they wouldn't make a sound. His brain couldn't take it. He hoped one day he'd be well enough to play it and make it sing, but for now, it was something he missed greatly and remembered fondly.

For the first few weeks, Campbell felt depressed about his situation. Visits from Chase helped and at times he'd bring Sonya with him. At first this pleased Campbell, but after a visit from a longtime friend, Campbell didn't trust the beautiful blonde and started feeling concerned about her, although at times he'd be confused and couldn't remember why.

Then one day, Chase showed up carrying a bundle with him. When Campbell looked inside the blankets he saw a beautiful green-eyed baby. The same eyes he remembered from very long ago belonging to a woman named Celia. She was enchanting! He loved the baby called Poppy. He loved her so much. She had the fingers of a great piano player and Campbell was suddenly very keen to get her in front of a piano but he needed to wait until she was older. That was fine; he wasn't ready just yet either but with every visit, Campbell would observe the child closely, looking for the sign.

One day, when Chase, Sonya and Poppy were visiting, Campbell was feeling particularly good and lit up when he saw the baby. He watched her with fascination and then interrupted Chase, completely distracted.

"Will you follow me?" he asked.

Chase stopped mid-sentence and stared at his father. Campbell's eyes were bright and excited. It was the first time in a long time that Chase saw some life in those eyes. He'd follow him to China if Campbell asked him to, if it helped to bring back the Campbell he remembered. He nodded his head affirmative and followed Campbell through the rehab facility until he came into the door marked "Gymnasium." Campbell threw on the lights to expose a 10 x 20 foot room with a piano in the far corner. He walked over to it and sat down at the bench lifting the wooden hinged cover and exposing the ebony and ivory keys. As if summoning an inner spirit, he took a deep breath and sank his fingers into the keys. His body became electric and covered in goose bumps; tears filled his eyes as he closed them and raised his head towards the ceiling. He imagined playing before an audience at Carnegie Hall. He played the hell out of a few classical pieces and then segued into a bluesy piece and then a whole improvisational piece, proving that he'd got his groove back! He impressed himself frankly, but mostly he wanted to impress Poppy and it worked. She watched him closely and didn't take her eyes off his fingers on the keys.

As Chase stood holding his daughter with his wife by his side, his father played the hell out of that old piano. Concussion be damned, Campbell was going to be fine! It may have slowed him down, but it didn't stop him in any way. When he finished his first impromptu show in many months he reached out for his granddaughter who was placed in his lap. She immediately stretched her long fingers out to reach the keys, instinctively using both hands and placing each finger on separate keys. Both her father and grandfather knew in that moment they were witness to the birth of a great and true gift; a calling being born. Pure discovery. Poppy took to those keys like they were her play toys and she understood their notes and tones without being taught. After all, Poppy Morningstar was the great-granddaughter and granddaughter of two excellent pianists. She came about her talents naturally, inherently. Her interest in those keys awakened something in Campbell that day that had been asleep for months. His progress increased from that day forward, but then, so did something else.

***

For years Campbell had been a single man. After his years as a traveling piano man and subsequent escape from Hennie's reach, Campbell hadn't really found himself a woman to love. His life was spent so hidden that he felt it wasn't right to ask a woman to live like that, nor did he trust a woman to know the truth, keep his secret and love him unconditionally. He'd had girlfriends briefly, maybe saw the same woman a few times over, but never any commitment; never allowing himself to daydream about a life with someone. He'd only allowed himself to indulge in that once and he never forgot it; once so many nights ago...

On the day that Campbell introduced Poppy to the piano, Campbell also introduced Poppy to Donna McIntyre. She was a platinum blonde in the rehab centre for a few months while she recovered from her double hip replacement. She was a spitfire! She spoke openly, had her own opinions and called a spade a spade. She also had a wonderful singing voice and Campbell couldn't take his eyes off of her from the moment they met. So, when Chase came by for a visit with Poppy in tow, Campbell made sure the two were introduced. As usual, Poppy didn't disappoint.

"Ba ba brrrrr," Poppy spouted, and her audience laughed at her antics which led her into even more rubbish words and sputterings.

"She's definitely my granddaughter," quipped Campbell, and all had a good laugh at that one. Donna paid close attention. Just because she had worn out her hips didn't mean her mind wasn't as sharp as a tack and her sense of style and of self was top notch. It didn't matter if it was bingo night or movie night, she always dressed with finesse. Donna was quite the fashionista! Probably because she was built like a sixteen year old. Her frame was small and her figure hourglass and firm. Donna was a power walking, yoga and Pilates enthusiast and had been so for more than 20 years. It had paid off; she really looked fabulous but it had worn down her poor brittle hips and she'd been in surgery to have both replaced when Campbell had been in the centre for a few months.

Her sense of style was the first thing Campbell noticed, although if she wore too vibrant a color, he couldn't stay around her very long in those earlier days of his recovery.

As time wore on, Campbell's ability to tolerate his environment began to improve. His doctors were reluctant to say he'd be back in the studio any time soon but felt that he'd be back leading a normal functioning life in no time. The truth was, now that Campbell had met Donna, he didn't want to leave the rehab centre. He knew she'd be a few months behind him and was reluctant to leave the facility without letting her know how he felt. Campbell was in love and he knew it. He only hoped he didn't blow it with Donna and once again lose the chance at having such a unique and fantastic woman in his life. If only he didn't have someone who was out to kill him.

***

Kyle was in the middle of a fun sexual encounter when the call came in. He wouldn't have taken it except he was hoping to hear from this particular person days ago, so the call was important enough to take.

"Make it quick," he answered, out of breath. His face registered an "I'm sorry" to the girl beneath him but his attention was totally on the call, regardless of his circumstance.

"Call everyone together. We should gather at Campbell's," Kyle's investigator said, showing consideration for the elderly man.

"I'll arrange it right away," Kyle said, as the call disconnected. He took a moment to digest the instructions from the caller and then proceeded to thrust into the lusty and busty brunette beneath him. Quickly, the other head took over and he was exploding into nirvana. Life was good for Kyle.

***

Campbell sat at the table wondering who all the places were set for. He'd been informed that Kyle reserved the center's private room for a dinner for eight attendees. The group would make a large donation to the center if they provided secrecy, confidentiality and dinner. No alcoholic beverages were necessary or allowed.

Chase walked into the room alone. He smiled seeing Campbell already seated at the table.

"Hey! You look great. How are ya feelin'?" he asked Campbell, giving him a strong hug.

Campbell broke into a huge smile. "I'm doing much better, son," he said affectionately. Since Sonya's funeral, Campbell had been very concerned about Chase and the baby. "More importantly, how are you doing?" Campbell asked him.

"I'm okay," Chase said, nodding his head. "I've… uh… taken some steps to ensure that no one ever gets near Poppy and I'll… uh… tell you about them after this meeting." Campbell cocked his head in question, but Chase just smiled and continued on. "You look like you're doing great, like the spark has come back to you," Chase said honestly.

Campbell couldn't help but break into a full blown ear-to-ear grin, making his son follow suit. Before one could explain to the other, Kyle and Paul Craven entered the room. The moment between father and son was broken by the entrance of father and son. Kyle, ever the businessman, realized that Chase and Paul had never met and therefore did the formal introductions.

"Chase Morningstar, this is my father, Paul Craven. Dad, this is Chase Morningstar," said Kyle.

The two men shook hands, each having respect for the others talents. Paul's attention turned to Campbell and he embraced him affectionately and had a few quiet words with him that the younger men weren't privy to. It interested Chase that these two had a strong relationship.

While still pondering their relationship, Chase was oblivious to the large man who entered the room. He had medium blonde hair with deep blue eyes and an easy smile. He had requested the presence of everyone in attendance but wasn't sure exactly who was who.

"Lucas?" Paul suddenly asked. The new attendee's head snapped around and he smiled a huge smile.

"Yes," said Lucas. He made an educated guess. "Paul?" he asked.

"Yes," said Paul, extending his hand to Lucas. "How are you?"

"I'm just fine," answered Lucas, with a large grin on his face. As they shook hands, Paul nodded his head and his smile grew wider. Both knew their meeting was important.

Chase was still in the dark as to what was actually going on. He was very intrigued by Paul and Lucas' relationship. How did they know one another? It occupied his mind so much that he completely missed Brad and Charlie's entrance into the room. They were greeted by Kyle first and it wasn't until Chase turned his attention from Paul that he realized his brother was there. Astonished at his presence, Chase walked over to him and embraced him.

"What the hell are you doin' here?" asked Chase, completely surprised. "And you brought your dad? Hey, Brad, good to see you, man," he said to Brad, as he shook his hand and then gave him a hug. Chase stood back, smiling his million watt smile, as he stared at the look-a-like father and son.

"I had no idea that you were coming! This is a great surprise. Are you in town for long?" Chase asked, looking at the two and then to Kyle who had come over to join them.

"We're here for a bit. Kyle called me and asked that Brad and I join you for this dinner," Charlie explained, but didn't go further.

"I asked for a meeting to fill us in on the investigators findings, and then we can decide what to do," Kyle explained. Chase had held his grin this entire time, but as he looked around the room and realized that everyone else looked very serious, his grin faded.

"Let's listen to the information that the investigator has come up with. If you have a hard time with it, then we're here for you and if you don't

then, I..." he hesitated and looked around at the room full of men, "...
we support whatever your decision is as to how to deal with it," Charlie
said.

Chase was really unsure as to what he was about to hear but he braced
himself for it all.

When they all took a seat, Kyle began the introductions. "I realize
that not everyone knows each other so let's go around the table and
introduce ourselves, shall we? I'll start. My name is Kyle Craven and
I'm Chase's representative at the record label Lapis Labels." He turned
to Paul.

"I'm Paul Craven, Kyle's father and friend to Campbell for more than
thirty years," he said, smiling and turning to Campbell, on his left.

"I'm Campbell..." he hesitated a moment. "Also known as, Mark
Hagen. I'm Chase's dad," he said proudly.

"And I'm Chase Morningstar. Younger brother to Charlie and son to
Campbell," he said to all.

Charlie was next. "I'm Charlie Morningstar, Chase's older brother." He
looked at all the attendees and then to his father.

"I'm Brad Dumont, father to Charlie and family to Chase too," he said,
smiling and nodding to Chase. Chase nodded back and smiled at Brad.

They all turned and looked at the only other person at the table. The
large man smiled at them all and said, "I'm Lucas Hollomby. I'm the
investigator that Paul called to investigate Hennie's whereabouts and
possible involvement into the threat made on Campbell and, of course,
Sonya Morningstar's murder." He paused a moment and swallowed.

"Wait... what?" Chase asked, obviously confused. "I thought the Hollomby cop was killed years ago. Didn't you tell me that?" he asked Campbell.

Campbell nodded and smiled at Lucas. He would never forget Christopher's face and he could see his father in the man before him.

Before Lucas could continue, Chase spoke up again. "Are we waiting for someone else?" he asked, referring to the empty place setting next to Lucas.

Lucas looked down and smiled. He took a moment and then said, "This place is for my dad. If you'll notice, all of you here are father and son. My father should also be here but he isn't," he said, nodding to confirm Chase's question.

"I'm the son of Christopher Hollomby – the cop you referred to. He was killed years ago. And the information I have here tonight will have an unpredictable effect on all of you. I didn't want to give any of this information to the police before sharing it with you. You can decide what happens with this," he said mysteriously. He suddenly had every man's attention who was seated at that table.

So they wouldn't be interrupted, Kyle made sure the doors were locked. Then Lucas began his story. He first told the men how he came to sit at this same table with them. He was contacted by Paul Craven after the launch party and the threat made to Campbell by an individual they believed was Hennie. Paul knew Lucas's father, Christopher, through Campbell's Aunt Pearl and recounted to Lucas, Campbell's volatile relationship with Hennie. Once Campbell moved in with Paul and his family, Pearl put Christopher Hollomby and Paul Craven in touch so that if anything were to happen to Campbell, Paul could call a cop he could trust and who was familiar with Hennie's history. Paul and Christopher spoke many times but never met.

Paul had called Lucas to ask if he knew anything about what happened to Hennie and if he knew of someone Paul could trust to investigate. He explained that a threat was made on Campbell's life and that it now encompassed more than just Campbell. Lucas informed Paul that he was in fact a private investigator and would love to take the case on.

Lucas then admitted to the table of men that he agreed to do the job because he always believed his father died as a result of being set up by Hennie. Once Lucas came of age, Christopher often told his son the story of the night he arrested Hennie. He also suggested that, if anything ever happened to him that didn't seem right, it was possible that Hennie had something to do with it. To Lucas, his father's death never seemed quite right. Taking this case on served a dual purpose for Lucas and he was determined to find out all he could.

***

Decades previous, Christopher Hollomby put Hennie into the back seat of his car having arrested him for the attempted murder of Campbell and Eric. Hennie was handcuffed and furious. He couldn't believe he'd been set up by someone as simple as Eric Hagen and his pain in the ass son, Mark or "Campbell" as Hennie knew him.

He watched as Campbell got into a silver car, said a few words to Eric, and then drove away into the night. This made him absolutely furious. He couldn't help himself. When Christopher got in the car, Hennie said to him, "If you think you've got me, if you think you won't somehow pay for this, you've got another thought coming. No matter how long it takes, no matter what I have to do, I will see to it that you pay for this," he threatened.

Christopher and Hennie locked eyes in the rear view mirror but, considering the position Hennie was in, he was the first to look away.

Christopher didn't mention Hennie's threats to anyone except his son and he then ingrained it into Lucas's mind. His threats, his promises to take his revenge out on Christopher, were not things that Lucas ever forgot. So when the call came in that his father had been shot during a domestic dispute, something he'd dealt with a hundred times before, Lucas was convinced that it was a hit. The police worked their best but couldn't find anything connecting the shooting to Hennie at all and that was what they told the boy and his mother. As a teen boy Lucas had no recourse but to wait until a time came when he could investigate this himself. He finished his schooling, followed in his father's footsteps and entered the police academy graduating and becoming a cop, just like his dad. After a few years he left the force to become a private investigator. As a cop he worked too many hours to devote any time to finding his father's killer. Once he became a private investigator he was able to work for clients as well as his own quest for truth. He had worked hundreds of cases, jilted wives, swindled business partners and once in a while a murder investigation, usually working for the victim's family.

During his work, he managed to find a few things out about Hennie along the way, which he kept in a file he carried with him everywhere. The attempted murder charges his father arrested Hennie for didn't stick. The evidence was weak and only one witness came forward, Eric, Campbell's father. By then, Campbell was long into hiding and the police couldn't locate him.

The judge had no other alternative but to dismiss the case for lack of evidence. Smiling like a cat, Hennie turned and prepared himself to walk out of the courthouse a free man, but Chicago's finest were there waiting for him and the moment he stepped outside he was immediately arrested for the murder of Warren Miller and his girlfriend Sondra Locke and this time, the charges stuck. He was sentenced to life behind bars without parole. He was a model inmate and died of brain cancer, while still incarcerated. That was the story told to the layperson anyway.

Through Lucas' investigations, he learned that Hennie was visited once a week by his family for a short time and then later by only the boy, his wife having divorced and remarried, his other children cutting him out of their lives completely. His shipping company was funding his legal fees and his family was left near penniless. Upon his death, his children received nothing. Case closed.

This didn't satisfy Lucas. It was too tidy. He wanted to know more about the wife and children, but it was one child, a boy, that Lucas grew more and more interested in. Hennie's son, from his mistress, visited his father on a regular basis, more than any of his other children and he would spend hours talking with him through the paned glass and phone handset. Lucas's research in Chicago led him to find an alias that Hennie used once to rent an apartment for his mistress and two children in Chicago. It was his mother's maiden name, possibly the "K" in his full name. He'd used it to hide his secret second family and it gave Lucas a lead to tracking down the other two children. That name was Hennie Kellerman.

Lucas searched all the databases in the Chicago area for Kellerman's. There were many that fit the possibility of being Hennie's children and the process was slow and arduous. Once he'd located and determined who the "Kellerman" was, he'd move onto the next on the list. He was going nowhere and came back to New York thinking there might be a lead in the shipping company. He was going to start looking into that next when he happened to catch the photo of Sonya Kellerman on the front of the newspaper the day she was released from the hospital. From the photo he determined that she could be a relative; a likeness about the eyes and chin. His keen intuitive sense knew he was onto something and he went straight to the newspaper to get some information. They told him that the picture came from an outside source and that there were no other pictures on file of Mrs. Chase Morningstar. Undeterred, he called and asked Kyle for as much information on Sonya as possible. Kyle wasn't sure why he was asking but gave him all he could. Kyle recalled Chase telling police that she had an absent brother and that they worked in the family business for some time. He also said she'd been helping work with a shipping company for the family. Hearing this made Lucas certain he was on the right track!

He then paid a visit to Campbell. Campbell was having a good day when Lucas came to speak with him and he was able to provide Lucas with some excellent inside knowledge that was going to blow the investigation wide open. Armed with the new information from Campbell, Lucas had a more refined search on the internet.

He found the shipping company through following a listing of ships travelling to Amsterdam and back. There were only three and although they were all owned by different individuals or corporations, "S. Kellerman," was the acting CFO for all three. Going down to where the ships were docked and speaking with some of the men, he learned that they rarely saw Ms. Kellerman or her brother, but that he frequented an East Indian place nearby.

Lucas decided that the only way to know for sure was to go undercover. He was hired as a dockhand that serviced the three ships and told only those men he felt were dangerous and involved with drugs that he had a shady past and wasn't above doing anything for money, hoping that Johann was swimming the dock waters looking for someone to take on his task. His risk paid off when his phone rang one day and Johann was on the other end asking for a meeting with him.

He wore a wire to the meeting and taped the entire conversation. He also wore a hidden camera in his coat button. Johann was on video confessing to Christopher Hollomby's death and hiring someone to kill Chase Morningstar, and Lucas was now ready to play the video for the men who sat around the table.

***

Chase's mind was reeling. He had about a million questions for Lucas and didn't know where to start so he began with Campbell.

"Wait… what is this? Sonya was Hennie's daughter? Seriously?" he asked Lucas. Lucas nodded in confirmation.

"She was the daughter of Hennie and his mistress."

Chase pondered this for a moment and then asked, "What was it that Campbell told you that blew the case wide open?"

Everyone looked at Campbell waiting for the answer. Campbell took a huge breath and looked at his son sadly.

"I told him that Sonya was a drug dealer, son," he said, holding his gaze on Chase. "That's how I knew Sonya; she sold me marijuana," he explained. "I'm sorry, Chase," he said, shaking his head.

Chase looked at his father in disbelief. "What?" he asked incredulously. "There's no way! How could I have not known that? How could I have been dating and then married to the woman?"

Charlie put his hand on his arm. Those who knew the truth, knew that Chase would take this hard.

"I invited her to the CD launch party because she didn't believe I was your father and I wanted to show her I was telling the truth." Campbell shrugged his shoulders. Even to him the story sounded pathetic now considering the pain it had caused Chase.

"Why didn't you tell me?" Chase asked Campbell. It was a question that many around the table wanted to know the answer to.

"I saw how happy you were. And she really seemed to love you and then you showed up announcing you were married and pregnant. By then, nothing I had to say mattered. I will tell you this; she didn't try any of the shit she sold, ever." he said emphatically.

"So, her brother had her killed?" Chase asked, again doubting the information. All of this to him was just too much to believe.

"Well, that's the thing, Chase. The morning the news broke of Sonya's murder, Johann phoned me and was completely freaked out of his mind. He thought I'd made a mistake with the hit and that Sonya was killed in error. But, obviously I never had any intention of going through with the hit. When I told him I wasn't even in town he told me I was to find out who did the murder. I believed him, Chase. I don't think Johann hired anyone else and I didn't do it," Lucas explained.

"He doesn't mention your father's name. How do you know it's your dad he's referring to?" asked Brad of Lucas.

"The one detail left out of all news and media surrounding my father's death was that my father was shot through the eye. There were also three shots fired from his gun but only two bullets recovered from the scene. They always believed that whoever shot him got hit as well. Johann admitted carrying a reminder of the job and his injury requires him to use a cane. That was satisfying to know in some small way," he said, smiling. The men collectively nodded, agreeing with the evidence offered.

"He also offers up the fact that he hired the first assassin on you," Charlie noted. "This Johann guy is the one who called the first hit for certain, but I don't know about Sonya's murder."

"I agree," said Paul. "If Johann is acting enraged and wanting you to investigate his sister's murder then he's as in the dark as we all are."

"He wouldn't be acting so upset if he'd hired a second person, would he? Do you think he'd want Sonya killed too but by someone else? I mean, I know it doesn't make any sense but none of this really does, does it?" asked Chase, to no one in particular. No one thought that was the case.

"Chase, I don't think Johann wanted Sonya dead. He was pretty clear in the meeting and, as you saw in that video, *you* were the target. He never once mentioned Sonya and he admitted to the first attempted hit which happened at your place when Sonya wasn't there. Clearly, you were the problem here. So, why would he put a hit out on Sonya at the same time with a different guy? That just doesn't make sense," Kyle gently laid it out to Chase.

"This means that if Johann didn't call the hit on Sonya, then we don't know who did. And we don't know who they were really trying to kill, you or Sonya," Lucas noted to Chase. He felt badly for him but knew that he needed to understand the danger at hand in order to make an informed decision.

"And so, the question is… what do you want me to do with the information I have?" Lucas asked.

He knew that taking this to the police could possibly expose Sonya's drug dealing to the world and Chase didn't want that for Sonya or for their daughter. It didn't impress him at all that drugs brought Sonya into his life but he could also say proudly that it wasn't a part of their life together. If she was selling drugs while they were together, she didn't allow it to affect their lives at all and he knew nothing of it. He felt like a fool; how could he not have known? His emotions were all over the place; from anger and frustration to humiliation.

He wanted Johann nailed for the first attempted hit for sure but it wouldn't do anything about whoever was responsible for Sonya's death. The more information that was divulged, the more he believed that moving Poppy to Switzerland was the best idea.

"You know what? This has made my decision easier. There's no way I want Poppy living here where she's an easy target. I think the move to Switzerland is a great idea," he said, nodding his head.

Most at the table weren't aware of his plans and it took many by surprise. Chase saw the looks on their faces and knew it was a lot to take in. He looked to Campbell and saw his face; the shock.

"Do you want to come along... Dad? I'm happy to take you with me. If you still needed care, I'd find you the best rehabilitation centre in the whole country," he offered.

It was a lovely offer and Campbell was extremely touched but it wasn't what Campbell wanted in his heart. "I... uh... can't, Chase. I'm... well, uh," he smiled as Donna's face popped into his mind. "I'm in love," he said, almost guiltily. The whole table erupted in whistles and hollers and general compliments to him.

"What?" Chase exclaimed, "Are you kidding me?" Another mind blowing moment. "Who is she? When did *this* happen?" Chase sat back in his chair. Had he really been so wrapped up in other things, he'd completely missed that his father was in love?

Campbell smiled shyly at all the questions and comments. He held up his hand, laughing, trying to keep them all at bay. "Hold on now. It's not like you all should be so shocked. A place like this is a great way to meet women, you know?"

Campbell said it with a serious tone but it caused the table to break out into laughter and took away the tension and anxiety that anyone might have been feeling, especially Chase.

When the comedy moment had settled, Chase got up, walked over to the doors and unlocked them. Before opening them, he turned to the group of men and said, "I think I know what needs to happen here. Lucas, go to the police with your findings, let those chips fall where they may. For all we know, it was a drug hit and has nothing to do with me or Poppy. I'm leaving for a few months and the outcry won't be so bad secluded in Switzerland. By the time I return, people will have forgotten about Chase Morningstar and his dead wife's connection to the drug underworld," he said, nodded to the group then turned and opened the doors allowing the servers to bring in the food. Forgotten about Chase Morningstar? He couldn't have been more wrong.

~

Chapter 13

The Distance Between Us

There were a lot of things to arrange before Chase, Luisa and Poppy were to board the flight to Geneva, Switzerland. Arrangements had to be made, contractual agreements had to be met, and Chase had to make sure that everything would be seamless for Poppy's transition.

Kyle worked tirelessly to get approval for this unprecedented maneuvering from the shareholders and big wigs at Lapis Labels. He got the lawyer, Dana Rose involved, much to her chagrin. She really didn't want to help this rock star bugger so shortly after his own wife's murder and, when she found out that Chase married the nanny a few short months later, she just about lost it. Of course, Dana wasn't told all of the gritty details at first so the lawyer in her was the one making all the judgements. Chase understood her dislike of him but had neither the energy nor the patience to try and convince her otherwise. He did, however, make a mental note that one day he would straighten it all out with her.

Lapis was providing a confidential flight to help keep the media unaware. They were leaving for Geneva and then driving for two and a half hours to a town called Brig. As far as anyone knew, no word got out that they were leaving. Chase was grateful for the privacy. It meant he could help Poppy deal with the flight and keep her calm; no group of people grabbing at them, calling at them, no paparazzi, no explanations that needed to be made spur of the moment.

Poppy slept for most of the eight and a half hour flight and was easily entertained for the rest of it. Luisa had packed her favorite movies and toys and she didn't seem to mind until the landing when she pulled at her ears and cried out. It took some time for the child to settle after that but between Chase and Luisa, she was no problem at all. Clearing customs was easy and before they knew it, they were loaded into a Range Rover with very dark tinted windows and driving off to their new home.

Kyle purchased a very private country home for them on the outskirts of Brig. There was a corner store and an English style pub down the road about five minutes' walk, but to get anything more sophisticated, it was a car ride into Geneva.

Chase was expecting mountainous vistas and girls in braided pig tails standing next to snow covered gingerbread houses. He was wrong. Geneva was a hustling bustling metropolis much like New York, but European. He was grateful for Luisa's ability to speak German, exactly the sort of thing he knew would help with their transition. As they drove closer to Brig, Chase looked out of the tinted windows to a flat landscape, farmer fields and small houses. Nothing like he expected.

Chase kept the relationship between him and Luisa strictly platonic. They were married in name only and for a reason. He didn't love her, didn't pretend to love her, but cared for her as a friend and someone who his daughter Poppy held dear. That meant she was dear to him also, but that was as far as it went.

Luisa felt completely differently. The more he included her in the planning, the more he asked her opinion on things, the more she took it to mean he was falling in love with her. It was going to take some time and she was fine with that. His dear wife had been murdered and he was still in a state of shock from that. Luisa would be the person he leaned on and in time, he couldn't help but fall in love with her. Especially if she was left in a very secluded town with just the three of them. She was almost certain that he would end up in love.

***

Lucas met with Detective Shepherd, the head investigating officer on the case for Chase's intruder and Sonya's murder. He gave him all the information he found including the video of the meeting between him and Johann. He explained briefly how he became involved and how Johann mentioned his father's hit during the video. As far as Lucas could tell, Johann had racked up numerous felonies on this one video. Who knows what else they'd find once they had access to his files and really started digging? Both men agreed that Johann needed to be brought in for questioning.

They shook hands and exchanged private contact information. Lucas would be informed of any further developments and brought in should the need arise. The next step was to find and interrogate Johann. *Good luck with that,* thought Lucas, as he left the police station.

***

The house in Brig was extremely welcoming. Fully furnished and decorated, Chase liked everything he saw. He wasn't sure if Kyle purchased it that way or if there was a crew brought in. Regardless, it was a happy, cozy home that received its new owners and weary travellers with open arms. The fridge had all sorts of meats and cheeses, fresh vegetables and fruit. There was also cold beer; something Chase decided would be a great way to celebrate their arrival once Poppy was settled. Her room, filled with soft pastel and white wood furniture, was next to his, a small bedroom with a double sized bed. Chase offered the master bedroom to Luisa realizing she would be the permanent tenant.

It took no time at all for the three to get settled. They ate a meal in the kitchen and took in their new surroundings. For a small home it was incredibly spacious inside. The main floor had a bedroom, the only toilet and water closet, the kitchen and an open concept living room. The black wrought iron stairs that were a main focal point of the house were without risers. As long as they put gates at the top and bottom of the two flights, Poppy would be fine.

After a meal, Luisa ran her a bath and had Poppy in jammies in no time. The child was handed to her father, and as she let out a huge yawn, Chase smiled to himself. She always made him smile. He had never loved someone as completely as he did his little girl. He knew leaving for weeks at a time was going to be difficult for him but he also knew that her safety was more important. He would do his best to come home as often as he possibly could. Soon, he'd get someone working on the built-in studio and then he could spend more time there.

Once Poppy was happily sleeping in her new room, Chase grabbed himself a beer and sat in the living room checking out the different TV stations available. He was glad to see CNN from Atlanta, Georgia broadcasting; he could keep up with American news while he was in Switzerland. Other than that, he was out of his element. Even the beer tasted different and he could feel a slight buzz within a few minutes of finishing it. He noticed that for the first time in a long time he felt relaxed.

Luisa came down the stairs and got herself a beer from the fridge.

"You don't mind, do you?" she asked, raising the beer at him before opening it.

"No, not at all. Go right ahead," Chase said easily, raising his beer to her.

She uncapped the bottle and took a big drink from it. Chase couldn't remember ever seeing her drink alcohol. She came and sat down across from him with a magazine and started flipping through its pages.

"Happy to be back in your home country?" he asked her.

She shrugged one shoulder not looking at him. "It's good," was all she'd offer.

Chase was puzzled by her. She hadn't been back since before he hired her. He thought she'd be anxious to show him and Poppy all the sights and cities of her beautiful country but she really seemed indifferent.

"Someday soon, we'll drive up to meet your family, huh?" he said, taking a swig of beer.

She looked up from her magazine with a blank face. "They live very far from here. I doubt we'll get the chance to see them," she answered, which puzzled Chase even more.

"Are you kidding? They're your family. Don't you want to see them after all these years?" he asked her.

"Well, there aren't very many of my family left," she said, turning her attention back to her magazine.

Chase wondered why she was being so mysterious. She once told him that her family lived in the north of Switzerland, loved skiing and spent summers renting a cabin in a popular camping area, and that she hadn't seen them for some time. He wondered what had changed.

"We could go skiing while we're there. I'd love to teach Poppy how to ski when she's old enough. And if she's going to be living here, I'd like her to get immersed in the culture, the different languages, all of it!" he said, thinking how great it would be to be able to offer Poppy such a culturally diverse childhood. It could never make up for the fact that her mother was murdered but he'd do all he could to try. He sat back on the couch and closed his eyes allowing his beer buzz to play with his head as he imagined a much older Poppy, so sophisticated and multifaceted. Life here for Poppy was going to be amazing.

***

As the days passed, Chase was not sorry at all to have made the move and found himself inspired. With no recording studio, he only had his guitar and a piano to work with. He'd never played the piano much and worked hard at trying to learn its music while in seclusion. He and Poppy would sit together on the bench, Chase playing certain keys and Poppy trying to mimic her father. She was too young to really pick it up but sometimes her ear would be bang on and it would surprise Chase that her natural instinct was showing through so clearly at such a young age. Poppy was going to be musically gifted, for certain. The Morningstar gene ran full on in her blood.

The threesome took day trips further north to see the Alps and the lush of the green pastures at their feet. The scenic vistas were like nothing Chase had ever seen before. Luisa took her time explaining different things about the country to Chase and Poppy, although Poppy was more amused by the hand puppet that Luisa brought along for her to play with during the trip. Luisa had already started teaching Poppy how to speak German (her natural language), French and Italian, as all three languages were spoken there depending on where you lived in the country. With Poppy's incredible ability to pick up on things, she was soon saying her sentences four times over; first in English and then in each different language one after the other. Chase was in awe at how quickly she picked everything up and how adaptable she was to the whole move. Everyone had settled in nicely and Chase felt safe there. He often thought of Sonya and how she would have loved Switzerland. How she would have fit right in with all the blonde haired people that lived there and he didn't doubt she'd have been as interested in the county and culture as her daughter was. Sometimes, he'd allow himself a few minutes of longing for her and wishing she was with them, but he never allowed it to last longer than just a few minutes.

He kept up to date with Dana and how the investigation was going into Sonya's death. She admitted to him that the police were fully investigating Sonya's background, as well as her slimy brother but they had no evidence that Johann had called that specific hit. Dana told Chase that soon he would have to come back to the U.S. and speak to the police again, but they weren't asking for him yet.

"I just want you to be prepared, Chase. They aren't any closer to finding a suspect but aren't willing to let it grow cold either. They may want you back in for more questioning," she warned him.

He had flown off to his undisclosed place against her legal advice, which didn't help her feel any better about him or the whole murder but, until the police came at her with an arrest warrant, Chase was still in the clear. It didn't sit easy with Dana, but that didn't matter. Her job was to defend Chase and that's what she was going to do. Liking him and trusting him weren't necessarily prerequisites.

While in Switzerland, Chase's creative juices really started surging. He wrote lyrics nonstop for a week, writing three songs and started to put music to them when he got a call from Cooper Jack.

"Hey buddy! How're ya doing?" Cooper asked him.

Chase could practically see Cooper's big toothy smile through the phone. "I'm doin' good, Coop!" Chase told him. "Could use your expertise on the ivories here, trying to compose some new songs and I would love you to hash it out with me. Can you talk to Kyle and see if he can get you over here for a few weeks? I could really do with some American help!"

"I'm there, my friend. I'll get Kyle to arrange it and be there as soon as I can. Can I crash with you or do I need alternative arrangements?" he asked. Cooper was anxious to see what life was like in a foreign country having never been out of the continental U.S. before.

"We'll make the space, Coop. Just get your ass on that plane as quick as you can. Get Kyle to send me all the flight details and I'll be sure to come get you at the airport," Chase said, not realizing that wouldn't be possible. Kyle would have a driver pick Cooper up and take him to Chase's home, thereby avoiding Chase being found by any paparazzi that might be at the airport. In order for Poppy to stay safe, Chase was to keep himself hidden for the time being. Once he flew back to the U.S. he could make all the publicity rounds again but until then, his whereabouts was not for public knowledge.

Cooper's arrangements were made and within the week he arrived at Chase's door, luggage in hand. The two men embraced when they saw each other.

"Lookin' good there, Chase. Your face looks as though you've had way too much rest and relaxation. Where are all the stressed out eyes and worry lines you had before?" Cooper ribbed him, jokingly. It was true though. Cooper could see and sense a mellowness in Chase that he hadn't seen for a while and rightly so. The poor guy had been through hell.

"Who needs them here?" Chase answered, leading him into the cozy home. "This place is a little slice of heaven on earth. It's quiet and peaceful, has beautiful scenery and best of all, Poppy is learning more than she did the entire time we were in the States," he told Cooper proudly.

As if on cue, Luisa walked into the living room carrying the child. Cooper's smile exploded across his face when he saw Poppy and he immediately reached out for her to come to him.

"And there's my little Poppy-poo! Come and give me a big hug and tell me all about your last couple of months here," he said to her, as she practically leapt from Luisa's arms to let Cooper hold her.

She gave him a hug around his neck, squeezing him tight with her eyes closed. "Coopa!" was all she said, but it was worth a million for Cooper to hear.

Glad she remembered him, he started walking around the house with her pointing to things and asking her what it was. As he was occupied with the child, Chase took Cooper's luggage into the other spare room and Luisa went into the kitchen to make them all something to eat.

When Cooper came back into the main area, Luisa was there with a tray full of sandwiches, hard cheese, crackers and wine. He continued to hold Poppy, enjoying her hugs and trying to understand her gibberish. He and Luisa made eye contact and Cooper felt obligated to say something.

"Hi there, uh…" struggling to remember her name. "Luisa, is it?" he asked.

She only nodded. Cooper was not really sure of her. He'd always wondered about her. She was too quiet for his liking and seemed to hover around Poppy and Chase too much for just a nanny. Cooper didn't get a great feeling from her but knew she was important to Poppy and figured that was what made her so important to Chase. Even so, Cooper didn't really like her or trust her. He knew nothing of their secret marriage or that Luisa was really in love with Chase, but it wouldn't have surprised him at all. Luisa gave him the creeps.

When Chase returned, he took Poppy from Cooper and offered him a plate and a glass. "Help yourself, buddy. The bread and cheeses here are excellent. I know, right? So cliché but completely true," Chase said, as he handed a cracker to Poppy and grabbed one for himself.

Chase watched as Cooper took a bite of a sandwich and started chewing. The look on his face said it all; pure nirvana. It made Chase smile immensely. He really enjoyed Cooper and missed the camaraderie they had shared in studio and just hanging out. They both loved the creative process of making great music and they thought alike in many areas. Where they disagreed, they had respect enough for the other to hear out the argument and often times they could convince the other to understand their reasoning. Chase thought of Cooper as his younger brother. He was full of piss and vinegar, sharp as a knife, funny as hell, and sometimes Chase could see the young mischievous boy in his curly-haired friend.

"So, what do you do for fun around here? Are you house bound?" Cooper asked.

"There's a pub on the corner I like to frequent. *Zey have great bee-ah, Ya!*" Chase said, mimicking a German accent.

Cooper busted out laughing and the two men exchanged a few "Ya's" between them, having fun at Luisa's expense. German was her native tongue and their mimic of her accent was insulting. She took note. She didn't like Cooper. Not at all, and he was to stay with them indefinitely. She wondered what could be done about that.

***

"So, seriously dude, what the fuck?" Cooper asked Chase, as they sat in the far back booth of the Switzerland pub, Chase in disguise with a baseball cap on and darker hair poking out. Cooper could barely contain himself when Chase put the hat on in the car before they entered the pub. Now, as they sat in private, Cooper wanted Chase's story, the full story.

Chase took a deep breath before answering his friend. "So, the disguise is so that no one realizes that I'm here. We've travelled the country but never left the car. I can't be out in public because I can't risk this for

Poppy. I mean, she never asked for this, you know?" he said sincerely, to his friend.

His fatherly concern was understandable. Cooper thought Poppy was brilliant, the best little person he'd ever met. She won his heart. He nodded his head in agreement at Chase's explanation.

"Okay. What's with Luisa?" Cooper asked him, straightforward.

Chase looked briefly at his friend, dropped his head and admitted, "We're married."

Cooper was absolutely shocked. His jaw literally dropped at Chase's confession. Chase raised his head as both men stared at each other, not knowing what to say. Chase broke the moment.

"She was hours from being deported, just months after Sonya's murder. I couldn't imagine Poppy losing both women within months; she was too attached to Luisa. At the time, I didn't have a better answer to the solution so I quietly married her to keep her in the country. I know it wasn't my most brilliant move but I was thinking of Poppy," he told Cooper honestly.

"And now?" Cooper asked. He wanted to know what exactly the relationship was between Chase and his nanny.

Chase immediately shook his head. "I've never touched the girl, except for a kiss on the cheek the day we married," he stated firmly, with his hands in the air. "The marriage was never consummated. I let her know from the get-go that it was only to keep her in the country and close to Poppy. But I decided Switzerland was a safer place for Poppy to live. If I can keep it quiet, she might actually be able to have a normal and safe life. Now, considering both sides of her family, I think my poor little girl has zero percent of that happening in the States. I feel so stupid putting her all over the internet and showing her off so brazenly. It was

287

such a stupid thing to do," he said, almost to himself. His guilt was almost palpable.

He didn't fill Cooper in on everything at this point. Lucas Hollomby and his information regarding Sonya's background wasn't something he was willing to open up about, but if he did, Cooper would be the one person he'd admit it too. They just understood one another.

Cooper was shocked to hear Chase's admission of his secret marriage to Luisa. He considered himself a close insider on all things Chase Morningstar. The secrecy of it spoke volumes to Cooper. He sat back in the pub booth and looked at his superstar friend, long and hard. Cooper wasn't someone who'd bullshit Chase. He recognized right from the start that Chase needed someone who would be his friend, not a "yes" man. Cooper didn't trust Luisa. He deliberated over telling Chase his feelings but only for a moment.

"Okay, well I understand your reasoning… I'd crawl through a fire for that baby girl, but Luisa creeps the shit outta me and I don't know what it is but I think she's not what she seems and you need to be careful of her. I realize this may not be a popular view but you need to hear it," Cooper said frankly. He took a large swig of his beer after he finished and looked at Chase thoughtfully.

Chase gave a moment for the words to sink in. He nodded in agreement although Cooper wasn't sure what Chase had agreed with.

"Here's to not regretting decisions made in the name of love," Chase toasted, raising his beer to Cooper.

You can't ask for more than that, thought Cooper, softening to his friend. He raised his beer and the two friends clinked their glasses. They remained silent for a moment, lost in their own thoughts.

"Well, I came here for a reason. Let's work as hard as we can and write some of the best friggin' songs ever written," Cooper said enthusiastically, and Chase knew it would happen. He needed Cooper there to complete his creative process. This time would not be wasted. They would create magic.

***

As Chase and Cooper were having their night out at the pub, Luisa was left at home watching over Poppy and reading. Her cell phone rang at precisely 9:00 pm. Luisa answered but said nothing, waiting to hear from the caller first.

"Are you there?" he asked, hesitantly.

"Yes" she answered.

"I've done all you've asked of me. Please… leave me alone now," he pleaded.

"I told you never to contact me on this line." She paused, then threatened, "You and I aren't through until I say we are. Don't call me again, I told you… I'll contact you!" she spit into the phone and then quickly disconnected the line.

Shit! He should never have called her. He should never have done a lot of things where she was concerned. He lowered the phone from his ear. He regretted ever having met her. Now, more than ten years afterward, he was paying for his sins, heavily. He realized that it wasn't worth it. Not anymore. At times he thought of a way out. He actually daydreamed about it but he had neither the guts nor the balls to do it; but he knew that one day he was going to have to end this.

***

An address for Johann was found and once located, a raid was strategically planned and pulled together lightning fast. To his pure joy, Lucas was invited to participate in the raid. He'd done all of the background and footwork, not to mention his father was a cop who died at Johann's hand. The department felt he deserved to be there.

Suited up with a walkie-talkie, a bullet proof vest and a badge on a lanyard, Lucas was part of the second wave of law enforcement to bust their way into Johann's apartment in the early morning hours. To their complete disappointment, Johann wasn't there. Nothing was. An apartment that had been fully furnished and lived in for God knows how long was completely emptied. Johann had disappeared. Chase needed to be informed.

***

The collaboration between Cooper and Chase was simply creative genius. They each contributed equally to the process and together eight new songs were written within a six week period. Their style crossed many genres but that wouldn't surprise Chase's hard core fans. They expected his individual style and the fact that they could tune in to most radio stations and hear his music, no matter the playlist. Chase Morningstar was a household name.

The title track was entitled "The Distance Between Us." He wanted his fans to know that he appreciated their devotion, even if he wasn't out selling his music. He wanted them to know that even though he'd suffered a great blow with Sonya's murder and needed time to retreat and heal, he was still writing and creating and thinking of them too.

Leaving you behind has been my sole regret,
Like losing a love you know is pure.
But my heart and soul knew my mind was set,
And my steps were strong and sure.
When I put this distance between us,
Little did I know.
That there'd be hundreds of reasons,
To lessen the blow.
To turn back my actions,

And return to square one,
To lessen the distance between us,
And get back to where we started from.

And now I'm set on my path,
Not knowing what lies ahead.
When I put this distance between us,
I didn't think much should be said.
And now that I know your devotion,
And understand love that's so pure.
Does it matter the distance between us?
If we still feel safe and secure?

Chase was once again in full creative mode. He worked with Cooper on the design of the CD cover. Keeping within the universal realm, they decided on a star shining far from plant earth, showing clearly the great distance between the two. The inside jacket featured pictures of his fans from all over the world, each holding signs stating their devotion to him and his talent. Within a few months, Chase, in collaboration with Cooper Jack, had created his second CD called "Light Years." The title said it all, at least to Chase and Cooper it did. It held a double meaning and Chase liked that.

Cooper explained to Chase, "This new unplugged version of Chase Morningstar is light years away from anything you've ever done, including all the years touring with Chasing Charlie."

Chase took that as a compliment. He thought highly of Cooper's musicality with his uncanny ability to create a musical balance to the words Chase had purged, making them touch the soul. He was also one of Chase's closest friends and together, Chase and Cooper wrote music that would appeal to all genres. Chase's guitar and voice accompanied by Cooper's expert piano playing and harmonizing was all that was needed for "Light Years" to become a record breaking hit. With no studio available, they would live feed their performance straight from

Chase's living room in Switzerland while Kyle captured it all and, with very little editing, spun it into pure gold.

The entire time this was happening, Chase and his small family remained in hiding. No one knew of their whereabouts unless they were living under the same roof as he, were blood related or had their signature on Chase's paycheck. The fans, fully aware of the murder of his wife and secretive flight from the country were satisfied with live interviews via Skype, YouTube videos and Instagrams. Kyle had a whole web design team that kept Facebook updated as well as Chase's personal webpage. Chase's contribution was generally a quote or two a week. For a man who could write a hit song in a day, it wasn't asking too much.

Once again, Lapis Labels put together a marketing promotion that had Chase and Cooper's songs all over the internet and on the lips of everyone between the ages of 19 and 55, Chase's demographic increasing with the addition of Cooper. "Light Years" sold 2.3 million copies in five days making it the fastest selling CD in three years, smashing Taylor Swift's record to pieces. Chase had dreamed that he would one day be breaking records and to see his dream come to fruition was incredible. His fans flocked to his website and Facebook page, followed him on Twitter and downloaded anything and everything available on Chase Morningstar, but the man himself was a recluse. He never made an in-person appearance despite repeated requests. He was happy to chat via live feed but to have Chase Morningstar grace your presence on live TV just wasn't going to happen.

When asked about his living arrangements or whereabouts during interviews, Chase would just laugh, flash his million watt smile and shrug away his response. Most interviewers understood his reluctance to answer the question and respecting his position as a father trying to protect his child, would move on to another line of questioning fairly quickly, but they all tried.

Cooper had been back in the U.S. a few months and Chase had all but lost himself in his new life when the phone call came that would change everything.

"Hello, Dana," Chase said. He almost hid his dislike for the woman, but not quite.

"Hello, Chase," said Dana. She didn't let him get to her. She only represented Lapis Label and was paid very generously to do it, so personally caring about Chase Morningstar was going above and beyond her pay grade. All she had to do was give him legal counsel.

"You need to come back to the States, quick as you can," she told him directly. "They're considering filing murder charges against you."

***

Not finding Johann home during the raid made Lucas Hollomby frustrated. It meant that he had failed his father and also Chase. He wanted desperately to see Johann pay greatly for his life of sins and decided that he wasn't going to leave it to the police to find him. Knowing Johann from his meeting, and with his cover still intact, Lucas tried contacting Johann hoping to bait his hook once again. It worked.

"What the fuck happened?" Lucas asked, playing his role out to Johann when he'd answered his call.

"I have someone on the inside who told me of a raid on my home. It's the first time that the police have got that close to me. I got out of there before they could arrest me," he told Lucas.

An awkward pause fell between them and Lucas realized he needed to convince Johann he wasn't out to betray him. "I'm not interested in sloppy seconds," Lucas said. "Someone else is after this guy, obviously, and now he's brimming with security," Lucas said, almost forced. His ninth grade acting teacher would be proud!

Johann waited a moment, weighing his odds. If he believed his hired assassin, he could avenge his sister's death but if Luke was playing him, it could cost him *his* life.

"I was hoping you could find him for me," Johann admitted. "He's left the country, I know this for sure. I also know he didn't go south, like to the Caribbean or South America. I have no idea where he is but I want him dead. Can you do this? Can you find him and kill him?"

Another pause. It was Lucas now weighing his odds. If he agreed he might find out Johann's whereabouts, leading him directly to the drug king. If he agreed he could fulfill his personal vendetta against Johann. He could kill him.

~

Chapter 14

Luisa

Her father was a carpenter, her mother a teacher, both from a small farm town in Switzerland. She was the middle of three girls born to working parents and sometimes lost in the shuffle of everyday life. Both sisters were demanding of her mother and father and when Luisa did get her mother's attention, she always seemed to say Luisa's name with a sigh. Luisa took that as a negative. She felt completely overlooked by her family.

By the age of thirteen, Luisa knew she wanted to live in the United States. Once she had access to a computer, she'd surf the internet and explore the world and America was the place she dreamed of the most. She would daydream about running away and making it to the States... somehow. She'd travel from one coast to the other and dip her toe in both oceans. She'd visit all the major cities and see all the tourist sites and then she'd find herself an all-American boy and fall in love and settle down. She'd find someone who'd notice her and pay attention to her. Someone who would love only her. Someday she'd be over there and she'd never come home.

As if by her sheer will, the family received a call from New York when Luisa was in her late teens. Her mother's second cousin, Aunika, was on the phone. Born and raised in the States, she had traveled to Switzerland and stayed with Luisa's mother's family as a young girl one summer. Aunika had stayed close to her Swiss family, writing and then calling periodically and keeping up to date. Her husband, a brilliant lawyer, was fifteen years her senior and had accepted a seat in the courts of New York as a judge. She was a socialite and he was a very powerful man.

Aunika complained to Luisa's mother that her nanny had resigned and she now had to go through the agony of interviewing for a new nanny. *Oh, the troubles of the rich,* thought Luisa's mother. Through the course of their conversation the idea came about that, either Luisa or her older sister come and stay with the New York family and act as nanny until things got straightened out. Aunika would take care of all the details and felt as though she would be giving the same kind of opportunity to one of the two girls that she had been given.

Luisa's mother knew that this was the dream Luisa had been envisioning. It was her prayer come true and she convinced Luisa's father to allow the visit. Her mother was sure it would only be for a few weeks, no more than two months tops, and was a great proposal for the sullen, sad girl. She also believed that, of all of her daughters, Luisa was the one that could best tend to children, although she had her concerns as well. Luisa was a master manipulator!

Luisa's family all gathered at the airport to say their goodbyes. It had only been five days since the phone call and Luisa was boarding a plane and on her way. She was still pinching herself. Her mother's words stuck in her head. "I hope this trip brings you exactly what you want. I hope it's all you dreamed of." Luisa was going to make sure it was!

When she landed at JFK she was greeted by Aunika and her daughter, Regan, age seven. She thought they were very glamorous. They were dressed alike wearing the latest fashion and dripping in jewelry. Both of them. Luisa felt extremely plain in comparison; very plain indeed. She was whisked into the back seat of a long dark car and grilled over everything from her German accent to the fact that she didn't have long blonde hair. She answered every question the two females hit her with and didn't have a chance to look out the tinted windows and see what America looked like.

The car pulled up to a very large apartment building and suddenly the doors opened. A hand reached inside and Aunika took it as she stepped out of the car. The same hand reached back in and guided Luisa out and onto the sidewalk. Everywhere she looked were large apartment buildings, as tall as the eye could see, and on both sides of the street too. She was amazed at how much cement was used in the city and wondered where all the trees were.

The doorman, who was dressed formally, followed them into the building carrying Luisa's luggage. They stepped onto the elevator with an iron gate that was closed by another man dressed in uniform. They rode up to the 11th floor and stepped off into a plush carpeted hallway with deep burgundy flowered wall paper and dim lighting. Luisa counted four dark wooden doors with golden numbers. They stopped in front of the one numbered 1102. The doorman put Luisa's bag down as Aunika retrieved a large bundle of keys from her handbag and handed them to the doorman to unlock the door. To Luisa it was a monumental moment and she stopped and took a deep breath. This was her dream come true. She was in America and she was going to live the American dream. She crossed the threshold with nothing but hope and the brightest outlook for the first time in her life. She didn't anticipate what it would take to make her dreams come true.

Aunika's son, Greyson, was a nine year old brat who was far smarter than any of the adults who occupied his days. He spoke his mind and had no problem loudly complaining upon their introduction.

"I don't care what my parents say, I don't need a *nanny*" he said, almost spitting the word. He was going to make her work for his approval.

"Alright, Greyson, I will only help you when you require it. Otherwise, I will assume you've got things covered," she said matter-of-factly. She smiled again and nodded her head at him.

He turned his head and marched off down a long hallway. He would be difficult to engage. Regan was a different story. She already liked Luisa and had pulled on her arm to follow her to her bedroom. Inside, Luisa was shocked by the beauty of the room for a seven year old. They had spared no expense. The whitest and finest linens and Battenberg lace adorned a beautiful queen-size canopy bed. Everything on the bed and about the room was white, the brightest, whitest white. Luisa had never known of a room so lovely and wondered how hard it was for Regan to keep it unstained. But then, it didn't look as though the room was played in much at all.

The rest of the apartment was equally impressive, even her bedroom was absolutely breathtaking. A blue-green color was prominent throughout the room and the bedding was the same blue-green piped in white fringe. It was a smaller room than the others in the apartment but Luisa was fine with that. She walked over to the window and looked out and to her astonishment saw a large park right in the middle of the city, not far from the building.

"Is that a park?" she asked, as Aunika walked into her room.

"Yes, dear," she told Luisa. "That's *Central Park*." She emphasized the name and then mumbled under her breath, "You have no idea how much we paid for that view." She rolled her eyes as she looked around Luisa's room.

Luisa turned and smiled at her relative with such a radiant smile, overcome with joy at seeing her dreams coming true. When she had daydreamed about living in America, she actually envisioned living in an apartment that would overlook a city and a park. It was exactly what she wished for.

***

At dinner that first night, she was introduced to Aunika's husband, Judge William Carmichael. Judge Carmichael was a successful lawyer and had been a sitting judge for just a few months when Luisa came to work for them. Judge Carmichael had married twice, Aunika being wife number two, and was the father to three adult children from his first wife as well as Greyson and Regan. Known to be an excellent lawyer and a strict and hard-lined judge, William Carmichael was revered by his inner circle and peers and respected by all. Luisa was intimidated by him and when they were introduced his handshake was firm and solid. She hoped she never had to deal with him. He didn't make her feel like family; he made her feel more like an employee, more like *the nanny*.

Unbeknownst to Luisa, William wasn't superhuman. Not at all. He had his flaws and once introduced to the new nanny, his wife, Aunika's, second cousin, his "flaw" started nagging at him. He hadn't really cared when his pain-in-the-ass of a wife told him her cousin's daughter would be coming from Switzerland to help as temporary nanny to their children. He paid no attention when Aunika told him she and Regan were going to pick the new nanny up at the airport. He only became interested upon walking into the dining room that first night and seeing for himself the new nanny, Luisa.

She was a small-framed girl with mousy hair. Her eyes were large and blue, almost ice blue and the irises were framed in black. William figured she was maybe 17 or 18, although he vaguely recalled Aunika telling him her age. He'd have to inquire tonight at bedtime. When she reached in to shake his hand he could see down her braless t-shirt to her fully exposed right breast. It was quite a thrill for him. He fancied a younger female body and, although she was a bit young for him, he would remember the brief glimpse of her supple right breast many times over in his fantasies. No matter how many times his wife went to the gym and watched her diet, William just wasn't turned on by her anymore. He managed to have sex with her at least once every month or so, which she didn't complain about. What he really lusted after was a woman who wasn't the mother of his children, someone who had young supple breasts, someone like Luisa. It broke up his first marriage too. Once his wife became pregnant and started giving birth, his mind told him that she was not to be lusted after; she was someone's mother. He loved his mother very much. So much so that wrapping his head around his wives' pregnancies was a very difficult time for him. By the time Aunika gave birth to Regan, child number five for William, he made up his mind that having sex with a woman who gave birth to his child was wrong. He managed to rise to the occasion, rarely, after the birth of the first born child in both marriages, enough to impregnate three more times. Otherwise, his sex life depended on a call girl named Charmaine or, as was often the case, his right hand and a porn video. Aunika knew nothing of her husband's sexual fantasies. She was happy not to have sex with him; he grunted over her like an animal and took no time or interest at all in pleasing her whatsoever. The less sexual interest he took in her, the happier they were as a couple. She really didn't care who was satisfying his sexual cravings, she just ignored that part of their relationship all together. This gave William the justification he required in order to have sex with paid women or to fantasize about inappropriate sex at his leisure. Luisa's arrival only put a face to the figure William had pictured in his mind's eye while achieving orgasm. She was exactly what he had wished for.

***

The first time the judge saw Luisa naked was purely by accident. She was taking a mid-afternoon shower after a bike ride through Central Park with Greyson and Regan. They had worked up a sweat and Luisa came home to enjoy the luxury of the Manhattan apartment's shower pressure. When she stepped out of the shower she realized she forgot a larger towel, leaving her with only a small hand towel that could barely dry her off, let alone cover her young naked body. Luisa hesitated, pondering her dilemma. If she stayed in the bathroom long enough to get someone to bring her a proper sized towel, she could be there all day. On the other hand, if she ran from the bathroom to her bedroom stark naked, she ran the risk of being seen by someone. Weighing her odds she decided that there was little chance of being caught by anyone, especially at this time of day. Aunika was attending a committee meeting for some-such charitable event she was working on and the judge was never around during the day. He usually arrived home after 6:30 pm. Luisa figured she was safe as both children were in the entertainment room watching their favorite video with an afternoon treat made by the cook. *These kids really have it made*, Luisa mused as she dried off with the next-to-nothing sized hand towel. She tossed it, well used, into the laundry hamper in the bathroom and walked out in haste to make it to her bedroom careening straight into the judge, nearly knocking him over. He managed to grasp her arms as she plowed into him and the two were both left stunned for a moment until the reality of the situation set in. Both stood agape, not knowing where to look, not knowing what to say. Luisa's eyes were as large as saucers as the judge fought for words, as his eyes feasted on the naked teen. He took in every morsel of her and left nothing to his imagination before blustering something inaudible and carrying on down the hallway to his own bedroom.

By the time Luisa got back to her bedroom she was ready to burst into tears and yet incredibly excited at the same time. She saw the look in his eye as he took in her naked form. She noticed how his pupils dilated as they drank her in, how his mouth hung open and how he seemed incapable of looking away. Luisa enjoyed the thought that she had that kind of power over a man, regardless of their age difference. As she raced to her bedroom and quickly closed the door, she collapsed against it and felt her heart race as she steadied herself. *The judge just saw me naked and he enjoyed it!* she thought. *He enjoyed it!*

For days afterward Luisa relived the moment. She became increasingly curious as to what had brought the judge home that day. She often daydreamed about another encounter between them. Although she wasn't attracted to him, it excited her to envision the judge forcing

301

her into various sexual encounters where he mounted her during her protestations and forced her (gently) to have sexual intercourse with him. Although she daydreamed about it, she never thought in a million years that it would happen. But then, she hadn't imagined her daydream of living in America would ever happen either.

The first sexual encounter occurred during a very severe thunderstorm one hot August night. The power was out in the pricey Manhattan apartment block and residents were dealing with a sweltering night, despite the storm. The thunder woke Luisa and she stood at her window watching the lightning show and listening to the noise of the thunder clouds as they rolled by. Her lean figure was illuminated by the storm's light show and William was transfixed on the sight as he stood beyond the door frame watching her. Initially, she had no idea of his presence but after a particularly close lightning strike, with her full naked form showing through the diaphanous sleeping dress she was wearing, Luisa caught the judge's reflection in the window. She waited for a moment before turning and acknowledging him.

"Did the storm wake you too?" she asked quietly. William panicked and remained hidden in the shadows behind the corner wall. "Judge Carmichael?" she whispered. She waited a moment and then asked again. "Did you wake up from the thunder?" She acted so innocent, so naïve, wanting him to acknowledge her.

He had been secretly watching her for a few weeks; now, suddenly, because of the storm, he was caught.

"I... uh... I was just finishing up in my office. I saw you standing there just as the first lightning strike happened," he lied. "I didn't want to embarrass you," he lied again, dropping his head.

It was a move he learned after many years in the court room. When someone was guilty, they tended to drop their head as they confessed their sins. It made the jury feel sympathetic towards the defendant, no matter how heinous the crime. Judge Carmichael knew that Luisa would be taken with the move and he manipulated her using this knowledge.

But Luisa was equally intuitive, even given her young age. She knew full well how her body affected the judge and she used it to her advantage. It was in her best interest for both Aunika and the judge to want her to stay longer than just a few months, so giving him a little peep show seemed innocent enough. After all, no one ever died from seeing a teenager's nipples, did they? No. So, Luisa made sure that she wore her skimpiest nightgown and that she was in just the right place at just the right time. Luisa was very aware of William's secret spying and used that knowledge to increase her chances to extend her stay.

Facing him with her naked body slightly visible through the night gown, she carried on, seemingly oblivious as to how she appeared. She asked him questions but he couldn't answer her. He knew she had spoken but all the blood in his body had rushed to his penis and nothing was left in his brain; nothing that would talk any sense to himself or to Luisa. He couldn't tear his eyes away. Her young body was now on full display for him to gaze upon. Her soft, young, pink nipples, stood puckered against the cotton and the nightie stopped short of her thighs. He could tell that she wore no panties at all. Trying hard to fight his own devils, the judge focused his eyes on hers and spoke quietly and clearly.

"You shouldn't walk around my house dressed like that," he managed, in an almost angry tone.

It surprised Luisa; she didn't want him to be angry. "I'm sorry," she said, and she dropped her head. She could play that game too!

Immediately, he felt sorry for sounding so angry. He acted flustered for a moment and then took her by the arm and led her back into her bedroom.

"I don't think anyone would appreciate seeing you like this, Luisa," he explained, in a hushed whisper.

He was actually out of breath and trying hard to conceal his erection. His grasp on her arm had cinched the lightweight nightie up her thighs and her soft, virgin, pubic hair was visible, if he looked hard enough, and he looked hard. When he spun her around her bare bottom was exposed as the nightie crept higher up her backside. He could barely contain himself and he quickly shut the door keeping them inside her room, alone together. He swallowed hard as he took a moment to catch his breath and think about his next move. He tried hard not to turn and look at her, but his desire was incredible and he lost to his basic animal needs and took her in fully. This teen girl had entered his home and occupied his sexual fantasies for many weeks and now he was alone in her room, with her wearing nothing but a nightie.

Luisa could feel her heart pounding in her chest and she swallowed hard. At 18, she was past the age of consent and she wanted to consent. She didn't want the judge to think of her as an innocent, but more as a young, ripe ingénue; someone with whom he would feel comfortable enough to act on his desires. It would take more than once. Luisa knew that he would have to return to her for sexual relief before she could manipulate him and she was prepared to do that. Quite prepared. Luisa had been formulating this plan for many weeks now. She knew that the only way to stay in the U.S. was to have the judge on her side.

She took three steps and was within inches of him. His erection stood closer and fought hard against his pants. She showed no knowledge of his obvious desire and reached out to his face and stroked it with her hand, looking deeply into his eyes.

"I've always loved the color of your eyes, Judge Carmichael," she said softly. "I've always thought I could see you weighing every option before answering every question you're asked," she whispered to him, taking a closer study of his face.

William didn't move, didn't touch her and barely took a breath while she was within such close proximity. He knew he was walking down an extremely dangerous and stupid path, but the man could not make himself turn around and go out the door, his desire for the girl being so great. She leaned into him as she continued to study him and he could see her full breasts exposed as her night shirt fell away. His mind continued to scream at him and he was about to turn himself around when her small soft hand reached down and took hold of the head of his penis and stroked it through his pants. He completely lost control. Within moments he had her in his arms and was stroking the soft skin of her bottom as he crushed her chest against his and dropped his head, covering her mouth with his.

Although Luisa was indeed a virgin, even to kissing, she had prepared herself for what was about to happen. She found several VHS tapes of men and women having sex and exploring each other's bodies, hidden in a box in the back of Aunika's closet and had snuck two of them into her room. She waited until late at night when everyone was asleep to secretly watch them and learn what sexually pleased a man. Luisa already knew the judge was interested; if she gave him enough of a show, he'd definitely play along. Luisa did not disappoint. William barely had time to enjoy her soft supple body before she dropped to her knees and took him into her mouth. With that he was sold; this girl had to stay. And with that, Luisa knew she had sealed the deal.

***

Before they knew it, the search for a different nanny was forgotten because everyone was in love with Luisa, except Greyson. Aunika had already asked Luisa's mom if she could stay on the promise that she would enroll her in school for the coming semester. The judge showed mild attention as Aunika explained Luisa's extended stay, but inside he was thrilled to hear of it and got excited just imagining their late night playtime. Regan truly loved Luisa. She was a big sister who wasn't too old to play with her but old enough to help bridge any gap between Regan and Aunika. But it was Greyson who wasn't swayed by Luisa. Even with her ability to manipulate and put everyone else at ease, Greyson wasn't convinced she was as wonderful as everyone made her out to be. He saw her manipulate Regan into keeping her secret that she watched TV late at night. Thankfully, the small girl had never seen exactly what Luisa was watching, but she'd seen the light flickering in her room under the door and mentioned it to Luisa one morning. Luisa explained that she missed home and was watching news from Switzerland. She told Regan that it was helping her deal with homesickness and if Regan told her parents, they may not allow it because of the hour at which she watched. Regan hung on Luisa's every word and swore that she would never tell.

Greyson knew better. He was an extremely smart boy; brilliant one could say. He was already writing raw computer programs in C+ to make his computer one of a kind. The boy had intelligence beyond reason and was intuitive like no other. In his opinion, Luisa was a manipulative bitch who had no business playing nanny, especially to him.

Luisa was wise to Greyson's attitude. She tried many ways to win him over and nothing worked. Nothing. Luisa started wondering what it was going to take to bring Greyson on board. If she had the whole family wanting her to stay then it was a foregone conclusion that it would happen. Luisa was quite perplexed by his hatred of her and worked hard to have an honest relationship with him, but it still didn't help. The one thing Luisa didn't count on was Greyson's interest in sex at the early age of ten. She didn't think of him in that manner, but he liked to steal his father's Playboy magazine and look at the pictures of naked women for hours on end. He may have been a brilliant mind but he was a boy, first and foremost. A healthy young boy. It became Greyson's favorite afternoon activity; to spend a few minutes after school peering in on Luisa who was undressing in her room. He caught her on one occasion and watched for a full ten minutes. He saw everything; her beautiful, milky, white breasts, her small waist and hips that were slender with long slim thighs. She kept her underwear on the first time he peeped on her, but later on he managed to catch her while she completely disrobed and he changed his attitude towards her altogether. Suddenly, Greyson was Luisa's biggest fan and #1 cheerleader, very interested in her whereabouts and activities. When the time came for Luisa to return to Switzerland, all four in the Carmichael household cried out to her parents to allow her to stay in the U.S. The judge was able to make it happen with a snap of his fingers, his power so great, and with one phone call and his signature, Luisa had an extended work visa and the family celebrated with a nice dinner out. Afterward, the judge visited Luisa's room long after everyone had retired for the night and she secretly showed him her true appreciation. All seemed well, everyone playing their part perfectly, especially since cameras were rolling the whole time.

***

Luisa was a neat freak. Her room was always in correct order with each and everything in its place. She first noticed the camera when she was dusting her room. It sat tucked away behind an 8 x 10 picture frame sitting on one of the built-in shelves that adorned the side wall of her bedroom. It normally would have gone unnoticed except that Luisa cleaned her own room and dusted each and every week. It didn't take long for her to figure out that Greyson had rigged up some way of videotaping her behind closed doors. This meant that EVERYTHING was videotaped including the judge's late night visits which were more frequent the last few weeks. Luisa found the camera and followed it along straight into Greyson's room where the brilliant mind had a whole taping system set up. Once found, anytime the judge visited her she managed to go in the next day as Greyson was at school and steal the tape, replacing it with a blank. Greyson didn't seem the wiser and it was never discussed, so Luisa wasn't sure if the blank tape ever perplexed him or if he was wise to Luisa's tampering. Regardless, he never said a word and Luisa managed to stockpile quite the collection of proof that Judge William Carmichael performed sexual acts of every nature with his children's nanny, in his own home. A very immoral act for a very distinguished judge. If the collection of tapes ever fell into the wrong hands, it would be the end of his career. One day, Luisa would remind him of that fact!

***

Luisa first used the tapes against the judge when she needed to manipulate the Department of Immigration. She needed to have her visa pulled for deportation. The very one that Judge Carmichael worked to get for her so she could remain in the U.S. All it took was one phone call to the judge, a delivery of DVD's showing the many, many nights he had spent in Luisa's bedroom in the Manhattan apartment, and Judge Carmichael's judicial signature appeared on a "Deportation Notice." Luisa knew that the thought of losing her would be enough for Chase Morningstar to agree to marry her in order to keep her in the U.S. She thought she had excelled at that point, but her manipulation of Greyson and his willingness to do anything for Luisa secured the death of Sonya Morningstar. Once again, video tapings of Luisa in her own private living space showed up at Greyson's home address in DVD format with a detailed knowledge of how he had set up the entire taping system. That, combined with Greyson's incredible computer capability and complete fascination of all things Luisa, once again enabled Luisa to manipulate him into helping her figure out a way to commit the perfect murder. Between Chase's lackadaisical approach to the household security and Luisa's knowledge thereof, Greyson had helped as she requested and Sonya Morningstar was dead. Luisa had weaseled her way into the life of Chase Morningstar and through her total manipulation of the situation, Luisa was now fully in control.

~

Chapter 15

Are You Kidding Me?

Dana paced the small room at JFK airport nervously awaiting Chase's arrival. He was coming in by private jet and due to arrive any minute, straight into the arms of the waiting police, who were holding a valid warrant for his arrest. Murder, in the first degree. Dana shook her head as she internally argued with Chase. She knew that he was going to flip his shit and she hadn't been able to prepare him whatsoever. Their last phone conversation ended with him coming home on the understanding that the police had more questions for him. Since then, less than 48 hours later, the D.A. had pulled together enough circumstantial evidence for the arrest warrant to be signed. When she arrived at the airport, she was shocked to find the police already there, warrant in hand. Chase was expecting to be picked up, but now, unbeknownst to him, he'd be riding in the back of a police car within moments of his arrival. Thank God no one else was aware of his arrival.

Dana was completely frustrated with Chase's nonchalant attitude toward this case. His wife had been brutally murdered in his home and within months he secretly remarried and spirited his new family to a neutral country across the Atlantic. Dana was convinced that this guy was either telling the truth or his ability to create incredible music did not translate into making him a smart killer. Not smart at all. She really wasn't sure about his guilt or innocence, she was still pissed that this was the client she was handed when the firm was dealing was so many more interesting, less self-consumed defendants. A mega music star... *Hmpf!*

Dana wasn't the least bit impressed. They were all the same. Self-centered, self-indulgent, self, self, self. For whatever reason, her firm had decided that she would be best suited to represent Mr. Self Selfingstar and although she debated with excellent key points, in the end, Chase's file was thrust towards her with a dismissive wave. Dana was livid. She didn't pay the money she paid for her education to end up representing the music stars of the world. She had no desire or interest in that whatsoever. What she really wanted was to fight the good fight for people who were up against the big bad guys; those who really needed help to save their ass; the little businessman who was being screwed over by big bad corporations, American or otherwise. She just didn't believe that Chase Morningstar was going to need anything more than cash settlements to disgruntled groupies, fans and hotel managers. Perhaps a few magazines would require nasty letters to keep them from publicizing bold faced lies about her client or paparazzi would be dealt with should they release a not-too-private picture taken at a far-too-private moment. Either way, she didn't consider it honorable work.

Yet here she was, many months later, with two dead bodies being found in Chase's home within a couple of years of one another. His actions were very strange and could easily be taken as suspect. All the while he produced platinum selling songs, his YouTube videos were constantly going viral the minute they were posted and he managed to keep his name and face in the forefront of the music industry while remaining in hiding. To her astonishment, she was now having to defend this guy on extremely serious charges that could end his career, and if he wasn't much of a fighter, quite possibly his life. It was just this sort of thing that got her lawyer juices rushing through her body.

When she was informed by the arresting officer that they were there to arrest her client and transport him to the station where he would be processed, her lawyer side snapped into place and she immediately went to work. She asked to view the warrant and had her office send over the file containing all evidence on the case, once it was received. She had scanned through the file and from what she could tell, they only had circumstantial evidence, and not strong evidence at that.

1. His fingerprints were found everywhere in the home. *Because he had lived in the home for a number of years,* she thought. She could argue the hell around that one and dismiss it as totally circumstantial. Frankly, she was surprised they had allowed it.
2. They were sleeping separately, and there were many months when Sonya couldn't be at home, due to her mental illness, all of which showed possible motive - discord in the relationship. *She could prove that it was their routine for her to sleep in the spare room when his snoring disturbed her. Chase suffered allergies and was on medication for it; he'd been snoring heavily that week. Not to mention there were obvious signs that the couple were living a healthy, normal, happy married life and she would make all those points known to the jury.* Another easily dismissed point.
3. The whole point of living in a gated community and having the kind of security that the house had, was so that no harm would come to those living inside. At the time of the murder, the alarm system had been disabled from the main program. Only someone with access to the main program could disable the alarm. *Many months had passed since the man who entered his home was shot and killed. Chase had not had any attempt on his life since then. He became lazy in making sure the alarm was set but that didn't make him a killer. She could prove that the alarm had been disabled for many days, possibly months before Sonya's murder and none of that meant Chase had done it.*
4. He had no alibi. He was home along with the nanny and Poppy. *She had to agree; a bit of a sticky point. That still didn't prove Chase killed his wife. It's purely circumstantial again; dismiss.*
5. He secretly married the nanny and moved to Switzerland within months of his wife's murder. *She was considering letting Chase tell his story. He was convincing and even though she hated to admit it, he*

was charismatic. The two things a lawyer absolutely loved in a defendant. He was used to being front and center and with some coaching he could handle being on the stand. His explanation of his remarriage and swift move across the ocean was credible when he presented it. She could also show that Chase and Luisa had never been seen as a romantic couple, not in the limelight, in public or in private. Perhaps call Cooper Jack to testify; he'd lived with them for months after they left the U.S. You can't deny a relationship of convenience and although it's an illegal way to obtain a green card, it hardly gives cause to throw him in jail for life!

Dana knew she had her work cut out for her but she must admit, she was more on fire than she'd felt in a long time. She pitied the poor bastard of a prosecuting attorney that came up against her in a court of law.

As she flipped through some back pages of the file, she made notes regarding the home security system and the nanny. She felt it was necessary to look over these two points with a fine tooth comb. The alarm system should have a way to record its activity. She assumed the police had dug that deep but there seemed no report on it. Duly noted.

She read about the nanny, Luisa. Under 30 years old, Swiss National, working here on a work visa. She'd been a nanny for a number of years for four different families, all raved her credentials and signed affidavits were on hand to state that she was as pure and innocent as she portrayed herself to be... but something nagged at Dana, something she kept going back to again and again. She grabbed her iPhone and called Lucas Hollomby. He proved that Johann wasn't involved in the murder of his sister, Sonya. Chase truly thought Hennie or one of his men was responsible, but the police then turned their sights on him. They seemed to have skimmed over Luisa and closed in on Chase, but Dana wasn't convinced that the nanny was investigated thoroughly enough.

When Lucas answered, she smiled to herself. She really liked Lucas. Unlike the police, he was very thorough in his work!

***

He's sitting on a bed, plucking away at the guitar he holds. The new speakers, purchased for his 18th birthday, sound perfect. He's concentrating on the chords he's playing, repeating them until they are natural to him. As he plays he can see smoke building around him slowly. He doesn't panic – he doesn't move except his fingers on the neck of the guitar, still repeating the chords.

Out of the smoke he sees a form walking towards him. He continues repeating the chords and the speakers get louder as the form gets nearer. He is now playing frantically, moving his head to the chords, lost in the music. The form becomes clearer… the shape of a woman appears. She is slight of frame, elderly, dressed elegantly and smiling. He looks up from where he sits on the bed and smiles at her, still continuing to play the chords.

Her lips are moving as if in slow motion but no sound comes out. He feels frustration, tenses his body and increases the intensity of his playing as he tries to watch the woman and play the chords at the same time. Her lips continue to move without sound until suddenly she leans forward and her face is all he can see – large, wide-eyed and penetrating. The speakers are now full blast.

Chase woke up quickly. He knew the sign! By now, he knew that when he dreamed the dream, she was speaking to him, trying to warn him. He hadn't experienced the dream for a long time but he would always know what it meant. His mother had followed him for years in spirit, always with the fire looming in the background. Perhaps because Chase knew it forewarned of a life altering event, at least it always seemed that way. Chase became extremely unsettled.

He felt nervous not knowing what the warning was. He worried knowing Poppy was thousands of miles away but he trusted Luisa explicitly and knew she'd be making sure that Poppy was well taken care of. Even so, he was anxious. He prepared for landing and closed his eyes, feeling the force as the jet flew into the airport like a thread through the eye of its needle.

Chase grabbed his carry-on bag and threw it over his shoulder. He had packed light, hoping that his stay would be short. He had managed to remain hidden for these past months and hoped to maintain that while he was back on U.S. soil. He hadn't even mentioned his trip home to Charlie, figuring Charlie wouldn't have the chance to make it to New York in time to see him before he was back on the jet headed to Switzerland. He took a moment to compare how different his life was now as to how he lived just a few years before. Before Poppy or Sonya, before he returned to New York, before Georgie chose Charlie. Before life became so sensational and convoluted.

He made his way through customs fairly swiftly and was headed for private arrivals when he spotted Dana walking towards him. She looked stern and focused. *Uh-oh!* Chase thought. He stopped dead and his heart sank to his socks. Two big guys that Chase could only assume were police officers were on either side of her. Chase knew right away by the way Dana kept staring at him as they approached, that they were interested in more than just a few questions being answered. He waited for them to reach him and took a deep breath.

"Hey," he said to Dana, as she stood before him. "What's this about?" he asked, dropping his carry-on to the ground.

As he did, the man on the right grabbed his hand and spun him around, pinning both hands behind his back and putting him in handcuffs. "Mr. Chase Nicholas Morningstar, you are under arrest for the murder of Sonya Morningstar."

"What the f…" Chase started angrily, but stopped himself short, aware of his surroundings. Although they were in a private setting there were still customs personnel and security people within earshot and eyesight of what was occurring.

The officer proceeded to read Chase his Miranda rights. Dana saw his face but couldn't gauge what was going on in his mind; she just knew she wanted him to say absolutely nothing. When the officer arrived at the part where he said, "You have the right to an attorney, if you can't afford an attorney one will be appointed for you free of charge," Dana caught his eye and he managed to focus, understanding immediately what she expected of him; *Answer "yes" and nod your head when asked.* The officer stopped and waited for Chase's response, but he was silent. He repeated the phrase and then asked, "Do you understand?" Dana and Chase continued to lock eyes as Chase managed to nod his head briefly and answered, "Yes". For the first time since she was "assigned" to him, Chase felt as though Dana was truly on his side. She motioned to him not to say a word and he complied.

As the policeman grabbed his arm to lead him to the cruiser, Chase's mind was shifting rapidly through all the things he could tell them that would prove his innocence. How could they get it so wrong? Chase knew he was the easy answer, but it was also so cliché. As his mind reeled, he said out loud to himself, "Are you kidding me?" It was the only thing the paparazzi heard when they swarmed around the doors as Chase was escorted out of the airport. The cameras went off like the sound of bullets and having been in hiding for so many months, Chase wasn't used to their mad frenzy. The two hands that gripped his arms were locked on tight and were pushing him forward, regardless of the mayhem that the paparazzi were causing. Both he and Dana were stunned. Neither could figure out how anyone found out about his arrival, let alone that he was going to be arrested. Now there were at least 50 cameras snapping shots of him in handcuffs and being marched along by police. Nice.

The money shot showed Chase between the two large men, arms behind his back with a look of astonishment on his face. The headline read, "Are You Kidding Me?" and it sold out at nearly every newsstand in less than three hours. No such thing as bad publicity, they say.

***

The moment the door closed upon Chase's departure from the Switzerland home, Luisa took action. She'd known for just 48 hours that he was having to return to the U.S. and she was fearful that they were finally going to acknowledge her involvement in Sonya's murder. After some debate, she decided she wasn't going to stick around to find out. She made one phone call, gave all the information she could and then swiftly moved about the small house gathering up all the necessities she'd hidden since Dana's call. Chase left her 1,200 euro, as well as access to his local bank account. Before she left the area she would drive to town and make as large a withdrawal as she could. It wouldn't draw attention, especially while Chase was still in transit. She could get enough money to sustain her and Poppy for the next little while and it wouldn't give away her whereabouts; after all it was local. She thought of everything. By moving so quickly she would get a great head start and disappear without anyone even knowing she and the baby were gone.

She loaded everything into the car and then went into Poppy's room and carried her out. Sleepy from her nap, Poppy stirred and then rested her head back down on Luisa's shoulder as the woman patted her back and shushed her questions and whines as she strapped the child into the car seat and covered her legs with a blanket. Poppy fussed for a bit longer and then settled into the seat, eyes drooping quickly with the hum of the car's engine.

Luisa went through the bank's drive-through automated machine and took a withdrawal of 1,000 euro. It was all she was allowed at one time. She debated going into the bank and speaking with the manager but knew that would be her biggest mistake. She needed to make the money last and spend it wisely. Given time, she'd be able to reemerge, but for now, she needed to stay in hiding.

As she drove away from the bank she wondered how long before he'd realize. When she thought about Chase, her heart sank. It was supposed to be wonderful living with Chase and Poppy and being married. It was supposed to be bliss. But it wasn't and it never had been. At first, Luisa thought she would be happy in a loveless marriage, but it wasn't just loveless, it wasn't a marriage at all. Chase just continued to treat her as the nanny, not the woman of the house, not the mother to Poppy, just "the nanny." She didn't like that and figured that she deserved so much more respect. Especially considering how she had been there for the child even before Poppy's own mother was and now Chase had left Poppy in Luisa's good care while he returned to the U.S.

Luisa's resentment had grown as time passed and when Dana's call came and she told him to return to the U.S., Luisa started plotting. His absence was the perfect chance for her to leave, and taking the child with her was sweet revenge. She loved Poppy and wasn't going to leave her behind. She also knew that it would shatter Chase to discover that his daughter was missing and that he'd never give up searching for her. That meant that Luisa had to make sure Chase couldn't find them. The more she thought about it, the more she realized there was only one way out. And then the rain began and like a dark cloud metaphor it followed her all the way along her journey.

She drove on until Poppy couldn't take it anymore. Through the driving rain she found a small roadside restaurant nestled in a welcome spot a few miles outside of a treacherous hill known as much for its climb as its casualties. Luisa's father had spoken often of the danger during family camping vacations in the summer. He always complained when he had to drive it with the girls in the car. Luisa remembered several times being in the car with her family and climbing the hill in silence, everyone holding their breath until her father navigated right to the very top. Back then it seemed daunting but now it was just another obstacle.

As she reached into the back of the car to remove Poppy from her car seat, she had another thought; she hadn't considered putting Poppy in disguise and wondered if she'd be recognized from Chase's YouTube and the music videos he'd spotlighted her in. Chase hadn't allowed Poppy to leave the house much and so she hadn't been out and about a lot in public. Now, they were going to enter a public restaurant and Luisa wondered if it was a mistake. She decided to see how many people sat inside and go from there. Regardless, both girls needed a bathroom break so she led Poppy to the bathroom. Luisa then looked in at the empty dining area and went in to find them a seat. She took a darkened booth near the corner. As she was attending to Poppy's questions regarding why they were there and different meal choices, a young girl about Poppy's age, poked her head over the booth next to theirs.

"Hello, I'm Rebeccah," said the child, all smiles.

"Hello," said Poppy, immediately standing on the booth's seat to see the girl better. They touched hands and smiled at one another.

Suddenly, the child's mother popped up from behind her daughter and said shyly, "I'm sorry. Step down, Rebeccah. She's excited to see your daughter," the young mom explained to Luisa, a little embarrassed. She grabbed the little girl by her waist and pulled her down onto the bench seat of their booth.

Luisa continued looking up to the other side of the booth, the seed of a plot began to germinate in her mind. She smiled to herself as Poppy stood up and called over the top of the booth.

"Rebeccah?" she asked. "Where did you go?"

Rebeccah popped up from the other side of the booth, smiling her large smile. "Hello," she giggled to Poppy, her infectious smile beaming at them.

Luisa couldn't help but smile at the two girls. She called out to the young mother who also popped up over the booth.

"I brought some crayons in with me. Would you and Rebeccah like to join us and the girls can color together? I know we'd like that," she encouraged.

"Oh, we don't mean to intrude at all! Rebeccah just hasn't had a lot of friends to play with lately and she saw you walk in and well… she was just happy to see another child," she explained.

Luisa nodded and smiled a large grand smile. "No, I insist." She patted the seat as she said it. "Come and join us… I could do with some grown up talk," Luisa told the young mother.

With that, she gathered up all her belongings and her child, and soon Rebeccah and Poppy sat across from one another, quietly coloring, while the women traded stories. The waitress came and went once in a while, leaving the women to their grown up conversation while their children chatted and colored happily.

"So, do you live up this way?" Luisa enquired.

"I do now," the young mother told her. "My mother left me a house with some property that was willed to her. I've been up here once before but that was just to check it out, to see if the house was habitable. It was in fairly decent shape so I figured we should move up here and start a new life. You know, before Rebeccah starts school and we make any roots."

"You don't have other family? What about Rebeccah's father?" Luisa asked the young woman.

She shook her head as she sipped coffee. "He's long gone. Haven't seen him since just after her first birthday. It doesn't matter; she's so much better off without him," she said, matter-of-factly.

Luisa pondered this for a moment. "Your mother has died? Can't your father help you?" she asked the young woman.

Again, she shook her head. "My dad died when I was 12. Skiing accident," was all she said.

Luisa stared at the young woman thinking about her situation. "That leaves you and Rebeccah all alone? Don't you have any family at all? No one that you could call out to should you ever need help?" she asked, sounding extremely concerned.

"Oh, we're okay," she assured Luisa. "I've done this for a while now and I've had to move on the spur of a moment a few times," she admitted, embarrassed. "We travel light and I managed to get it all in the car. I'm anxious to get us home but we're just going to wait here until the trip is less dangerous up the hill and then head out."

Luisa nodded. Smart idea. Especially if she was unsure of the road. But she then got an idea.

"You know, we could travel in tandem together up the hill. We could watch out for one another and be on our way once we get to the top. I've done it quite a few times and it isn't that bad but I have to be honest, another set of eyes would be nice," Luisa suggested.

The young woman thought a moment and shook her head no.

"No?" Luisa exclaimed, surprised. "Seriously? Listen, I've driven that hill a hundred times and it's a lot more talk than anything," she assured the young mother. Still, the woman wasn't willing to do the drive. "Are you scared? Are you afraid your car won't make it?" Luisa asked, pressing the issue.

Finally, the young woman relented and nodded her head. "It's a standard drive car and new to me," she explained. "I don't think it would be smart of me to try to go up that hill in this weather, in that car," she stated.

Luisa thought for a moment and then her face lit up. "Let *me* drive your car!" she said excitedly. "I've driven a standard car for years and could make it up that hill blindfolded. We could get you up there quick as can be, safe and sound. My car is a four wheel drive, you and Rebeccah will be very safe and I know what I'm doing. I'll get your car to the top," Luisa said confidently. For a moment the young woman thought about it but again shook her head. Luisa looked over at the two girls; both were resting their heads on the table and had drifted off to sleep.

"Look, don't you want Rebeccah to sleep snug in a warm bed tonight?" Luisa pointed to her.

The young woman looked over at her little girl, fast asleep at the table. She felt badly that they were stuck in the restaurant until the weather broke and if Rebeccah could sleep in a warm bed tonight, she'd do all she could to get her there.

"Yes, I do, but I can't ask you to risk your life for us," the young mother explained. "Besides, the rain can't go on forever," she said, not entirely convinced that was true.

"C'mon. I promise you, you'll be home before you know it. I'll get you there safely," Luisa said, trying to ease the young woman's worry.

The young woman sat there for a moment contemplating Luisa's offer. The only deadline she faced was her own; however, she recognized that her young daughter, fast asleep on the table at a roadside restaurant, was paying the greater price. She sat silent for a moment and then asked, "We need to go and use the bathroom before we leave, okay? Rebeccah won't make another long car ride without it," she explained, almost apologetically.

"Of course!" Luisa exclaimed, thrilled that she had managed to change the young woman's mind.

She watched as the young woman woke her sleeping daughter and escorted her off to the bathroom. In her absence, Luisa paid the bill for the whole table and tipped the waitress generously. She chatted happily with a sleepy Poppy and made a few adjustments to her clothing and herself. When the young woman and her daughter returned from the bathroom, Luisa was all set to go.

"I didn't expect you to pay the bill!" she exclaimed, overwhelmed by Luisa's generosity.

Luisa smiled sweetly as she helped her into her coat and managed to zip up Rebeccah's and Poppy's coat before the young woman had a chance to see to Rebeccah herself. Having had many months of being a caregiver to her ailing mother and her young daughter, this young woman welcomed the help. Outside they traded keys.

"Do you need a quick tutorial, or are you good to go?" Luisa asked the young woman, who smiled back at her, shaking her head.

"No... thanks, I'll be okay. It's you and your daughter I worry about. Hope you know what you're doing!" she said, as she stopped in front of Luisa's vehicle. She hesitated a moment, looking at Luisa, and stopped herself from saying something. Suddenly, she started shaking her head and then said, "No, I can't do this," changing her mind again, as the rain began to beat down harder on them.

Luisa stopped dead in her tracks and looked wearily at the young woman. "Are you kidding me?" she said to herself, under her breath.

***

The vehicle moved slowly through the winding climb. It fought for every inch and the driver's grip on the steering wheel was turning her hands white and stiff. She kept wondering why she thought this was a good idea. As the ascent progressed and the rain's intensity increased, it became more difficult for her to see. She was very scared and regardless of her earlier bravado, she now wished she hadn't attempted the climb at all.

She closely followed a vehicle in front and together they worked through the winding road almost to the top of the hill. In the back seat, the young girl slept peacefully, unaware of the danger their journey entailed. With every twist and turn, the driver highly regretted her decision and wondered if she could somehow pull over and turn back.

Her thoughts wandered to problem solving that scenario and she let her tired mind shift for just a moment, long enough for her car to slide and then hydroplane on the slick, wet roadway. She slammed the brakes and ploughed into the back end of the vehicle in front. It hit hard. Her car's bumper took most of the impact and crunched only a little, but the inertia and the slick roadway propelled the car in front forward. She watched in awe as its lights spun around once, twice and then were lost from view. She gasped as her foot kept hard on the brakes and she prayed her vehicle stopped and didn't race out of control. It, too, started to spin but she had the sense to keep her foot from the gas and steer into the spin, avoiding any further damage. The car came to a complete stop, lurching from side to side. When it had settled she became aware of a tremendous thundering crashing sound, making the ground beneath her shake. She tried to see what was going on outside her window, but the rain was hard and relentless. As the crashing sound increased she realized what was happening, *a landslide!* she thought, full of panic. Acting quickly, she cranked the wheel to get the car turned and get the hell out of there. She wasn't sure if the vehicle she'd been following was still ahead or not. She decided to keep on with the plan and get to the meeting place to wait for the other driver. It was hasty to make any assumptions, but her heart was beating like a drum and she knew she was lucky to be alive.

~

Chapter 16

Trial and Error

"Have you heard from Luisa yet?" It was the first thing out of Chase's mouth after Dana walked into the room.

"No, I haven't. I've left quite a few messages too," she answered, as she dropped her coat, handbag and laptop case all onto the table. That and two chairs were the only furniture in the room. Chase was being held in the local jail just like any other person charged with committing a crime; regardless of the fact that he was now worth millions of dollars with a face and a voice known around the world, and that his name "Chase Morningstar" sent grown women into hysterical crying akin to the sighting of a boy-band member by a tweenager, and that his music was playing in the officer's lounge at any given time during the day with fans of every age, ethnicity and gender keeping a mini protest alive and well outside the jailhouse promising their loyalty until Chase was exonerated and released; regardless of all of that, he had spent six weeks in a cell awaiting his trial.

The prosecuting attorney, a real asshole named Martin McAllister, was keen to race to trial. He wanted to see Chase vilified and pulled apart and made it his personal quest to send Chase to jail for the rest of his life. He was ready to prove that Sonya's murder was not only committed by Chase but that he'd planned it all along. Chase was in for the fight of his life and he knew it.

Given all of that, his main worry and concern was Poppy and Luisa. Where the hell were they? Why wasn't Luisa getting back to Dana? His mind reeled with worry.

"I called Lucas Hollomby. I've sent him to Switzerland with your address and pictures of the two of them. If anyone can find out what's going on, he will," Dana said confidently.

It made Chase take pause for a moment and he wondered if something romantic existed between Dana and Lucas. It would make sense given that their professions sort of intertwined. Each had a very high level of integrity and work ethic and Chase could see how their personalities would work well together. He studied Dana for a moment. She was maybe in her early to mid-thirties, a smart dresser with a touch of flare and drama for shoes. She kept herself trim and lean and she always wore heels which made her legs look incredible, not that Chase had noticed. Chase was increasingly impressed with her ability to hold her own and work for him, represent him and stand up to anyone. She was incredibly smart and Chase had begun to see her in a new light. She'd become a ray of hope to him and her expertise at arguing a case and representing him made him need her all the more. She was an attractive woman and Chase could easily see how she and a man like Lucas Hollomby could grow close. For some reason, he hated that thought and no matter how hard he tried to erase it, it stayed with him. Her voice brought him back to present.

"I've subpoenaed Judge William Carmichael. He can prove that Luisa was to be deported and the only thing to save her was a marriage, basically." She hesitated a moment and then carried on absentmindedly, "Funnily enough, Luisa worked for him for a few years as a nanny to his two kids – about 10 years ago, and he was the judge that signed her deportation papers and then her last work visa. Frankly, I could see this as a conflict of interest. He should have stepped away from the case and offered it up to a colleague," she admitted. She stopped short of saying any more but Chase knew it only meant she was keeping her tongue until it was truly worth it.

"I would also like to subpoena Cooper Jack to testify. He was living with you for many months while you worked on "Light Years." He could state for the record that your marriage to Luisa was only to keep her in the country," she stated, as she wrote herself notes.

Chase looked at her quizzically. "Do you believe me?" he asked her bluntly.

She looked up from her notes and studied his face. He looked tired and worn. The worry of not knowing the whereabouts of his daughter was clearly taking its toll on him, not to mention the trial he faced before him.

"It doesn't matter if I believe you, Chase, it's whether a jury of 12 of your peers does. So far, the police have you on circumstantial evidence only. If I do my job right, they'll believe that you were in the home, fast asleep, just as you have stated, when the murder occurred and that you have no idea who committed this crime." She smiled briefly and looked down to her notes and continued writing.

If I can't get her to believe me, how the hell do I convince 12 strangers?" he thought, his heart sinking. Chase wondered if he was going to spend the rest of his days in jail.

All the while, his music soared to the top of the charts. Despite the murder charges, Chase Morningstar remained a music superstar!

***

When Lucas landed in Geneva, Switzerland it was 10:17 am and he felt pretty rough having flown through the night. To his body it was four in the morning and he wasn't quite top notch. He checked into his hotel suite and grabbed some sleep before driving to the address provided by Dana. He found the small house with no lights on and no one home. The curtains were drawn and Lucas could get nothing from his search of the outer grounds. It was completely deserted. He couldn't gain access into the house itself, no matter how hard he tried. Probably Chase's decision to have it locked up tight.

Plan B: He then visited the bank that Luisa went to before she and Poppy vanished. The bank's surveillance system no longer had video or data in their files from six weeks ago, but they could confirm a 1,000 euro withdrawal from Chase's personal account at the same time that the airline confirmed Chase to be on board the jet. Ergo, Luisa either made the withdrawal of her own accord or she was forced, but it definitely wasn't Chase. No other video existed of Luisa's transactions at the bank and that was where Lucas' trail went completely cold. He had no idea where to look for her and hoped her family might give some insight.

Travelling to the north was picturesque and thoroughly enjoyable. Lucas took the time to appreciate the scenery and thought to himself that one day he would bring a woman he loved with him on a drive like this; it was more than enough to share for two. Once he reached the town where her parents lived, he pulled his car over and called the phone number on the fact sheet he had on Luisa's parents.

"Guten tag!" a male's voice answered.

Lucas hesitated, wondering if they spoke english.

"Uh… guten tag. Sprechen sie englisch?" he asked, hoping like hell the man said yes.

"Uh-huh… yes… I speak english. May I ask who is calling?" the man asked, becoming suddenly suspicious.

"My name is Lucas Hollomby. I'm a private investigator from the United States, sir, and I'm looking for your daughter, Luisa." A long moment passed before Lucas continued. "I uh… wonder if you'd agree to meet me or may I drop by your home to ask you a few questions?" Lucas knew this was a long shot. He'd really like to have a look at the home and get an idea of Luisa's upbringing.

"Oh dear!" the man said shocked. "I… I… uh… we haven't heard from Luisa in years. I don't know what I could tell you," the man admitted to Lucas. *She'd come back home to Switzerland and in all this time she hadn't contacted her parents? Interesting,* Lucas thought. *I wonder if that was Chase's idea?* and made a note to himself to discuss it with Dana.

"I would really appreciate being able to meet with you. I promise not to take up your time. She hasn't been answering calls for a few weeks and we believe she's got my client's young daughter with her. Anything you could tell me would help me to figure out where she might be," Lucas explained. He held his breath hoping that mentioning the young girl would tug at the man's heart and, being keenly attuned to human emotions, he was bang on.

"I see… uh… yes, of course. Uh… where are you now?" he asked.

"I'm actually just a few kilometers from your home. I've been in Switzerland for a couple of days now but I've had no luck finding Luisa. Can I come over now?" Lucas asked persistently.

"Yes, that would be fine. I'll see you soon then. Goodbye," he said, and then hung up.

Lucas sat wondering what kind of a man he was. Hopefully, he was concerned about his daughter's well-being despite not keeping in touch. Lucas was counting on this, otherwise any leads and trails went cold and so did his way to find Chase's daughter, Poppy Morningstar.

He started the car and turned the wheel to head back on the road. Even though it took only a few moments to arrive at the home of Luisa's parents, Lucas couldn't help but think it was another picturesque drive. Switzerland was becoming his new favorite place!

***

Dana was extremely busy now building Chase's defense case in the murder trial of his wife Sonya. The media was in a frenzy, constantly bombarding the law offices of Dana's firm and broadcasting from morning until night every nuance of every moment they spotted Dana or anyone closely related with the case. The internet was ablaze with blogs, discussion rooms, chats and every different kind of conversation imaginable about the Chase Morningstar murder trial. Forget O.J. Simpson, this was the trial that was going to monopolize the news, social media and water cooler or lunch room conversations for months, possibly years to come, and all the while Chase's music rose and stayed at the tops of the charts. Kyle Craven and Lapis Labels couldn't explain it but reveled in it none-the-less! Chase Morningstar was selling more music as a possible murderous criminal than any of Kyle's other artists combined. His fans must know something the police didn't!

Chase knew only what he was told by Dana or Charlie, who had visited him a few times since his arrest. Charlie trusted Dana Rose and believed that she would be able to get Chase a fair trial, regardless of the fact that it was topic #1 with everyone having an opinion. It was a great comfort to Chase to see Charlie, knowing he had his support and that he believed in Dana. It helped bolster Chase's spirit who was still consumed with worry about Poppy and Luisa being missing.

All pretrial hearings had taken place with the judge finding enough evidence to proceed with the trial. A jury of 12 peers and six alternates was chosen. Dana subpoenaed Judge Carmichael, Cooper Jack and other music professionals as witnesses who could vouch for Chase and the circumstances he was under when he made some very suspicious decisions. Although she had compiled a varying list of people from Chase's past and present life, she knew that no one would influence the jury more than Chase himself. He was genuine in his love for his daughter and the pain he felt when Sonya suffered with post-partum depression, was truly gut wrenching. Any woman on that jury would absolutely melt as Chase told his story and explained how he managed to get through a very difficult time in his life. Dana began to understand how incredibly tragic Chase's life had been with the loss of his mother, his wife and now his obvious concern for his missing baby girl. Against her better judgment, she started warming to Chase Morningstar and if she could, then she knew Chase could absolutely affect a jury's decision.

***

"Hello, hello, come in," said Rainer Von Zeeban.

A lean man with a small patch of grey hair and a smile that exposed perfect white teeth all his own. Rainer was a carpenter by trade but he had many interests and hobbies to occupy his ever-working mind. However, his posture was another story. He had been surrounded by women for many years and they had worked him over into a bit of a stoop.

These were the observations Lucas Hollomby picked up on just entering into the vestibule of the house. Rainer shook hands with Lucas and that alone told him all he needed. The man had nothing left, no backbone or voice. His handshake was limp, clammy and unimpressive. Rainer lacked confidence so Lucas hoped that there was someone else at home that could shed some light on where she might be. Hopefully, her mother would be of some help.

Rainer Van Zeeban took Lucas' coat and ushered him into the living room; a large open area with soft white couches and pillows in different beige tones. At one end of the room was a solid wall of windows out to the backyard and deck. Lucas was impressed with the room and took a moment to appreciate the view; another incredible vista. He wondered how it must have been for Luisa if this had been her view growing up.

"Please have a seat. Can I get you something?" Rainer asked Lucas.

"No, nothing, thanks," he answered. He really just wanted to get to the business at hand. "I... uh... was hoping that we could just get to you answering some questions," Lucas admitted honestly.

"Of course... of course. We are anxious to help you in any way we can, obviously," said Rainer. He sat down and motioned to Lucas to do the same across from him.

"So, first off, I want to know when the last time you heard from Luisa was?" Lucas asked, and pulled out his notepad.

"Uh... probably four years ago. She left the employ of my wife's cousin and after that her communication with us was very limited. We never knew who she was working for or what she had been up to most of the time," Luisa's father told Lucas.

He noticed the man's body language; he sat on the edge of his cushy chair, hands clasped as he leaned forward. When he spoke he hung his head. Lucas also noticed *what* he had said. *"We never knew who she was working for or what she had been up to most of the time."* It intrigued Lucas immediately.

"Was she a mischievous child?" he asked, his first thought going straight to his lips. Rainer looked at him inquisitively, wondering where his questions were leading.

"What do you mean by "mischievous" Mr. Hollomby? Do you mean, was she always getting into trouble because of her inquisitive nature? No, I don't think that she was. No more or less than any of the other girls. Are you asking me something more than that?" he inquired of the private investigator openly, his shoulders shrugged in confusion.

Lucas felt for the man. Considering his surroundings, he seemed so pathetic. As this thought crossed Lucas' mind, he heard a sound that

331

made every sensory receptor rise to its highest peak on his body. It broke into his thoughts and shattered everything clear in his mind.

It was laughter; more specifically, a woman's laughter. It resonated through a hallway and into the room before she had even entered, as if to keep the room waiting in anticipation, and when she did appear, there was no disappointment and Lucas was struck dumb for the first time in his life. Despite everything that was going on, Lucas believed he'd just laid eyes on his future. She stopped dead when she saw him and visibly blushed, which made Lucas's heart leap even more.

"I'm sorry, I didn't mean to interrupt," she exclaimed breathlessly, as she locked eyes with Lucas. "We haven't been introduced; my name is Leena Van Zeeban. I'm Luisa's oldest sister."

She offered her diminutive hand and Lucas all but gasped as he grabbed it and felt the confident strong handshake. Despite her slight frame and dainty, delicate features, her handshake told Lucas immediately who was in charge.

"Hi, Leena," he hesitated, enjoying saying her name. He held her hand slightly longer than was appropriate and it made him feel awkward. Lucas was a large, wide shouldered man who commanded attention simply because of his size but somehow Leena Van Zeeban, a tiny bird of a woman had reduced him to a puddle of insecurity.

She stopped shaking his hand but held onto it as if to make him feel at ease. A smile spread across her face and it immediately settled him down. She was simply lovely; blonde, blue eyes, a natural beauty. She was dressed just in grey leggings, a cream colored thick sweater and large bootie slippers. He just wanted to curl up on a couch and cuddle with her.

She gave him some time to introduce himself and when he hadn't offered up his name, she was left to ask, "...and you are?" She tilted her eyebrows and her head as she asked, which he thought was completely adorable.

"Lucas Hollomby," he told her, unconsciously standing at his full height and puffing his chest out.

Oh, he's a proud man! thought Leena. The vertical difference between them was ridiculous and yet they were opposites attracting. She once again pumped his hand reigniting their handshake. They shared a smile before Rainer cleared his throat to remind both of them that he was still present in the room.

"I... uh..." Lucas cleared his throat. "I'm here to get some information about your sister, Luisa. She's missing along with a small female child." His eyes never left hers.

"Yes, my father was telling me," she said, gesturing to her father and then joining him on the couch. This left Lucas standing, the tallest thing in the room. Intuitive to his discomfort, Leena directed him to a nearby chair.

"Take a seat, Lucas, please," she offered.

His heart was now beating so hard and fast that he thought the whole house could hear it and it might actually thump out of his chest. He sat and smiled at her gratefully.

"What is it that we can tell you to help find our sister," Leena asked him.

He referred to his notes and asked them, "It's been many years since you saw Luisa – is there a reason for that? Was there an argument or an estrangement for a specific reason?" he waited and then realized he had asked an extremely personal question.

"I need to understand *why* Luisa is missing," he continued. Was it her wish or was she forced, or something else? She works for a public figure who has experienced some unsettling and unfortunate incidents and we aren't sure what's happened but she's been missing for about six weeks." He explained. "…and she's been taking care of his young daughter… who is now, also missing." He knew they had no idea that she was working for Chase Morningstar, let alone married to the man, even if only for a green card.

Both Leena and her father weren't quick in responding and the room went quiet for what felt like an hour to Lucas. He was just about to speak when Leena stood up and began speaking as she walked away toward the big picture window. She stood in the middle of it making her seem even smaller and incredibly vulnerable.

"Luisa was never happy in our family, Lucas. From an early age she dreamed of not being here, of being somewhere else, some other city in the world. I suppose in some way my youngest sister and I are responsible; we were extremely demanding of our parents as young children. I think Luisa felt like she didn't belong and in spite of a lovely family and an incredible home to grow up in" raising her hands outspread appreciating the view before her "…she wanted to be anywhere else but here, with us." She stopped for a moment, wondering if her father would speak. When he didn't, Leena continued.

"Luisa is a very bright girl who works hard and her mind is as sharp as a tack. She would be a great nanny to children…" she turned around facing both men and raising a finger she spoke again, "…except for one single thing. Luisa manipulates. She works and twists and manipulates so that you think things have naturally fallen into place when all along she's had her hand in it." Leena stared hard at Lucas and he knew she was speaking the truth. He looked over at Rainer who remained sitting, hands clutching and writhing. He sat like a father who knew his child well enough to know Luisa had displayed less than perfect behavior.

"She went to America to be a nanny for relatives of my mother's and she never came home. Now we are told that she's been living in Switzerland for some time and hasn't bothered to let us know she's here? We're concerned but have a lot of questions ourselves, you understand?" Her father nodded his head in agreement to what she'd said and then also looked up at Lucas. Seems as though the Van Zeeban's were as in the dark about Luisa's whereabouts as he was.

He pondered Leena's words for a moment wondering if they weren't so very worried about Luisa's disappearance. He then asked "Is there anything you can think of, a place she might go to here in Switzerland? A favorite place or childhood spot? I'm at a loss here and anything you could tell me would be appreciated." Father and daughter looked to one another, each looking for permission from the other. Rainer nodded and acquiesced to his daughter, once again.

"We spent summers in a cabin in a small town north of here. Luisa loved our time there. She might be there." Leena shrugged her shoulders, as much in indecision as in confidence. It didn't matter, Lucas believed it to be true. In his mind, Leena simply wasn't capable of lying.

"Okay... that's excellent information. I'll look into that. Anything else?" he asked innocently. There was a long pause before he got his answer.

Leena hesitated before answering. "Luisa was a difficult person to understand. She had a lot of resentment towards all of us. It's frustrating to the family, hard for us to understand her feelings. Anyway, you should know she isn't above doing whatever it takes for her to get what she wants and that includes lying to anyone and everyone." She took a moment to catch her breath, long enough for Lucas to catch his. They stared at one another for a long moment both understanding the importance of the unspoken thoughts. "Please let us know what you find" she said and smiled weakly. He would do what he could to help her and her family. Whatever he could.

***

He left the Van Zeeban household and drove north towards the address of the summer cabin Luisa loved so much. In his mind he had gone over and over different scenarios of why she had left and where she might have gone. With really no leads at all he knew he would have to be methodical. This wasn't going to be a quick fix. He would have to stop at every establishment along the way and leave a photo and information sheet on the missing nanny and contact information hoping someone had seen them *if* they travelled this route; all of it a long shot.

He was hoping to hear something within a week assuming that most staff would be at their place of work within that time and see the photo and information on Luisa. It didn't take him long to reach the restaurant near the bottom of the hill. He decided to stop in at the roadside restaurant for a meal and a coffee. He entered the restaurant, spotted a booth and immediately sat in it. He put the paper about Luisa on the table face up and sat back in his seat closing his eyes.

"Guten tag," he heard the waitress say.

He peeked one eye open and saw a middle-aged woman with short brown hair standing in front of him with a nice smile. He returned her smile.

"Guten tag. Sprechen sie englisch?" he asked.

"Yah, I do," the waitress answered, nodding her head.

"Coffee and a steak dinner please, baked potato and steamed vegetables," he ordered, without looking at a menu. The waitress nodded politely and wrote it all down.

"Eez that all?" she asked smiling.

"Is the manager here?" he asked straightforward.

"Yah, shall I get her?" she asked him, nodding her head again.

"Please," he said.

She turned and left the table, returning shortly with his coffee and a glass of ice water. He had half the coffee gone when a short grey-haired woman approached the booth.

"Can I help you, zir?" the woman asked him.

"I'm hoping you can. Please have a seat. I'm searching for a missing woman. Her name is Luisa and she may be travelling with a female child," he told her, as she sat across from him and studied the paper he moved in front of her. The woman looked closely at the photo.

Lucas gave her a moment and then continued. "We don't know if she travelled this way but her favorite summer cabin was just on the other side of that hill so I'm hoping she came through this way. I'd like you to show this to your staff and see if anyone saw her, or spoke to her. I've left photos all along the route here hoping to hear something. Do you think you could do that for me?" he asked her.

"Yah, I will hang it in the staff lounge. I will make sure everyone zees it and we will call if we know anything," she said agreeably.

The Swiss are such nice people, Lucas thought. He enjoyed his steak dinner, drank two more cups of coffee and was getting ready to leave when a waitress approached him holding the photo.

"My manager said you wished to speak to anyone who zaw this woman. I did. I remember her, with a little girl. I served them," she said, as she wiped off his table slowly.

"What can you tell me?" he asked her.

She looked at him from top to bottom, not giving anything up easily. Lucas decided that some of the truth was better than an outright lie, but then he didn't have to give up the whole truth and nothing but.

"I'm looking for them. Their family wants to know where they are," he admitted.

He said nothing more as the waitress studied his face determining whether or not to say anything more. She decided to have faith.

"She had dinner with another young woman and child. I don't know if they knew one another but they had dinner and then when they were done, this one," gesturing to Luisa's picture, "paid for everything with cash and they all left together."

"Did you hear where they were going?" he asked, excited to have the first confirmation of a sighting of Luisa since the withdrawal at the bank and of Poppy, confirming she was with Luisa. Lucas wasn't sure if he was relieved by that thought or not. "Or did you see which way they went when they drove off? Anything you could give me would really help," he said anxiously.

The waitress closed her eyes and gave it some serious thought. "It was a while ago. Actually, I remember now. It was the night of that bad storm. It rained for almost two full days. It rained so much that they had to close the road going up the hill after the landslide. I didn't see them leave but if they went up that hill, they'll be lucky to be alive," she said ominously.

Lucas took this in for a moment as she continued looking at Luisa's picture. If she was headed to the cabin, how else could she get there?

"And can you please tell me, if I wanted to get to where they rent the summer cabins, would I have to take that hill?" he asked.

"Yes, yes, you would. As a matter of fact, it's the only way to that particular area. The road was closed for a little while afterward. I'd say about six weeks ago," she reminisced, "trees down, high winds and hard rain. I can't imagine that they risked it with their young children," she said. Smiling at the picture of Luisa, she handed it back to Lucas and went to walk away.

"Uh… you said she was with another young mother and child? Had you seen them before or know who they were? Perhaps they live around here?" he asked, hoping for anything else she might know. It was the first time he'd heard about them and wondered what they had to do with it all.

"No, I'm sorry, I had never seen them before or since. I don't think they were from this area," she said confidently, then motioned her thumb towards a table of hungry patrons who had just sat down and walked off towards them.

Lucas left the restaurant and climbed back into his car. Six weeks ago. It fit the time frame when Chase returned to the states and Luisa and Poppy went missing. Now another person and small child has been added. He shook his head unable to answer the many questions that were circling in his mind.

He pulled the car back onto the road and began to climb the hill slowly, keeping his flashers on at all times. Looking at the road ahead with a keen eye, trying to look for something, ever mindful that even on a good clear day, it was a very scary climb. With every few hundred feet the drop down to the bottom got steeper and steeper and not a railing in sight. He got to the very top and pulled over and got out to once again survey the landscape. There were trees for miles and down the approximately 400 foot drop was a river, about 70 feet wide. He could make out where the landslide had taken out a huge swathe of the hillside. Lucas figured 200 trees were gone because of the slide, some stuck in a heap at the bottom, not having reached the rushing waters. It was vast, so much for the eye to take in. Lucas scanned the surroundings carefully, taking in every detail he could. He found nothing. He thought he'd hit it lucky finding the one waitress who might have seen Luisa and Poppy in such a short time. Unless he was contacted by anyone else it was all he had and with only the rest of the week to look. He continued on beyond the hill and stopped at a motel past its peak. As he stood at the front counter he noticed a small convenience store beyond the main reception area. He got his room key and entered the store, walking through the few aisles. He picked up a bag of potato chips and two cans of beer. As he stood at the checkout his eyes took in all the items surrounding the counter. It was littered with small hand-held camping items. As he scanned each item his mind wondered if any of it could be of use to him. He hadn't expected to have to go in to a wooded area in his search and felt ill prepared. His eyes rested on a small pouch containing binoculars. He grabbed the pouch, brazenly opened the Velcro and examined the glasses, raising them to his eyes and turning the lenses to focus. Surprised by their quality, he put them on the counter along with the chips and beer and paid for the lot. What a find! He would take them back to the hillside tomorrow morning at sunrise and put them to good use!

The next morning, early and eager, Lucas stood on the top of the hill scanning the area with the newly purchased binoculars. They increased his ability to pick out the smallest of objects tenfold, but still he found nothing. He started at the top of the hill and slowly worked his way down, foot by foot surveying the area with his binoculars.

He'd been at it for the better part of the day, standing about 140 feet from the top of the hill and was debating breaking for food when he spotted something shining in the sun down at the bottom of the ravine near the edge of the water. He tried adjusting the focus but couldn't quite make out whatever the shiny object was. He tried from several different vantage points but to no avail. Whatever it was, it lay hid beneath a large pile of broken trees and mud held at the side of the river. It was too far down for him to traverse himself and without something tangible he wouldn't be able to get police or rescue teams out to help. He waited until the sun had set to make sure the perspective didn't reveal anything new and left the area being sure to mark where he had left off. He'd pick up there the next morning.

And so he did, continuing from the 140-foot vantage point down along the hillside from the road, surveying the entire ravine area and inspecting the shiny object closer. He needed another rainstorm equaling the magnitude of the one that caused the landslide for the mass of tree debris to give up its secrets. Until then, if there was anything hidden amongst that debris at the edge of the river, those secrets were going to be kept.

His prayers were answered 36 hours later when another weather system raged through the area bringing torrential rains and flash flooding. Lucas was certain that the river would churn up something but hopefully wouldn't take it so far down stream it would be hidden forever. Lucas had a theory about the shiny object and if his theory was correct the raging waters could be the best or the worst thing that could happen. At the first light of dawn, Lucas was at the side of the hill, rain slicker protecting his clothes and binoculars improving his vision. He scanned the river's edge closely seeing what secrets the waters revealed. It was difficult for him to pinpoint where the shiny object had been, the area was changed with the fast-moving water. He followed the river's edge upstream and stopped short about 50 feet past where he last saw the shiny object. Uncovered, but wedged in by trees, a mangled heap of what was once a vehicle lay broken and beaten and stuck in the rushing waters. It wasn't completely submerged; the trees kept it up out of the water and Lucas could make out the Range Rover insignia on the vehicle. Shit. He hated it when his theories were right.

The police arrived within the hour and after confirming the sighting of the vehicle, called in a tow truck and forensics to look over the scene. Lucas managed to make the Chief of Police understand the need for absolute privacy in the matter and he agreed. When the search and rescue team arrived on the scene they found neither Luisa nor Poppy; they did however find the vehicle's registration number and confirmed it was in fact Luisa's. Lucas' suspicions about the river washing away all contents was right, except for a small child's soft cotton doll. It was stuck into the seat of the vehicle keeping it safe for someone to find.

Lucas wasn't sure if it was Poppy's or not and took a picture of it with his phone, texting Dana right away, asking her to show it to Chase. Maybe he could identify it.

The text came back about a half hour later. All it said was, "Its Poppy's, what's happened?"

***

The second time Lucas drove up to the Van Zeeban house, he was anxious as hell. The police were ahead of him by 15 minutes to tell them the news. Lucas was not looking forward to seeing Leena learn some very sad news and although his heart ached with sympathy, it also raced in anticipation of seeing her again. This put him into a very emotionally confused state and he braced himself with some deep breaths before knocking on the door.

Leena answered it within a few moments and immediately began asking him questions, her eyes red from crying. Leena searched his face and then drew him into the house, again into the living room with the large windows. This time, there were two other females, along with Rainer, sitting in the living room. They all looked up at Lucas as he walked in. Two officers were standing to the left of the room obviously in an uncomfortable position. Leena led Lucas over to the women.

"Lucas, this is my mother, Caroleena and my sister, Nadia. This is Lucas Hollomby. I have filled them in on your efforts to find Luisa and how integral you were in locating her car," she said, choking back tears. The two women shook their heads at Lucas, waiting eagerly for him to speak, both sets of eyes welling up.

Lucas could see where the family all had their father's features in the face, but were all built like their mother. Small framed, but with strength and pride. Once again, Rainer stooped in his chair, wiping his nose with a tissue.

"Was the child with her?" Luisa's mother asked, her voice just above a whisper.

It stopped Lucas a moment and then he realized she had a scarf around her neck, possibly hiding a surgical scar. Her raspy voice was more than just a cold or sore throat.

He took another deep breath. "I believe so," he said, holding his breath.

Luisa's mother brought her hand up to her mouth.

"We believe she attempted going up the hill that takes you to the summer cabins and went off the road during the storm." Everyone gasped. "A landslide must have happened shortly after her fall and wiped out any evidence until last night's storm."

Her father shook his head. "No... no... no, she knew better than to do that!" he insisted. "We never travelled that hill if the weather wasn't just right. She knew not to try something like that."

"The vehicle went off the road? Where, at what part of the hill?" Leena asked, trying to find more answers.

"Near the top," he told them sadly.

"She's dead, isn't she?" Leena asked outright, clenching her hands as she remained standing, her feet firmly planted.

Lucas wasn't sure how to answer, so he just told them the facts. "The storm was very bad. As the police told you, the water was raging in the river that night. Judging from the position of the vehicle and the state of the scene, the water took everything; they found nothing inside except a small cloth doll that we have confirmed belonged to the young girl she was in charge of," he told them.

Still not satisfied, Leena asked, "No bodies were found, Lucas?" her head shaking as if to answer her own question.

He confirmed her thoughts. "No, I'm afraid not. Neither Luisa nor the young girl have been found. They are scouring the river's edges as much as they can, but it's been about six weeks. The water's been rushing fairly steadily and then another storm last night." He paused... "It's possible they may never be found."

"Dear God!" Caroleena's raspy voice cried out and she fell sobbing into Nadia's arms.

Rainer sat there, stooped over, shaking his head, mumbling his disbelief. Leena stood before Lucas, unable to speak, her eyes welling with tears. The officers stepped away from the room for a moment to allow the family some privacy.

"We always hoped that one day she'd want to have us in her life again. She's missed so many things in these past four years – mother's illness, my sister's marriage. All things that we hoped she'd contact us about, but she never did. And now, we know it won't happen," she said sadly, as a single tear cut a path down her beautiful skin.

It cut Lucas to his core. "I'm not able to stay here," he said gently. "I must get back to my client and deliver this news, personally. I must ask that you keep this information to yourself for the next 48 hours while I get myself back to New York. I can't explain why, but I'm asking you to trust me and allow me some time before you say or do anything," he asked, hoping Leena would give him that chance.

She looked slightly perplexed but nodded in agreement.

He smiled weakly at her in thanks and offered, "I'm very sorry for this news. I had hoped to have found her safe and sound for both your family and my client. I'll be in touch," he said, and nodded to each family member and then left the room.

Before he made his way to the door, Leena caught his sleeve and asked him, "Is there something more you aren't telling us? We are a proud family you know; Van Zeeban is a royal name here. If there is something we should know, you would share it with us beforehand, correct?' she asked.

Lucas wondered how intuitive or informed Leena was. There was no way she could know of the connection to Chase, but Lucas didn't doubt that she might have been able to figure it all out.

"I promise to keep you informed. I just need to share this news with my client first. He's potentially lost his young daughter and I think he needs to know this first before it hits the news."

He took a moment to study her face, knowing it could be some time before he'd see that beautiful face again. Oh, but he planned on it. As soon as this trial was done, he'd come back to Switzerland and find Leena again and then they could be together.

***

Dana waited for Lucas to return from Switzerland before telling anything to Chase. They would tell him together. She informed the judge and district attorney that she would be filing for an extension due to unforeseen circumstances. She knew this news would hit Chase hard; it would shake him to his very core. She needed him in top shape when the trial began.

Chase was seated in the meeting room as Dana entered with Lucas. Immediately, Chase stood up.

"What have you found out? Where is she? Where are they?" he asked all at once.

Lucas had difficulty hiding his emotions from this man who was obviously in great distress. Chase Morningstar's music was still playing on every radio station, his face was plastered all over the news media showing his good looks and charisma, but the man who stood before Lucas was a different man. He had been through hell and it was starting to take its toll. Chase was looking weary.

"The Swiss police are still investigating, but they believe that Luisa and Poppy were lost in a car accident during a very bad storm." Lucas let out a long breath. He watched as Chase's face froze and his lips began to tremble. Lucas, at Dana's eyeing urge continued, "The Range Rover went over the side of a hill, ending up at the bottom of a very deep ravine and then was caught under a landslide. It hadn't been spotted for all these weeks. I caught the shine off one of the side mirrors and that's how we found it. I'm sorry Chase," he said sadly.

Chase hung his head, the tears flowing quickly down his face and falling onto his jail uniform. He looked up quickly at Lucas. "Where is she?" he asked.

Lucas shook his head. "They can't find either of them. They fell near a river. They're still looking but they..." He shook his head again.

Chase fell back into his chair, leaning into the table as he began to sob. His body shook with the emotion.

Lucas felt his heart constrict and a lump form in his throat. He didn't believe Chase Morningstar was guilty of murdering Sonya and now, under this amount of pressure, he has to learn of the death of his daughter and the girl's nanny. He couldn't make sense as to why, publicly, his fame was climbing, when privately his life was going to hell. Life just wasn't fair.

Dana moved over to Chase and knelt beside him at his chair. She rubbed his back as he sobbed and tried to comfort him. Her heart wasn't just breaking for her client but for this gentle kind man she had come to know and care about. A man who had tried to be the best father to his young family and made decisions based on that priority alone. During his entire time in hiding, his family remained safe and yet he had still managed to create music and send it out into the world. She was impressed by his integrity, admired the love he had for his daughter and his dead wife, and afraid that if she wasn't careful, soon her emotions would be crossing a line.

Chase's emotions completely overtook him. He believed he needed to stay strong while they tried to find Poppy but now, it was too much. It was all too much. The news of Poppy's death burst open the flood gates and Chase cried and sobbed like he never had before. He cried for his mother, his beautiful mother Celia who was taken so tragically all those years ago. He cried for his beautiful murdered wife, Sonya. He felt so robbed; her mental illness preventing them from being a family for so long and then, when she was finally healthy enough, her life was so brutally taken, and by who? He didn't even know! And now, his beautiful baby girl, Poppy. He had loved her instantly and unconditionally. She was his child, his first morning smile and his sleepy-headed cuddle-bum. Never again would he hold any of them; never again would they grace his table, his presence or his life. Chase sobbed and sobbed for all that had been lost, while Dana knelt beside him, spoke softly to him and rubbed his back. Even for a man of Lucas Hollomby's size, it was truly gut wrenching.

***

Upon Dana's appeal, the judge granted a two week extension, noting that should Dana's client require more time, another request would have to be put forward and another review done. Dana was pleased at the outcome knowing that if she had to push things off two weeks at a time, so be it. Poppy's death had destroyed Chase and he had become quiet and sullen. He'd lost his will, Dana believed, and she'd tried everything, even having Charlie and Georgie visit him a couple of times. He was unable to get himself together and would weep off and on, uncontrollably. It broke Dana's heart to see him like this, but more importantly it had her worried. If he wasn't able to get on that stand and defend himself, the jury may feel as though it was out of guilt and lean towards the prosecution's case; that was the last thing she wanted. Chase must take the stand, but only if he was able.

She had him working with a therapist while she gathered as much information as she could, knowing full well that it gave the prosecutor time to strengthen his case as well, circumstantial or not. The more witnesses they could find, the more attacks on Chase's character, the more likely they were to find probable cause for murder. She needed to defend Chase's character at all costs.

The first place to start was any loving caring actions witnessed towards Sonya while she was ill. She got numerous affidavits stating, "Chase would come by with Poppy and stay for long periods of time trying to keep them all together, letting Poppy know who her mommy was." She subpoenaed the night nurse as a witness because she described a night when Chase brought in his own mattress and slept on the floor of Sonya's room when she'd had a particularly bad night. Dana figured this would build a strong case for the man's love for his wife, rather than supporting a motive for murder.

The one thing she had to refute was the belief that Chase wanted Sonya out of the way to marry Luisa. She would prove that it was exactly as Chase has said; it was done to keep her in the country. Judge William Carmichael would be able to prove that it was his insistence on this that drove Chase to act so impetuously.

Although, Dana was still stuck on the fact that Luisa was a family member to the judge, so why had he been so insistent? She was pondering that very fact when her phone rang. She reached for it and answered Lucas' call as she reclined in her desk chair throwing her pen down.

"Hey, Mr. P.I. Hollomby, how's it going?" she asked, as she let out a long tired breath.

"Been a few shitty days, Dana, if you'll pardon the expression," he said apologetically.

"Well, it's a pretty shitty expression," she said, laughing easily. Lucas was a great guy. She liked him a lot. She figured he had a pretty tough job finding this all out and wanted to make him smile if only for a moment. It worked.

"Thanks, Dana, I needed that," he admitted. "Where are you at with things? How's Chase?" he asked, wanting quick answers.

She let out a huge sigh and rubbed her eyes. "Uh, he's a walking mess. I'm worried he's given up and just doesn't care anymore. Like he almost wants them to find him guilty so that he can drown in his tears for the rest of his life," she said dramatically, and then apologized right away. "Sorry, that's not fair – he's been through hell, I know, but it's my job to save his ass and it's hard to do if he doesn't want it bad enough too, you know?" She didn't mention the fact that it was also breaking her heart, which was totally unprofessional and would probably give the P.I. reason to worry about her ability to defend him.

"Anyway, I'm trying to work on his character defense and was just going over what I want answered by Judge Carmichael. Hey…" she stopped, thinking out loud. "This Judge is the same judge who she's related to. She was their nanny for a number of years which is how Luisa came over to the U.S. in the first place. Interesting, huh? I think there's something to that," she told Lucas.

Remembering his conversation with Leena, Lucas said, "I think that's an incredible coincidence. Bet it wasn't a fluke at all." He then proceeded to tell her all about his trip to the Van Zeeban home, leaving out the gushing over Luisa's older sister, Leena. He informed Dana that Luisa had become estranged and, when asked, he was informed that Luisa was very manipulative.

That was all Dana needed to hear. Suddenly her focus was on the male members of the Carmichael family and with the appropriate documents signed and dispersed, the judge and Greyson Carmichael were subpoenaed. She would get to the bottom of the reason Luisa was being threatened with deportation by the very family that helped her get into the U.S.

***

The news of Luisa's and Poppy Morningstar's death leaked out three days after the report that an extension had been given in the case, for undisclosed reasons. Someone made themselves a fortune leaking to the entertainment and cable news networks, that Chase Morningstar's small family was tragically killed in a horrific fall off the side of a large treacherous hill in Switzerland. Some papers were incredibly insensitive as to show a photo of the landslide's broken trees with the erroneous caption, "Fall of the Morningstars", with earlier pictures of Poppy andLuisa taken by none other than Donny Doan.

Lucas was having a drink with a bartender friend at the Old Owl Tavern when CNN's Anderson Cooper broke with the news. The large 50-inch TV screen blazoned pictures of all three, Poppy, Luisa and Chase, the music superstar, who was now the grieving over the death of his daughter and "secret" wife and nanny.

Lucas felt sick to his stomach. Another thing that wouldn't bode well for poor Chase, and yet, Anderson was reporting that in a strange twist, all of Chase's music and video's referring to his daughter had once again climbed back up the charts to #1. Lucas shook his head. It didn't make sense. Not wanting to hear it anymore, he said goodnight to his buddy and left the pub.

***

Donny Doan spent weeks trying to contact Luisa. He blew through the first installment and now wanted the rest of his money. He knew he had enough on the little bitch to get her into a whole heap of trouble. If she wanted to continue with her cushy life, she'd better pay up or else he would start talking. Of course, he wouldn't implicate himself; that would be stupid. He'd just let the right people know that Luisa had wanted that Morningstar bitch dead.

His frustration also brought him into the Old Owl Tavern to spend his last $50.00 on a few drinks and maybe a bite to eat, only he forgot about the food once the news broke. *SHIT!* he thought. *She's dead?? She was supposed to be good for another $30,000.00!* Now he wouldn't get his money and now he truly was flat broke. He hadn't taken a picture of anything in weeks, figuring he didn't need to. He'd even gone so far as to sell his camera so that he had enough to tide him over until he could get Luisa to transfer the funds to him.

Now he was shit-out-of-luck and getting drunk with every shot he ordered; after all he did have $50.00. By the time he'd had his fifth shot, the bartender cut him off. He made sure Donny didn't have any keys to drive with and let him sit at the bar where he could keep his eye on him, all the while Donny kept his eye on the breaking news.

"Stupid bitch," he muttered. "STUPID BITCH!" he then yelled out loud. The bartender stayed near and told him to simmer down.

"She's a stupid bitch… driving off that hill like that. Never gonna get my money now, STUPID BITCH!" Donny yelled at the TV.

Now the bartender was intrigued. He'd spent nearly 35 years tending bar and had heard a lot of sins and sorrows. But this Donny Doan was a really bad guy who he didn't trust. He'd smile at your face while robbing you and would do anything for a dollar. Anything.

"You don't know her, do ya Doan?" the bartender fished. "Nawwwww… come on," he said, in hopes that the drunk paparazzi would give up what he knew.

"Let's jus' say, I did her a huge favor to help her secure her future and she still owes me mine," he slurred, trying to navigate an unlit cigarette into his mouth.

The bartender wasn't sure if he understood exactly what Doan meant but he wanted to hear more. "Oh yeah? You know her well, do ya? Well enough to go to her home?" he asked, wondering if it was a sexual relationship. If so, Doan was a pig enough to tell him; in great detail too.

Donny started to giggle, holding an unsteady finger to his lips. "Shhhhhh… up through the living room, through the kitchen and down the hall. First bedroom on the left," he giggled again, nodding his head the whole time.

The bartender stared hard at the little shit of a man. He didn't trust him, especially not when he'd been drinking, but something about this made him think twice.

When he got Lucas's voicemail, the bartender left the message, "Hey man, call me," and hung up.

***

Dana's appeals ran out after only four weeks. The judge ordered the jurors sequestered so that all the sensational news about the death of the defendant's family wouldn't be heard by any member of the jury. But four weeks into it, they'd had enough and started to insist that the trial continue. The judge agreed that he could no longer hold off the trial and set a date to enter back into court. Dana was informed that Chase had been ordered back near the end of October. Just a few short days away.

As the trial began again the prosecuting attorney, Martin McAllister, presented a strong circumstantial case, just as Dana predicted. Some of his witnesses dated back to when Chase was still with Chasing Charlie and before he became a superstar. Dana was able to poke holes into a few of those witnesses' testimonies. The nurses who had seen Chase's frustration during his wife's illness, testified to seeing moments of caring when questioned by Dana. The prosecutor ended his case by bringing in one final witness who claimed to have heard Chase profess his love for Luisa. There was an audible gasp in the court room and the judge banged his gavel demanding order in his courtroom. Dana didn't protest knowing full well that Judge Carmichael's testimony, along with Cooper Jack's, would settle any question about Chase's supposed love for "the nanny."

Dana began presenting her case on November 8th. She opened with an explanation of what the jury could expect; evidence that someone other than Chase Morningstar killed his wife, Sonya. She would prove without a doubt that Chase Morningstar loved Sonya very much, had displayed incredible caring towards her, and had been an excellent father for his daughter, Poppy.

She brought the three night nurses forward and questioned them on Chase's behaviour during his wife's post-partum depression. After she finished questioning them, Martin McAllister had his turn but failed at getting them to say that Chase didn't love Sonya and didn't support her through an extremely difficult time in their marriage.

Dana then reiterated the prosecutor's theory on Chase's killing Sonya because he was in love with Luisa and brought Cooper Jack on as a witness.

He was in a deep blue suit, white shirt and dark tie, looking respectful and responsible; the trustworthy close friend. He placed his hand on the bible and swore the oath to tell the truth. He cleared his throat, adjusted the knot at his neck and rested his eyes on Chase who sat at the defendants table, looking down, sadly. He swallowed hard and sat in the witness seat.

Dana gave him a moment to get settled and then she began. "Mr. Jack, can you please state your name for the records?"

"Cooper Ryan Jack... but most everyone calls me Coop... or Coop-Dawg," he said, smiling.

The courtroom broke out into a short burst of laughter and the mood immediately lightened. Dana knew he would have them mesmerized. He might just become Chase's best chance right now.

"Thank you," she smiled at him, then added, "I'll just call you Mr. Jack, if that's okay?" and again the courtroom shared a laugh. She gave it a moment.

"Mr. Jack, please explain to us your relationship with Mr. Morningstar," she asked.

"I became the piano man for Mr. Morningstar's band, Supernova, when his former piano man suffered a concussion," he answered.

"And when was that?" asked Dana.

"Approximately three years ago now," Cooper stated.

"And in that time, were you present when Sonya Morningstar and the defendant were married?" she asked.

"Yes, I was – I was the best man at their wedding," he answered.

"And was it a happy wedding? Big ordeal?" she asked.

"Uh… no. Hardly. Cha… uh, Mr. Morningstar flew the four of us down to Vegas and they were married within 12 hours of him proposing," he stated.

"Four attendees? Who attended the nuptials?" she asked.

"Chase, myself, Sonya and her girlfriend, Darla," he answered.

Dana walked over to the table and wrote on a notepad, *Darla?!* She then pushed the notepad closer to Chase. She returned her attention back to Cooper.

"And they were happy?" she asked.

"Oh, yeah. They were in love, for sure."

He smiled and looked to Chase who looked up and brightened a little. It was the first sign of light that Dana had seen from Chase in a long while. It was obvious that Chase trusted Cooper.

"And did you ever note any troubles between them, any displeasure from the defendant towards Sonya Morningstar during their married time together?" she asked.

"No. I mean, Sonya was around a lot at first and they were pretty inseparable but once the baby was born, she got ill and then Mr. Morningstar spent a lot of time with her at the hospital. I didn't see much of them together after that," he told the courtroom.

"Were you in the home a lot once Mrs. Morningstar returned?" she asked him.

"Well, we were recording at his home by that point. Mr. Morningstar had gone under lock and key after an attempt was made on his life. The whole band would go over and record in his studio."

Dana paused for a moment. "Did you notice any strange behaviour from the defendant? Anything that would suggest he was unhappy with Sonya?"

"No", he shrugged. "Mr. Morningstar was thrilled when Sonya came home and he pretty much kept things low-key so that she had time to adjust to being home. Didn't seem like that was something he'd do if they had troubles, right?" he answered.

"I object – the witness is making assumptions," Martin McAllister stated, rising to his feet.

"Your honor, Mr. Jack was there to witness the couple as they married, he was there before Mrs. Morningstar had her baby and then later when she finally returned home after her illness. If Mr. Jack witnessed a change in the defendant's behavior it would support discord in the marriage; but he didn't. He is only stating that, from his perspective, there didn't seem to be any troubles, and that Mr. Morningstar's actions led him to believe there were no troubles," she countered.

The judge thought this over a moment. "I'll allow it. Please continue."

Martin McAllister sat down disgusted.

Dana smiled and continued with her questioning. "Mr. Jack, after Mrs. Morningstar's murder, were you able to speak to the defendant?" she asked.

"Uh… no. I actually didn't see him after that until Sonya's funeral. I don't remember speaking with him at that time, either. He was really broken up," he answered, his voice going softer.

Cooper's big brown eyes looked down for a moment and then over to Chase, his friend. Chase looked at him and the two exchanged a sad, weak smile. Both men dropped their head, both fighting back tears.

Dana allowed the moment to hold, perfect for the jury to see this nice piano man care for the defendant; however, inside her heart was near shattering. She too swallowed the lump in her throat and continued. *Jesus Christ girl, get a grip!*

She cleared her throat and proceeded. "Mr. Jack, shortly after Sonya's murder, Mr. Morningstar married the nanny, Luisa. Were you aware of this?" she asked Cooper.

He shuffled in his seat and cleared his throat. "Uh... no, not at first. But when I flew over to Switzerland he and I had a long conversation about it one night," he admitted, nodding his head.

"So, Mr. Morningstar didn't let on about his new marriage at first? Did he tell you why?" she asked, hoping he understood why she was asking.

"Yes, he told me that he knew it would be mistaken for more than it was," he answered, being careful to keep his answer short. *Let Dana ask the questions she needed the answers to – don't offer up more than that,* he figured.

"And what was it?" she asked, thankful for his intuitiveness.

"A marriage of convenience," Cooper answered firmly.

"A marriage of convenience," Dana repeated. "Did Mr. Morningstar explain to you why he married his nanny out of convenience?" Dana asked.

"Yes, he told me that she had received a deportation notice and when she'd gone to court she was told that she had to marry in order to stay in the country. He said that with his wife having already been taken from his baby girl's life and facing losing the girl's nanny, he did what he had to do. He didn't love her; I know that for a fact." He nodded his head as he made his last statement.

"How so?" asked Dana

"I spent six months living under the same roof with them and it was a much smaller house than the one here. Never once did I see anything remotely close to romance between them. They had separate bedrooms and kept the employer/employee relationship. She cooked and cleaned and cared for the baby and was paid for her work. There was a real love between Sonya and Chase. There was nothing but a licence and a business arrangement between Luisa and Chase. I mean, Mr. Morningstar." Cooper's voice was full of conviction.

Dana smiled. *Good job, Coop-Dawg!* she thought.

***

Lucas smiled at Cooper's last statement, and judging by the silence in the room and the satisfied look on Dana's face, he believed the case had started leaning more towards Chase's side. He mentioned to Dana that, if needed, he would take the stand to explain how he'd been hired by Johann to kill Chase, but only if the case was tanking. He hadn't finished his job yet and to blow his cover would mean he'd never be able to get vengeance for his father's death. After the trial is over, Johann must be found and Johann must die!

***

Martin McAllister tried hard to trip up Cooper in his testimony but Cooper was solid and answered every question with ease and credibility. The attorney knew when he wouldn't be helpful to the case and stated, "No further questioning, Your Honor." The judge gave a brief recess and the court was adjourned.

Dana sat down with as heavy sigh next to Chase. "Who the hell is Darla?" she asked him, under her breath.

"She was a friend of Sonya's. She was a soap actress or something…" was all he answered.

She gave her head a little shake as she looked at him with thunder in her eyes. "Excuse me, Mr. Morningstar, but I'm trying to save your ass here, do you get that?"

She waited a moment as he looked at her, a little surprised. So far, she'd been very tender with him since Poppy's death but now she looked ready to scrape his eyes out.

"*Who... the... fuck... is... DARLA!*" she whispered harshly. "Why am I only hearing of her now?" she asked angrily, still keeping her voice lowered.

Chase sighed and rubbed his face, trying to remember Darla. So much had happened since then. He could barely recall her face and no wedding pictures existed so, all he had was her first name and that she was a soap actress.

He shrugged his shoulders, "Jesus, Dana, I'm sorry. I don't know that much about her. She was Sonya's friend. Maybe she bought drugs from her and that's why I wasn't in the loop about her. I don't know," he answered. He hung his head in his hands and let the tears fall down his face, hitting the tiled floor between his feet.

"I'm so lost, Dana. Part of me wants to fight, but my heart hurts so much I can hardly breathe," he told her honestly. His voice was full of pain and anguish.

She knew he was in a very bad way but she needed him to fight, especially now. Now that her heart was also involved, she did not want this man to give up on himself. She wasn't going to, that was for sure! She sat looking at him, wondering what it was he needed to hear to make him snap out of it.

She got up from her chair, knelt before him and grabbed his chin in her hand so she could look directly into his eyes. "Both Sonya and Poppy are up there right now, together, screaming their heads off, trying to tell you to fight for yourself! You keep that in mind." She paused, letting him acknowledge what she'd said with a nod of his head. "Do you really believe they'd want Mr. Superstar Morningstar to spend the rest of his life rotting in jail, rather than living out there, making his music? You didn't kill her Chase, so you shouldn't be convicted for it. Poppy's death was an accident; you shouldn't convict *yourself for that!* You're an innocent man; fight for yourself for Christ sakes! You're not really helping me do my job here!" she said, rather bluntly.

She let go of his chin, stood up and turned from him and sighed heavily with more than frustration behind it. For as much as she tried not to, she was falling in love with him and knew it was the worst thing she could do. For him and her and the case.

Lucas approached them both and sensed some tension. Not a good sign but he didn't want to get sidetracked.

"Can I have a word with you?' he asked Dana, gesturing off to the side.

Dana nodded, told Chase she'd be back in a moment and they stepped out of earshot of him.

"Who are you bringing up next?" Lucas asked her.

"I think Judge Carmichael and then Greyson are up. I want to continue with the questioning along the lines of the marriage of convenience," she explained.

Lucas nodded in agreement; she was doing a great job. "Cooper was excellent – you could have heard a pin drop," he said, smiling.

Dana nodded and smiled too. "I think your sworn statement will be all that we need at this point, Lucas. I don't think you'll need to blow your cover. I haven't asked for a subpoena yet and doubt I'll need to after that. But, I'll keep you informed," she said, smiling.

"Listen, I got a call from a bartender friend of mine who told me that sleazebag paparazzi dickhead, Donny Doan, was spouting off about Luisa not paying him the rest of the money she owed him. The guy said that Donny had some instructions on how to get through Chase and Sonya's house, making like he knew a lot more about these things than he's letting on. I let the police know and they've put out an A.P.B. on him. They're going to question him on what he knows," Lucas told her.

Dana was shocked. She had a million questions but couldn't vocalize any of them, trying to process this new information. If what this Doan guy was saying was true and could somehow be verified, then it could prove that Luisa was the one who hired the killer, not Johann and certainly not Chase!

"Holy crap! This case would be dismissed immediately with this kind of information. Keep me informed of what you hear! In the meantime, this recess is about to end and I want to make sure Chase is ready for the next round. Thanks for letting me know." She squeezed his arm and went back to Chase. Lucas nodded over to Chase and went back to his chair in the spectator's seats.

As the trial continued, Judge William Carmichael was called to testify. A hush came over the courtroom and the two judges nodded at one another as Judge Carmichael was sworn to tell the truth.

Dana started her line of questioning with the most recent events in which Judge Carmichael was involved with Luisa – the deportation notice.

Judge Carmichael gave an easy testimony stating that it was regular practice for someone in the nanny profession to be asked for a deportation inquiry from time to time. He explained that Luisa had changed employers a number of times during her visa status and that was not allowed; she had gone against the rules of using a work visa.

It was because of this that he ordered her deportation, he explained to the courtroom.

She then asked him about Luisa's employ with his family and the fact that she was also a niece to the family. He seemed uncomfortable answering these questions; uncomfortable and unnerved.

Lucas watched Judge Carmichael as he seemed to dismiss Luisa as though her family status and employment was inconsequential. *For a judge, he isn't that smart,* thought Lucas, *he's hiding something!* His mind wandered back to Leena's conversation with him, how she'd stressed Luisa's ability to manipulate and he started to wonder. He jotted down a question and handed it to the bailiff standing close to the back of the room. He whispered, "See that Ms. Rose gets this, please," and sat back in his seat.

As Dana ended her questioning, the bailiff approached the defendant's desk and put the piece of paper on Dana's notepad. She looked down at the paper, snapped her head to look over to where Lucas sat and watched as he nodded his head slowly.

She cleared her throat and said out loud, "Uh… actually, I apologize. I do have one more question…" she hesitated and waited for the judge to allow or deny. He nodded her on.

"Judge Carmichael, did you ever have an intimate relationship with Luisa Van Zeeban?" she asked confidently, and the courtroom erupted!

Both judge's mouths dropped and it took a moment before the judge brought down his gavel for order in the court. Keeping his temper in check, he called both lawyers to his desk. "In my office, NOW!" he ordered and then adjourned the court for 15 minutes.

Once behind his office doors he asked Dana angrily, "Ms. Rose, are you aware of the seriousness of the accusation you are bringing to Judge Carmichael?"

"Yes, your Honor, I am. I believe that Ms. Van Zeeban was more than just a nanny and now have reason to believe she manipulated the marriage between herself and my client. I believe that Judge Carmichael had more to do with that deportation notice than he's making out."

She halted catching her breath. It was now or never and she knew it. Chase wouldn't be able to testify in his present state. The case hung on the answer to this one question. She trusted her gut and her gut told her to trust Lucas Hollomby's question.

"I'm fighting for the innocence of my client. This line of questioning will determine if Judge Carmichael acted through manipulation and, if so, then it will point the finger of guilt for Sonya Morningstar's murder, towards Luisa and away from my client," she said emphatically.

"Oh, you can't be serious," Martin McAllister said in frustration. This was the first he was hearing of this defense theory. "You're claiming that Luisa killed Sonya and the judge had something to do with it?" he asked incredulously, throwing his hands in the air and shaking his head.

"I'm stating that Luisa had more motive to want Sonya dead than Chase ever did. Perhaps Luisa set things up and, if she did, that makes her far more a suspect than Chase Morningstar," she countered.

The judge sat back in his chair, looking at the two lawyers, both of whom he respected. It was going to be a bitch if she was wrong; he'd take real heat for allowing the line of questioning. He'd needed more than what Dana had stated.

"Where is this coming from?" he asked her.

"I have an investigator who was told that an ex-con turned paparazzi was complaining out loud that he wouldn't be getting the rest of his money from Luisa, now that she was dead. He knew she was Chase's nanny and had undisclosed knowledge of the house's interior where the murder occurred. He mentioned it to a bartender who told my investigator. The police have been informed; they know the guy and are out looking for him," she explained.

"So, right now it's just hearsay?" Martin claimed, shaking his head. "You're going to do this against a judge based on what a sleazebag said in a bar?" he asked her, as if she were a fool.

"Look, it's compelling and could break the case wide open. After she hires a killer and he succeeds, Luisa manipulates the judge for her deportation, forcing Chase to marry her. Extremely plausible. All you have against Chase is circumstantial evidence at best," she countered.

They both looked to the judge who sat quietly. He knew Judge Carmichael well – enough to recognize that he'd seen him squirm and hesitate before even trying to answer the question that Dana posed to him. It intrigued the judge; enough to compel him to believe that Dana was onto something.

"I'll allow it, but you'd better be prepared for the fallout, Ms. Rose. These are dangerous waters you're swimming into," he told her sternly. "If you're wrong, he'll want your licence and you'll be unable to practice ever again – anywhere. That's a lot of faith you have, Ms. Rose."

More than you'll ever know, thought Dana.

***

Donny Doan was picked up just as Judge Carmichael was being seated in the witness box. Donny was ushered into an interrogation room and told that he was going to be questioned about his relationship with Luisa Van Zeeban and then left alone.

As the police watched on closed circuit monitor, Donny Doan began to squirm in his chair, stand up and pace back and forth. He then began swearing over and over again about the "stupid bitch" and how "she'd blown everything for him" and "it would have been a perfect murder had she not got herself killed," which the lead investigator found very interesting. Without even being asked a single question, Donny Doan had sealed his own fate. Stupid dick.

***

Johann sat watching his TV, smoking a joint. He had remained out of sight ever since Sonya's death, but had stayed glued to any news on the trial of his sister's murder and the son-of-a-bitch music star that killed her. He had wanted Chase Morningstar dead for a long time and now even more so, but that useless prick Luke hadn't come through. Now, watching CNN with more "breaking news" stating that the trial had taken a short recess as some furor had broken out in the courtroom, Johann seethed. He had watched after each day's proceedings as a breakdown of the courtroom's events were given. He just knew that Chase would not be found guilty. The prosecuting attorney was a stupid fuck who couldn't prove a sunny day! And this Rose chick was sharp as a tack! Johann knew what had to be done. He walked into the bedroom with a plan for how to take this job on himself.

***

"Judge Carmichael, I will ask the question again. Did you have an intimate relationship with Luisa Van Zeeban?" Dana directed at him.

Again, the courtroom went still, awaiting the judge's answer. He looked around the room as his mouth went dry. He knew it was his penance. He knew as soon as it had started with Luisa that it would be his downfall. He found his wife and daughter staring at him, wondering why he was taking so long to answer the question, a look of complete shock on their faces. Judge Carmichael took one last look at the judge, his friend and colleague for a number of years, but found no understanding in his eyes.

"Please answer the question, Judge Carmichael" he stated.

Knowing he had no recourse but to tell the truth, he simply answered, a quiet, "Yes," and dropped his head.

The courtroom once again erupted as Martin McAllister sat back in his chair, absolutely stunned. Chase looked equally stunned and he made eye contact with Dana, who saw a flicker in his eye. A small understanding of what had transpired and how, he too, had been manipulated. For a long time Chase had no idea how he'd ended up in this position. Now the clouds were lifting and the picture was becoming perfectly clear.

Dana did a fantastic job getting Judge Carmichael to relate the story of how he had been in an inappropriate relationship with Luisa. Furthermore, when she left his employ, he hadn't heard from her in a while, but then she contacted him out of the blue, possessing video tapes of them having sex in her room in his house. Not criminal, but certainly not something a man of his stature should be doing. She told him that she needed to be sent a deportation notice and that she needed to be told she must marry in order to stay in the country. The judge admitted that he'd agreed to help her, not knowing what her real purpose was. When she returned with a marriage certificate he accepted it, hoping it was the last time their paths would cross.

When Judge Carmichael finished his testimony, he looked as though he had aged 20 years. Martin McAllister knew everything hung by a circumstantial thread and waved Judge Carmichael off the stand. This case was going to hell in a hand basket.

Dana next called Greyson Carmichael to the stand. When he took the seat, Chase's mind went reeling. He knew this guy! He couldn't remember where but he'd met him somewhere before.

Dana began asking him how he came to know Luisa and Greyson answered that she had been his nanny for a number of years. Not knowing if the pattern ran down the male line, Dana asked Greyson directly about anything inappropriate he may have done with her and, once again, just as his father had done, Greyson hesitated. He looked stunned. Not being in the courtroom during his father's testimony and questioning, he could only wonder at what had been discussed. He started feeling an ache in his gut and when he looked over at the faces of his mother and sister, he knew. He knew that his father had opened up. You only had to see his mother's face for him to tell she had heard something truly unbelievable about her husband, the judge.

Greyson let out a heavy sigh and began. "I had a fascination with her. When I was younger, I rigged up a video camera in her room, taping all her bedroom activities," he said, ashamed.

The courtroom reacted loudly. Some gasped, some cried out, his mother screamed, sobbed loudly and then left the courtroom, unable to hear any more. His astonished sister followed after her, all eyes watching as they exited.

In all the uproar, Chase had an epiphany. This was one of the coke snortin' IT guys from Lapis Labels who Chase met at the dinner party for the release of his first CD. The stockholder's party. Of course, *Greyson* Carmichael. How could he forget? The name was fresh in his memory now, being that he commented on it that night. And now here he was, testifying to something he had done years before meeting Chase, something that would have a profound effect on Chase's life! Chase sat in shock at the turnaround of events. *Karma is certainly a bitch, Greyson Carmichael!*

"Mr. Carmichael, can you please tell the courtroom, if you were also being blackmailed by Ms. Van Zeeban?" Dana asked, almost knowingly. The courtroom looked towards Greyson, all deathly quiet.

"Yes, she blackmailed me. She told me if I didn't teach her how to work the computer program for the house security system, she was going to go to the police with what she had on me and on my father," he explained, clearing his throat nervously.

"And did you, Mr. Carmichael? Did you teach her how to use it?" she asked him.

"Yes. I sent her instructions on how to go into the program and disable it for a period of time and then enable it again, undetected." He answered honestly and then sighed heavily, a huge weight lifting from his shoulders. He hadn't known what he had done at the time, but after a while he started wondering if Luisa was involved in the death of Sonya Morningstar. When he read that the security system was off at the time of the murder, he began to do his own questioning around the Lapis Labels offices and found out that Luisa was, in fact, Chase's nanny. Not something known to all.

Dana knew immediately that the case against her client had fallen apart. She quickly requested that, given the circumstances and the testimony of the last two very credible witnesses, the murder charges against her client be dropped and a new investigation be opened into Luisa's involvement in the murder of Sonya Morningstar.

The judge banged his gavel twice and called for order in the court. "I hereby dismiss this case on the grounds of insufficient evidence. Mr. Morningstar, you are free to go!" He banged his gavel and left the court immediately.

All media personnel raced from the courtroom to get the news to their newsrooms, their cameramen at the ready and their questions set to go as soon as Chase was ready to leave the courtroom.

Chase sat stunned, unable to fathom what just happened. Dana approached him and, as he stood, he pulled her into a great big hug, a smile of realization spreading across his face. Before he knew it he was being slapped on the back by Charlie, Georgie, Cooper, Campbell and Kyle, all who had been in the courtroom, day after day; Chase was unaware of them until now, his mind clearing as the moments progressed.

"I'm not too sure what just happened but I can't thank you enough for your help," he said quietly, in Dana's ear.

She stood back from him and smiled. As quick as she could, she would now insist upon being let go as Chase's lawyer. This just wasn't professional anymore.

***

As the courtroom let out and the news broke, Lucas' phone vibrated in his pocket. He didn't recognize the number and was curious as to who it might be.

"Hello?" he answered.

"I knew that bastard would get off scot free. Time to take matters into *MY* hands now!" Johann spat into the phone and quickly hung up.

Immediately, the hair on the back of Lucas' neck stood up. He slipped out of the courtroom, quickly making his way to the outside where reporters were setting up for a quick news briefing. He positioned himself so that he could scan all around without being seen. There was a lot of commotion as everyone left the courthouse, spectators talking of the shock of what they'd been witness to, reporters quickly reporting their feeds and many awaiting Chase Morningstar's walk of freedom, straight into the hundreds of waiting microphones and cameras.

As the crowd began to maneuver to the briefing area, another furor emerged from the courthouse as Chase, his supporters, and lawyer, Dana Rose, were presented, arms raised triumphantly!! The crowd erupted in cheers. Dana and Chase exchanged a few words and Chase stepped forward to the microphone.

"This afternoon, justice has been served. In the past few years my personal life has taken many hits and, although I sometimes lost faith, I can't thank you all enough, my fans, who supported me and believed in me. My lawyer, Ms. Dana Rose, did a fantastic job and I'd be remiss if I didn't mention her hard work and her dedication to my innocence."

They shared a look and Dana watched as Chase Morningstar began to finally emerge from his long nightmare. As questions were thrown at them, a larger crowd formed. Lucas kept his keen eye watching for anything suspicious when someone caught his attention. The person was wearing a large floppy hat and a long coat. Although it was November, the fall air was fresh but not crisp or cold. The person seemed over-dressed and very intent on squeezing through the crowd, slowly making their way towards the group standing in front of the microphones and cameras. Gut instinct kicked in and Lucas started walking towards the figure, his hand on the hilt of his handgun.

Just as he was about to make it to Chase's side, he heard a woman shout, "He's got a gun!" and screams and shouts rang out as people dropped and dispersed immediately. Four shots were fired and two bodies dropped to the ground, with Lucas Hollomby being the only one standing in firing position, feet firmly planted beneath him.

~

Chapter 17

Let the Tour Begin!

It took only a few hours for the police to break Donny Doan's story wide open and he was subsequently arrested and charged with the murder of Sonya Morningstar. After a thorough search of Luisa's things left at the house in Switzerland, the police found the account she used to transfer the $10,000.00 to Donny Doan. With that, he confessed immediately and was sent back to jail, this time for life.

The news broke all over the world that Luisa Van Zeeban, nanny and secret wife to music superstar, Chase Morningstar, hired Donny Doan, sleazebag paparazzi and ex-con, to kill Sonya Morningstar, Chase's first wife. Many wondered if Luisa committed murder-suicide driving herself and the baby off the side of that hill. The media wasn't kind to her at all and thoroughly vilified her.

The shooting outside the courthouse left Johann dead and Dana Rose injured, with a shot to the arm. She had seen Johann pull the gun and heard a woman's voice call out and instinctively moved to protect Chase. The doctors said if she'd been a second faster, she'd also be dead.

Chase, holding her still until paramedics arrived, fired her on the spot. He had better plans for Ms. Dana Rose than being his lawyer, but Chase knew he'd need to give her some time.

After being questioned by police, Lucas made a phone call.

"Hello?" the voice answered, teary.

"Mom, it's me," he said softly. He waited a moment. It had been his lifelong dream to say this to her. "He's dead, Mom," he told her. He heard her gasp at first and then her tears turned into sobs. A lump formed in Lucas' throat and he allowed the silence.

"Thank you, Lucas. Thank you," his mother said.

"Can you come home?" she asked him.

"Soon. I have one more trip to make, but I'll be home soon, okay? Just know that it's over now," he told her softly, and hung up. He'd make sure the police had all they needed and then he was on the first plane out.

***

Kyle Craven clinked beers with all the members of Supernova, Chase, Charlie and Georgie in a celebratory drink.

"So, now that you're a free man, Chase Morningstar, what the hell are you going to do?" he asked. He hoped that it wasn't lost on Chase that Lapis Labels had stood by him, unconditionally. Most labels would have cut short and run at the first sniff of trouble, but Lapis Labels had believed in his talent, his earning ability and his innocence! Everybody's pockets were lined from Chase's publicity, be it musically or otherwise; he was a money-maker.

"Well, I've had some time to think," he said, smiling softly. Laughter went round the table. "I think it's about time that the fans were treated to some live performances," he said, completely serious.

Everyone froze, looking around to see who would be the one to give up the joke, but no one laughed.

"Are you serious?" Cooper asked him.

Chase nodded his head and guzzled down some beer. He swallowed the mouthful and smiled his million watt smile. "I do believe I am, *Coop-Dawg!*" he emphasized the name. "Can I call you that?" he laughed at him and rubbed his curly head. Everyone laughed and then the table fell quiet again.

"Yes, I am serious. It's time we work on touring. I've been writing this whole time and some of it is shit, but some of it's pretty good and, with you all behind me, how can we go wrong? I owe it to my fans who stood by me and bought my music, even when things were going for shit!" he told them.

"I'll start booking practice time in the studio, whenever you need," replied Kyle, encouragingly. You could tour just on the CD's you have out now, Chase. No one has seen you do those songs live."

God knows, Chase had created enough music in the past few years to keep a tour going through at least 25 countries, if not more. And, now that he'd been cleared of all charges, he was able to travel freely. This tour could be the biggest thing since his murder trial.

"I'm on it for you, Chase," Kyle said, as he pulled out his phone and started making some phone calls.

"Yeah, well before you do, there's one or two phone calls I need you to make for me, okay?" Chase looked at Kyle, a plan unfolding.

***

She'd been restless and uncomfortable all day, as if she knew he was coming. It would be hard to face him after all that had transpired. Would he look at her differently? Would she be able to overcome everything? She knew he had feelings for her, she was sure of it and even though they hadn't spoken since the day he left, she had this sense that he wasn't far. She wasn't wrong.

His car pulled into the driveway midway through the day. Immediately, she began to feel light headed. It was the fight or flight reaction she knew she was experiencing and she admonished herself for being so ridiculous. Her pride was at stake here and she knew that no matter what he said, no matter what he did, she needed to stay strong. Her feelings aside, she strode towards the door when he rang the bell.

When she opened the door, his breath was actually stolen away. She was as exquisite as he remembered. A lot had transpired since they last saw one another, but he believed in his love for her and had waited for this day for some time.

"Hello, Leena," Lucas said softly.

"Hello, Lucas," she replied. Her face gave nothing away. She registered neither happiness nor sadness at his appearance at her front door.

"I had hoped to speak with you again, especially now with the case being over," he told her.

She looked at him. At first he thought she was studying his face fondly, but then it changed to a look of sadness.

"I cannot speak with you, I'm afraid. Our family has been horribly shamed by the news of Luisa's involvement in the death of Mrs. Morningstar. We've been hounded by the police and news media here; not-to-mention the American news constantly at our front door. It's been hell and our name has been dragged through the gutter," she told him, holding the door partly closed between them. Her eyes welled up as she continued.

"It meant nothing to you to allow that to happen to us. Our family wants you to go away and leave us in peace," she told him. She went to close the door but he quickly jammed his foot in the way.

"Wait… wait here. I had no control over any of that. I was unable to call you to tell you that Luisa was being implicated in some pretty awful things because of my involvement in the case, don't you understand? If I'd divulged that to you before it came out in the courts… in my country the courts would have had reason to make the information inadmissible. It was because of those implications that the truth was found out," he explained, hoping she understood that he had to act on behalf of his client, an innocent man.

"Oh, I understand, all too well. My family, also innocent, is now unable to be seen in public without stares and ridicule and gossip. You could have at least given us the chance to leave here and go into hiding, something your client was successful at doing for years, am I right?"

Her words cut into him. He could see she was hurt as she dropped her resolve and started to weep at the door. Lucas took the moment to step forward but his foot came away from blocking the door and, in anticipation of his move, Leena took that opportunity to slam the door on him and lock it.

Lucas knew when he was done. He was done, for now.

***

She'd been restless and uncomfortable all day. Painkillers did that to her; they made her edgy and twitchy. After being discharged home from the hospital after only 48 hours, with some pretty hard narcotics, she spent the day sleeping them off and drinking water. She looked like crap and was completely useless with one arm in a sling and hurting like hell. Lapis Labels had sent a driver to get her home and a nurse who was willing to be on call for the next few days should Dana require anything.

The bullet didn't do any major damage, but she was truly lucky to be alive. What the hell was she thinking, leaning *into* a friggin' bullet? That was way above her pay grade!

She kept CNN on in case anything more transpired and sure enough, Judge William Carmichael was found inside his garage, sitting behind the wheel of his beloved 76 Mustang, its motor running. Tragically, without realizing it, his century home allowed the carbon monoxide to seep into the rest of the house. Judge Carmichael had also asphyxiated his wife and daughter, Regan (home for moral support) and the family pets who were all asleep in their beds at the time.

Dana just couldn't believe how things had turned out so tragically for everyone that came into Luisa Van Zeeban's path. She was simply evil personified and all those around her suffered for knowing her. Even down to little Poppy, who she was hired to care for. Tragic and ironic all at the same time. Dana sighed a heavy sigh. She was tired of being cooped up but really couldn't go out in her present state. She sat staring out her living room window at the cold November day, when a black limousine pulled in. She blinked hard and wondered if she was seeing things. She nearly fell off the couch she leapt so hard, when Chase emerged from the vehicle and walked briskly towards her door.

Dana ran to the nearest mirror and tried patting down her unwashed hair, raking her hands through it to tame it and bring it under control. She straightened her pajamas, not so proud of the Tinkerbell theme, now that she was going to be seen by Chase. Her sling made everything difficult and, in the end, she decided she'd do her best to assure him she was fine without letting him in! Good plan!

Her doorbell rang and she stopped herself first before answering. Deep breath *(oh shit! Had she brushed her teeth?)* She opened the door with her good hand, only wide enough for a quick conversation and smiled.

"Hey. Thanks for coming by. I'm uh… not really having visitors right now but…" she stopped, hoping he'd get the hint.

Instead he shoved his foot into the small space and gave it a bit of a push, enough for Dana to lose grip of the door and for it to swing wide open, exposing her in all her Tinkerbell pajama'd beauty. Chase smiled and it lit up like a million watts. It made her stomach flutter a little.

"Tinkerbell's my favorite fairy," she told him, as she caught him glancing her over.

"Oh, yeah," he said interested, "Elton John is mine," he said, deadpan and walked past her into her house, uninvited.

A smile broke across her face which hadn't been there in a long time. Damn, if Chase Morningstar wasn't the best pain killer a girl could ask for!

***

They married a year to the day of Chase's exoneration. It happened to be November 11th, Poppy's birthday. Chase and Dana both thought it fitting that the date be remembered for so many happy things. Chase had a few pictures of Sonya and Poppy throughout his office and in parts of their home but, for the most part, they lived on in his music.

Supernova and Chase Morningstar toured for almost two years straight. Dana travelled with them, being a legal advisor for the group and helping them navigate the laws in other countries.

Chase Morningstar and Supernova were the first American group to tour Cuba, once the embargo was lifted. They toured the historic city of Havana and spent three nights rocking the Cuban people with his musicality. He was surprised to find that Cuba had a huge wealth of musically talented people who had learned his music by ear and had been playing it for tourists for years. He was entertained one night in a small club located off the main island of Cuba; a small island called Santa Maria. There, he and his whole crew, including Dana, were entertained by a phenomenal guitar player by the name of Yosvani and a cellist named Suilady. These two musicians impressed Chase and the group so much, that Chase asked them to join his tour and play along with him. They readily accepted and Chase Morningstar once again made news headlines around the world. "Morningstar gives rise to new talent!" He had no idea how much!

~

Epilogue

He's sitting on a bed, plucking away at the guitar he holds. The new speakers, purchased for his 18th birthday, sound perfect. He's concentrating on the chords he's playing, repeating them until they are natural to him. As he plays he can see smoke building around him slowly. He doesn't panic – he doesn't move except his fingers on the neck of the guitar, still repeating the chords.

Out of the smoke he sees a form walking towards him. He continues repeating the chords and the speakers get louder as the form gets nearer. He is now playing frantically, moving his head to the chords, lost in the music. The form becomes clearer... the shape of a woman appears. She is slight of frame, elderly, dressed elegantly and smiling. He looks up from where he sits on the bed and smiles at her, still continuing to play the chords.

Her lips are moving as if in slow motion but no sound comes out. He feels frustration, tenses his body and increases the intensity of his playing as he tries to watch the woman and play the chords at the same time. Her lips continue to move without sound until suddenly she leans forward and her face is all he can see – large, wide-eyed and penetrating. The speakers are now full blast.

Chase awoke with a start, his heart racing... no, thumping in his chest. It had been years since he had the dream. At least 18 years.

He looked at the clock on his phone. 6:18 am. God, why did it always have to be an early morning dream for him? He knew what it meant – he always had. He was being warned. It made him feel incredibly unsettled. Tonight was his last performance and he was quitting touring for a while. He'd been back on stage for nearly all of the past 18 years and, although he loved it and played to more numbers than he could count, he was ready to get back into the studio, to be a creative force and team up with others. The new music makers out there were impressive as hell and if he didn't keep up with them, they'd surpass him. Right now, he was on top, even after all these years, but Chase Morningstar needed to keep on his toes to stay there.

Tonight's performance was going to end a long journey for Chase. In the past 18 years, he'd mended his broken heart and found love again with Dana by his side. They'd never had any children, so they started their own foundation called "The Morningstar Foundation" that provided funds to help children, aged 1 – 18, to access any kind of musical program they wished. The fund wasn't exclusive; anyone from all over the world could apply. The Morningstar Foundation was responsible for more than 20,000 children receiving music lessons throughout the 18 years it had been operational. Dana and Chase also believed in anonymous philanthropy and would sometimes, over breakfast, scour the newspaper for hard luck stories or organizations that could do with some financial help and, suddenly, there would appear a cashier's cheque for tens of thousands of dollars. It made Chase think back to the day of his birth and his mother receiving a check that changed their lives. Chase liked that, in homage to his mother.

Chase was very happy in his life and his past tragedies made him stronger. He remembered Celia saying something similar once. His mind wandered to his mother and those first 30 years of his life, as he prepared for his final concert that night. He was anxious for some much needed rest and looking forward to the torrent of creative juices he usually experienced on his downtimes. Sometimes he wrote, sometimes he painted, whatever his creative outlet, Chase usually excelled at it. Some of his paintings sold for tens of thousands, all of which he donated to a charity of the buyer's choice.

He reminisced throughout the day, thinking back to a time when he made music video's with a chubby faced, little girl who stole his heart from her first blink. He thought of Poppy often and sometimes he looked for a child similar to her and would watch her play, remembering a time when he held the young child in his arms. How brief and fleeting life could be, he thought. He was now so grateful for the few short years he'd had with her and the many that had passed since then.

***

The audience's anticipation was palpable. They had all come to see his final live concert tour. If you hadn't seen Chase Morningstar perform live, then you hadn't lived! His tour sold out year after year. Each time, he'd change it up, never giving the same performance twice. Ever.

Only a select number of tickets were sold and of those, only four were given an "Exclusive Pass" which gave you an all-access backstage pass to Chase and the entire team. Chase was assured that each purchaser was vetted and that they passed through the highest of security. If there was anything that even seemed slightly suspicious, the pass would be redeemed for cash and access denied. No questions asked.

She was thrilled to even be in New York, let alone at the Chase Morningstar Final Tour concert! Just a few short days before it was only a brief thought, one quiet whisper out to the universe and before she knew it, she was living her dream!

The stadium held more than 56,000 people and not a seat was empty. Security was ridiculous but considering all that had happened, she understood. She stood patiently in line with the other fans seeking their seat. After showing her tickets to the outside teller, she was ushered in with a personal navigator through to the backstage area. She watched as everyone prepared for the electricity that was about to surge through the venue when Chase took to the stage. She had watched it numerous times and it never grew old to her. How he mesmerized his audience, how he held them in the palm of his hand and carried them with him.

He never failed to entertain his audience and for that, they were truly grateful, showing their appreciation with thunderous applause and whistles.

She watched from her VIP access seat and felt as though he played right to her. It was exactly what she needed. After the show she would then get treated to a Tour Finale party, only one of four fans included. Her father had really gone all out to do this for her and she swallowed hard when she thought of him. He was such a lovely man. She could only hope to find someone like him to love. She dearly loved her father and it was because of him that she was here.

With the final performance complete and the after party in full swing, she raised a glass of champagne to her dad and took a swallow. She could see Chase Morningstar being greeted by many people and she waited patiently for the opportunity to be introduced! She secretly wished her dad could be there to witness it!

Chase made it through his last live concert without a hiccup. He'd never admit it, but it unnerved him, wondering what the hell was coming. He knew the dream meant something wasn't right, *but what?* Yeah, that part was never clearly divulged!

The after party was full of nearly 100 people (too large when Chase had asked for an intimate group) but, realizing that most were his band and crew members, he didn't complain.

His favorite part of the night was always meeting the fans and tonight's fans were very special. They were chosen out of the 20,000 children that had received musical training through The Morningstar Foundation.

The first recipient was a very grateful blind guitar player who had an incredible gift, but no funds to see him through college. Chase and Dana shook his hand and marveled at his ability as he played an original piece for them.

Next was a young boy who was orphaned in China but whose violin ability was beyond incredible. He was now 15 years old and had been attending school and violin lessons for nine of those years, all because of Chase and Dana.

Third was an 18 year old girl from Vancouver, British Columbia, who was also a guitar phenom. She could outplay most guitarists with double her experience and she was generally half their age.

By the time the last recipient was ushered in front of Chase and Dana, both were very tired. It had been a long tour and an even longer week with TV appearances, interviews and all sorts of media meetings scheduled in anticipation of tonight's performance. Chase and Dana were long past exhausted and were grateful for the last recipient's very wide and endearing smile. She was very attractive with a mane of blonde hair and exquisite green eyes. Right away, Chase was very interested in her and her story.

"Hello, my name is Chase and this is my wife, Dana." He offered her his hand, smiling wide himself, despite his need for rest.

The bright young woman took his hand and shook it very hard, very confidently.

"Hello. It is such an honor to meet you!" she gushed. "I cannot thank you enough for your support of my lessons for all these years!" she said, to both Chase and Dana. This was truly the part that gave them the energy to go on for hours longer. Someone like this bright recipient was the whole reason they started the philanthropic organization in the first place.

Chase was so taken with the young woman he had not bothered to ask in what way they'd helped her. He couldn't stop looking at her, thinking he had seen her before, maybe at another concert or some charitable event.

"I'm sorry, we didn't catch your name, sweetheart," Dana asked innocently.

The young woman looked star struck. "Oh, I'm sorry. How silly of me!" she laughed out loud and it made Chase laugh too.

She was very refreshing and made him think of the memories of a time long ago when someone's giggle could melt his heart.

She thrust her hand into Chase's once again, pumping it hard as she said, "My name is Rebeccah. Rebeccah Baumgartner," she said, smiling. Then she pulled Chase a little closer and whispered, "You probably remember me as Poppy though, huh?"

Chase's face fell as his heart lurched. *Poppy?*

The End.

Watch for #3 in The Morningstar Trilogy
Rise of the Morningstar!
Release date fall 2016

About the Author

Spurred on by her readers, DJ Sherratt explores the Morningstar's story further in this second book in the series The Morningstar Trilogy. Creating a tumultuous, gripping, and captivating story, DJ has expanded the Morningstar's journey with this novel. "There were too many who had questions after the end of Chasing Charlie for me to leave it alone. I had to finish what I'd started."

DJ Sherratt lives in London, Ontario, where she works full-time in the health-care industry. DJ has been married for more than twenty years to her beloved, Mark. They have two daughters, three grandchildren, and their beautiful rescue dog, Rosa, a terrible attention seeker but incredibly loveable distraction.

Visit my website at http://djsherratt.ca

Printed in the United States
By Bookmasters